D1193609

Project Samuel

Project Samuel

J. P. Polidoro

Longtail Publishing

ISBN: 0-9677619-1-3
Library of Congress Control Number: 2001-135018
Cover design: Pearl & Associates
Typesetting, design and production: Tabby House
Printed in The United States of America

Any resemblance to any person, either living or dead,
in the novel, *Project Samuel*, with the exception of Ted Williams,
George Grove, Charlie Sherman, some vintage ballplayers and other
contemporary personalities, among them, O. J. Simpson, Ken Burns,
James Watson and John Elway, is purely coincidental.

Longtail Publishing
1391 Old North Main Street
Laconia, NH 03246

For my father,
Anthony Giulio Polidoro,
(1913-1987)
He loved baseball, and the Boston Red Sox,
and was the only true gentleman I've ever known.

Acknowledgments

First, to my wife, Brenda, and children, Michael, Christopher, Kimberly, Stephanie and John Perri. I thank you for the love, support and freedom to pursue my literary dreams.

I am indebted to Paul Shea, Ph.D., and Andy Michael for inspiring me to follow the sport of baseball and the hobby of sports memorabilia collecting. I wish to thank George Dearlove, Ph.D., who aided me in my scientific literature search in the field of biotechnology.

I am grateful to authors Peter Mars and Peter J. Marchand, Ph.D., and to Professor Donald L. Black, Ph.D. (University of Massachusetts) for their kind words on the back cover. Thank you for reviewing the manuscript.

Prologue

When he was five, Joseph Rizzo arrived in America from Reggio Calabria, Italy. His town faced Sicily, a short distance away. A channel of the ocean separated those two parts of Italy. His mother only wanted the best for him as they docked in New York City. She knew, in time, that Joseph would love America. She had heard good things about the country, America. It was the land of opportunity and many of their predecessors had immigrated there and written home of their opportunities and wealth.

"Follow me, son," she said in Italian. "We must stand in line. Be patient, young one. We must follow procedures to enter this new land.

He replied in the same dialect, the only one he knew. "Mama, I am scared and I miss my friends."

Sensing his fear she replied, "You will be fine. We will be fine. You will make many new friends in America. Look around you. These people are your friends. They all came on the boat together. They were with us. Look at them. They are not scared. They are happy to be here."

"Yes, I see, Mama. They seem happy outside, but inside they are scared, too," he said with youthful candor. His mother was impressed with his observation. She was also scared but did not want to let on. She knew it would make matters worse for the youngster.

"I don't know anyone, Mama."

She took Joseph's hand and held it tightly. She knelt down and hugged him. Grasping his face in her hands, she gently kissed his cheeks, first one, and then the other.

"My son," she said quietly in the hall of loudness, "we will be fine and you will be fine. New surroundings are strange to everyone. But if you look and listen carefully, you will find happiness. We came to this country to be happy. You will make many new friends that will be nice to you. America will be nice to you. You might even be famous someday. It happens here in America. Do you understand?"

"Yes, Mama, I hear what you say, but I am still scared. Please don't be mad at me," Joey cried out in pain. The trip had been long across the ocean and he did not know where he was.

"My son, I love you more than anything in the world. I would never see you harmed. This is only the beginning. We are in New York, a very big city. But we will go to Boston, a smaller city. You will know many people there. We have relatives there, remember?"

"I remember the pictures that you showed me, Mama. When do we go to Boston, Mama?"

"Soon, my son . . . we will go soon," she replied with tenderness. "We must fill out some important papers first. It will take a while, but we will be free to go after that."

"OK, Mama, I want to see Boston," Joey said calmly.

"Look up!" she said. "See the lady—the tall lady?"

"Yes, I see her, Mama."

"Guiseppe," she said more formally. "She holds her hand up to greet you. She is the famous Statue of Liberty. She welcomes you, me and all these people in line, to America," she reassured him. "Son, after New York, we will take a train to Boston. You can sleep on that train and when we get there, there will be people to greet us . . . friends, relatives; people that know of us. They live in the North End of Boston. It is where Italian people live and speak our language. We will live there and learn a new language, too . . . the American language, English. You will know two languages then."

"I think that will be nice, Mama," he said, seemingly comforted.

"Son, see the lady, see the torch?"

"Yes."

"The torch will light our way and guide your life," she added. "You will never be alone, not here in America. Hurry, son! We need to move forward. It is almost our turn."

Joseph Rizzo's mother hurried him along. They had two small bags to carry and a large trunk of clothes would follow them to Boston. That is all they had.

Young Joe Rizzo was now on American soil. His life would change forever, especially in Boston. He would have a very long life and be surrounded by family. He would become a barber and own his own shop in the Fenway area of Boston. He would marry, raise children and become well known. He would make hundreds of friends, work hard, and live a simple life. He would succumb to old age in 1998. In the end, just like a cat, he would experience more than one life.

One

Jack Danton traveled extensively in his job. As director of business development for a preclinical toxicology laboratory in Cambridge, Massachusetts, he often called on the biotechnology and pharmaceutical industries. His travels took him throughout North America and his clientele were in New Jersey, Philadelphia, Chicago, Denver, San Diego and San Francisco. The biotechnology clients were heavily concentrated in San Diego and the San Francisco Bay area.

Jack recently returned from a sales trip to San Diego and his client appointments included the La Jolla and Del Mar areas. He often stayed in the greater San Diego area or sometimes downtown. His favorite hotels included the U.S. Grant Hotel in downtown San Diego and the Hotel del Coronado, on Coronado Island to the south of center city. On this trip, he decided to be near the Gas Lamp District, which is close to the U.S. Grant. One block from the hotel were some of the finest restaurants in San Diego. The cafés, bars and restaurants started from Fifth Avenue and Broadway and ran all the way down to the San Diego Convention Center located on the water.

When Jack Danton had free time between appointments, he would wander over to a sports memorabilia shop on Sixth Avenue. It was a two-minute walk from the Grant. There, he would peruse the autographed photos, baseballs and other sports-related items to potentially add to his collection. On this trip, he had picked out an autographed plaque signed by Joe DiMaggio. Danton loved the players from yesteryear. He favored the Ted Williamses, Joltin' Joes and

Mickey Mantles of the sports world. Jack would often seek out the famous players' boyhood homes, when he was in their town. Few people realized that Ted Williams, star slugger for the Boston Red Sox, grew up in San Diego in the North Park section of the city. Jack had already been to San Francisco's North Beach area and Fisherman's Wharf. That is where he had located the boyhood neighborhood of Joe DiMaggio. Joe's father was a fisherman and Joe and his brothers, Vince and Dom, helped their dad at the fishing pier. Jack Danton felt chills when he stepped along the same streets that Joe or Ted probably walked as kids.

On the recent trip to San Diego, Jack found his way to University Avenue in the North Park section. He stopped at a local pharmacy in the center of North Park and asked for the location of Utah Street. The pharmacist pointed to the next corner and said, "You're only a block or two away! Just go out the door and left."

"Thank you," Jack replied, "I must have passed it on the way in."

He left his car in front of the closed-down movie theater on University Avenue, grabbed his camera and started to walk toward Utah. Most of the surrounding streets were named after states. As he passed a coffee café and the Salvation Army store, he thought of how it must have been to grow up in that part of San Diego. The homes were older but well maintained. Rounding the corner at University and Utah, he walked toward the 4000 block. He still had three blocks to go. He felt his heart race as he neared the address, which he had found in a biography of Ted Williams.

It was a beautiful day in San Diego and the sun shone warm on the pristine street. A few cars were parked in front of the homes, but the one that Ted grew up in had no car in the driveway or directly in front of it. Overgrown bushes stood to the sides of the front steps and the small front yard now had a chain-link fence in front of it. Jack remembered that it didn't have a fence in the photo in the book that he had read. Perhaps the current owners had become tired of people coming up to their door to ask if this was Ted's boyhood home. After all, he thought, there was no plaque to commemorate the site. One would have had to known that Ted was born and grew up at 4121 Utah. *Many people could care less,* he thought. Not everyone had

Jack's desire to find the home. Some people thought he had grown up in Boston.

As Jack walked slowly by the home, an older gentleman stopped and caught him staring at the little house.

"Ted lived there, son," he commented. "I knew him as a child!" he boasted.

"Really? Ted Williams?" Jack offered coyly.

"Yep! Played ball with him as a kid," the old man said. "Right over there," he pointed to a field a block away. "It's now a baseball park for kids. T'was just an overgrown field back then."

Jack was excited. "You played ball with Ted Williams? *The* Ted Williams?" he asked.

"Yep, son, I did! Right over there!"

"Show me please. . . . Do you mind showing me the field?" Jack asked.

"Nah . . . don't mind at all . . . be happy to, son. What's your name? Where ya from?" the old man asked.

"The name is Danton . . . Jack Danton . . . from Boston. Yours, sir?"

"My name is Robert Bennett . . . lived here all my life . . . right here in North Park."

"Nice to meet you, Mr. Bennett . . . nice to meet someone who grew up with Ted," Jack added.

"Nice to meet a man from Boston . . . ya know . . . Bean Town!" Robert Bennett said.

The old man stopped on the sidewalk and took Jack's arm. He said quietly, "She was never around ya know. Never around."

"Who was never around?"

"Ted's mom . . . his mother . . . she was never around . . . worked all the time," the man added.

"She was active in the army, ya know . . . the Salvation Army," he stated. "Always downtown tryin' ta save people. Teddy raised himself . . . always by himself. My mother would feed him . . . felt sorry for him." The man said sadly, "He'd be on the porch with his bat in his hand waitin' for his mom . . . in the dark. Always had a bat in his hand."

Jack was entranced by the conversation as they walked the one block over to the ball park. The old man shuffled along and became quiet as they approached the chain-link fence. It was as if he was entering a church sacristy. He revered the field as if it were Fenway Park. To the old man, it was Fenway. He just pointed to the area where they used to play ball. Now it was a field with a plaque commemorating it as TED WILLIAMS FIELD. On the fence was a sign with the figure of Ted swinging a bat. It was a small sign and offered little information on Williams's career. Jack thought it odd that there wasn't more fanfare over Ted's accomplishments. *After all*, he thought, *Ted was no fly-by-night player.*

Jack had taken one or two photos of the house and now positioned himself behind home plate to photograph the baseball field. He would perhaps have the photos enlarged and send them to be autographed by Ted himself who was living in Florida. Jack had found Ted Williams's official Web site on the Internet. It was www.tedwilliams.com. The Web site provided a Florida address for fans to mail memorabilia to Ted for his signature. For a price, Ted would sign all flat items. He could no longer autograph bats and baseballs. Two recent strokes prevented him from easily signing anything that wasn't flat. These photos would look nice signed, matted and framed on the wall of Jack's den.

Robert Bennett was very impressed by Jack's desire to know more about Ted Williams's boyhood. He decided he would chat with him some more. He would sit in the bleachers and tell him stories from the old days and Jack would end up postponing his afternoon sales appointment in La Jolla. This was far too important an occasion for him to miss. After all, the next time he returned to San Diego, the older gentleman might not be there or even be alive. *If Ted was in his eighties, then the old man probably was also an octogenarian,* Jack thought.

After a while, the old man departed from the bleachers, reminding Jack that he needed to pick up a prescription. As Jack remained seated, he watched the old man turn the corner and head toward University Avenue. He would not see the man again. It would be months before Jack would return to the San Diego area.

That night in the hotel, Jack had a strange dream that would not go away when he awoke. He dreamt that he was about to leave a ball field and that he saw some children approaching him from the right field fence of the ballpark. He decided to see who they were and reminisce about his own days in Little League baseball. The children looked about the age of Little Leaguers. Some were eight years old and some looked twelve. Underneath the perfect San Diego blue sky was a warm breeze from the west. The temperature was about 74 degrees with low humidity.

In the dream, which seemed to be never ending and real, Jack sat and watched the kids line up to hit. Some ran to the outfield. They were happy kids and obviously loved to play the game. They would take turns pitching and hitting. Some of the kids were beginners and swung late on every pitch. Perhaps their bats were too heavy. *They need to choke up on the bat,* Jack thought. One of the kids ran in from right field to take his turn at bat. He was a handsome kid, tall and thin. He towered over the other kids and seemed to be respected by the others. He fidgeted a lot and seemed to have a lot of nervous energy that kept him from standing still. Waiting his turn to bat, he would swing left to right, then right to left. His motion was fluid. Someone had instructed him well. It was as if the kid had been play-ing baseball for years—but he was just a child. He was a *natural.*

From the other side of the field, someone yelled to the kid, "Swing level! Just meet the ball . . . keep your eye on it, and meet the ball," the man hollered. "Don't try and kill it. . . . Just meet the ball!" The kid did not listen to the man and instead swung with a slight upward angle. He knew exactly when to meet the ball. One of his hits cleared the right field fence and he smiled gently at the plate. He was not about to swing level and hit line drives when he could pop them over the fence. *The kid is talented,* Jack thought.

Jack checked his watch and knew that he had to go. In the dream, he had arranged a dinner appointment with a client at 6:00 P.M. He needed to get back to town and meet the client at The Fish Market restaurant on San Diego Bay. He smiled to himself as he walked away.

As the dream continued, Jack approached his parked car near the strange ballpark. He could only think of the young ballplayer who played the game like a fourteen- or sixteen-year-old, not a boy eight to twelve. He was good enough to be in the Babe Ruth League, not Little League. *Who the heck was this kid,* he thought.

He awoke from the dream and was haunted by it. It was the second day of his appointments in San Diego and the unusual dream, he figured, was something that he would think about all day.

Two

Joe Rizzo owned and operated a barbershop near Fenway Park in Boston. For years, he catered to the locals as well as an occasional ballplayer, coach or manager of the Red Sox. His shop was located diagonal to the ballpark, near ticket entrance "A" and was surrounded by sports bars, souvenir shops and ticket agencies. The barbershop was small and dark, and reminiscent of the 1920s.

He often told his customers of his first experience with America and seeing the "lady's torch" for the very first time after crossing the Atlantic with his mother when he was only five. Joe's wife, Rose had passed away years ago and some of his children had moved away as well. He lived alone in an apartment above the barbershop. The apartment had only four rooms—a kitchen, living room and bedroom with a bath. His abode was as old as the barbershop, but he made it his home. He did not need much room to live. When not working, he watched TV. He had a few friends that he got together with but mostly he stayed to himself. He visited friends in the Italian North End across town to play bocce or to just sit and have espresso with them. His forty-year-old barbershop business was evidenced by an old barber pole outside the door. It was a peppermint stick-like pole that was dimly illuminated and rotated clockwise. It was meant to draw the attention of customers walking on the street. Joe didn't need any new customers. He was popular enough with his regulars. Every day, someone that he had known for years appeared in his shop. There were no appointments for haircuts with "Joe the Barber." If you wanted a haircut, you sat and waited for the next available slot. Stacks of sports magazines kept his clients occupied.

Joe had two old barber chairs, the kind with real leather and a foot pump to elevate or lower the customer's seat. The foot pedal made a *gush-gush* sound when he applied his foot to it. When done with a haircut, he would hold the pedal down and the chair would lower with a *whooshing* as the hydraulics released the pressure.

Part of the ambiance of the shop was Joe's rare collection of sports-related memorabilia on the wall and on the shelves. Visitors in the waiting area would sit in straight-back chairs and notice the numerous eight by ten photos that were framed on the wall. Most were black and white, and almost all of them were autographed by someone of notoriety. There were many Red Sox players, politicians and even a couple of presidents, framed inexpensively and mounted around three of the four walls. The other wall had a large mirror facing the two barber chairs. In addition to the photos, were autographed baseball bats and baseballs. The balls were in a glass cabinet that was never locked. If customers wanted to hold a ball, Joe didn't mind. He was proud of the collection, which he had acquired through the years. Some of the photos and baseball signatures were faded from their age and handling; however, all were authentic autographs that Joe acquired himself. Many items were dust-covered or covered with small hair clippings, which had been lofted airborne by years of sweeping the floor after a haircut.

Babe Ruth signed one now faded but noteworthy photo. The Babe had autographed it during his brief stint in Boston and was traded to the New York Yankees shortly thereafter. Between the baseballs in the glass-walled china cabinet were small glass vials about three inches long. Each one was capped and labeled with a set of initials. Usually they had a date on them as well. In each vial were clippings of hair. There were literally hundreds of them in makeshift wooden racks. They stood like test tubes in each homemade rack. Some clients considered Rizzo's hair collection grotesque since some of the samples were from people that had passed away over the years. Other people found it odd and interesting—a conversation piece. It was assumed that the hair clippings were from notable clients, the sweepings gathered off the floor after they had left. Joe Rizzo didn't care what people thought. He enjoyed everything that had to do with haircutting, baseball and sports memorabilia. His shop was his life, and his soul was in that one, small room.

Some years back, a man from Texas had stopped by Rizzo's shop on his way to a Red Sox game. He was aware of Joe the Barber's notoriety and decided to get his hair trimmed. The Texan was fascinated by the sports collection because he had one of his own. The Texan's collection was vast and comprehensive. It included game-worn uniforms, original "model" bats, team hats and baseballs and baseball gloves from the Draper-Maynard days in New Hampshire. The D-M Company made baseball equipment. The Texan's collection was proudly displayed in his massive home outside of Dallas. The man from Texas had told Joe that he had items in his collection that no one else ever thought of collecting.

"If you ever want to get rid of the stuff, or sell it, please let me know," he told Joe. "I'll pay the highest price of anybody! Guaranteed!" he said confidently. Joe just smiled as the Texan left him his business card, which read "E. R. MacD., Dallas, Texas" and had a phone number, 1-800-BASEBAL on it. After the man left, Joe flipped the card into the drawer in front of the chair. He had offers all the time for single and multiple autographed items that surrounded the room. He would not sell them because they meant a lot to him and they drew his clientele into the shop. New customers always wanted to hear the stories of how he acquired this or that piece.

⚾ ⚾ ⚾ ⚾

Jack Danton had never met Joe Rizzo and had never been in his barbershop. Sometimes on the way to 7:00 P.M. games, Jack would stand outside the heavy wood- and glass-paneled door and peer through the window into the shop to admire the collection of memorabilia. In the dimly lit room, he could see photos and baseballs. Often there was nothing more than a night-light left on near the barber chairs to prevent Joe from tripping if he had to go downstairs to get something that he had forgotten earlier in the evening. Jack hoped that one day he would have time to get his hair cut there to learn more about the items.

A few months would pass before Jack had the opportunity to visit Joe's shop. In the meantime, the barber became ill and his health began to fail rapidly. Jack would not know of the old man's illness.

Three

The funeral of Joe Rizzo was held three days after he died. The service was held at the Immaculate Conception Roman Catholic Church not far from his barbershop. Dignitaries from in and around the Boston area attended, including Charlie O'Neill, mayor of Boston, and Red Sox notables including management and players. Burial would be in Sacred Heart Cemetery in Brookline, Massachusetts, and he would be interred next to his wife, Rose.

His close Italian friends and many of his clients were also there to pay their respects. Even the local TV news and Boston newspapers had reporters covering the service. It was more than news. It was a "human interest" story about a noted and respected Bostonian. He was the common man and worked hard all his life. Joe's picture accompanied his obituary in all the papers. His life was his friendships and those included hundreds of famous and common people. Sports columnists and reporters of all the local newspapers knew Joe Rizzo. Their columns in the papers the next few days would eulogize Joe as a true Boston sports fan and servant to the "sports stars."

Joe Rizzo had three children: two sons, Joe Jr. and Tony, and a daughter, Paula. They grieved during the Catholic "high mass" in their father's honor. In time, they would need to settle their father's estate and possessions.

Joe Jr. was executor of his father's estate and will. For weeks the barbershop remained closed with the window shades drawn in both front windows. The children would await the legal process and subsequent action by the probate court in Boston. Even in the best of uncontested death settlements, it was a long court process in the Commonwealth of Massachusetts.

Four

Jack Danton and his wife, Fawn, headed for the annual Old-Timers'
Game at Fenway Park. They found a spot in a parking garage adjacent to Boston University and made the usually seven-minute walk to
the ballpark in five minutes. They crossed the bridge over the Massachusetts Turnpike extension and then turned onto Yawkey Way, named
for the former and now deceased owner of the Boston Red Sox. Many
Sox fans revered him. His wife was also respected and ran the team
after his passing. She was known only as Mrs. Yawkey.

Tonight's game was a first for Fenway. Most Old-Timers' games
were held during the day. Tonight, they would perform under the massive lights of the park. Game time was 7:05 P.M. and Jack and Fawn
were there at 6:45 P.M.

The Dantons often went to games. They had season tickets and
they tried to attend when he was not traveling on business. Sometimes Fawn would bring a friend if Jack was out of town. Her girl-
friends enjoyed the games as well. The seats were box seats seven
rows behind the Red Sox dugout. This was a prominent area in front
of section 15 and along the first base line where the view was spectacular. Batters on deck were virtually in front of them.

The Danton family had been season ticket holders for those same
seats since Jack's dad had acquired them years earlier. They were
passed on to Jack after his father had died two years earlier. Due to
the small size of Fenway Park, any seat promised a good view of the
field. There were about 34,000 seats total and views from the first

and third base lines also were excellent. In the first row ahead of them, were three or four seats that were reserved for visiting dignitaries. Quarterback John Elway, from Denver, who was passing through Boston the week before, sat ahead of Jack and Fawn just that prior week. Jack got to shake his hand as Elway left the ballpark. It was a thrill for all the fans who recognized him since Elway and the Denver Broncos had just won the Super Bowl. Elway was in a hurry so Jack did not bother to ask for his autograph for his collection. He was just happy to have had the opportunity to shake his hand.

The baseball game this night would marry the players of old, with an historic ballpark built in 1912. It had character and ambiance like no other ballpark. Jack knew that they were eventually going to build a new ballpark and Fenway would be history. It saddened most Bostonians, but the corporate gurus and Red Sox management were greedy. By building a new ballpark they could add more corporate boxes and suites that would generate more income for the owners. That supposedly would allow management to acquire more expensive players of note. In return, Boston might have a shot at a World Series. They hadn't won a series since the early 1900s. After Babe Ruth was traded to the Yankees, they appeared cursed. Often referred to as "the curse of the bambino," it was Ruth's way of getting back at the Sox for trading him to New York. Folklore or not, the Red Sox had made it to few playoffs after that. Nineteen seventy-five and 1986 were their last good years. The Red Sox had just acquired Pedro Martinez at $75 million dollars. That alone would take a ticket price hike, just to pay for his salary.

This game was even more special. In addition to the old-timers playing on the field, there would be dignitaries watching from the reserved seats in front of them. It had been rumored that many stars from the '50s, '60s and '70s would be there. Among the players would be "Yaz," Carlton Fisk, Dom DiMaggio, Dewey Evans, Luis Tiant, Johnny Pesky and several recent retirees such as pitcher Dennis Eckersley.

Jack enjoyed seeing the game each year since many of these players were his heroes when he was a boy. He could boast to Fawn about his knowledge of their batting records and averages. He became a little boy when he talked about these "silver-haired relics" of the past. She enjoyed seeing her husband happy.

"Peanuts! Peanuts, he . . . ah!" said the kid. "Peanuts!"

"Over he . . . ah!" said Jack, mimicking the boy's accent. "I'll take two bags!"

"That'll be $3.75," the kid replied. He compressed the peanut bags into a baseball shape and fired them to Jack. Fawn in turn, passed a five dollar bill down the short row of people to the aisle. The kid smiled and asked if they wanted change.

"Keep it kid!" Jack said back. "If you see someone with Cokes . . . send him here, will ya?"

"Sure," the kid said. "Peanuts! Peanuts, he . . . ah!" he shouted, as he continued up the steps of section 15.

Having season tickets to Fenway so close to the dugout enabled him to acquire signed programs, balls, bats and baseball caps from many players for his collection. He would go early to games and visit behind the opposing team dugout, as well. He had met Cal Ripken Jr. recently during a Baltimore Orioles visit to Fenway. Jack managed to get him to autograph a baseball. Cal was a great people-person and took the time to sign before and after most games. He was at the point of challenging Lou Gehrig's record, and had only twenty-seven games to go to beat the goal of the most continuous games played. The figure to beat was 2,130. He eventually would beat Gehrig's record at his home park, Camden Yards in Baltimore.

Jack went to the men's room and upon his return noted some commotion by the Red Sox dugout. He had gotten some hot dogs and two pretzels on his way back. As he emerged from the concrete tunnel and in front of section 15, he could see some people assisting a gentleman in a wheelchair, directly to the left of the dugout. Behind the older gentleman was the famed "Green Monster," the left field wall at Fenway. Just over thirty-seven feet tall, it towered over the man in the wheelchair. Surrounding the austere figure were TV cameras and bright lights for live coverage. Sports announcers from Boston, and regional TV stations, such as New Hampshire's Charlie Sherman, were there to cover. Jack Danton knew Sherman well and was envious that Charlie had this rare opportunity to be right there tonight with the apparently distinguished gentleman in the front row. Sherman often interviewed the older ballplayers one on one and was respected in New England for his sports broadcasting and general knowledge of sports.

Jack got excited when he saw whom the sports announcers were interviewing—none other than the most famed Red Sox player of all time, Ted Williams—The Kid! Jack was astounded that he was in a wheelchair and that he needed assistance getting to a front row seat adjacent to the Red Sox dugout. Jack was so shocked that he dropped one hot dog. It rolled under a distant seat, but he didn't care. He would give the other one to Fawn. Flashes from cameras saturated the section of seats where Ted sat. Even people in other sections were snapping shots of "The Kid," "The Splendid Splinter," "Teddy Ballgame," as they affectionately called him. His son, John Henry Williams, who had accompanied him from their home in Hernando, Florida, was extremely protective of his famous father. He was always at his side, and had run the family business of Ted Williams Enterprises for many years. Their memorabilia Internet site helped generate business. As a businessman, John Henry was often accused of exploiting his father's name at autograph shows, and having him appear at public signings and other functions at the expense of his health. Ted was no longer the six-foot, four-inch, 198-pound hunk of a man from the 1940s. His health was now in question.

It was clear, however, that Ted enjoyed his son. He loved him dearly and defended him against the press. Some of the press had disliked Ted when he played ball and carried their grudge over to John Henry. Tonight Ted was the focus of all the people in the stands and on the field. He was "Mr. Fenway Park."

Channel 20-TV covered the event live and area newsmen also interviewed other people on the field. Having Williams, Johnny Pesky, and Dom DiMaggio there was incredible to the older fans. In another five minutes, Bobby Doerr would emerge and join Ted in the seat next to him. Doerr remained a close friend of Ted's. The crowd would erupt with cheers all over again. Even if no one took the field to play, the night was already special. Jack Danton flushed as he saw Doerr hug Williams. This would be a night to remember. Soon organ music would be heard overhead. The national anthem would be played against the backdrop of the American flag flying over center field. Behind the flag was the famed CITGO sign . . . a fixture for three-quarters of a century of Red Sox baseball.

Ted Williams had a love affair with Fenway Park. As the crowd chanted "Ted . . .Ted . . . Ted!" he turned and smiled at the patrons at Fenway. He tipped his hat, something that he rarely did during his years of playing ball. The crowd gave him a standing ovation. Jack Danton and Fawn stood to honor him, as well. Jack leaned into his beautiful wife and said, "See, they love him!"

"Yes, they do, honey, and I think he loves them, too!" she shouted over the roar of the crowd.

"There was a time when he didn't like the crowd, or the writers," he continued. "The Boston sports writers were always in his face."

"Really?" Fawn asked. "Why?"

"They thought he was a brat!" Jack paused, then added. "He was spoiled from the day he went pro. He dropped a ball once at Fenway and the fans booed! So Ted spit back at the crowd."

"Spit?" she asked, surprised.

"Yeah . . . he was pissed at them, I guess . . . did it a couple of times. Spit at the writers once . . . crossin' home plate after a home run. Looked up at them and hurled one!"

Ted Williams had a love/hate relationship with the press. When he needed the exposure in the press, he would nurture them. When they wrote something bad about him, he avoided them and kicked them out of the clubhouse. That was back when sports writers had access to the players in the locker room after a game. Ted would manipulate the press when it was to his advantage. On the positive side, Ted drew crowds to Fenway. He was a draw. He was the last man to hit over .400 in a single season. His .406 in 1941 was a record that still remained. He maintained a lifetime batting average of .344. His swing at the plate was the sweetest ever, many people thought. He was the Sam Snead of baseball. At the plate, he had the eyes of a hawk and his vision was purported to be 20/10!

Jack looked lovingly at Fawn. "You are looking at a legend, honey. The man could see the stitches on a fastball comin' straight at him.

His eyes were *that* good. He would wait for the right pitch and then put it in the right field stands."

"Really? He could see the stitches?" she asked with surprise.

"Yah . . . he could focus on that ball at 80 or 90 mph," Jack responded.

"See that red seat in the sea of green chairs out there in right field?"

"Yes," Fawn said.

"Ted put a long ball there . . . over 500 feet! The man was awesome," Jack smiled.

"This really makes you happy, doesn't it?" Fawn said to Jack lovingly. "I mean, he meant something to you when you were a child . . . that's a nice memory, honey."

"Yes, sweetheart, he was my hero . . . I had his number on my back in Little League . . . number 9!" Jack boasted.

"I love you, Jack . . . I love it when you are happy," Fawn said leaning into his shoulder.

Jack smiled back at her, "You're the best, Fawn. . . . Who else would put up with me reminiscing about baseball and the days of old?"

"Reminisce anytime you want, honey," she replied.

"No one can ever replace a man like that . . . no one! They broke the mold when they made him. He's a one of a kind ballplayer . . . just look at Ted. They adore him," Jack said fondly. "Wish people adored me like that," he added.

"I adore you, Jack boy . . . I adore you. . . . Just wait till we get home! I'll show you adoration!"

"Really?" he said coyly.

"Yes, Jackie boy, bet Ted never got what you'll get tonight when you get home!"

"Really? What would that be?" he asked.

"A grand slam!" she said, winking.

Fawn was very much in love with Jack. She loved to make love to him and tonight she would pamper him. *Seeing the legendary Ted Williams and getting laid, all in the same day! Doesn't get much better than that,* he thought in anticipation.

Jack could hear Ted Williams chatting with his son, John Henry. His voice boomed over his son's voice. Ted was known to innocently use obscenities like "hell this" and "hell that," as well as "Christ" and "shit." Those words would preface a statement such as, "Hell, I can remember when. . . ." Jack thought that it was funny to see how Ted was dressed—he avoided ties with a passion. Most of the time he wore slacks and a polo shirt from a golf club in Florida. Tonight was no different for Ted; he sported a Red Sox cap and blue nylon jacket over the polo shirt. Even when they dedicated the newest tunnel in Boston in Ted's honor, he didn't dress up for the occasion.

Jack Danton's own collection of sports memorabilia included Ted Williams as well as many other Red Sox players. He did seek out the most unusual "Ted pieces" when they were available. Jack had found many autographed photos of Ted Williams as a younger man. They included photos of him practicing at Holy Cross College in Worcester, others of Ted in his flight uniform in Korea and pictures of him with Jimmy Foxx at Fenway . . . in their jock straps and flexing their biceps. The most cherished photo that Jack possessed was the one Ted preferred himself. That one showed a young boy in a Minneapolis Millers's uniform. Ted played minor league for the team and the boyish, happy smile was a beautiful picture of Ted at nineteen years old. Jack's other favorite shot of Ted was that of the Brearley Collection—*the classic swing* picture of Ted swinging at the All Star Game in 1947. Brearley was a noted photographer in Boston. He captured the rhythmic swing of Williams, with the catcher and the umpire looking up while watching "the shot" going over the wall of Fenway Park. The black and white pictures were often developed in sepia or brown tone finish, making them reminiscent of baseball photos from the 1800s.

Fishing and hunting became his life after he retired from the game. Ted was even known to shoot a few pigeons from the rafters of Fenway Park until someone complained to the humane society. He and Mr. Yawkey thought that it was a way to eliminate the filthy birds from the rafters of the Fenway overhang.

Tonight, the legendary Ted Williams would watch three or four innings and then retire to his hotel. His health, deteriorating from two strokes, prevented him from watching the whole game. Jack and Fawn relished the fact that they got to see him. It would be a lasting memory for both of them.

Five

The offices of attorney John Campari were located on the fifteenth floor of an office building that overlooked Boston City Hall and Faneuil Hall marketplace.

As the months passed, the family of the late Joe Rizzo met to settle their father's estate. A lawyer would finally read the last will and testament of Joseph Rizzo after it had cleared probate court and the family gathered at the lawyer's office near Government Center.

The Rizzo family sat in a large cherry-paneled conference room of the Campari Law Offices. Tony Campari, one of the partners, proceeded to read Rizzo's will to his children, their wives and husbands. It was a simple will. The three children would split equally all of Joe's personal possessions and revenues from his bank accounts, stocks and trust funds. His personal articles, jewelry and other possessions such as his furniture, the barber business and automobile would be dispersed according to the children's wishes. There was a statement in the will that ordered his three children not to bicker over his possessions. It was a statement that was unnecessary, since the three offspring were close and would easily decide who best needed the articles to be disseminated. Paula would get the automobile. She had none.

The lawyer then addressed a footnote at the bottom of the will. It stated clearly that *the sports memorabilia in his barbershop was to be sold or auctioned and the revenues from the sale were to be dispersed equally among all three surviving children and their families.*

The grandchildren's names were also included in the list of beneficiaries. Since Joe Sr. knew that no one in the family had an affinity for the odd collection of trinkets and autographs, he felt it was best that they benefit from the revenues of its sale instead. He possessed good forethought on that one. He did not want his kids bickering over one baseball here and one baseball there. Besides, he had many offers for the collection and knew that the value was high. The three kids could use the cash and someone who really cared about the memorabilia might appreciate the collection.

The clause at the bottom of the will also referenced the name of a Texan who had expressed interest in the collection. The will stated that the man lived in Dallas and was to be contacted relevant to his prior interest in the memorabilia collection. A flat rate of $60,000 was the figure that Joe and the Texan had agreed upon, if there was ever to be a sale. Joe had negotiated the 60K flat rate with an *E. Royston MacDonald,* a Texas oilman and collector of baseball and other sports memorabilia. If he no longer had interest in the collection, then the entire lot was to be auctioned by a reputable dealer for the most money that the children could get.

MacDonald would have first shot. His home and display in Dallas was a museum unto itself. It included game-used uniforms belonging to Gehrig, Ruth, Mantle, Williams and DiMaggio. His collection was highlighted in sports collectors' magazines and some of his possessions were revered as one-of-a-kind items. The collection was valued at between five and nine million dollars. The Rizzo children were not familiar with E. Royston MacDonald, but knew that most Texas oilmen had large sums of money. If their father had agreed to a $60,000 deal with the man, then that was fair enough for them. They would honor the arrangement and the lawyer would call Mr. MacDonald that very day.

The lawyer also had an inventory list that accompanied the will. In that way, Joe Sr. guaranteed that the collection would be complete no matter who desired it or ended up with it. Royston MacDonald also had a copy of the inventory list, which Joe had given him during a visit to Boston. They each felt that someday they might work out a deal while Joe was still alive.

Attorney Campari, contacted MacDonald in Texas, by calling the 1-800-BASEBAL number on the business card. Royston MacDonald called him back in twenty minutes. It was clear from the conversation between Campari and MacDonald, that the Texan was still very interested in the sports collection of Joe Rizzo. Royston also expressed to the Rizzo family his sincere condolences on the loss of their patriarch. He had grown genuinely fond of Joe Sr. and had visited him on numerous occasions when his travels took him to Boston. Most people were unaware that they had met more than one time. As a courtesy and extension of his condolences, MacDonald sent each of Joe's children a very expensive floral arrangement and a sympathy card. He also hoped to treat them to a dinner when he was next in Boston. He was not aware of Joe's passing when it happened, and he was away on business oversees in Scotland when the funeral had occurred. There was now ample reason for him to go to Boston as soon as possible. The reason was Joe Rizzo's agreement with him, in Rizzo's will.

One week later, the contents of Joe Rizzo's sports collection in the barbershop were carefully inventoried, packed and en route to Dallas. MacDonald had hired a national moving company and had also sent one of his trusted employees to Boston to oversee the transportation of the memorabilia to Texas. Joe Sr.'s lawyer would oversee the family's end of the deal because none of the children wanted to see their father's prized collection physically removed from the old shop. That would mean closure to them, and they really didn't want that yet. Royston, knowing their sensitivity decided not to go to Boston. Instead he sent some representatives to handle the details, in his absence.

The Rizzo children toured the shop the week before and reminisced about each part of the collection. It was clear that the collection was a part of their father's life and they would miss it. They realized that the collection was going to someone who appreciated it as much as their father did. *Someday,* they thought, *it might even end up in Cooperstown, New York . . . in the National Baseball Hall of Fame.* Some of the collection certainly deserved to be in the hall.

The truck was loaded with the collection in less than five hours. Among the treasures placed on the van were the autographed photos collected during the forty years Joe spent in the barber business. Additionally, there were team-signed baseballs, bats and multi-signed balls by Williams, Joe Cronin, Jimmy Foxx and many others. Interspersed in the baseball collection was a single-signed Babe Ruth signature on a Gold Smith ball. The baseball, manufactured at one time in Cincinnati, was old and had imprinted on it below the logo GOOD FOR 18 INNINGS. It was the predecessor of the official Rawlings and Spalding baseballs, used today. The stitching on the ball was red and blue and Ruth's signature was in near mint condition. It was personalized on the "sweet spot" and said "To Joe the Barber, Your friend from Sudbury, Babe Ruth." It was a classic Ruth signature—perfect in penmanship and each letter of his name was clearly legible. The ball was worth about ten thousand dollars by itself . . . perhaps more now that a famous Boston Italian barber was also deceased.

Added to the collection on the moving van, were the carefully packed vials of Joe's hair clipping collection. Many of the vials had handwritten labels, which were illegible. Many others were still clear and easily read. Eventually, some would be tossed out, but MacDonald would determine which ones would go or be retained. The Rizzo collection was not limited to ballplayers. Royston figured that some of the clippings were from celebrities and even presidents. *They would go on display by category,* he thought. Joe's collection would expand MacDonald's own and encompass some of the most famous people in the world. At one time or another, many of them had stopped by Joe Rizzo's barbershop.

Once the shipping containers were opened, E. Royston MacDonald would find that the hair samples varied in texture and color. There was every color from black to white and in between. It would take weeks to sort through the collection and Royston would start doing that the day after they arrived in Dallas.

MacDonald insisted that each vial be individually packed. They were to be shipped in isolated containers packed with plastic popcorn-shaped shipping material. They were not to have contact with any other vials or packages. MacDonald had ordered the shipping to be precise and methodical. It took three hours of the five just to pack the vials in accordance with MacDonald's instructions.

The unusual collection was now loaded and the doors to the van closed. It would make its journey to Dallas in about two to three days. No one could ever predict construction and traffic delays en route to Texas. Drivers of the van would rotate turns so that they didn't have to stop, except for gas and food to go. MacDonald paid extra for the continuous service and didn't care if the ICC or DOT rules of the road were followed. He was anxious to get his new collection to Texas. He monitored the van's progress by calling the drivers by cellular phone to determine their location. His spokesperson from the oil company, who accompanied the shipment, drove in a Cadillac behind the moving van all the way. Once in Texas, the drivers of the van and the man in the Cadillac would each be rewarded handsomely with a check—a very large check. The car and van drivers switched as needed.

Thirty-six hours later, the van pulled into E. Royston MacDonald's massive estate complex. Workmen at his home would unload the shipment in an hour and a half. MacDonald would then personally allocate each package to a specific area in the receiving room of the museum. He would oversee every move that the workers made. He wanted nothing to disappear from his strange, new collection.

"That box will go there," he said to the two men. "The other one goes in the vault, please." The vials were locked immediately in a vault adjacent to the museum entrance. Only MacDonald had the combination of the massive metal doors. The same company that also made commercial vaults for banks (Diebold) made the thirty-by-thirty-square-foot vault exclusively for him. Complete with electronic sensors and virtually indestructible, the massive metal container was fireproof, waterproof and burglarproof. It was a fortress by design and housed much of MacDonald's one-of-a-kind collection items. It was humidity and temperature controlled with alarms that were relayed to the local manufacturer. Security officials were immediately dispatched to the estate if a problem arose with the monitoring and alarm system. MacDonald's alarm company put him in the loop for any emergencies that might occur whether he was in or out of town.

"Who built this fortress, sir," asked a workman. MacDonald merely told him it was a local company. "Come on, guys! No small talk today. I need this stuff in the museum quickly!" he barked.

"Yes, sir, we're on it," replied the workman who now realized that he needed to move a bit faster. "Damn, I need a cig break," he whispered to the other man.

The Babe Ruth ball was immediately secured in the vault. The remainder of the collection could wait before being stored elsewhere and eventually displayed behind the glass-encased mahogany wall units of the personal museum.

Six

The MacDonald Oil Company in Dallas had interests and investments in biomedical research around the world. Because Royston MacDonald had an interest in the latest research in pharmaceuticals and biotechnology, he had acquired many friends in the San Diego area. In addition to his San Diego connections, he maintained friendships in the biotechnology industry in Cambridge, Massachusetts; Denver, Colorado; Research Triangle Park, North Carolina; San Francisco, California and Seattle, Washington. He made his millions from Texas "black gold," but felt that the biotechnology industry was the wave of the future. He was curious about diseases and their eventual cures, hence he invested in companies in the health care area in hopes of funding the next Nobel prize-winning scientist in physiology or medicine. That person might have the ultimate cure for HIV, or the cure for central nervous system diseases such as ALS or Parkinson's Disease. Royston felt that that would gain him fame as well, if he were supporting their research. If they were awarded the Nobel prize, he would be recognized as the financier behind the research. His contribution might deem him the award as well. The thought excited him.

Because of his San Diego connections, MacDonald either stayed at a hotel in Coronado, or he rented a small condo in La Jolla. His living room overlooked the Pacific Ocean along Coast Boulevard. It was the most exclusive property in the area. From his living room window, he could see surfers, sea lions, a migration of whales and the pounding surf of the Pacific. The surrounding homes and condos belonged to very wealthy, health conscious elderly people who decided to retire with a constant view of the ocean in front of them. Each morning they walked their dogs along the beach or sidewalks, which overlooked the cliffs below. Some jogged or walked with hand weights and dressed as if Nike or some other sports clothier sponsored them. Even on the warmest days, they wore logo wear from head to toe. They were fashion statements of the rich and famous.

Royston would laugh at the ones who jogged below his living room window. Some of the supposed athletes were quite heavy for the task at hand. It was comical to him to compare the shapes and sizes of the bodies under his window. He could laugh to himself because he was totally out of shape and made no attempt to correct the situation. Years of over indulgence in fine food and booze had resulted in Royston MacDonald becoming a very large man. He often dressed in expensive tailored suits to hide his enormous stature, but most people could see beyond the clothes. *Someday,* he thought, *I might start an exercise program.* But for now he was an extremely busy man. His fully equipped exercise and weight room in his Dallas home went unused most of the time. The door to the modern, state of the art gym was rarely even unlocked. Royston's personal trainer had all but given up on him.

Royston MacDonald was a philanthropist to many research institutes in southern California. He had often donated large funds to "start-up" companies and "spin-offs" of universities in the San Diego area. Many institutes, such as the renowned La Jolla Research Institute, benefited from his anonymous donations each year. Usually it was only the top management of each company or institute who was aware of MacDonald's generosity. He enjoyed the biological sciences and favored premed courses in college. He never pursued a career in the biological sciences because he was handed an oil company to play with from his wealthy father. Royston never knew what it was like to earn a dollar until he was placed at the top of his oil empire. He then learned what business was all about. His interest in biology presented him with the opportunity to meet prominent scientists and medical doctors. He would befriend anyone who was into basic research of life-threatening diseases.

One of Royston's cohorts in San Diego was Dr. Dwayne Blackburn. He was a Ph.D. biochemist and scientific director at an emerging biotechnology company called Mesa Biotechnology, Inc.

MBI, as it was called, had located its new facility fifteen miles north of center San Diego, just off the Roselle Street exit. Close to La Jolla, it was nestled in the valley between Route 5 and the 805. Mesas, hills and dark green scraggly shrubs common to the southern California coastline, surrounded MBI's facility.

MacDonald liked Blackburn because he was a prominent researcher first, and a sports fanatic, second. The two men enjoyed both the seriousness of the science as well as their fondness for sports. Blackburn had season tickets for the San Diego Padres's home games at QualComm Stadium located just off Route 8 and east toward La Mesa, California. The baseball team touted sluggers the likes of Tony Gwynn, Greg Vaughn and pitcher Kevin Brown. They finally had a team that might go for a World Series championship. All they had to do was beat the New York Yankees, regarded as the finest team ever. The box that Blackburn had at the stadium was enclosed and air-conditioned with a buffet table and an open bar. It overlooked the first base line and had a wonderful view of the entire ballpark. Dr. Blackburn had joined The Padres Club, an upscale social club, and knew many of the Padres players personally. There were always meet-and-greet sessions for prominent ticket holders. Acquisition of autographs from top players was simple if you were a member of "The Club." Both Blackburn and MacDonald were fans of Tony Gwynn. Tony was considered to be the next Ted Williams in notoriety. He was a slugger for the Padres and well liked by everyone. Since Ted was from San Diego, the two players were often compared. Gwynn didn't see the match. After all, "The Splendid Splinter" was a hero to him, not someone to be compared to. *No one could be another Ted Williams,* he thought. *They broke the mold after Williams was born. Who would break his record batting average of .406 in a single season?*

Dr. Blackburn had his own sports memorabilia collection. It was not as large as Royston's but it was a nice compilation of artifacts from baseball, football and basketball. Blackburn had grown up in San Diego and went to the same Hoover High School that Ted Williams had attended years earlier. That alone inspired him to collect Ted Williams memorabilia. Because of the difference in their ages, Blackburn, however, never got to Fenway Park and never saw Ted play there. He regretted the fact that he never saw Ted play, but still admired Ted's career and stylistic autograph.

Blackburn and MacDonald would share duplicate items of memorabilia with each other, especially if a player that they admired signed the items. They would look for unique collectibles while traveling around the country. Many major cities had autograph shops in malls and each man would go out of their way to see if the shops had anything worth acquiring for the other. MacDonald would always go to visit San Diego Sports Collectibles north of San Diego. Unfortunately, the last time he tried to stop by the shop, there were chains on the doors and a bank notice posted for an auction. He was saddened by this event since he thought that they were solvent. He used to buy unique Red Sox memorabilia and baseball cards there. Had he known that they were in financial trouble, he might have bought their entire stock.

Because of their strong bond in science and in baseball, MacDonald and Blackburn became close friends and Royston invested heavily in Mesa Biotech. Blackburn would benefit each year from the endowment since MacDonald funded seventy-five percent of the research and development activity at MBI. The preclinical research areas were of interest to Royston. Mesa Biotech was on the forefront of science. As scientific director, Blackburn oversaw the DNA and protein discovery group. Mesa Biotech was gaining fast on several therapeutic areas. Its future products would be in the areas of diabetes, Alzheimer's, and ALS or Lou Gehrig's diseases. It also dabbled in the infertility area and focused on female antibodies to the protein content of human sperm. In some couples, this resulted in infertility, if the sperm were killed or incapacitated. Other research in this area focused on *in vitro* fertilization, a way to increase fertility in infertile couples. MBI had isolated a protein that made the egg more susceptible to sperm penetration *in vitro*. This greatly increased the chances for more viable eggs to attach to the uterine wall after the *in vitro* procedure.

Because of their promising research programs, Mesa scientists often collaborated with the Fertility Clinic at Torito Bay Medical Center. Dr. Blackburn knew Dr. Jonathan Bradshaw there quite well. They often attended symposiums together and cooperated in hosting seminars with prominent speakers as guests. The local universities also fostered the academic and pharmaceutical interaction by allowing most biotech companies to use their library facilities. Scientific knowledge was shared throughout the San Diego community.

Before MacDonald had gone back to Texas, there was a discussion with Blackburn that focused on building a specialized research team. Royston had asked Blackburn if he knew of any candidates for a project management position that he was considering. There was a need for someone to oversee the group and help build a prominent research team. Blackburn mentioned that he could think of only one person who was connected with biotech and pharmaceutical firms across the country.

"Who's that?" asked Royston with serious interest.

"Roy, the man you want to talk to is a fellow named Danton—Jack Danton in Boston. He's damn well-connected and a personable sort. We deal with him and his contract lab for toxicology testing on occasion. He comes out here often to see biotech clients."

"Really?" said MacDonald with piqued interest. "You like this guy?"

"Talk to him," added Blackburn. "I'll get his number for you. . . . Ah, better than that, here's his card!"

"Thanks, I'll try and reach him," said Royston raising both eyebrows. "Danton, eh?"

"Yep," responded Blackburn. "Worth talkin' to."

Royston would return to Texas before he contacted Jack.

✐ ✐ ✐ ✐

The phone rang at the Danton residence and Jack noticed a Dallas area code on the caller I.D. The phone number was not familiar to him but he decided to answer it. Had it said "out of area," he knew it would be an irritating telemarketing call and he would let it ring.

"Hello, this is Jack Danton."

"Mr. Danton, this is Royston MacDonald in Texas. You don't know me, but we have mutual acquaintances and interests."

"Really, Mr. MacDonald?" Jack responded politely. "Can I ask the nature of this call? I'm a bit busy right now," he said thinking it was some sales pitch.

"Yes, sir, Mr. Danton," MacDonald said with reassurance. "A client or two of yours in San Diego suggested that we talk. They regard you highly and recommended that we touch base. There might be opportunities for mutual enhancement, and mutual interest."

"Really?" Jack asked impulsively. "What client was that?"

"Jack, you and I have friends and business acquaintances at Mesa Biotech in San Diego. It turns out that all of us, individually, collect baseball memorabilia. They thought that you might like to see my collection in Texas. It is rather vast and one of a kind. Do you collect, Jack?"

"Yes, I have some items, mostly Red Sox, but nothing that would be vast," Jack replied with significant interest.

"A lot of my pieces are Boston-related, Jack. . . . By the way, may I call you Jack?"

"Sure, that would be fine."

"The collection I have includes many artifacts from Boston players . . . both the Red Sox and the old Boston Braves teams. There is a lot of Ted Williams, Yastrzemski, Cronin and Foxx pieces. Some Ruth memorabilia is here, as well. He played for Boston for a short time."

Jack was enthused by the conversation.

"I have a tiny collection. Some signed photos of Ted and some baseballs from the '75 Impossible Dream Team. I have a lot of Tony Conigliaro pieces. I really liked him."

Royston listened patiently to Jack's account of Tony's untimely death. He died on February 24, 1990 at forty-five years of age. The 24th of February was also Jack's birthday.

"That's good, Jack! 'Tony C.' was awesome. Anything by him is of value. He was a singer, too. He had a band and had done recordings. He sang very well. Do you have any of those, Jack?"

Jack was excited now. *A Texan who knew who Tony Conigliaro was! Amazing!* he thought.

"Yes, I have some old 45s by Tony," Jack added proudly. MacDonald didn't tell Jack that he had the original tapes from the studio where Tony C. recorded his songs. He also had many baseballs signed by Tony. Jack was somewhat embarrassed that his collection was so small compared to Royston's.

"Jack, I wanted to mention some business opportunities as well," Royston changed subjects. We both have a commonality of being in the pharmaceutical business. I like biotech as well. It's exciting. I invest heavily in research. . . .That is, research . . . with potential!"

"Really?" asked Jack. "Is that how you know Mesa Biotech?"

"Sure is!" said Royston. "They are one of many I have interest in. Many companies are into cardiovascular research, some into the central nervous system diseases (CNS), and others into immunology, like HIV and AIDS research. We even support a local fertility clinic in San Diego for people who can't conceive. We help them have the children that they normally can't have."

Jack was now into the conversation. He knew the reproductive biology field well and found Royston's comments of interest.

"This is fascinating. Most of my clientele are on the West Coast: San Francisco, Seattle and San Diego. My company performs safety testing of new drugs for those clients."

"Jack, my boy, that is precisely why I called you. You seem to be connected nationally, according to my Mesa sources. They say you know everyone that is anyone in the biotech and pharmaceutical field," Royston said warmly.

Fawn looked in to see whom Jack was talking to. He gently gestured with his hand as if to temporarily wave her off. It was a signal that he would be done soon. She could see that he was excited.

Royston stepped ahead in the conversation. The niceties were over. He wanted to meet Jack and discuss some potential interaction in business. "Jack, because of our mutual interests, I thought I might come to Boston and take you and your wife out for dinner. Would that be acceptable? I need your input on something and would pay you handsomely for your help."

"I *am* employed," responded Jack. "I can't work for two companies."

"Jack, let's do dinner and then you can tell me what you think. There is no obligation. I'm merely coming to Bean Town to say hello and meet with you, briefly. I need to get back out to San Diego after that. What do you say? Dinner?" Royston was persistent.

"Your wife is Dawn, ah . . . sorry . . . no, Fawn, correct?" said Royston with some confusion.

"Yes, her name is Fawn." Jack was amazed that MacDonald knew his wife's name. *Someone at Mesa Biotech must have spilled the beans,* he thought.

"And, Jack, please call me Roy or Mac or whatever. Don't be formal. Only strangers, or insecure people call me Mr. MacDonald. I feel like I know you, boy."

"Me, too, Roy," replied Jack.

Royston now was on a roll. "I can come up next week. Jack, are you in town, or travelin'? Is it convenient for you?"

"I'm here catchin' up on paperwork. What evening works for you, Roy?"

After a few minutes of discussion, both men agreed to meet at the restaurant, Grille 23 in Boston. It would be Tuesday at 8:00 P.M. MacDonald said he would cab it from Logan. They would meet at the bar and go from there. The restaurant specialized in steaks, chops and seafood and Fawn would surely enjoy the night out.

Fawn was approaching Jack just as he was saying good-bye to MacDonald. "Honey, who was that? You sure hit it off well if it was a stranger! You were on the phone for an hour!"

"Sorry, babe, it was an unusual conversation, but interesting," Jack responded, but stood there thinking.

"This MacDonald character from Texas wants to treat us to dinner next Tuesday. He's a friend of a friend, he says. He sounds rich and prominent. He knows of me through a client on the West Coast, a San Diego client. Fancy this! He also collects baseball memorabilia. He has a house or mansion full of it. Wants me to see it someday."

"Is this guy for real, hon?" she asked with some concern. "You must trust him or you wouldn't have been on that phone for so long."

Fawn walked over to the calendar in the kitchen cabinet. "Oh, honey, Tuesday evening I have my hair appointment with Mr. Michael.

I can't just 'bag' on him. He gets so annoyed when I reschedule. He pisses and moans for hours. Are you sure he said Tuesday?"

"Yes, hon, it's Tuesday. Can your appointment be changed to the day before or after? I think this dinner meeting will be important," Jack begged.

"Yah, real important! Since when is baseball memorabilia all that important?"

"Not just baseball, hon. The Texas cowboy hinted at a job in the 'field' with high salary—lots of bonuses and other perks," Jack added with excitement.

"Job?" she asked, almost annoyed. "What about a job? I don't want to move. We just got this fabulous home and stuff! Dammit, Jack, you promised we'd settle in here and start that *family,* remember?"

"Hon, relax! I didn't say we would go for it. It is worth meeting him and seeing what's up. Anyway, I want to go to Texas and see his collection. We owe him a dinner discussion. I tell you . . . this guy is loaded and seems nice to boot!"

"Why have me go?" she asked. "What will I talk about? That I saw Ted Williams at Fenway, recently? I have nothing in common with this stranger or your business," she said sarcastically.

"Honey, it's only dinner and I need you there. He invited you too, but did toss around a couple of names before he got yours straight. He did end up with Fawn!"

"Oh, that makes me feel just wonderful," she smirked. "What did he call me . . . Susan?"

"No, sweetheart, Dawn! At least it rhymed. What do you say? Can you reschedule that 'Mr. Henna' appointment?" Fawn laughed at the comment and said she would try to change it.

"I have this feeling there is a lot of money involved," Jack added softly. "He had *that* voice about him. Money seemed to be no object and the man was confident, but not forceful. This guy pulls strings, no doubt about it."

"Is this a dress-up thing, Jack?"

"Yes," was the reply. "It's at Grille 23 over by Stuart Street. You need to wear something wonderful and impressive."

"Impressive? Are you using me to impress this Texan? I don't believe it. You want me to let one breast hang out, too? You're a male chauvinist pig!"

"No," Jack replied, sensing that maybe he had crossed the line with his wife.

"I need you to look like you always do when we are out . . . total class and beautiful!"

"Better quit now, hon, or I'll *keep* the damn hair appointment!" she said, smiling back at him. She loved him dearly and saw how happy he was on the phone. He was really into this Texan thing and she would follow his lead. If there were money to be had, she would want to scrutinize this Texas cowboy's integrity. She read people well and Jack would value her opinion. She was beautiful, sexy and smart.

"When this guy sees you, he'll know I *too* have class!" Jack laughed.

"Jack, you are such a bullshit artist! But I still love you." Fawn kissed his cheek and wrapped herself around him.

"Hey, forget about the potential job on the phone! Are you going to finish the 'job' you started before the call?" she said coyly.

"Job? What job?" he responded.

"You kind of left me in limbo. You were being affectionate and loving before the damn phone rang. Would you like to finish what you started, Jack man?"

Jack became silent and smiled at her. He took her hand and gently kissed her behind the ear. He grabbed both cheeks of her ass and slowly removed her underwear. She only had a T-shirt and panties on anyway. Fawn playfully jumped on his back and rode him piggyback and was laughing. He swung her around so that she was facing him and looked for the closest wall for support. In the vertical position, he pressed her against the wall and made love to her in a standing position. She was totally into it and had no problem climaxing. They were both amazed how fast they both came. He had not had a rush like that since they dated; the lust of it all was still there. The primal instinct was ingrained in both of them.

They headed for the shower laughing and playing. They would wash each other for a good fifteen minutes. They were soul mates and each of them was pleased that the desire was still there. Jack was amazed that this all occurred after a phone call. *People should call more often,* he thought.

Fawn kissed his nose in the shower and pressed her breasts against his chest. She could feel his excitement as it pressed against her. No way would she let this moment pass. She gently lathered him up in the genital area and reintroduced him inside of her. . . . One of her knees was against the shower stall for support. He had his back against the wall this time.

Afterward they gently dried one another off. Totally irrelevant to what had just occurred, she whispered to him that they needed to go grocery shopping if they were to make dinner for tonight.

Jack had no intention of shopping. He was wiped and so was she.

"Never mind, hon, I'm buyin' tonight. We ain't shoppin' nowhere," he said with a slight Texas twang. You and me, pardner, are goin' out for grub!" he joked.

"You make me laugh, honey. One phone call and you are a Texan in your own mind! But, I'll take you up on the hospitality, bucko!"

They would go out to dinner at Joyce Chen's in Central Square. It was a perfect finish to a great afternoon.

Seven

E. Royston MacDonald arrived at Logan Airport on Tuesday and took a cab to the restaurant that he had discussed with Jack Danton. It took some time to get to the Back Bay area of Boston. He had scheduled an early flight so that he would be there on time. The cab ride to the financial district and Boston Common was slow, but he was still early. Traffic was the normal snail's pace near Beacon Hill and Tremont Street. Royston would stop briefly at the Boston Common to watch people ride the swan boats—a famous, historical adventure in central Boston. Willow trees and maples surrounded the pond where people rode the boats that, at least from the side, looked like swans. There were also real swans that slowly paddled in meandering paths through the coves and nooks of the pond. Royston thought that they were the most beautiful birds he had ever seen. *They sure didn't have a whole lot of swans in Texas,* he thought. The beauty of New England was its diverse fauna and flora. It was always so green in Boston in the spring and summer.

"Pull over here please, and wait for me," he instructed the black cab driver. "I want to walk a bit through the park. I'll only be a few minutes."

The cabbie responded with a grunt and pulled to the side of the common near the Bull Finch Pub, known as "Cheers" for the television show inspired there. The driver waited and read the *Boston Globe* for a while. The meter was ticking and Royston returned from his stroll twenty-five minutes later. He was winded from the exercise.

He had killed enough time and now instructed the cab driver to head for Grille 23. He knew that Jack and Fawn Danton would be heading for the restaurant shortly from an area north of Boston.

Royston went up the stairs of the restaurant and headed straight for the bar. He ordered a Chivas scotch on the rocks. When he was in a business deal mode, scotch was his drink of choice. It fired him up pretty well. He swirled the drink and ice with his finger and gently wrapped the napkin around the base of the glass. The bartender was attentive to his needs bringing him some "upper end" snacks.

"Mr. MacDonald," the bartender said, "Nice to see you again, sir! How's the great state of Texas?"

"Fine, son. . . . 'Don't mess with Texas,' they say!" he joked, citing the famous rhyme.

"I remember you from last time, sir. You like that twelve-year-old scotch! I have a rare twenty-five-year-old version. Care to try it?" the bartender remarked.

"Sure, son, but I'm expecting some guests. Don't get me all liquored up before they get here. Scotch can do that ya know," Royston responded, sampling the twenty-five-year old liquor.

"Damn, that's fire water, son. Man! What's the proof?"

"'Bout 87, sir . . . but smooth, right?"

"Nice stuff, son. I'll switch to that, if you don't mind. Put some over ice, please." Royston was impressed with the bartender's taste and recommendation.

"I'll let the maître d' know you are awaiting some guests, sir. I'll be right back."

"Thanks, son," replied MacDonald. "Plenty nice of you to do that. Their name is Danton—Dr. and Mrs. Jack Danton."

"By the way, what's the special tonight, son?" asked Royston to the bartender as he returned to his post.

"Sir, the special is always steak *au poîve* here. I always recommend beef. It's the best!"

"Really?" MacDonald replied. "I'll have to try it."

"Yes, sir, it's the cracked pepper that grabs you. The flavor is intense and the beef is tender. Nice, consistent meal here. The chef's specialty."

"Fine, you've convinced me, son. How about some more of those enticing nuts and twigs?" Royston said, referring sarcastically to the munchies in front of him.

"Comin' right up, sir," the bartender responded attentively. Between sips of scotch, Royston devoured the bowl of nuts.

Just then, Jack and Fawn Danton arrived. They had the doorman valet park the BMW directly out front, walked up the steps and quickly noticed the man sitting alone at the bar. Jack just knew from his dress and his enormous size that it was E. Royston MacDonald. He remembered him sounding just as big on the phone.

Royston, in actuality, was always impressive. He was impeccably dressed with a suit, shirt, and tie that came from a New York haberdasher; all handmade and fitted to his massive body. Jack, in turn, was dressed in a blue suit and monochromatic shirt and tie. Both men's shoes were Italian and shone like patent leather. MacDonald had his shoes shined on his way through Logan Airport. Jack, on the other hand, did his own at home.

MacDonald peered over his glass at Fawn. The peach summer suit highlighted her perfect tan and made her look even darker than she actually was. Subtle overhead lighting in the reception area graced the henna of her brunette hair. Royston just knew from the description that the Mesa people had given him that Jack and Fawn Danton were entering the bar. They were an impressive and attractive couple and exuded class. Royston loved that—charisma in a couple.

The maître d' was quick to notice Fawn as well. He thought that she was a strikingly beautiful young woman and a potential model. She certainly had the facial structure and stature to be one, and he was right. She had modeled for a while. He quickly brought them over to meet Royston as he had been instructed to do.

"You must be Jack and Fawn. Pleasure to meet you both," Royston said as he stood up and kissed Fawn's hand. He mentioned how he had heard nice things about both of them. "Let's grab a cocktail at the table. That way we can chat and be comfortable. Is that OK?" Royston asked.

"Yes, Roy, that would be just fine. Honey, please go ahead," he gestured courteously to Fawn. The maître d' guided them to a table by the window, but in full view of the piano player who was entertaining on the lower level.

"Pleasure to meet you as well, Roy. I feel like we've met before or that I've known you," said Jack.

"Yeah, son . . . feels the same here. I enjoyed our recent conversation on the phone. But, you didn't tell me that your better half sittin' across from me was so beautiful. You are a lucky man, son."

"Thank you," Jack and Fawn replied almost simultaneously. They laughed at their mutual timing and response. "Welcome to Bean Town, Roy, I sense that you've been here many times before."

"Yes, Jack, I have. I love this town and even went to the Boston Common to see those gorgeous swans of yours," Royston said as a pleasantry. "They sure are a unique and graceful bird."

Fawn commented with some knowledge and authority, "I'm glad they have them back. They were ill, you know. Perhaps you didn't hear about the problem down south. Had some disease a while back and some of them died. I'm not sure they figured out what was wrong, but the supplier of the swans was in question. There was no apparent problem with the pond or their veterinary care here."

"Really?" said Royston with interest. *She's not only attractive, but a very intelligent woman,* he thought. She was obviously tuned in to the Boston scene and caring enough to show some concern for the swans. He wanted her to expand upon the issue and encouraged her to elaborate further. Jack and Fawn seemed to be a good match.

"There were only two or three birds there," Royston added to her conversation. "I always remember more. Have they reduced the number of birds?"

Fawn continued, "They're the new ones, I believe. The others were removed to be examined, as well. The ones that died underwent necropsies by veterinarians to diagnose the problem. It was a mystery disease."

Royston was aware that a necropsy was an autopsy on an animal. Autopsy only referred to humans. He became more impressed with Fawn as the conversation expanded. Jack added some avian viral information to the discussion as a potential cause of the swans' predicament. Soon all three people relaxed.

Fawn was impressed that this enormous man, who was dressed "to the nines," was sensitive and an obvious gentleman. She thought he carried himself well for his enormous stature. Her original impression of him was that of a sugar daddy who paid a lot of money to get laid by gold diggers from Texas. She caught him staring at her body on occasion and self-consciously adjusted her outfit as often as necessary. It was not an unflattering look, but she realized that he often checked out her chest and face in appreciation.

Jack sensed that Royston was mentally groping his wife, and changed the subject. "Roy, how was the flight?

"They actually did OK today and I was pleased to see that they really can run on time," Royston responded.

"They can really stack them up over Logan—at least that has been my experience."

"Perhaps the weather was in your favor. It sure was a pleasant day here today," Jack added.

Royston laughed. "It's a bit crowded here up north. We have lots of airspace over Texas. We rarely get delays at Dallas-Fort Worth. They can stretch 'em out for miles on final approach."

"You're a lucky man," Jack replied. "We are kind of close-knit up here. Lots of people in a small area and tough access to commercial travel, especially Logan International."

The waiter politely interrupted the conversation to mention the dinner specials. He recited "the fish of the day" and the four specials of the house. Royston already knew what he wanted, but casually let Jack and Fawn peruse the distinctive menu. A candle centered on the circular table glowed warmly in a hurricane glass shell. Around the base of the globe was a ring of fresh flowers. The ambience of the evening could not be more pleasant, or the setting more beautiful. A scotch, a vodka tonic and a glass of chablis were ordered for the table. As they finished their drinks the waiter returned for their main course orders. After a bit of thought, Fawn ordered salmon; Jack ordered filet and Royston the steak *au poîve.*

While waiting for appetizers and bread, the conversation went from pleasantries to a more serious tone. Royston MacDonald had business to discuss.

"Jack, I'm glad that you both could come to dinner tonight. I am pleased that Fawn was able to change her original plans. I have heard good things about you from my West Coast affiliations in biotech. Everyone seems to know you, or of you! Better than that, they respect you in business."

Fawn interjected, "That's been my experience, too. He really is well liked. I'll vouch for that."

Royston smiled and continued, knowing that Fawn was referring to her love for Jack.

"I have a research plan, a 'project' of sorts, that may make history in medicine and in science. It is unlike any project that other U.S. scientists have going—at least that we know of.

Jack, I would like you to be involved in a portion of the overall program. I will reward you handsomely with a significant salary and incentives to help me build the perfect research team. There is program management needed as well. I really need a 'hands-on' manager for this sophisticated scientific endeavor."

Jack was shocked at the bluntness of the initial offer of employment. He could see that Royston was serious and that he was on a "mission from hell," so to speak.

"Roy," Jack replied, "I have been out of direct science and research for years. I haven't published a paper or abstract in a very long time. I don't even read journals in my field anymore! How could I possibly help your program?"

"I know!" interrupted Royston. "Don't sell yourself short! It is not your direct scientific training that I need here. It is your knowledge of the pharmaceutical and biotech industry—your knowledge of the best scientists out there and your levelheaded approach to getting things accomplished. I could tell on the phone that you are organized and methodical . . . perhaps analytical. You also know the basic research programs of the biotech industry and where progress is being made and what promising new drugs are emerging. Although this knowledge is confidential to your clients, I would value your input on which overall medical R&D areas are 'sexy' and moving forward: cardiovascular, CNS, arthritis, anti-inflammatory. You are also a trained reproductive biologist and have a scientific mind from that background. We have programs ongoing in fertility and infertility, cloning and basic embryonic development. Your prior experience there, *is* relevant. For instance, the mechanics of reproduction have not changed. Right?"

"Yes, that's true about my prior background—but when I did research years ago, *we* dealt with whole organs and beasts with four legs. Today, it's all cellular stuff, and I'm way behind on that kind of detailed science," Jack said sheepishly. "I don't have a clue about stem cells, cloning, DNA or any of the stuff that is so controversial today."

"Jack! Look, son. If I needed a crackerjack endocrinologist or protein chemist—if I needed a specialist in biological sample analysis or the best technicians in *in vitro* technology, you might know of capable people in those areas. Right? That is what I need *you* for, not hands-on science! Besides, Jack, I've begun pulling together the team. I've done the groundwork with some prominent scientists. You can help me fill in the missing links."

Jack felt better after hearing what Royston was looking for—a coordinator, a program manager and ambassador between multiple scientists and research facilities involved in the project.

"I guess I might have some contacts for you, if this were to work out between us," Jack replied with confidence.

Fawn, at this point, sensed seriousness on the direction of the dialogue. She listened intently to both men and casually sampled the bread on the table. She nodded when she felt it was appropriate, but at this point she could see that Royston was intent on hiring her husband, almost immediately. *What could be so urgent?* she wondered.

"Jack, I want you to come to San Diego for a visit and meet some people. Some you already know, because they know you now. I will let you know the date that you are needed. We can further the discussions there if you have interest. You can meet some of the people I have on the project and tell me what you think of my hires, thus far. Meeting them should give you some perspective as to what I am trying to do. You would then become a part-time human resource person for me to find the people to fill the missing slots. You will be my 'prospector of talent' so to speak."

"You really want me to be part of this plan I can tell," Jack said with conviction.

"That is true, son! I need a guy like you to make all this work. The finances are in place. The project is designed, the facilities are set and now we need the talent to make it all happen."

With that, Royston backed off a bit. The meals had finally arrived and were presented before them in an elegant fashion.

"For now, let's enjoy the meal. It certainly looks wonderful, right?" Royston said, raising his glass. "To you both!"

"Thank you," said Fawn. "And to you, too."

Fawn now felt comfortable to say something.

"Roy, this looks wonderful. The salmon is very fresh and the vegetables are cooked perfectly."

"Mine looks great, too," remarked Jack. "The filet is covered with a light béarnaise sauce."

Royston just smiled and sampled his steak. It was an incredible dish, just as good as the bartender had said it would be. On his way out, he would have to remember to leave the kid behind the bar a handsome tip.

Royston indicated that he would be going to Dallas or San Diego in the next day or so and that he wasn't sure which would occur first.

"We'll talk more about the opportunity in a day or so. OK?" Royston added.

"Yes, that's fine. I'll need some time to talk over this opportunity with the beautiful woman to my left—my wife."

Fawn was appreciative that Jack was not deciding on a career move without first discussing it with her in detail.

The meal was exquisite and the wine selection by Royston for dinner was most appropriate. He was an expert in both red and white wines. He selected a white that complemented Fawn's salmon and a spectacular red that embellished the beef that both he and Jack had ordered. The dessert tray and coffee followed.

The Dantons and Royston laughed like old friends as they discussed Boston, baseball, Cape Cod, Texas Longhorns, the JFK assassination and a host of topics of mutual interest. Later, they had a cordial to finish off the meal.

Royston had the maître d' package up the ring of flowers center-piece for Fawn to take home. The leftovers were wrapped in aluminum foil and presented to them in the shape of swans. It was a classy, prearranged gesture by Royston, and the waiter obliged.

During the ride home, Fawn bluntly asked Jack if he trusted MacDonald. She was a bit skeptical about the Texan earlier in the evening, but could not put her finger on what bothered her.

"Fawn, for some reason, I am fascinated by this man. I need to hear what he has to say in San Diego. I'm flattered that he wants me involved. I was a bit concerned about him at first, but when we were in the men's room, he kept saying, 'Jack Boy, this is Project Samuel and you will be famous like the rest of us. I need you to help with the program management. Think about the opportunity!' "

Fawn half listened to her husband. Music from the car radio was low and soothing. She had one ear tuned in to her husband, but she was also tired from the evening's intense conversation. She put the seat back in the car and rested while Jack reviewed the evening discussions out loud.

Before the Dantons left the restaurant, Royston reminded Jack that he should also come to Texas to see his baseball memorabilia collection. Jack would try to work it in so that it involved a weekend and didn't affect his current job needs or travel.

Ultimately, Jack and MacDonald would end up having much in common. He had not accepted a position as yet, and he still deemed it necessary to meet with Royston in San Diego, and on the man's own turf in Texas. He needed much more information.

Royston MacDonald spent the night at the Bostonian Hotel adjacent to Quincy Marketplace. He managed to include a walk around the Fenway Park area the next morning. He loved to see the bars and shops on Yawkey Way. He touched the brick wall of Fenway's main structure and felt a kindred attachment to the grand old park. Pressed for time, he took a quick ride to Logan Airport by way of the Massachusetts Turnpike extension adjacent to Fenway. He had decided to fly home to Dallas instead of on to San Diego. He had a trip to San Diego forthcoming anyway and needed to check on his home and oil business enterprise as well, especially before heading west.

Eight

The Torito Bay Medical Center, ten miles north of San Diego, was situated high above an affluent residential section. It offered standard medical care and a few specialized medical units. The medical center was known for its heart teams as well as its fertility clinic. The heart team specialized in invasive surgery and was staffed with former members of the Cleveland Clinic. The Cleveland group had developed and trained others in coronary bypass procedures in the late 1960s. Torito Bay offered angioplasty and the newest methods for correcting coronary occlusion, such as stents. They had moderate success with the latest in medical devices. They were also one of the first clinics to utilize biotech drugs for busting coronary clots. The center's surgical unit was the best in California and most new cardiovascular drugs went to them for preliminary phase I and phase II clinical trial evaluations.

With respect to fertility enhancement in infertile couples, Torito Bay Medical Center had acquired Dr. Jonathan Bradshaw from England. Bradshaw, a fertility expert, had been chief of staff at a Cambridge, England foundation and hospital. He was a welcomed addition to the Fertility Clinic at Torito Bay. In England and in the United States, Bradshaw had a high rate of success in assisting couples who were childless but passionately desired pregnancy. His specialty was *in vitro* fertilization (IVF), and he was a coauthor of one of the original publications on enhancing success with the technique. Twenty years earlier when his publications appeared in the journals *Nature* and *The Lancet*, Bradshaw's fertility enhancement success rate was above seventy-five percent. Infertile couples traveled from all over the world to utilize his expertise and become patients in his clinic. Although the evaluations and follow-on procedures were costly, the affluent community around San Diego fostered a clientele for which money was no object. Additionally, some health care providers and insurance companies supplemented the cost of the treatment. This was especially true if the medical problem was the result of a prior reproductive disease state, or was a genetic anatomical anomaly. Fallopian tubal blockage in the female reproductive tract was a common occurrence in women who had prior pelvic inflammatory diseases or sexually transmitted diseases, such as gonorrhea. Often the female patient was unaware that her reproductive organs were blocked due to scarring. They were merely aware that they failed to get pregnant. Prior diseases were sometimes asymptomatic.

The Fertility Clinic at Torito Bay also provided services in ovulation induction and *in vitro* fertilization for those wishing to become pregnant, but they also catered to patients that desired contraception. They performed vasectomies and tubal ligations, if requested. A satellite office of a Planned Parenthood-like group was maintained on site to accommodate the contraceptive needs of promiscuous teenagers in the local area. They provided courses and consultation for the teens that desired to be educated in their sexual health and well-being. It was clear from the number of young clients that visited the clinic, that southern California was a hotbed of the sexual revolution. If clients were going to be having casual sex, the clinic wanted to promote safe sex and protection from unwanted pregnancy and sexually transmitted diseases (STDs).

Nine

Tom and Vicky Palmer were married ten years and had no children. They had practiced birth control for eight years and now had decided they wanted to have a family. Vicky had gone off the low-dose contraceptive pill about two years earlier, but although they were attempting to get Vicky pregnant, they had not met with success. Tom was now thirty-six and Vicky, thirty-two. If they were to have a family, they wanted to do it as soon as possible. Neither Tom nor Vicky had a desire to have children in their mid-forties. They decided that they would seek the assistance of the fertility clinic at Torito Bay Medical Center.

Tom Palmer was a successful stockbroker. His annual salary was in the $250,000 range. Tom and Vicky lived in a beach house overlooking the coastline in La Jolla. They had recently found their Spanish-style dream home, surrounded by an acre of land—an almost impossible find. Most of their other neighbors abutted one another since land on the Pacific coast was at a premium. Vicky had been a nurse for years and had friends who helped her contact Dr. Bradshaw. Through her friends, she was able to make the "short list" for a consultation with Dr. Bradshaw. With a long waiting list of fifty potential clients, her connections got her moved to the top four on the list. It helped that the Palmers' income was in a bracket that could easily pay for the services required. At this point, they were desperate to start a family, and Dr. Bradshaw and his colleagues were the Palmers' first choice.

Two months into their fertility evaluation, it was clear that the problem was Vicky's. Tom's sperm evaluation was normal in all respects. Vicky had also been cleared of any anatomical problems, but she had a prior history of an irregular menstrual cycle. The hormonal imbalance of reproductive steroids, estrogen and progesterone, had resulted in her inability to predict when ovulation might occur from one month to the next. On occasion, there was no cycle to speak of, hence ovulation was absent. Even if she did get pregnant, it was unlikely that she would go to term without supplemental hormonal treatment. The brain and the ovaries were out of synch with one another. The condition resulted in occasional ovarian cysts and infertility.

Dr. Bradshaw was confident that it could be corrected. Bradshaw's evaluation was confirmed by the fact that Vicky had confessed that she had been pregnant once before, but had never gone to term. She spontaneously aborted the fetus at two months of gestation. Tom was not aware that his wife had ever been pregnant, since the pregnancy had occurred when she was in nursing school and before they had met; the result of a fling with a then-resident doctor. She didn't care to share those facts with her husband of ten years. *It was best kept secret,* she thought. She did, however, have to tell Bradshaw in confidence, since she was asked if she had ever been pregnant. That information was part of the overall evaluation. She had checked off "yes" on the medical history chart and it remained confidential to all of Bradshaw's staff.

Dr. Bradshaw called Tom and Vicky into his office.

"Please sit down," he said warmly. "I think we have a logical approach to the problem."

"Really?" Vicky replied enthusiastically. Tom perked up as well.

"It would appear from all the tests to date, that you two can become parents! That is to say, that it is certainly feasible."

"How? We've been trying for two years," Vicky said.

Bradshaw continued, "It's not how hard you've tried or the length of time that you have tried. You have an endocrine imbalance that thus far has prevented you from conceiving easily. There is no anatomical reason that we can find to prevent you from having a child. Your reproductive system has all the parts, but your brain does not regulate your cycle properly. It has to do with the pituitary gland, but I don't want to bore you with medical jargon."

"Brain?" she asked, "Something's wrong with my brain? I'm a trained nurse. You will not scare or bore us. Please elaborate."

"OK, then," said Bradshaw. "There is nothing that can't be corrected from a hormonal point of view. That is where we can help. You need to have your menstrual cycle regulated to where we can predict ovulation. Your estrogen level has been high as the result of cystic ovaries. This apparently happened after you ceased taking the pill. Normally the body goes back to a normal cycle after the pill, but in your case, the ovaries were over stimulated by pituitary hormones."

Vicky and Tom listened carefully to the options.

"If supplemental hormone replacement creating a proper cycle doesn't work, we would induce ovulation, harvest some of your eggs or ova and then fertilize them *in vitro*. We would then place them in your uterus at the appropriate time when the womb would accept them. You would have hormonal treatment as well to prepare the uterus. The necessary extra hormones to keep the pregnancy going would continue through gestation. This makes the body think that you are undergoing a function natural to the body. In the end, you should be able to have a child or perhaps more than one. What do you think of this approach?"

Vicky responded with some apprehension. "Does that mean that the baby will be normal? I mean with all those chemicals?"

Bradshaw assured her, "Yes, the hormones that we use are natural to your body. Please be aware that if the *in vitro* method is used, you may have more than one fetus developing. This often occurs in this procedure. Multiple pregnancies are common because we return more than one fertilized egg to the womb. This is to insure that you have at least one egg implant in the uterus, resulting in a baby. Questions?"

There was a sigh of relief as both Tom and Vicky said almost in unison, "Instant family? That's OK! So, doctor, when can we start?" asked Tom.

"Anytime. Looks like we've got you penciled in to start hormone treatment next week! Is that OK?"

"Yes!" Vicky piped up, "That will be fine. Thank you, Dr. Bradshaw. Thank you so very much!"

"Then, see you next week . . . check with the receptionist out front for the time and have a great weekend."

Tom and Vicky left the office arm in arm. They were smiling at the thought that they could finally start a family, with the help of Dr. Bradshaw. He made them feel confident that the problem could be resolved. If there were more than one child as a result of the treatment, that would be OK. Relatives in the area could help them if needed. It might even be fun with two or more kids at once.

Ten

E. Royston MacDonald had been in touch by phone and soon invited Jack Danton to Texas to see his sports memorabilia collection when Jack was between sales trips. Jack planned to incorporate a weekend with MacDonald with a visit to some of the Texas biotechnology clientele in The Woodlands area near Dallas.

It wasn't long after their dinner that MacDonald called Jack and said, "My boy, I've added some new Red Sox items to the collection. Time for you to get down here and see it before I sell any of it. I need to talk to you some more about the project."

He was laughing since he was not known for selling any memorabilia that he had stockpiled over the years. "I'll give you a private tour of the vault, as well," he added as enticement.

Jack was so excited at Roy's call that he barely asked Fawn if it was feasible for him to get away. She sensed that it was forthcoming and encouraged Jack to enjoy the invitation and tour of MacDonald's mansion. They were still undecided on a job change.

"Thank you, Roy, for the invite. I'll check with Fawn to see if there is anything that we had planned for those dates that I might have forgotten. I really want to see all those Ted Williams and Babe Ruth pieces that you've hoarded away." Jack was so excited that he couldn't stand himself. He would see items never seen by other collectors at baseball card shows, or even at national sports memorabilia conventions. Even Cooperstown's Baseball Hall of Fame didn't have some of Royston's artifacts.

"Check with Fawn, son, and then get your ass down here. You won't regret it," Royston said with the voice of authority. "Don't make her mad now, ya here? Tell your beautiful woman that I merely want to have you see this collection and talk some more business opportunities with ya. She sure is lovely Jack. You keep that one, ya here? No matter what—you don't lose that nice lady!"

"Yes, indeed!" Jack replied.

Royston continued, "Thought you might like to see what oil money can buy, son. I'm surrounded here by memories as we speak—Fenway memories, Boston memories and Ted Williams memories! You gotta see it, son!"

What Jack Danton did not know was that a "famed collector" of memorabilia had decided to auction off his entire collection to pay some elaborate debt owed the IRS. Christie's and Sotheby's vied for the privilege of handling the vast collection of memories. Royston MacDonald had sent one of his confidants from Texas to the auction in New York City to acquire "the best of the best" items—within reason. MacDonald guided the man through the auction by cellular phone, picking and choosing the critical items for acquisition or bid. MacDonald knew the going rate for most items by reviewing the preliminary list and photos. He would select only the most unique pieces of memorabilia. He focused on Ted Williams. There were uniforms and gloves, bats, shoes and warm-up jackets. There were war artifacts of Ted's from Korea, including parts of the fighter planes that he had flown. In general, each item was unique to Ted's career and life. Baseball, WWII and Korea were all part of that career.

"Jack boy, you know when Ted Williams hit his last home run?"

"Think so, Roy. It was his last 'at bat,' right?"

"Right, boy! You're a smart man. It was 1960 and Ted's last step up to the plate, before he bowed out of playing baseball. His last 'at bat' was a home run off pitcher Jack Fisher of the Orioles on September 28, 1960."

"You're right, Roy. It was a great way to close out a career!"

"Well, Jack, while I'm talkin' to you I'm holdin' a plastic display cube with a ball in it. Know which ball it is, son?" asked Royston, exhibiting great pride and mystery during the phone call.

"No, Roy, I don't know what ball it is. I'm friggin' 2,000 miles from Texas and you've got lots of baseballs, I would think." Jack was waiting in anticipation for the answer.

"I'm holdin' the ball that Williams hit over the fence at Fenway—during his last 'at bat.' I found the guy who caught it years ago and tracked him down. I paid him a bundle and now *I* have it. It was stuffed far away in his bedroom closet where no one could see the damn thing. Wasn't even protected from dust and stuff. He bought a cheap bleacher ticket and caught the friggin' ball . . . Ted's last hit, home run and baseball, hit by the slugger!"

"Jesus! You've got *that* ball? Must be worth a mint. I imagine Ted wanted it as well," Jack said politely.

"Hell, son, I might just give it to Ted. Have to think about it though. Bet he'd actually like to know who has it. But one thing for sure, son, it doesn't belong in a closet! It needs to be displayed and I'll do it!

You comin' down here to see it?" Royston asked, growing impatient.

"Yes, I'm comin' down. I have to see *that* ball!" Jack added. "When can I come down? What's convenient?"

"Get a ticket boy!" barked MacDonald. "Call my assistant down here and have her arrange for the plane and limo. You plan on stayin' here with me. And dammit! Bring me some of that maple syrup from New Hampshire, will ya? Love that stuff on pancakes and grits."

"Yes, I'll call her and arrange for the trip. I'll get you some maple syrup—know just the place that has it. I'll have them ship it direct from Mason, New Hampshire, to Texas. I'll get the gallon size! Liquid gold!"

"Thanks, Jack boy! You're all right. You are fast at decisions and getting things done. I need you to get some things done for me in San Diego. When you come down, we'll sit and chat." Royston carefully added the business needs to the conversation. "By the way, son. Liquid gold is black and it's right here under my feet deep in the ground. It doesn't come from no damn maple tree!"

"Right," laughed Jack. "But have you ever tried *your* liquid gold on pancakes?" Jack snapped back. "Pretty dark and messy, as crude goes!"

"Nope! Ya got me there! Ya got a sense of humor, too. I like that! I'll be in touch and see you soon in Texas!"

Both men hung up and chuckled to themselves. The rapport and level of comfort was building between them. Jack liked Roy and Roy liked him.

Jack took off a couple of days from work and headed to Texas on a Thursday. He would spend the weekend at Royston McDonald's extensive estate and tour his home, museum and vault of sports memorabilia. There would be items from Mantle, Williams, DiMaggio, Ruth and Gehrig. It was a miniature hall of fame in its own right. Some Cooperstown plaques were duplicated there, as well. Jack would end up viewing racks of uniforms like at a dry cleaner. It was all self-contained behind a glass viewing area and motorized. The uniforms were from Satchel Paige, Ruth, Foxx, Hornsby, Mantle, DiMaggio, Williams and other sluggers of the '40s and '50s. All were original and had been "gamed used." Jack was allowed to go inside and hold one or two uniforms. The Babe Ruth uniform was his favorite. He felt his pulse rush and his face go flush.

Royston also collected items from the famed Negro League players, and the female ballplayers from the league, which dominated the years of WWII when men were called to action. There were items from Major League Negro players such as Jackie Robinson and Larry Doby, as well as an Hispanic collection including some Roberto Clemente authentic memorabilia.

After Jack arrived in Texas, he was driven by limo to the MacDonald spread about thirty miles from the airport. MacDonald would wine and dine him, put him up in royal decadence and treat Jack to incredible discussions of old-time baseball and its history. As a gift to Jack, Royston gave him a signed copy of Ken Burns' book on the history of baseball. Jack knew of Ken Burns through his film of the same subject and another on the Civil War. Jack was aware that Ken lived in Walpole, New Hampshire, but had never met him. Walpole was located above Keene, and not all that far from Boston. Jack was overwhelmed with Royston's generosity. After all, in advance of his trip, he had only sent Roy some maple syrup from Parker's Maple Barn in Mason, New Hampshire.

Royston shared stories on how he acquired many of the items, but never let on to Jack how much he had paid for them.

"Bet ya never saw one of these collections!" Royston boasted to his guest. "Seen this?"

"No, Roy, I haven't," Jack responded in amazement.

"Ted Williams endorsed Sears & Roebuck's sporting goods after he left baseball. This is a collection of every Sears's item that bore his signature or endorsement in the catalog. Even the Sears catalogues themselves from those days are collectable. They were the catalogues that one asked for and Sears mailed them to you for free. The checkmark/tick and Ted signature were on all these items. There was clothing, too. The labels on the clothing had his facsimile signature on them as well."

"Jesus," said Jack. "How many are there in here?"

"Hundreds, son! There are boat motors for fishing and fishing reels and rods, guns, ammo, balls, bats, vests, boats, rifles, pants, jackets, and so on. It goes on forever. I even have the boys' and girls' bicycles that he endorsed. Just look at those white wall tires! They're as good as the day they were made." Royston waved his right hand over the collection and continued his lecture. "Williams was as good a fisherman and hunter as he was a baseball player. He managed to land some big ones in Florida.

So, what da ya think, son? Nice collection?" he asked Jack candidly.

"Roy, it would take me two years to see it all. Can I come back someday and see more?" Jack asked with a sigh. He had sensory overload.

"Sure, son, anytime. I only show it to people that appreciate baseball and Ted Williams. He was the best ever!"

"Roy, this is probably the greatest collection in the country . . . perhaps in the world!" Jack exclaimed loudly. "I don't know anyone who has even thought to collect this stuff on Ted W."

"Right, son, no one can match it. No one!" Royston said emphatically.

Jack's eyes panned the room and wandered back and forth in amazement. He could not comprehend the whole collection. Royston left him alone for the moment and knew that Jack Danton was impressed with his achievement. Royston was happy to show him what he had collected. After all, Jack was from Boston and would understand the significance of the baseballs, bats, gloves and Red Sox clothing that Ted Williams once wore. The Sears's stuff was just fluff over and above the rest.

"What's this?" Jack asked. He was staring at a number of boxes that said "Rizzo-Boston." They intrigued him since most of them were unopened.

"Ah, Jack, that is my latest acquisition from up your neck of the woods," Royston boasted.

"Really? What's in the boxes from Boston? What's Rizzo?"

"Well, Jack boy, I recently bought the Joe Rizzo collection after he passed away. Bought it from the family after the estate was settled. Ya know, Joe, the barber?" he tested Jack.

"No, Roy, I never met him. I know there was a barber near Fenway Park who ran a small shop. He had some memorabilia on his wall. They say he used to cut the ballplayers' hair from time to time. Is *that* the guy? *That* Rizzo?" Jack asked with interest.

"Joe Rizzo, God bless his soul, was a decent man and a man of his word. He had this collection and, yes he did cut some players' hair as well as other notables like JFK, prominent politicians and baseball owners and managers. He and I had a pact of sorts. He promised me that if he ever sold his collection, I would get first dibs!"

Jack piped in, "Looks like he kept his promise, Roy. Just look at all the boxes!"

"He did, son, but it was after he had died. He mentioned me in his will, and his family honored his request."

Jack added, "I read of his death. There were many noted dignitaries there for his funeral. He was elderly, right?"

"Yes, he was an old man who loved baseball and lived very simply. His collection of photos kept people busy with conversation, while waiting for a haircut or a shave. It was like an amusement park of memorabilia there. No one ever stole his stuff either. No punk ever dared to steal it. The old man lived upstairs and had the ears of an elephant. If someone was near the door, he heard his or her footsteps. He had the collection gathering dust all those years. Much of the dust was hair and dander, I suppose. If you had allergies, his shop was not the place to go," Royston laughed.

Jack told Royston that he had stopped by the shop on numerous occasions to stare from afar at the baseballs and photos. He mentioned to Royston that he always wanted to meet the barber and chat about his memories of Fenway from 1912. It was new then and the town had no need to expand the seating, like today. They both knew that Fenway was going to change soon. Even Royston was opposed to the new plan to change or move the ballpark. He loved the tradition of the older parks, long before money had precedence over the actual sport.

"Too bad you never got a trim or haircut at the barbershop, boy," Royston said with raised eyebrows. "You might have been in that box over there!"

"What the hell are you talking about? Are there heads in there from his slip of the razor?"

"No, son, there are vials in there. Hundreds of them filled with hair clippings. Some of the vials even seem to have hair follicles attached to the hairs. Rizzo must have plucked a few hairs as well. Weird, eh?"

Jack just stared at Royston and was confused. He looked at Roy then back at the boxes and then back to Roy.

"The hair clippings are sweepings or apron collections from people who had their hair cut at Joe's. They are labeled with initials and the year. He apparently swept up some cuttings when finished with the customer and saved the samples for posterity. He didn't do it for everyone—just those that were prominent figures.

Jack interrupted, "Roy, are you saying that JFK or Red Sox ballplayers' hair samples are in those vials . . . like that of Ruth and Williams?"

Royston smiled and replied, "Yep. Home team and visiting team players are in there, most probably. We haven't gone through the whole lot yet. It just arrived. We think most of the vials are well-known players. There's a DiMaggio vial in there. We think it's Dom, not Joe. His brother Dom played for the Sox. The vial said 'D. DiM'."

Jack stood there and thought for a while. He looked at MacDonald and was pale. He envisioned Babe Ruth's hair in one of the glass vials and it was scary. It was like science fiction to him.

"So, why do you want these vials of hair? It is rather a macabre and unique thing to collect," Jack quizzed him. "You can't be sure that the hair is really who you think it is, right?"

"The date on the vials is a good indicator that the hair belongs to who we think they are. It is uncanny how the dates correspond with major players' careers. It is almost magical."

"Perhaps you are right, Roy," Jack said, shaking his head back and forth as he looked at the boxes. "What will you do with this, this collection of dead protein, anyway? Display it in a cabinet?"

"No, son, the plan is to see what the hair is made of. We want to analyze the hair, out in our San Diego lab," Royston volunteered.

"Why?" was Jack's response.

"Son, if you decide to join my team of experts, I'll tell you much, much more. Until you take the job with me, I can't tell you much. Let me just say, it's *big* son, *very big!*"

Royston now had Jack in the palm of his hand. Jack was so interested in what he had going on out west in San Diego, that he could hardly contain his emotion.

"Son, biotechnology is the wave of the future: a *tidal wave* of sorts! You can be part of that future. You need to consider my offer seriously. There's no time to waste. Are you on this train, Jack?" Royston asked him directly. "Are you ready to board?"

Royston was now fired up. He wanted Jack Danton to answer right there, to *commit*. Jack, on the other hand, was cautious. He hardly knew MacDonald and had no idea if the man was crazy or demented. *Vials of hair,* he thought. *What would someone do with vials of hair?* MacDonald seemed normal and bright and was successful and respected. Jack wanted the same for himself. He would need to know more about what San Diego personnel were doing. *What did Royston MacDonald have up his sleeve?* Dead protein and locks of hair were the clues, but Jack did not immediately put two and two together. He had to know what the hell the job was about but Royston would not share the information until Jack committed to the job offer.

Royston MacDonald allowed Jack some space and sensed that Danton was in a quandary. Royston would change the subject to politics just for fun. He would have some wine with Jack and tell him whom he knew well in Washington, D.C. He often lobbied for the petroleum industry. Some senators and congressmen were in his hip pocket, so to speak. Royston sat in the large leather chair across from Jack and told him of the presidents that he knew or had met. He knew Lyndon Johnson from Texas well, but did not elaborate on *that* particular president. Danton could not conclude whether Royston was Republican or Democrat. He surmised that he favored the Republican side. He was into big money and influence and so were the Republicans. Some labor unions and the big corporations leaned toward the Republican side. Since MacDonald was a huge oilman and rich, Jack pretty much guessed which way he leaned. The guns over a fireplace convinced him of that.

By the time Jack left Texas for Boston he was exhausted. How could he tell Fawn about all he saw and talked about? He would not stay in Texas to see clients. He no longer cared about hooking up with those biotech firms. His mind was on a potential new job and hair clippings. Jack would tell Fawn about the four days in Texas and about the Rizzo collection. She would listen intently but knew from Jack's excitement that he was strongly considering joining the MacDonald team.

❧ ❧ ❧ ❧

Jack Danton was now close to saying yes, but needed to make a sales trip to San Diego. If Royston was out there, they could hook up again and further the discussions. Jack needed to talk to Mesa Biotech scientists to determine who had recommended him to MacDonald. They would be able to enlighten him about this E. Royston guy from Texas.

Eleven

Dr. Dwayne Blackburn at Mesa Biotech perused the monthly research journals on his desk. The latest issue of the journal *Proteins* had not yet arrived.

"Sandy?" he called to the administrative assistant, "have you seen the new copy of *Proteins*?"

"Yes, Dr. Blackburn, it just arrived today. It's in the pile on the left side of your desk," she replied.

"Many thanks," he said shuffling papers around on his cluttered desk. "It's right here all right . . . need new glasses, I guess," he laughed.

He fumbled a bit more and proceeded to flip the pages to the back of the journal. On the last few pages, there were advertisements for faculty positions, people seeking jobs in industry and symposium advertisements for forthcoming meetings around the United States and Europe. An advertisement grabbed his attention. The National Institutes of Health (NIH) in Bethesda, Maryland, were sponsoring a symposium relevant to the "application of cloning in the biomedical industry." The preliminary program highlighted the topics of increased beef production through cloning as well as other sessions on the basic methodology of the cloning process. It would be an excellent review of the latest technology in that biomedical area. It would also highlight the cloning of cattle in order to harvest human proteins in bovine milk. The animals that had been genetically altered would produce more protein in their udders than could be produced in a chemistry lab. The natural means was seen as a way to produce large quantities of therapeutic proteins in a short period of time. The cow, sheep or goat would be a "protein factory," right in her own udder. The economics were mind-boggling.

Just a few years ago, "Dolly" the first cloned sheep, had been created in a laboratory. More recently, the first cow to be cloned was achieved in a collaborative effort between a university and a bio-medical company in Massachusetts. The cloning of pigs would follow in the year 2000. The research, although benign, started speculation that man was next, and that the first cloned human was only a short time away. This sent fear into the general population; a fear that emanated from the university boards of directors right to the White House. There were public outcries to ban such research and regulate it at the highest level.

The ethical and moral issues of potential human cloning would be addressed, in part, by the forthcoming symposium in the D.C./ Maryland area. It was sure to be attended by politicians, government medical officials and the top scientists in the field of genetic engineering. The program highlighted some of the most prominent researchers that were presenting their research at the prestigious symposium. In the conference's advertisement were the names of Sir Jon Edmonton and Dr. Bruce Kettinger from the United Kingdom. They were proponents of the future cloning of humans and saw the research as a potential approach to curing genetic diseases that were fatal to man. Their intent was not to create a copy of themselves or someone sinister just for fun, or to prove a biomedical point. It was to eliminate certain diseases such as cancer and central nervous system anomalies or disorders. Because of the human cloning controversy, both Blackburn and Bradshaw decided to attend the conference in Maryland. They would travel together to the East Coast.

✪ ✪ ✪ ✪

A month passed and the San Diego scientists arrived at Washington's Dulles airport. They took a cab to the NIH conference, a thirty-minute ride on major highways. The two-day symposium highlighted the historical perspective of the science of DNA, proteins and cloning. It was well attended by some two thousand conferees. The previous year's meeting had drawn about one thousand attendees. However, this year's program was a stimulus for others to hear what was thought to be a very controversial subject. The media room had some three hundred personnel e-mailing and faxing highlights of the lectures to their respective news organizations around the globe. Delegates from Europe and Japan saturated the international conference. All attending seemed to focus on specific agendas and missions.

One or two of the morning symposium sessions focused on the methodology of cloning, and its successes, pitfalls and failures. The Scottish researchers seemed to have the jump on the American researchers. Therefore, most presentation rooms were *standing room only*. Everyone seemed to want to hear what the Scots were presenting for data. The attendees were in shock at the announcement that a fertile woman in Scotland was actually awaiting an embryo transplant of a cloned egg. No one was aware that they had even entertained attempting that feat. Farm animals, yes, but humans, no, was the supposition among researchers around the world.

All that the Scottish researchers would share with the attendees, was the fact that the woman was living in the Highlands and that more data would be forthcoming about her planned gestation. The woman was scheduled to receive a genetically-engineered human egg, but no one knew when. Ultrasound would be performed each month, if confirmation of a pregnancy was achieved. The pregnancy would then go to thirty-six weeks after which a cesarean delivery might be performed to remove the baby.

However, with little specific information, many attendees assumed wrongly that a woman was already with child, in Scotland.

Drs. Blackburn and Bradshaw, and many other scientists, hurried to the telephone area. They would call their friends and fellow scientists regarding the Scottish researchers' revelations. One of the people to be called *immediately* was E. Royston MacDonald. He had a keen interest in the symposium, but could not attend. Blackburn would try to reach him. He was successful since MacDonald always kept his cell phone turned on.

Blackburn quickly relayed the advances in Scottish research and that the first planned pregnancy of a human clone was close to being initiated. The Scots were able to get a human egg to divide, after some DNA manipulation. That was only step one, but a major break-through.

"Can you get a synopsis of the Scottish study to date?" Royston asked with impatience. "Is there hard data on the procedure?"

"Don't know if there is a copy of their presentation or a hand-out," Blackburn responded in rapid fashion.

"Talk to the Scots and see if there is a 'preprint' of an anticipated publication. It's too early for a reprint! Tell Dr. Edmonton that it's for Roy. You know. Tell him it's for me! He knows me and might give it to you."

"I'll ask," Blackburn said, as he raised his eyebrows to Bradshaw. He felt that the chance of getting advanced information was nil since newsmen and TV cameras were bombarding the two Scottish scien-tists with questions. Instead, Blackburn left a message at the Hyatt for them. If anything might gain them access to either scientist, it was a personal note or voice-mail message at their hotel where both San Diego men and the Scottish researchers were staying.

In less than fifteen minutes, the news of the intent to develop a human clone was being broadcast on CNN and C-SPAN TV. The Catholic archbishops in the United States were already denouncing this "science" as playing God. The ethical ramifications of the "new science" shocked them. Washington, D.C., was abuzz with the news for days.

Edmonton and Kettinger appeared on every TV talk show that could book them. From morning to late evening, the talk shows hosted the potential future Nobel laureates. After a day or two of intense interviews, the two men secretly flew home to Scotland. No way could they travel on a commercial flight. The press would have occupied the entire flight behind first class.

The chartered flight overseas was private and paid in part by NIH funds. NIH administrators had made the decision to assist the Scots by pre-booking the secret departure from Dulles International. It would leave Dulles at 1:00 A.M.

As planned, the two men were on their way home before the news organizations would even know of their hastily prepared departure.

But before the researchers left for Scotland, Drs. Blackburn and Bradshaw were able to meet with them in secret. Both Edmonton and Kettinger were pleased to see their fellow colleagues again. Bradshaw was from the United Kingdom, and Blackburn's name was known to them through MacDonald.

Edmonton and Kettinger shared their recent unpublished research results with the San Diego scientists and passed on their best wishes to E. Royston MacDonald. They indicated that they would be in touch with Royston very soon. They valued his financial support in the past and he was on their board of directors in Scotland. Neither Blackburn or Bradshaw were previously aware of that association. *Had MacDonald been to the UK,* they wondered?

Both San Diego scientists returned to the West Coast with a renewed excitement in the research area of cloning. They wondered if the Scottish feat of DNA injection into a human egg could be duplicated in the United States. *What would be the ethical and moral ramifications? What would be the success rate?* The restrictions for basic human research in the United States were stringent and there were rumblings that the guidelines for that kind of human research would be tightened, certainly after the recent advances by their Scottish colleagues. The manuscript, which they had confidentially secured from the Scots, elucidated in the "methods section" how they successfully achieved the current microinjection technique in the human egg. It also mentioned the need for an "electrical current" to stimulate the egg. No embryo transfer had occurred as yet. Although the intended surrogate woman remained anonymous, she was referenced in the preprint, as "Lassie."

Time and *Newsweek*'s covers would feature articles on the ethical issues of genetically engineered humans. One cover showed a Xerox-like machine spitting out carbon copies of the same person. The featured articles emphasized the fact that humans were not cows, or sheep. The editorials questioned the direction this "science" was taking.

Blackburn and Bradshaw sat together in first class on the flight to San Diego. They decided that they would contact MacDonald again as soon as they arrived home. During the conference call, they would suggest a meeting for the three of them in San Diego. Royston was due to return to San Diego in another week. By then the two U.S. scientists would have a secret draft of a business plan for the first human cloning in America, as Royston had requested. MacDonald was a gambler and sought recognition in the field of biomedical science, as well as in the oil business. If they presented their case to him logically and truthfully, he would fund the program. Along the five-hour flight, the San Diegans drafted their presentation to MacDonald. They utilized the relevant information from the Scottish research paper to make their case. They had garnered other data from researchers at the two-day conference in Washington. Success of a cloned human would surely yield the Nobel prize and there was no guarantee that either the Scots' current research or their own plan in the United States, would take a pregnant women to "term." If the planned pregnancy in Scotland failed and Royston's team were to succeed, the first cloned human would occur in the United States, not overseas. Ethics no longer played a part in their minds. . . . Royston's and their quest was the Nobel prize, and MacDonald would surely buy into the potential notoriety.

The technology for cloning the first human was right there in their briefcases. *Who would Royston wish them to clone?* They wondered. *How would they initiate their collaboration?* It was critical that they contact MacDonald as soon as possible and set up the secret meeting. It would be held at the "Hotel Del" in Coronado.

Twelve

In the "personal" section of the *San Diego Gazette* was an advertisement that had been printed in bold typeface. It was highlighted with a boxed, shaded border. The header read:

> WWW.SURROGATEBABY.ORG
> NEED MONEY? EARN $5000 CASH!
> WANTED: YOUNG, HEALTHY, FERTILE
> WOMAN (21-24 YEARS OLD)
> **FOR SURROGATE PREGNANCY.**

The advertisement was also printed in the local college and university newspapers. The ad generated strong interest by e-mail through the Web site. Local university coeds flocked to the Internet by the hundreds. Friends told other friends. One young woman, who worked laboriously as a chambermaid at a hotel on Hotel Circle off of Route 8 West, was also told of the advertisement. She did not have a computer, but she had a girlfriend who spent time surfing the Internet. The friend of the chambermaid printed out the details of the ad for the young woman of Mexican descent.

The chambermaid studied the two-page document, which had been given to her. She closed the door to the hotel room that she was cleaning, sat on the bed and read the description in the advertisement. The young woman's eyes widened as she read the amount of money involved. It was more than she earned in six months. The body of the advertisement read:

WANTED: YOUNG, HEALTHY, CHILDBEARING WOMAN BETWEEN
THE AGES OF 21 AND 24 TO CARRY THE CHILD OF AN INFERTILE
COUPLE. EARN $5000 DOLLARS FOR THE COMPLETED
PREGNANCY. FREE HEALTHCARE AND MEDICAL MONITORING PROVIDED.
ROOM AND BOARD PROVIDED.
PREGNANCY BY *IN VITRO* FERTILIZATION (IVF).
DONOR EGG AND SPERM PROVIDED.
SURROGATE MOTHER MAY BE OF ANY NATIONAL ORIGIN.
CLINIC IS IN SAN DIEGO AREA. INTERESTED WOMEN, PLEASE RESPOND TO
"BLIND E-MAIL" BELOW, OR CALL 1-800-FERTILE.
-ALL INQUIRIES CONFIDENTIAL-

The young Mexican woman placed the piece of paper in her apron pocket and finished the room that she was cleaning. During her afternoon break at two-thirty, she would call the 800 number. When the opportunity presented itself, she left a message on the answering machine, which included her home phone number. The call would be returned by the clinic that evening at eight o'clock. The maid would call in "sick" to work the following Friday. She was scheduled to initiate the elaborate interview and preliminary medical screening process that particular day.

Thirteen

The San Diego Forensic Toxicology Laboratory located in downtown San Diego was active with a recent murder case. A crime had been committed and the body of the victim was subsequently mutilated. The laboratory had received a portion of a finger from one hand and their job was to establish to whom it belonged. The murder occurred somewhere near the Gas Lamp District, an area of San Diego which had been recently renovated. What remained after the Gas Lamp district renovation was the constant flow of transients and homeless who found the weather of San Diego to be attractive and accommodating year-round.

At night, tourists and convention attendees from hotels near the Convention Center on San Diego Bay migrated up Fifth Avenue to seek out the cafés, bars and fine restaurants. Every night, there was a crowd of visitors from whom the homeless would try to conjure money. If the conventioneers wore their meeting badges outside the Convention Center, the homeless would target them specifically. Small bills or spare change was the order of the day.

The forensic toxicology lab had the gruesome job of trying to identify fingerprints and matching any mutilated remains to the victim or body of its rightful owner. They often did not even have recognizable tissue samples to work with, which meant that they had to resort to DNA analysis in order to confirm the identity of samples found by the San Diego Police Department. Sometimes there would be more than one murder on a given evening and the forensic lab would be busy resolving a combination of cases during any particular week. On this specific night, another murder had occurred across town. It was not considered related to the first murder. The lab would be extremely busy tonight.

Dr. Robert Johnson, DVM, Ph.D., was a forensic pathologist, who had spent a portion of his training in medical school. As a trained veterinarian, his human anatomy training was garnered from med school courses. His knowledge of general pathology transcended both human medicine and animal medicine. He was well versed in toxicology and cell biology. He fought hard to get the most modern equipment for forensic analyses. His career had started in biotechnology and he was a protein biochemist at a local biotechnology firm prior to vet school and taking the head job at the forensic lab.

Added to his academic accolades was his postdoctoral experience, which he had gained at a well-known cellular biology laboratory—The North Shore Cellular Biology Institute—on Long Island in New York. He had worked with some renowned scientists at that facility, located one hour east of New York City. Nobel Laureates in medicine often visited the lab and presented their most recent data in DNA technology.

Dr. Johnson was a specialist in DNA research. He was often an expert witness in murder cases, and he had the grim task of presenting to juries the DNA evidence substantial to the county prosecutor's cases. The difficult task for him was the presentation of medical pathology information in a manner that a layperson on the jury could understand. Dr. Johnson was good at communicating the science to the average person. Johnson knew that the field of forensic toxicologic pathology had risen to new heights after the legal case against O. J. Simpson. It was clear, in Johnson's mind that the O. J. case lacked the presentation of the considerable DNA evidence found at the scene and in his Ford Bronco. It was perhaps the only time in the history of a murder case, that DNA data was disregarded and not even submitted into evidence. Johnson was appalled at the thought that the sophisticated DNA data was not admissible to the court, or ignored by the courtroom participants. *Damn those lawyers!* He thought. *Always finding a legal, but immoral, unethical "out"!*

Because of the O. J. case, Johnson vowed that he would never testify in any case related to a prominent figure. *Too much politics,* he thought.

Dr. Johnson spent time in Scotland and England during his graduate school days. As a postdoctoral student, he had visited Dr. Kettinger's lab. Johnson had studied molecular pathology under Kettinger, and Johnson also knew Dr. Blackburn locally at Mesa Biotech. They had attended the local pharmaceutical discussion seminars in the greater San Diego area. Because of their academic history and common research interests, they socialized and kept in touch with each other on scientific issues of mutual interest.

Prior to his forensic studies in toxicology, Dr. Johnson focused his research on expanding the Watson and Crick theory of DNA molecular function. He also participated in the Human Genome Project between the United Kingdom and the United States. The project was mapping the DNA and genes of man. Each of the two researchers sometimes collaborated in professional journal publications. They co-authored many prominent and respected scientific articles in the field of DNA research.

Applying his previous postgraduate research to his present job at the forensic lab, Dr. Johnson was an expert in DNA extraction of tissues, blood and hair samples from crime scenes or corpses. One of the reasons that he was selected for the current job at the forensic lab was his extensive experience in the area of DNA extraction and evaluation of proteins and amino acid sequences. During interviews for the job, no one matched his credentials. He was the logical choice for the position and he quickly became director of the facility. He was an obvious candidate for the Royston MacDonald team and for his special research project.

Fourteen

E. Royston MacDonald stepped off the Boeing 757 from Dallas and onto the jet way at San Diego International Airport. The flight arrived at Gate 15. He draped his raincoat over his arm and proceeded through the airport terminal toward the baggage claim area, rocking slightly as he walked. He was overweight from years of eating poorly and consuming alcohol. He attended too many functions and social events to remain healthy. He was well dressed for his size and purchased most of his clothes from the 1888 Shop in New York City. Contrasting his business suit attire of the day, was an enormous ten-gallon hat, which he proudly wore so that people would know he was from Texas. His outfit had no place in San Diego, neither did his raincoat. It never rained in southern California, but he was prepared if it did.

A limousine driver met Royston near the baggage claim area. The sign that the limo driver held up for all passengers to see read: MESA BIOTECH. Royston identified himself to the driver, Max, and awaited his checked luggage. Lindbergh Field in San Diego was not known for its fast delivery of bags to passengers. MacDonald stared out the front windows of the North Terminal. The palm trees were swaying in a light breeze generated from nearby San Diego Bay. After about five minutes, the bags arrived on the carousel.

"Mr. MacDonald, how many bags are we expecting, sir?"

"Two, Max," the large man responded still staring out the window, "Just two. Two black, hard-shell Samsonites. . . . Oh! There's one, son!" Royston pointed.

"I'll get it, sir . . . the car is right out front if you care to head out there," Max continued.

"There's number two!" Royston shouted.

"Got it, sir!"

Royston followed Max out to the black Mercedes in front of the terminal. He only had a briefcase in hand and his raincoat. Max carefully dragged the large Samsonite bags to the rear of the car. He popped open the trunk with a remote device.

"Please get in, sir. I'll be right there after I load your luggage."

MacDonald looked at the shiny car. It looked freshly waxed. The license plate read MESA1. He knew the company well, since he was a major investor in the firm. He practically created it. Royston invested in many industries, but biotechnology companies were his favorite investment strategy. *It was a gamble,* he thought, *since many start-up companies never made it to Wall Street.* He had faith that the next unique pharmaceutical therapeutic product just might evolve from a small start-up company with excellent staff and ideas. Perhaps the next cure for a major disease was right around the corner and needed financing to facilitate the venture. Hence, he became a venture capitalist in the industry. He picked only the prospects that had sound management and scientific foresight.

Mesa Biotech might be that kind of company with a future, he thought. In the biotech industry of some two thousand companies, one thousand operated on the West Coast and they ranged in location from San Diego to Seattle. Some were emerging in Vancouver, B.C.—Canada as well. The universities in California often spawned the start-up ventures.

The limo that he had just entered had been leased with his investment in Mesa Biotech. He just wasn't aware of it. The vehicle was new and would always be at his disposal. It was also used to shuttle other Mesa investors and other visitors back and forth to the facility.

Royston had a keen interest in all biotech research, not just Mesa's forte in the industry. He considered it the forefront of science. He really was aiming his sights on funding the research of the next Nobel prize scientist in medicine or physiology. He imagined that a researcher of that critical acclaim would need to solve a significant breakthrough in one of the following areas of disease: cardiac, pulmonary, central nervous system, diabetes, immunology/AIDS or infertility. He had learned that the U.S. government in Washington, D.C., was funding research in those fields so that biotech firms would naturally follow suit. The NIH and FDA focused on these areas when awarding grants or approving drugs from universities, biotech firms and private foundations. That often meant that the FDA would look kindly on reviewing new drug applications that mimicked their own in-house research and NIH collaboration.

MacDonald's trip to San Diego this time was to attend a board meeting of Mesa Biotech. The Hotel Del was a short trip by car down Route 5 and over the San Diego-Coronado Bay Bridge. There to the left stood the "grand lady" of hotels, the Hotel Del or "The Del" as the local residents affectionately referred to it. Her majestic red-roofed peaks stood out as a perfect contrast to the pure blue San Diego sky. The white wooden structure had been constructed in 1888 and her U.S. flag waved high above the tallest peak. The hotel had been the host of twelve presidents of the United States, assorted dignitaries from Europe as well as numerous movie stars. Marilyn Monroe and Tony Curtis filmed *Some Like It Hot* on the Hotel Del beach. Their pictures adorn the hallways of the lower level of the hotel.

"Nice trip, sir?" Max asked, as they drove south on Route 5.

"Yes. . . .Very nice . . . smooth flight," said MacDonald.

"Will you be staying in the area long, sir?" Max asked, courteously.

"No . . . just a couple of days. . . . How's the weather been?"

"Well, sir, you are lucky. . . . we have had 'June gloom' for the past week. The rest of the week should be nice, sir."

"June gloom? What's that, Max?" asked Royston.

"Ah, sir—that's when the desert to the east of us gets so hot that it pulls in the cooler marine air from the ocean. Usually covers the city with a cloudy haze—happens in June each year," said Max, the San Diego native, authoritatively.

"Well, it sure looks good today. How close are we to the hotel?" Royston asked.

"Five more minutes and we'll be there, sir," Max replied.

Royston fumbled with some glass vials in his raincoat pocket. He took them out of the pocket and studied the labels. Two of them said, "T. W. 1950" and "Ted W. 1959." He was silent as he shook the dark brown hair clippings inside each vial.

MacDonald relaxed on the leather rear seat and looked out over the bay as they crossed the bridge to Coronado. As they crossed the blue center span, MacDonald commented to Max, "It floats, ya know!"

"What does, sir?" Max asked.

"The bridge—the center span under us!"

"Sir?" Max asked with interest. "Floats?"

"Yes, the center span of this bridge is designed to float. If we were ever attacked . . . ya know, like Pearl Harbor was in the '40s, if the bridge was hit, it could never block our Navy ships from getting out of the bay! See all those ships?"

"Yes, sir."

"Well," Royston added, "Can't have them trapped in the bay. The Navy would be paralyzed so they designed the bridge to float so tugs can push the spans out of the way if we were attacked and they fell into the bay."

"Didn't know that, sir," Max replied.

"I was a Navy man, Max . . . that's how I know that."

Royston became silent as he recalled his Navy days. The glass vials in his hand made an irritating, clicking noise. Max wondered what he was playing with. He could not see Royston in his rear view mirror, so he had no clue as to what was in his lap. Royston had been stationed in the San Francisco Bay area, but had been on shakedown cruises that had taken him to San Diego Harbor and the naval yard.

MacDonald was a bright man with a Lyndon Johnson demeanor. He was slow to judge people, but sure in his ways. A deliberate thinker and excellent listener, Royston despised ignorance and incompetence. He enjoyed good, intelligent conversation. He felt that people in the United States had every opportunity to be educated and that they should strive for an adequate one. He believed in the saying "there is no free lunch." If you want something, get the education to get it, he always said. On the other hand, he often sided with the "little people," the down and out and the less fortunate. Life dealt many people a bad hand and he did not criticize the downtrodden. Not many of his friends knew that side of him, but it was there. He was a firm believer that people should at least skim a newspaper every day. An awful lot of information was there for less than a dollar. Aside from increasing one's mind relative to world events, reading a newspaper also made people and their conversations more interesting to others.

He enjoyed Max and they would become good friends. Max liked to listen to Royston. He learned from Royston and in turn, Royston learned from him. Max continued to call Roy, "sir," even though Royston asked him not to be so formal. But Max had respect for the large man from Texas and insisted on addressing him in a professional manner. Even in front of other friends, he called Royston "Mr. MacDonald." Royston finally gave up on Max converting to a more informal address. He respected Max's professionalism and appreciated it.

In front of the Hotel Del a bellman warmly greeted MacDonald as he opened the rear door of the limo, then led him to the enormous wooden doors at the front entrance. Opening them for the impressive-looking guest, a separate doorman welcomed MacDonald with a casual sweeping wave of the hand in front of his body.

"The name is Babbitt, sir—that's Babbitt with two 't's, sir. If you need anything, please let me know. 'Been here thirty-three years! Need a tour of the place? Just ask, sir."

"Thirty-three years?" asked Royston. "That's a long time! Hell— you must have known Marilyn!"

"Monroe, sir?"

"Yeah, Marilyn Monroe—the movie star!"

Mr. Babbitt leaned over and whispered to Roy.

"That sack 'a shit!" retorted Babbitt. "She was no fuckin' good!" he responded firmly to MacDonald. "Trollop!" he continued. "Mr. DiMaggio, God bless his soul, should never have married the tramp. She was like the Lincoln Tunnel, ya know?" Babbitt said.

"Really? Why?" Royston laughed at the apparent honesty of the old bellman.

Babbitt responded with a smile, "Just like the tunnel, everybody's been through her!"

The Texan roared with laughter. He went inside and passed the registration desk of the hotel. He took the left past the desk and headed for the conference room at the end of the hallway. The entryway to the hotel was the original dark stained wood of the 1800s. The original elevator still worked and was enclosed in a mesh cage for safety. The bell in the elevator rang out as it went up and down. It signaled every floor on which it stopped. MacDonald's bags would automatically be sent to the Presidential Suite on the top floor. Royston stood in line for no one, especially a hotel registration line. The manager of the reception area knew what to do when he arrived—give the usual red carpet treatment.

Tourists gathered in the lobby and stared at the intricate woodwork in the ceiling. It was truly an historical landmark and people came from all over the world, just to have brunch in the Grande Hall on a Sunday morning.

Max passed the bags from the limo to a waiting bellman and surmised that MacDonald was not new to The Del. Max concluded that Royston was pretty familiar with the old place and knew his way around. MacDonald reached the end of the hallway and after a quick right, he stood outside a series of small conference rooms.

In a meeting room were gathered various representatives of Mesa Biotech, the Medical Center at Torito Bay as well as the Forensic Toxicology Laboratory from downtown. MacDonald had asked all of them to attend, as an adjunct session to part of the board of directors meeting for Mesa Biotech. The agenda of the ancillary meeting was not known to anyone except MacDonald. He had a highly confidential idea for a collaborative research project that would startle the research world.

Royston had hinted to individual attendees in the room that he was creating a research team for a special project, yet he had never gathered all of them together in the same room to discuss it. The lives of the individual attendees at this meeting would change from that day forward. The future funding of their respective institutions would also be dependent on their confidential participation in MacDonald's novel research project. The project was to be referred to, in the future, as "Project Samuel."

Fifteen

One of the critically important attendees awaiting Royston Macdonald at the Hotel Del meeting was Dr. Dwayne Blackburn. When he was not at Mesa Biotech, Inc., he dabbled in research in the molecular biology laboratory at Torreyana College in La Jolla. The school was located a short distance from MBI. The university setting was spectacular since it was located on the cliffs overlooking the Pacific Ocean fifteen miles north of San Diego. Students went to the school because of its academic standings as well as the sheer beauty of its liberal arts campus. The college was only ten years old, yet it drew the finest faculty from around the country. The school paid their full professors and associate professors more than most schools that size. Their enrollment was limited to four thousand students so that class size was small and professor/student relationships fostered individual attention. Many scientists at local biotechnology firms had joint appointments at Torreyana College. They would lecture on occasion without being full-time instructors on staff. Blackburn was called upon to lecture a few times a year. He enjoyed the interaction with students yearning to learn about the advances in cellular biology.

In return for their lecturing, some of the biotech researchers could utilize the research facilities on campus. They had total access to the extensive college library as well. An entire floor of the library was devoted to the biological and medical sciences. One section favored the biotechnology area. The library subscribed to every journal that fostered the biomedical sciences. Torreyana College offered a premed academic program to their serious biology majors desiring the field of medicine.

Blackburn liked to perform basic research in his spare time. He could not readily do that at MBI, so he shared a small lab and desk in the Department of Molecular Biology at Torreyana College. His research interest was in DNA replication. He had free access to a small animal colony of rats and mice at the college. Blackburn had applied for and received a small NIH grant to pursue his scientific studies in DNA. Helping to map the Human Genome Project was fun for Blackburn. It kept his brain stimulated and took him away from the day-to-day management responsibilities at Mesa Biotech. His resume was always up to date with recent scientific publications. He knew that one day he would be president of a larger pharmaceutical company and that having both the management and scientific experience on his resume would be beneficial. It also allowed his colleagues and peers to see that he was an active player in the DNA research area.

Blackburn's desk at the college was in a corner of one of the biochemistry laboratories within the molecular biology group. His desk was a mass of publications and books piled high on top of it. Many of the scientific reprints that were in the stack were publications in the fields of protein chemistry, DNA, and reproductive and developmental biology. On top of one of the piles of literature was an article in *Scientific American* relevant to DNA analysis of forensic samples. A contributor to the article and a coauthor was none other than Dr. Robert Johnson of the local San Diego Forensic Toxicology Laboratory. In the same pile of scientific literature were the latest articles on the cloning of sheep and cattle. The articles were about the most current methods of cloning at both the Scottish laboratories and those of the U.S. laboratories in the New England area.

Prior to the meeting at the Hotel Del, Blackburn had spent time at his desk in the lab reviewing the articles for issues related to Royston's project. He had synopsized the methodology for DNA extraction from biological samples. Royston MacDonald had asked him to do that in advance of the meeting. He would be presenting a synopsis of the methodology to the attendees of Royston's special meeting.

The *Scientific American* article had an extensive reference list at the end of the article. It provided Blackburn with additional information that he could present at the meeting. His presentation at MacDonald's meeting would specifically focus on the extraction of DNA from tissue samples, i.e., tissue, blood and hair. Blackburn was not aware that Robert Johnson would also be presenting his knowledge of DNA technology. That, combined with the third presentation from Jonathan Bradshaw, the fertility expert, would make for an intense afternoon of scientific reports. Royston figured that each presentation was related, and that it would foster an excellent discussion for the framework of Project Samuel.

Blackburn was amazed and reminded by his review of the literature on DNA, that a simple strand of hair contained the genetic code for a complete individual. To him, hair was basically dehydrated, dead protein. At the base of a hair strand was a live follicle with active cells. The follicles contained the same viable genetic information, but were not dehydrated like hair samples.

DNA extracted from hair or other tissue is a tool often used to determine who might have been present at a particular crime scene. The DNA sequence of a person can help identify the perpetrator of a crime. In a struggle with an assailant, a victim might have strands of the assailant's hair on their clothing, or skin scrapings underneath his or her fingernails. Many murders in San Diego had been resolved using these DNA analytical techniques and Johnson's presentation would embellish Blackburn's talk.

Johnson knew that the methodology for extracting DNA from tissue, blood or hair was straightforward. Hair was a bit more difficult because it was not living tissue. He experimented with extracting his own DNA from blood. He wanted to know what his own genetic makeup was . . . sort of his "biological roots." He also asked friends to give him blood samples under the guise of a useful experiment. He really wanted to surprise them with an analysis of their DNA—a unique "present" for sure. He even surprised Royston MacDonald with the gift of his own DNA printout. Royston was pleasantly surprised by Johnson's gesture. He had the document framed on an expensive cherry wood plaque.

In experiments at the college, Blackburn had collaborated with Dr. Bradshaw from the Torito Bay Fertility Clinic. They had performed some studies in the mouse where a surrogate female mouse carried the fertilized eggs of other genetically different strains. The transplants were successful and the recipient mice delivered the donor mouse's young.

They also tried a cloning technique in mice. They successfully transferred the DNA from one mouse egg into another mouse's egg using micropipettes. The task was completed under a microscope of high magnification. Successful reintroduction of the cloned egg back into the animal was easier to perform in the mouse, than in other species. The mating and hormonal synchrony of the two female mice (donor and recipient) made the procedure feasible. They were relying on the methods of scientists from the 1960s. The earliest studies with transferring nuclear cells were performed in frogs' eggs. The procedure was not all that different in approach, in mammals. The men presented this data to the group as well.

⚾ ⚾ ⚾ ⚾

Royston MacDonald, had on his last trip to San Diego, presented Dr. Blackburn with some of his recent memorabilia acquired from the Rizzo collection. They were duplicate items which Royston thought Blackburn would enjoy for his own sports collection. Some were faded, autographed baseballs and smudged or less perfect items from being improperly stored over many years. Royston kept the most perfect autographed baseballs for himself. They were worth far more than the pieces that Royston shared with Blackburn. Even at that, it was a nice gesture on the part of MacDonald. Blackburn did the same for Royston when he acquired duplicate collectibles.

MacDonald also gave Blackburn some vials of hair clippings from the Rizzo collection. They were extra hair samples from apparent celebrities, but there were no baseball players in the lot. Blackburn enjoyed the macabre samples anyway. Some were movie stars or famous Massachusetts politicians. Blackburn had hoped for a sample from a well-known baseball player. He thought that would be more valuable.

Wouldn't it be fun to know the DNA of a Joe DiMaggio, a Mickey Mantle or a Ted Williams? Blackburn knew that Royston had acquired some Red Sox players' clippings in the numerous sample vials of hair. He was just not aware of who might have visited the Rizzo Barber Shop in the old days. Blackburn consulted the real expert, Dr. Johnson, at the forensic lab, and would end up practicing the extraction of DNA from those samples to see if the varying years of collection, noted on the vials, were a factor in isolating the DNA. He found no real difference in the results. Hair was hair, whether old or new.

During this particular trip to San Diego, MacDonald had other samples for his colleague, Blackburn. The vials, which Royston had carried in his raincoat, were surmised by Dwayne to be the hair clippings from two of Ted's visits to the barbershop. When analyzed for DNA, both of Ted's samples would look the same in DNA sequencing. MacDonald needed the research team in the meeting room to garner that information for him. It was critical for the success of Project Samuel. MacDonald apparently had multiple missions running concurrently with Project Samuel.

The men in the room today were not aware of the potentially unethical plan which E. Royston MacDonald was about to reveal to them behind closed doors. They *did* know, however, that the discussion was going to be confidential. The memo that Royston had sent them in advance emphasized that fact.

Sixteen

A week passed after Vicky Palmer was evaluated for her infertility. The results confirmed that her hormones were not in synchrony and *in vitro* fertilization of her harvested eggs would be the proposed next step. In order to obtain the ova, she would undergo a series of injections to stimulate the ovaries to produce numerous follicles. Using an ultrasound or laparoscope, Dr. Jonathan Bradshaw would be aware of the optimum time required to retrieve the ova. The eggs would be harvested from the ovaries by the trans-vaginal wall approach. They would be fertilized with Tom's sperm and reintroduced back into Vicky's womb.

Vicky was scheduled to return to the clinic at eight on a Saturday morning. She would undergo extensive blood work and then be prepped for ovum retrieval. The initial use of the laparoscope or ultrasound would be to visualize the ovaries in search of mature eggs for harvesting. The doctor would then aspirate the eggs from each of the largest follicles he could find by using a micropipette and catheter. Both ovaries would contain many eggs that were readily accessible by this trans-vaginal procedure.

Seventeen

The young Mexican girl finished cleaning her last room at the hotel. It was Thursday and she knew she would not be in on Friday. She had already confirmed her appointment with the surrogatebaby.com clinic and was due to have an interview and physical on Friday morning.

She was a beautiful young woman who hid her figure well beneath her hotel uniform. She was 5"6' tall and weighed 107 pounds. *I'll probably pass the physical with flying colors,* she thought. She had no known prior history of family diseases or genetic abnormalities. She anxiously waited for the next day to arrive.

In anticipation of the physical exam and interview, she thought of the $5,000 that she might earn if she qualified and was selected for the surrogate mother program. She was also sensitive enough to think that she was doing something wonderful for an infertile couple— giving life and a family to people who were unable to conceive. She revisited the thoughts of the $5,000; that was a lot of money to her. Her family in Mexico would also benefit from the large sum of money. The peso was at an all time low and $5,000 was more than the annual salary for many people south of the San Diego border.

Friday morning came quickly. The young woman arrived at the Fertility Clinic at Torito Bay well in advance of her scheduled appointment. She entered the lobby and followed her instructions to go to the second floor of building G. In confidence, someone would greet her. For the initial interview, she would not use her real name. She would be coded with a color and number initially. The young girl was told in advance that she was designated "Red 5" for the purposes of accounting and interviews. The use of the candidate's real names were avoided for confidentiality, in case the review committee did not select them after the initial physical examination. Only after close scrutiny of her mental and physical health, would she meet with the clinic's medical team. Separate interviews would be needed with them.

"Good morning," the receptionist on the second floor said warmly to the young woman. She responded with a cautious nod and caught herself saying "good morning" in Spanish. She quickly corrected it to English and smiled. She did not know that the receptionist was bilingual.

"May I have your code, please?" The receptionist asked.

"Yes, ma'am," the Mexican woman responded. "My code is Red 5."

"Yes . . . yes, I see you right here," while looking at the list. "Welcome!" She handed the young woman a clipboard with a medical questionnaire attached to it and asked her to complete it for the clinic's records. It was a standard medical background form, which required completion in advance of the physical. Fortunately, it was printed in both English and Spanish. It would be confidential and included a release form to absolve the clinic of any mal-intentions with the written information she was about to provide them. It basically allowed the clinic to share the information with other medical collaborators-interviewers in the clinic and at other relevant facilities, if needed.

Twenty minutes later, the young woman handed the completed form to the receptionist. She was asked to remain in the waiting area. She sat down and perused a *People* magazine. The cover story was the death of the rock star/singer Selena. It saddened her to see the beautiful photos of the star and to read of the tragic ending to her life.

While the Mexican woman was in the reception area, two other young women entered the waiting area. Both were blonde, Caucasians and similar in stature to the Mexican. They smiled at Red 5 and were given the clipboard and medical form to fill out as well. They introduced themselves to the receptionist as "Yellow 3" and "Blue 2." As competitors for the $5,000, they seemed afraid to communicate with "Red 5," although they each knew why they were there.

Each girl appeared nervous, occasionally exhibiting long restless sighs. Just as the Mexican finished reading the Selena article, the reception-ist called out, "Red 5? Please step forward to the reception desk." The girl stepped up and was greeted by a nurse wearing a pristine, white lab coat.

"Red 5?" she asked pleasantly. "Please follow me."

The nurse took her to a large and impressive conference room where she was told that she would be interviewed and have her medi-cal record form reviewed. If all went well, they might elect to do a preliminary physical, if time permitted. Usually, that occurred during the second visit. In an adjoining laboratory near the conference room was the capability to collect and evaluate bloods, urine and perform obstetrical-gynecological exams. A pregnancy test, if positive, would obviously rule out the patient as a candidate for the surrogate proce-dure. Both a generalist and obstetrician/gynecologist were available if needed.

Red 5 had no problem with the medical evaluations anticipated, or outlined to her in advance. As she sat there, she looked at the framed pictures of the success stories on the wall. There were numerous black and white photos of children at play, or sleeping. *Each child,* she thought, *belonged to a happy couple that had received a child from a surrogate pregnancy.* She also noticed the pictures of fraternal twins. Occasionally, multiple births could result from the procedure for which she was being considered.

The room in which she sat was tastefully warm, quiet and well insulated. She could hear no extraneous noises or distractions. She felt herself hold her breath, and then sigh.

After a minute or so, the door opened and two men and a woman entered the conference room. The woman was a nurse and did not speak, except for a quick hello. The nurse was really there for legal purposes—a witness of sorts while the two male evaluators questioned Red 5. This was common practice at the clinic when professional medical men met with female patients. One of the two men was of very large stature.

The other gentleman introduced himself as Dr. Emilio Sanchez, a medical doctor, a fertility specialist and psychologist. He spoke English and Spanish fluently. He smiled softly at the young woman and greeted her with *hola*. She responded with a smile and timidly said, *"Buenos días, señor."* It quickly became apparent to both men that "Red 5" was comfortable speaking English since she responded easily to the larger gentleman with, "Good morning, sir." That was fortunate since E. Royston MacDonald did not speak fluent Spanish.

At first, the young Mexican woman felt intimidated by the size of MacDonald, but she quickly warmed up to his unassuming demeanor and the gentle shaking of her hand upon meeting her.

"Welcome, Ms. Red 5. We are glad to have you here," said Dr. Sanchez.

"Gracias. I mean thank you, doctor," she replied. "I am happy to meet you as well."

"We have asked you to come here this morning because you have responded to our advertisement. It is necessary for all of us to understand what the surrogate process entails and whether you, as a patient, understand the task at hand. Are you comfortable with our conversation in English or would you prefer I speak in Spanish?" he asked thoughtfully.

She responded, "English is fine, doctor. I will let you know if I have trouble with some phrases or medical terms . . . if that is OK?"

"Sure. That will be fine. Please let us know if there are any concerns at all."

MacDonald immediately was drawn to her and expressed his desire for her to feel comfortable. "Please let us know if we are not clear in explaining the clinic's policies and your responsibilities if you are chosen for the surrogate pregnancy."

"Yes, sir, I will be sure to let you know," she said softly.

MacDonald continued. "We want you to know that anything that you say to us will be held in the strictest of confidence. If at any time you feel uncomfortable with a comment or question, please let us know. If you do not wish to answer a question, or wish not to continue with the interview, we will respect your intent. You are not obligated, and we can stop at any time."

"Yes, sir, I know. I will let you know if I feel uncomfortable," she replied.

"'Red 5? Your preliminary records indicate that you have never been married, and have never given birth to a child. Correct?" Dr. Sanchez asked forthrightly.

"Yes. That is true," she replied confidently.

"I did however, once have a miscarriage . . . so, I have been pregnant in the past. I was young and became pregnant in high school. My boyfriend . . . he did not know of the pregnancy. I was young . . . fifteen years old."

"Was there an abortion performed?" asked the doctor.

"No, oh no. The baby was lost at eight weeks . . . I was ill with a fever at that time . . . the flu."

Both MacDonald and Sanchez were actually happy to know that she was *fertile*. They appreciated her honesty. The occurrence of the flu and subsequent spontaneous abortion would not preclude her from being a candidate for the surrogate pregnancy. *One could not predict the flu,* Sanchez thought. It was more important to them that she was fertile and probably cycled regularly. Her records indicated that she had a twenty-eight-day menstrual cycle. Carrying a child for even two months requires a hormonal balance between progesterone and estrogen and there was no indication that she could not carry another child to full term. If chosen, her endocrine hormone blood levels would be monitored for a month or two. Follicle Stimulating Hormone (FSH), Luteinizing Hormone (LH) and her estrogens would be monitored to establish normal background levels in serum.

"Red 5? What interested you in the surrogate program that we have here . . . I mean what made you contact us to be considered for the program, and needs of the clinic?" the doctor asked.

"At first, doctor, it was the money . . . the $5,000 dollars. I have family south of San Diego, near Puerto Nuevo, Mexico, and they are poor. I wished to maybe help them with the money. The more I thought of it, the more I wanted to help a couple that can't bear children. It is sad when they can't be blessed." She added, "Blessed by God with little smiling faces."

Red 5 was almost embarrassed by the admission of her desire for money. She thought they might end the interview right then and there.

"I'm sorry . . . I should not have mentioned the money."

"That is all right, miss. We appreciate your honesty," said MacDonald.

The more honest she became during questioning, the more he liked her. Dr. Sanchez was also quite taken by the beautiful young woman.

MacDonald humored her by adding, "That kind of money was meant to attract a woman in need of financial help. That was the purpose of the advertisement and the lure of $5,000 in bold print. We don't expect someone to become pregnant for our clinic and carry a baby to term without some reward. It was normal for you to feel that money was important to you and to your family down south."

She responded with a *gracias* to both of them.

"Miss, are you aware that there are risks to this procedure to become pregnant?" asked the doctor. "This is a real pregnancy and the only difference between this being your own child and that of another woman's egg is exactly that . . . you will be carrying another woman's baby. It is not your natural egg and an unknown man, the woman's husband, will fertilize the egg *in vitro*. Is that OK with you? You are merely the *carrier* for the infertile couple that desires a child. It will be their genetic child inside of you. Do you understand that concept?"

"Yes, I understand that the baby will not be mine. I know I can't keep it. It would not be right," Red 5 replied.

"Correct!" insisted the doctor emphatically. "You will not be able to keep it. You signed a document to that effect in advance. Correct?"

"Yes," she nodded. "I understand that it is not my child . . . to keep."

"I must tell you that you will not see the child once he or she is delivered. That is the procedure here," Sanchez commented. "It will be taken to another area of the clinic. This is so there is no direct attachment to the child once he or she is born. Does that bother you? Will that procedure affect you psychologically after carrying the child for nine months?" He peppered her, "Can you deal with that reality?"

"I am aware of that, sir. I read the form that you had me sign . . . I am aware of the procedure after it is born," she said solemnly.

MacDonald who had been observing and listening, piped up, "Ma'am, would you like some coffee?"

She nodded yes and said, "Thank you." Royston whispered to Dr. Sanchez for them to take a break. It was an intense and emotional situation for her, and a ten-minute reprieve was welcome at that point. Red 5 asked to be excused to the ladies' room. The nurse would accompany her as far as the bathroom stall, just in case a candidate might like to shoot up or snort something while alone. There were no doors on the stalls so there was little chance of a candidate doing drugs during an interview, even if they were addicts of some sort. In Red 5's case, she only needed to urinate, but the clinic preferred to cover all bases even though there was no inkling that she was a recreational drug user.

All the time that she was in the conference room, Royston studied Red 5's posture, her demeanor and her mental stability during the intense review of her life and medical records. He noted her beauty and intelligence. *How was it that she became a chambermaid?* he wondered. *If properly nurtured and directed she could have been a model or actress in Hispanic advertisements or movies.*

She was not unaware of every passing glance by Royston, but she occasionally played up her positive attributes when she wanted them to know that she was serious about carrying the child. She caught MacDonald eyeing her breasts on occasion. She was not immune to gawks at the hotel. After all, she was a beautiful woman with a splendid figure. Royston could never "have her," except in his wildest dreams and fantasies. It had been a long time since Royston had been with a woman. But despite his money and power, he would never have a chance with this woman. She was too proud to be bought or bribed. *Besides,* Royston thought, *the mission of selecting the right woman for the "Project" was of paramount importance. His zipper and fantasies could not take priority over the work at hand.*

The interview continued. At the end of an hour and a half, MacDonald began asking some unusual questions.

"Is there any reason why you wouldn't be able to relocate from where you now live?" he asked Red 5.

"Sir? Why do I need to move? To where?" she responded, surprised. "I guess if I had to I could," she stated in confusion. "But why would that be necessary? I live close to the clinic."

"Not far from here," Royston commented. "It is still in San Diego, but east of center city, in a nice residential area. We had hoped that the final candidate would agree to live rent free in a prearranged house in North Park, off University Avenue."

"Where? North Park? That's a nice area but far from the clinic or my friends. They will wonder why I moved there."

"Not to worry, young lady," was Royston's response. "If chosen, the final candidate will need to be in the North Park area for reasons that I cannot explain right now. Do you think that would *not* be possible for you?" he asked with a raised eyebrow.

She hesitated, while her mind went blank from sensory overload, and then responded, "I can live where you wish me to live. If that is important to your clinic, I would agree to move."

"Good! That is helpful," added MacDonald. "You are a flexible woman and I admire that in a person. If you are chosen for the program, we will make sure that you are happy in North Park."

"Thank you, sir. I hope to be chosen for the surrogate pregnancy."

She was then told that the interview was over for the day and that they would contact her when they had reviewed the other candidates. They shook hands and she quietly left the conference room. The nurse who had initially greeted her escorted her back to the lobby. MacDonald could not help but focus on her figure. She was truly a very attractive woman.

After she had left the room, Royston was quick to prejudge the woman. It was all positive. He looked at Dr. Sanchez and said, "If she passes your mental and physical exam, as well as the gynecological/ obstetrical review, I think she is the one for Project Samuel."

He was emphatic. "I like her looks, her attitude and her responses to the questions today. I think we have found our woman, even though there are others out there waiting to be interviewed. What do *you* think?"

Sanchez responded in the affirmative. He would not disagree with MacDonald. Ever! Royston paid him handsomely. *If MacDonald wanted Red 5, then Red 5 is the one,* Sanchez thought. They would merely go through the motions with interviewing the other candidates.

"I really liked her," Royston said. "She exudes truth!"

Sanchez agreed by saying, "She did well in the prelim, sir. She did well."

"She did more than well, doctor. She won the contest before it happened. Just make sure she is really fertile and has no skeletons in her closet. Make sure she doesn't have any drug issues or other hang-ups. This project is too important for us to jeopardize. My first impressions are usually pretty good, my boy . . . *she's* the one in my book!"

"Yes, sir, if you say so," Sanchez said in agreement.

MacDonald repeated, "She exudes the truth. I mean she actually wants the money! Many women want to keep the baby, and that has been a problem for other surrogate women. She never showed us that emotional bond to kids or babies. She won't have a problem giving the baby up at term."

Sanchez whispered, "Sir, they have been known to change their minds—I've seen it before. We must be careful about the selection. There are two more women out there waiting to be interviewed—today."

"I know," said Royston confidently and half listening to Sanchez. He was still fixated on thoughts of Red 5.

"Let's see how the other clinicians read her," replied MacDonald. If they see no negatives, she will be my choice for sure."

"Fair enough," responded Sanchez. "If the physical and emotional parameters are positive, I agree that she would be a good candidate for Project Samuel."

Dr. Sanchez felt that MacDonald was being premature in his decision, but Sanchez kept his thoughts to himself. He could see that Royston was not anxious to interview anyone else but it was necessary to go through the motions. They would honor the commitment to the other candidates waiting in the lobby.

Royston was Royston and he got what he wanted. Oddly enough, his demands were usually based on educated guesses and perceptions, yet he was often right on those occasions. His intuition often "drove him" in business and in pleasure. Sanchez was well aware that MacDonald was footing the bill on the project.

The women coded Yellow 3 and Blue 2 were next to being interviewed, but separately. Spending an hour on each person, Sanchez knew that MacDonald appeared almost disinterested in the other surrogate candidates. He would fidget and drift off in an apparent daydream. The nurse and Dr. Sanchez knew where Royston's mind was, and it wasn't on the two sequential candidates. His mind was on the young, Mexican girl—Red 5.

The remaining candidates were blonde and American-born. Both had graceful figures and very little upstairs. Royston later commented, as an arrogant Texan, that the blondes of Dallas were not like the ditzes and bimbos of California. These two candidates, in his mind, were not intelligent. They lacked the desire needed to commit to the program at hand. It was determined that one of them would not be able to move to the North Park section of San Diego. There was no desire on her part to relocate. The other woman had a potential drug problem in her past.

After a brief discussion amongst the professionals in the room, they concurred that Royston was probably right. The Mexican girl was the best candidate of the day. She led the list by day's end and would need to have further evaluation to be selected as the final candidate.

Red 5 was summoned back in a week, and examined by more clinicians. She was found to be of known fertility, able to ovulate and without any anomalies of the reproductive tract. Her cervix, uterus, fallopian tubes and ovaries functioned normally. The blood work showed her pituitary gland adequately controlled her ovarian cycle. Radioimmunoassay values of her progesterone and estrogen blood levels were normal in all respects.

The clinical chemistries of her blood and urine were without comment. Her blood type was A+, and that was about as normal as one could get. There appeared to be no Rh factor incompatibility, either.

It would be two or three days for the results of the HIV test, and whether she had been subjected to any sexually transmitted autoimmune disease or other common microorganisms such as syphilis or gonorrhea. Except for an occasional bout of monilia (*Candida albicans*) or yeast infection, Red 5 was "clean" from a clinical point of view. Her last monilia infection was a year earlier. The drug, Monistat cured that problem in a few days. Of particular interest to her clinical evaluators was her menstrual cycle length. It was so predictable that she normally felt ovulation. The pain she felt each month was referred to as "mittleschmerz." Knowing her exact cycle would increase the chance for a more precise timing of egg transfer for the surrogate pregnancy. The uterus would need to be in synchrony with the dividing egg at transfer. If the hormonal balance of the endometrial lining were off, the fertilized egg would be rejected, and would not adhere to the uterine wall.

The two other women also returned for their physicals. This was a mere formality. One had a confirmed case of endometriosis, which precluded her from the study. The other woman had prior incidences of vaginal infection, which may have adversely affected her anatomy. The reproductive organs can become occluded or scarred from sexually transmitted diseases (STDs); this might interfere with a successful pregnancy.

The blonde, coded Blue 2, also tested positive for prior drug use, including cocaine. She had come from a broken home, and had some psychological issues from that experience. It was unlikely that she would be a good match for any surrogate project. She probably wanted the $5,000 to feed her habit, Royston and Sanchez concluded.

The young Mexican woman had no record of drug use and tested negative for substances of abuse. Neither cocaine nor THC from marijuana was detected in her system. She also did not drink alcohol, the result of having had an alcoholic father.

MacDonald also ruled out the blonde, Yellow 3, in an unprofessional and subjective manner. He said, "Her breasts were too small." No one laughed at his joke but they were finally getting the picture that the Mexican chambermaid was his only choice for Project Samuel. Obviously, breast size had nothing to do with the overall research project.

Dr. Sanchez knew Royston was joking and just rolled his eyes at him, in dismay.

Royston did not bother to meet any additional women who responded to the advertisement. He let Sanchez and the nurse go through the motions and later would reconvene with them and other clinicians and psychiatrists when Red 5 returned for subsequent evaluations. She continued to be their lead candidate.

The young Mexican woman returned for further discussions and it was decided that the confidential code name, Red 5, would be dropped and her real name would be used from that point on. All members of the team would utilize their first names for the convenience of everyone. Royston had instilled in them that there was no place for egos, Ph.D. titles or M.D. accolades.

It was at the next formal meeting that Red 5 officially became Ms. Teresa Cordero. The former chambermaid, "Ms. Terry," as Royston affectionately called her, underwent elaborate discussions with the final medical team. She would be the one chosen to potentially make MacDonald and the Project Samuel team notorious.

In a week, Phase II of the Project would be initiated. Little did Teresa know that she would be relocating sooner than expected to the 3000 block of Utah Street in the North Park Section of San Diego. The arrangements and expenses for the move would be completely covered by MacDonald. All Teresa Cordero had to do was be there on moving day and get herself settled into her new abode. She would be shocked at the amenities that were prearranged for her new home. She never would have seen all the conveniences that Royston bestowed upon her, had she remained in Mexico or continued to work as a chambermaid.

Eighteen

Jack Danton was still employed by the Cambridge firm when he had last called on Mesa Biotech six months earlier. This would be his last sales trip before committing to Royston. Mesa had a new "therapeutic," which promised to be the next cure for Parkinson's disease. The dopamine-like chemical analogue was derived from a plant source, which had been genetically altered to express the drug in the plant leaf. It was hoped that it could eventually be mass-produced in genetically modified corn, at a later stage of development. It had shown some preclinical effectiveness or efficacy in rodents, especially in the mouse model. Jack's contract toxicology laboratory in Cambridge would have the opportunity to bid on the safety evaluation testing of the new drug entity. His mission was to have a face-to-face discussion with the client and researchers at Mesa Biotech in order to secure the deal. To follow-up by phone or e-mail would not be appropriate at this time. A review of the overall research project on the potential Parkinson's drug required a detailed review of the relevant animal model needed, and the estimated budget to actually get the drug through the FDA in Washington. Since most drugs cost some five hundred to eight hundred million dollars before they make it to the pharmacy, Mesa Biotech would need a large pharmaceutical collaborator to eventually help fund the clinical program. Human studies would be costly. Three large drug firms were vying for that collaboration and Jack could suggest personal contacts at those firms that dealt with new acquisitions and mergers. His contacts in the industry afforded him the opportunity to help start-up biotechs collaborate with large pharmaceutical companies. The same knowledge, personal connections and strategies that E. Royston MacDonald saw in Jack Danton's talent, would come to bear in the Mesa Biotech meetings.

Danton exited Route 5 north at the Sorrento Valley exit and headed east to Mesa Biotech. It was only four miles from the highway, atop a mesa near the junction of routes 805 and 5.

The meeting with staff toxicologists and pharmacologists from the drug discovery division of Mesa was scheduled for 10:00 A.M. The present need for safety evaluation of the promising therapeutic was in a nonhuman primate model. The rhesus or cynomalgus monkey had been the recommended species. A simulated state of Parkinson's was available in the monkey by using a chemical that depleted the brain of dopamine. The new drug would then be tested in numerous monkeys to see if the symptoms of Parkinson's were ameliorated. This study was designed to show efficacy. . . . Did the drug counteract the effects of the synthetically-induced clinical signs of Parkinson's? Subsequent toxicology studies would also be run to evaluate the problem. It would not make sense for Mesa Biotech to develop the drug any further if primate efficacy or toxicology studies showed adverse effects to the animal's health or major organs. The liver, kidneys, brain, or blood clinical chemistries might be affected.

The meeting at Mesa progressed well for an hour and a half and Dr. Dwayne Blackburn peeked into the room to say a quick hello to Jack. His schedule was intense and he had little time for meetings. He had met with Jack Danton on several prior occasions and knew that he was from Boston. Both men followed baseball, and specifically the Red Sox. There would be no time at this meeting to discuss where the Red Sox stood in the American League East. Blackburn, however, did want to meet with him separately, if Jack had time.

"Jack, how long will you be in S.D.?" Blackburn asked.

"Couple of days," Jack replied with interest. He sensed that Blackburn wanted to see him socially. "Then I'm off to Denver and Boulder. More biotechs out there ya know!"

"Got time for lunch today?" Blackburn asked.

"Sure, but who's buyin'?" joked Jack. "Me again?"

"Yes, you, of course. We're the client and you folks have the expense budget!" smiled Blackburn. "We have no budget for lunch at Mesa Biotech. We're on an austerity program here. All the money goes for monkey studies, right?"

Everyone at the meeting smiled and joked about not being able to travel to scientific meetings that year. Each scientist had his or her own poverty story to tell, it seemed.

"OK, OK, you win again . . . stop your cryin'," Jack joked back to Blackburn. "Where we goin'?"

"Don't know. I'll see you in a few minutes and we can decide. Stop by the office when you are done with these folks."

"You got it!" Jack responded. "See ya in a few."

Once Jack was done with his meeting he contacted Dr. Blackburn's office and met him in the lobby of Mesa Biotech.

Danton had found a new rental car agency that specialized in exotic cars. It was located a mile and a half from the San Diego Airport off Grape Street. It was called "Rent-a-Vette." They had given Jack a fire-engine-red Corvette that only had 1,800 miles on it. It was a "rocket" and a definite California car.

"Jesus, Danton!" said Blackburn with envy. "Where did you get this ass machine? Did you get a bonus or somethin' back in Boston? I'll bet Mesa paid for this, in monkey studies."

"Nah, this is from a local rental right downtown and not all that far from the airport. You like?"

"Are you kidding?" responded Blackburn, "I once had a '63 Vette almost the same color. Man, have they changed!"

"Hop in, doctor," Jack commanded. "Let's get some chow."

Blackburn jumped in the passenger side, and felt like he was sitting on the street. The cabin of the red rocket was about four inches off the ground. It was basically a fiberglass shell surrounding a "motor from hell." His jaw dropped as Jack nailed the gas pedal and headed toward Del Mar on the Pacific coast. They would take Torrey Pines Boulevard north to get to the restaurant. Jack took a left on Fifteenth off Camino del Mar. He passed the Americana Café. They decided to have lunch at a restaurant by the beach.

Jack Danton had looked for another rental car agency when on the West Coast. Avis and Hertz were OK, but he was tired of the Ford Taurus and Pontiac Sunbirds in their fleets.

"How much for the day?" queried Blackburn.

"Not much more than the Hertz-mobiles," Jack replied, with a smile. "They do make you fill out a form for extra auto insurance and tell you not to cross the Mexican border. If you do, you may be left with just a "frame" and a large bill. They want the car back in one piece. The Mexicans near Tijuana tend to strip vehicles, especially rentals, and then resell the parts," Jack added. "An $80,000 car is worth three times that in parts! The Mexicans resell those parts back to the U.S. buyers in need. They charge less than the NAPA parts dealers down the road and make a killin'," Jack said with authority.

Blackburn's hair was swept back by the wind and he was in awe of the power of the convertible's engine. After lunch in Del Mar, Jack would let Dwayne drive it back to Mesa Biotech.

At the Wingless Pelican Restaurant, the two men were seated at a table near the windows overlooking the beach. The waves were only seventy-five yards away and the restaurant was at sea level. There were distracting bikinis and thongs everywhere. Blackburn had arranged the lunch at this particular restaurant to impress Jack and knew that he would appreciate the view. A discussion of thongs and baseball promised to be most entertaining.

Jack was impressed with the menu, as well. He would take a business card from the reception area of the restaurant. The card was for future reference in his Rolodex file.

"Hey! . . . Business aside for the moment . . . guess who got the Rizzo collection of baseball memorabilia back in Boston?" asked Blackburn with raised eyebrows.

"You? . . . was it you?" asked Danton. "Did you acquire old man Rizzo's barbershop collection?" Jack did not let on that he knew Royston had scoffed it up, or that he had been talking to Royston about a potential job.

"No . . . no, not all of it. Just some pieces, odds and ends . . . the dregs," answered Blackburn with a Cheshire-cat smile. "But I know who got the good stuff!" Blackburn added as a teaser.

"For God's sake, you're in California. How'd ya get any of the collection? Were you at an auction or somethin'," Danton asked with significant interest.

"Nah . . . we have ways . . . and connections," he added.

"Actually, a colleague of ours at Mesa acquired the memorabilia. E. Royston MacDonald, a board member and a very rich man, from Texas, bought the whole shebang!"

Jack asked with furrowed brow, "*The* MacDonald from Dallas? That guy with the enormously valuable, prized collection? I've read about the man. He supposedly has everything in a vault, right?"

Jack was coy, not knowing what Blackburn might already know about his potential hire by MacDonald. Jack needed to know more about MacDonald and Blackburn could shed the light.

"Uh-huh! It's the same guy, and yes, he has a bank vault in his home loaded lots of Ted Williams, DiMaggio and Mantle stuff."

Blackburn continued, "MacDonald is a 'heavy' on our board of directors at Mesa and gives us megabucks in research money. He invests heavily in potential biotech companies. He has an avid interest in research areas like cardiovascular, CNS, immune diseases and fertility enhancement and control. I guess he's lookin' for the Nobel prize someday, and damn well just might get it!" Blackburn confided.

A waitress brought each of them their soup and sandwiches. They thanked her for her prompt service and continued the discussion.

Jack commented, "I was wondering what happened to that collection in Boston. I think it was hung up in probate court for a while. It was certainly unique. He had some pretty wild stuff . . . even hair clippings from older, now-deceased ballplayers . . . that is morbid at best." Danton continued to play Blackburn along.

"Right," added Blackburn. "It was a macabre collection of trinkets. Almost everything was personalized to Mr. Rizzo. Everyone loved the old man. It was an apparent honor to have your hair cut by the Italian immigrant."

"So why did the family not keep the stuff he had collected over the years?" asked Jack.

"No use to them, and Rizzo had promised the collection to MacDonald, in advance. Heard the Rizzo kids got 60-100K for it,"

Blackburn added. "Knowin' that I also have a small collection, Royston gave me some of the rejects or duplicates from Rizzo's glass case. Ya know—signed balls and stuff, smudged or dirty."

Jack asked quietly, "Tell me about the clippings, the hair clippings. Were they from famous people or from regular Joes that lived in the neighborhood near Fenway?"

"Don't know the details but some may have been older ballplayers that played for Boston. Either the Boston Braves or Red Sox way back when."

Jack allowed Blackburn to continue to talk. He still did not let on to him that he had met with MacDonald in Boston and in Texas.

Blackburn sat back and thought for a moment. Then Dwayne mentioned the celebrities. It was known that JFK and others of note occasionally visited Rizzo because they grew up in nearby Brookline, Massachusetts. Blackburn then blurted out the fact that there were no "broads" in the collection. Rizzo never cut women's hair except his daughter's. Jack found it amazing and odd that the whole collection of hair clippings came from men of notoriety. Jack was beginning to understand some relationship between the vials of hair and Royston's supposed "project" in San Diego. He began to correlate the two pieces of information.

"What about Ted Williams?" asked Jack, still playing dumb. "Was he ever there, to get a haircut?"

"Sure! At least we think so," remarked Blackburn. "We actually have some on-going experiments at my university's lab trying to extract his DNA from one of Rizzo's vials of Ted's hair. The vial said T. W., so we assume it's him. We don't know for sure and may never know. The experiments are practice for MacDonald's Project, a DNA project that is top secret in the San Diego area. I'm a member of the team doing the research."

"Really? What's the secret?" asked Jack.

Blackburn went silent for the moment. He had overextended himself by providing Jack with information, and quickly changed the subject. Jack now had a good idea what was going on.

"It's all proprietary. I can't talk about it just yet and we probably need to get back, Jack. I have a meeting at 1:30 P.M. Thanks for the sandwich, beer and sights on the beach. Didn't mean to detract from the beach with all that baseball stuff."

"Sure," said Jack. "I need to get moving as well."

Jack pondered the whole conversation and the sudden change in demeanor of Blackburn. It made him all the more curious. Jack paid the bill with his Amex card and handed Blackburn the keys.

"Here! Try it out, when they bring it around," said Jack enticingly.

Once the valet brought the car forward, Blackburn would take a slightly longer way back to Mesa Biotech. He would find some local roads near the beach in Del Mar and then circle back through La Jolla. Except for an occasional comment on the car's suspension, there was little conversation and nothing more was added to the prior discussion on the project. Driving the Vette, he seemed less worried about his 1:30 P.M. meeting.

Jack said good-bye at Mesa and thanked Dwayne Blackburn for a great lunch.

During the lunch, Jack Danton had continued with his discrete questioning of Blackburn. He asked if MacDonald ever came to San Diego. Blackburn confided that Royston would be in town the next day and that Jack could meet him if he wanted. They could talk baseball, he had suggested. Jack was unaware that Blackburn had already set the whole thing up and had recommended Jack to MacDonald in the first place. They both seemed to be playing a game with each other. What Blackburn didn't know was that Jack had sales appointments scheduled for the next day. One was at 10:00 A.M.

Jack Danton had never let on that MacDonald had actually sought him out to be part of the team. That was the dinner at Grille 23. Blackburn would find out about the possibility of Jack joining the team the next day, at the afternoon meeting with MacDonald.

Jack headed to downtown San Diego. His meetings were over for the day. After a couple of drinks at Croce's, Jack returned to the inn at Torrey Pines. It was still light out. He stayed there out of convenience to the clientele in the La Jolla area. It was much cheaper than the nearby Hilton or Sheraton, and he had access to some golf at the inn, on rare occasions.

Jack called Fawn from his room overlooking the ninth hole. They would chat for an hour. He missed her dearly, and road trips, although sometimes glamorous, were basically a lonely time for him. He would tell her of his investigations concerning the Rizzo hair collection, his lunch with Blackburn, and his plans to maybe come home a day early if he could shorten the trip. He would buy her a gift from the road; perhaps some jewelry from a shop in Del Mar. He had seen a piece with onyx and silver. That would look great on her, especially with the black dress that she had in the closet. *Perhaps some earrings, as well,* he thought.

After the phone call, he lay back against the pillow and watched a foursome hit shots outside his doorway on the South Course. He fell asleep in no time, as the breeze from the Pacific Ocean reeled through the open curtains and doorway. He began to snore noticeably and woke himself up briefly on two occasions. He clicked on a pay-for-view cable TV station called "Exotic Plaything." Before he even saw a naked body on the screen, he was fast asleep again and would not awaken until he heard the greens keepers watering the ninth hole at 5:00 A.M. His bill would include a charge of $8.95 for a movie that he never watched.

Nineteen

The next day, Danton finished his 10:00 A.M. sales appointment at Nucleic Acids, Inc. and left at 10:45 A.M. He proceeded to his next sales call on Science Park Road off Torrey Pines Road in La Jolla. His first appointment had gone extremely well and he was pleased. It was clear from the discussions with his client that they would need multiple toxicology studies in monkeys. Their protein drug at NAI was close to its first clinical trials. The studies that they needed in primates would total a million dollars and he was proud that he had landed the contract.

While en route to his second appointment at Rx Pharmaceutical, he stopped the car near a pay phone. He turned down the radio in the Corvette and shut off the engine. He had three messages in his voicemail. The third was from E. Royston MacDonald and it merely told Jack to call him on his cell phone as soon as possible. Jack had Royston's cell phone number in his electronic Rolodex. He decided to call Royston since the message was urgent. The next appointment, at 11:30, would wait but Jack was also to do lunch with them at a restaurant called Japengo. Rx Pharmaceutical's toxicology needs were pressing, but Jack knew that Royston waited for no one. He called him back immediately.

Jack dialed MacDonald's number and was nervous. After one ring, MacDonald answered. He was antsy.

"Jack, is that you? Did you get my message on your voice-mail? What took so long, boy?" asked MacDonald impatiently.

"Ah . . . sorry, I just retrieved my messages a few minutes ago and I'm late for an appointment," he said.

"Appointment? What appointment?" asked MacDonald.

"Sir, I have a meeting at Rx Pharmaceutical in a couple of minutes and I . . . "

Royston cut him off. "Rx? Why them? They don't have any promising drugs, boy. They got 'jack-shit' for 'lead' compounds! For Christ's sake, go see someone with a product and money! Rx doesn't have a pot to piss in! They don't need your services. Hell, they got nothing. You're wastin' your time! I checked them out ages ago. They're two months away from goin' belly-up."

"Really?" Jack interjected.

"Really, son, they're circlin' the drain. Understand?"

"Yes, sir," Jack replied. "Understood."

"Call the bastards and tell 'em you're ill. Tell 'em ya got *diarrhea* and you have to cancel!" MacDonald laughed. "No one wants to talk to anyone with diarrhea, boy!"

"Yes, I'll call them," Jack said, snickering. "The diarrhea idea *is novel.*"

"Atta boy! But hey, that is not why I rang you," MacDonald continued. "Should I have paged you, Jack?"

"No," said Danton. "I don't have a pager."

"What? No pager? Son, I'll have to get you one. You will be needing it if you're workin' for me!" MacDonald exclaimed.

"Roy, I'm still deciding," said Jack with surprise. He was feeling the pressure.

"I like ya, Jack, my boy. The guys at Mesa said you might come by their place this morning. I hope to meet with you while I am in town."

"I met with them yesterday, Roy," sighed Jack.

"That was yesterday. What are you doin' for lunch? I need to talk to you, son. Today! Let's do lunch!"

Jack interjected, "But, I have a lunch planned. I can't just . . . "

MacDonald cut him off.

"My boy, bag it! I need to see you today. I need you at the Hotel Del for a meeting—the Del at noon. You know the one in Coronado."

"Yes. I know the Hotel Del. I've been there," Jack added.

By now, Jack was confused about the urgency of MacDonald's needs.

"I'll be there, sir—at noon," he responded.

Royston suggested that they meet first at the gazebo bar over-looking the pool. Jack agreed to meet him there.

"We'll have a drink," suggested MacDonald. "Then I'll introduce you to some of my friends. Sound OK, boy?"

"I'll be there before twelve then," Jack indicated.

"You're learnin' kid, you're learnin'. See you in an hour or so."

After Jack hung up, he returned to his Corvette and pondered the conversation. He felt bad that he was not seeing the scheduled client. They were expecting him but Royston was intimidating. *He manipulates people well,* Jack thought.

Jack called his client and told them he was ill and would have to reschedule. They understood. He avoided using Royston's suggestion about the intestinal issue. He promised the client he would treat them to lunch the next time he was in San Diego. Jack, at that point, needed to head south to Coronado.

Twenty

Jack Danton drove past San Diego's downtown on Route 5 south toward Coronado. He was about ten minutes from the Hotel Del, and
would be there in time to meet MacDonald before the formal afternoon meeting. After crossing the Coronado Bridge, he paid the toll
and, about a mile west, took a left onto Orange Avenue and headed
for the hotel straight ahead. He drove behind the Hotel Del and parked
in the large lot to the right of the massive wooden structure. This
parking area was less popular than the one the tourists used. They
always parked on the south side, which was already congested.

E. Royston MacDonald left his room on the top floor of the Del.
He was dressed informally for a change. He did not have a suit on and
was dressed "smart casual." Anything else would have been over-
dressed at the hotel. His polo shirt had a logo of a famous Texas golf
course on the pocket, complete with crossed golf clubs and a golf ball
embroidered on it. His slacks were perfectly fitted as he headed down
to the barbershop to get a trim. He would meet Jack in about forty-
five minutes. His exquisite Gucci shoes clicked softly as he entered
the elevator. The elevator attendant, an older gentleman, greeted
Royston by his first name as MacDonald entered the "cage" of the
antiquated, but functional device.

"Mornin', Mr. Roy," said the elevator attendant with a smile.
"Lobby as usual?"

"No, Carsten, please take me down to the lower level . . . need a
trim at the barbershop. I guess they call it a salon now, don't they? I

like the old days when they were called barber shops . . . complete with the striped, barber pole and all."

"Right, sir. *Those* were the days!" said Carsten.

The elevator stopped at two and an older couple entered the elevator cage. The crosshatched mesh elevator door from the 1880s frightened the woman of elegant stature.

"This thing work?" she cried out to her husband.

"Sure, hon. Been around a long time, but it works!" he replied in a reassuring manner. She held on for dear life to the brass railing.

At lobby level, Carsten opened the cage with a quick motion of his arm and everyone departed except for Royston.

"Bye, ma'am," he said. "Goin' down?" Carsten said to no one else waiting nearby.

He and MacDonald proceeded to the lower level where the shops and hair salon were located.

"Have a nice day, Mr. Roy! I'm sure we'll see you later."

"You, too, Carsten, my man. I'm sure I'll catch you this afternoon. Got meetings all day."

Twenty minutes later, MacDonald left the salon and headed down the cavernous hallway of tourist shops to emerge by the veranda overlooking the pool. He proceeded out into the sunlight and shaded his eyes from the intense change of darkness to bright glare. He squinted as he scanned the total view of the beach, and then headed toward the gazebo bar above the hotel pool. The walk took him past the pool to his left and tennis courts to his right. The short walk was pleasant and the view of the beach and ocean superb.

Taking a seat on a stool he said, "Beefeater and tonic with a lemon twist, please."

"Yes, sir, comin' right up," responded the young male bartender. The blender to his left was noisily mixing a piña colada for a woman sitting nearby. The bartender added a slice of pineapple, a straw and a maraschino cherry to the frozen concoction and took it to her. The woman sat under her wide-brimmed straw hat and sipped the drink.

She is probably a tourist looking for a sugar-daddy by the pool, he thought. Royston paid her no attention, although she was attractive.

Jack arrived at the gazebo bar and accidentally startled MacDonald from behind. He had tapped him on the shoulder.

"Well, hello there," Jack said with a smile. "I thought I would beat you here."

"Hello, Jack boy," Royston responded. "Have a seat! What can I get you, son?"

"Is it noon? Can't drink before noon!" Jack laughed.

"Damn close to it, son. Two minutes to twelve!"

"Bartender! Please get this gentleman whatever he wants," commanded Royston.

"Sir? May I offer you a cocktail this fine day?" the bartender asked Jack.

"Sure! May I have the same thing that he has? Looks refreshing!" responded Jack.

"Beefeater and tonic? Comin' right up, sir!" replied the bartender.

Jack sat down next to MacDonald and saw him staring out across the glass-enclosed patio. The glass shield was a half wall that cut down the wind on the deck. It often had dried sea spray on it, which partially obscured the view of the beach where Marilyn Monroe filmed the movie *Some Like It Hot*. Royston was looking northwest and scanning the skies.

"Ah, son, there's one!" he said confidently. Jack looked up and saw a Navy S-3B Viking aircraft descending toward the Naval Air Station (NAS) at North Island. They were part of the VS-35 Blue Wolves squadron.

"They're shootin' landings, son . . . look at that SOB bank left! Awesome power for a small plane. They do this all day long, it seems."

"Quite a machine. That's our defense budget at work!" Jack added with a smirk.

"Waste of gas, I'd say," added MacDonald. "Pissin' away the budget every day," he mumbled under his breath.

"Guess you're right, does seem like a waste, if they do it everyday."

With that, Jack excused himself for a moment and headed for the men's room. The coffee from early morning had caught up with him. MacDonald sat there sipping his drink that was now virtually gone.

He chewed on an ice cube or two and spit one back into the glass. Fixated on the view of the ocean and sky, he waited for Jack's return. He passed the time reflecting on his oil company holdings and other investments. His stock was doing well. As well as he had done with his investments in oil, he still desired to be an icon in the biomedical field. Project Samuel would potentially get him that notoriety. He had planned the adventurous program well, and was pulling together the noted scientists that would make the project feasible and eventually successful. Danton would be helpful in that area, if Roy could coax him on board.

MacDonald was startled again from his thoughts as Jack returned from the men's room. Royston's drink almost tipped over and an ice cube popped out of the glass.

"Sorry. Didn't mean to scare you again," said Jack.

"No problem, son. Was just thinkin' why I brought you here. Barkeep! Get us two more please, and put them on my room if you don't mind. That's MacDonald. Top floor."

"Yes, sir, comin' right up!" came the reply from behind the bar.

"Jack, my boy. I appreciate your coming out to meet with me. I hope I didn't mess up your day too bad, but this is important."

Jack replied pleasantly, "No, I was able to reschedule the appointments from this morning and the luncheon as well."

"I like your style, boy. You care about your clientele and you are able to juggle more than one task at a time. That's admirable."

"Thank you. I was intrigued however by your comments on the telephone. You seemed eager for me to make a decision on your company," Jack said.

Just then, two Navy S-3B's passed over them abreast and in formation, and the roar of the engines was deafening. The massive jet turbines shattered the air as the pilots "goosed" the throttles on their final approach. It mimicked a *whooop-whooop* sound as they dropped rapidly toward the end of the runway. They were affectionately called "hoovers" because of the sound that they emitted upon landing. It was like a giant vacuum cleaner sucking air into their engine intakes.

"Awesome, eh, son? Guess we're secure for another day," Royston commented.

"Yes. Seems like we are protected pretty good on the West Coast," Jack responded with a smile.

"Jack, I suppose you wonder why I urgently called you here today. The job that I alluded to in Boston and at the ranch and on the phone, is real! The fact of the matter is, that I *need* you on a team that I'm formin' here on the West Coast. You have added value that you don't know about. Or, perhaps you do."

"What do you mean, sir?" Jack asked.

"Well boy. I'll cut right to the chase! What are you makin' in your current job with the Cambridge tox lab? I mean what's the total compensation? Including salary, commission, bonuses—all that?" Royston asked, as he leaned back in the bar stool. He crossed his arms in front of his chest.

"Ah, I'm doin' pretty well. They treat me well back in Cambridge," Jack said with pride.

"Total, Jack! What's the total?" Royston said as he belched from the cocktail he had rapidly consumed.

"I believe 135K!" Jack responded. "I think it's about 135K. It varies from year to year with the bonus thing."

"Hell! I'll pay you 200K plus all expenses, and give you a car— a nice one! Heard you like 'Vettes. I'll buy you one!"

Jack was startled by MacDonald's surprising offer and intent. Jack didn't even know what the job *was*, and here the man talking to him at the Hotel Del was offering him a substantial increase on the spot. He needed to have a job definition.

"Your present salary is basically 'chicken shit' for what ya *know,* boy," added Royston. "You're worth more than that to me. Don't they know back there in Cambridge what your value is? Don't you bring the clients to them? Don't they profit from you? Hell! You pay their salaries, and they get off cheap. Without you boy, they don't have many clients. You're out there prospecting for gold everyday and they're reapin' the profits!"

"But that *is* my job . . . to *get* the clients," Jack said in defense of his employer.

"Jack, that's jack-shit they're givin' you! No pun intended," Royston chuckled.

"I'll practically double that salary and if we succeed in my project, *you'll be a millionaire!* I'll throw in some biotech stock as well. We're about to be famous, son, and you can be a part of it!"

With that, Royston slipped off the stool and headed for the men's room himself. The gin finally caught up with his bladder. Jack sat there astounded by his forthright comments and cast his eyes out over the breaking waves to the west. *What the hell is so urgent*, he wondered.

Even the bartender commented, "Jesus, man! Take the fuckin' job! I couldn't help but hearin' what the man said. Even if it's illegal, take the job! If you don't, I will!" he walked away smiling. Jack smiled back and nodded in the affirmative.

When MacDonald returned, he continued with the conversation, picking up where he left off.

"Listen, Jack, this job will make you rich—salary and stock in Mesa Biotech as well," said Royston.

"To do what? You haven't said what I'd be doing. What exactly *is* the job? I can't move my wife out here without an explanation of the new job."

"We'll get to that, son, trust me. First you'll have to move out here to San Diego. Boston's too friggin' cold anyway— temperaturewise and otherwise. Damn people out there are cold! All those intellectual snobs from MIT and Harvard are there—lookin' cool and puffin' their chests all the time. The real scientists and biotech stuff are out here on the West Coast! Not back there in friggin' Bean Town."

"You haven't told me about the job yet," Jack reiterated. "Can you share more of that with me? In Texas you spoke of a 'project' and hair analysis. Is that it? Hair analysis?"

"Can't elaborate," said Roy. "Basically, it's my pet project that will make you and me famous. I need you for project management of the program, and you will still be connected with the biotech industry. I need some research staff of the highest caliber and you know who are the best out there—scientifically, that is. You are connected and will add value to the project," MacDonald repeated in a whisper. He leaned into Jack as if no one else could hear him. "Son, the boys at

Mesa Biotech and at the local university speak highly of you. They say you are well organized and also a *people* person. Like I told you at dinner at that steak joint in Boston, the project I have in mind needs someone of your caliber to manage it—ya know—the day-to-day bullshit. Scientists are prima donnas and I need someone to keep them in line and focused on this project."

"Why must I move," asked Jack with some concern. "We like Boston. My wife and I are settled in there."

"I can't be here all the time, Jack. I need you *here,* where the action is. I'm a busy man with many irons in the fire . . . all over the country," added MacDonald. "What do ya say? Will you help me?" asked Royston grabbing Jack's shoulder gently. "It's a win-win situation. Trust me!"

"Well, it does sound interesting and I have felt of late, that I was due for a change. The current job is fine but its becoming old hat to me. There is little appreciation these days of my efforts. Perhaps this would be a refreshing restart of my engines," Jack responded with a look of concern.

Jack became deep in thought and stared at the ocean to his right. He would need to convince Fawn and that would be tough. She was a Boston native and most of her life had been spent in that town. It would not be easy for her to leave their new home. He would call her to advise her that Royston was still after him, and then head home for Boston.

"Go home to Boston, Jack boy . . . and think about it. I wanna make sure that you are happy with the idea, son, and have a chance to discuss the specifics with your wife. Change ain't always easy and 'transplantation shock' of a move west can make things difficult with the family," Royston said sincerely.

"Yes, I know that," Jack added. "I need to convince the bride. She has a job that she likes a lot—*and* a new house. You're asking the impossible."

"I know," said Royston. "You have an nice woman there. Must keep her happy, ya know! The beauty of San Diego is that it's better than Boston! More to do here, son. Better weather, too. None of the snow and shit like back east! Hell, you can beach it here on Christmas! Just like Texas—no ice!" Royston laughed. "Go home and think about it! We've got forty-eight hours to get rollin'."

"Forty-eight hours? You want my decision in forty-eight hours?" asked Jack, with surprise.

"Sure, son. You can do it. Life's short and we got work to do. This project won't wait. Forty-eight hours will determine if you're serious. See what magic you can work with Fawn in forty-eight hours. This is business, son! It's like takin' a piss. 'You can just stand there and piddle like an old man or you can get the job done in record fashion.' Ah, sorry, son—probably not a great analogy, but you know what I mean. More than three shakes and you're playin' with it!" Royston roared.

Jack was laughing as well. The tension was broken.

Royston finished off the conversation with Jack by saying, "Instead of attending today's project meeting, son, we'll have you make the next one if you decide to join the team. I think it would be premature for you to attend today. I need a firm commitment from you and an agreement of confidentiality from all participating members first. We are about to attempt to make history and you can be a vital link in the program. The commitment and confidentiality are a critical first step."

Jack Danton bid Royston good-bye with a firm handshake while leaving behind half a cocktail on the bar. He would call Fawn and then head east that evening. With a deadline of less than forty-eight hours hanging over his head, he would need to get his ticket and flight changed as soon as possible.

"I'll talk to you soon, son," Royston said as Jack departed. MacDonald then left the gazebo bar and headed back to his room at the Hotel Del.

Jack was able to change his flight and red-eyed it back to Boston that night. He would arrive between seven and eight o'clock in the morning. Prior to boarding the plane in San Diego, he had a few cocktails at the airport bar near Gate 14. That way, he knew he would sleep during the long journey home. He needed to chill out, since Royston's offer was both confusing and interesting to him. The money and perks were exceptional. He needed to take a break from the confusion in his mind. He also had to convince Fawn to consider moving west. *That would be no small task,* he thought, and he knew it.

∅∅∅∅

That afternoon, Royston MacDonald convened his meeting in a first-floor conference room at The Del. He met for four hours with Johnson, Blackburn, Bradshaw and Sanchez. The attendees and team on Project Samuel were still not aware of the overall program endpoints. The preclinical scientists working on the rodent studies were not yet integrated with the members of the clinical group. Jack Danton would be needed to help in that area and Royston needed forty-eight hours for Jack's decision. It killed him to wait for two days since time was money and there was no guarantee that the Dantons would accept the offer.

During a break in the afternoon meeting, MacDonald wandered outside the dark hotel decor and was blinded by the afternoon sun. He headed for the jetty on the beach. The Navy Vikings above continued to circle the NAS at North Island to his right. Their engines were deafening, as an occasional plane flew near the hotel's beach. He proceeded to walk back to the passageway that ran parallel to the beach and returned to the hotel near the tennis courts. The breeze from the ocean and a near-perfect sunlit sky were enticing. He cast his eyes upward to the U.S. flag flying above the center of the large red-peaked roof of the wooden complex. He never ceased being impressed by the hotel's history. MacDonald wanted his piece of history as well. It was actually beginning to come together in the meeting room on the first floor.

He grabbed an ice tea from the table just inside the meeting room, rejoined his colleagues after break and recommenced the meeting at 4:00 P.M.

∅∅∅∅

At 6:00 P.M. Royston departed The Del in a limo. Max was instructed to take him to the North Park section of San Diego, east of Coronado and San Diego proper. Max drove through the predominantly gay area of Hillcrest in order to get there, then proceeded east on University Avenue. He turned left at Royston's suggestion, passing the run-down movie theater in North Park and then drove slowly down Utah Street. It was becoming dusk and the street was not busy. Royston instructed Max to stop the limo on the 4000 block. He rolled down the back window and stared into the living room of the boyhood home of Ted Williams. It sent chills up his spine. The living room window that he was looking into from a distance, was the same window that Ted looked out of as a toddler. Royston said nothing and the only sound he and Max heard was the idling engine of the limo.

Max then took a left and passed Ted Williams Field, which at that hour of the evening was empty. He then took Royston back to the Hotel Del.

Royston would fly to Texas in the morning and await Jack Danton's call from Boston.

Twenty-one

Jack Danton had mentally accepted Royston's offer while they were having lunch, but needed all of the forty-eight hours of Fawn's time to discuss the new opportunity for both of them. He spent the entire time sitting with her, walking with her and discussing the pros and cons of E. Royston MacDonald's verbal proposal. It was tentatively decided that Jack would accept the offer to work with Royston and Jack decided to take a week off from his present work to get Fawn out to the West Coast at Royston's expense. She knew for several months that Royston wanted him badly. It was also not a surprise to Royston that Jack was in a quandary over a very hard decision in life. He knew he loved the Boston area.

"If my wife likes San Diego, I will accept your offer," said Jack by phone to Royston in the forty-sixth hour of the forty-eight that he was allotted.

"Great, Jack! You and Fawn won't regret it. Get her out there and take a look around. Once she sees La Jolla and Del Mar, she'll probably be hooked on the area. Every day is a 72 to 74 degree perfect day. She'll love the classiness, as well. You can always go back to Boston to see the relatives. It's only a plane ride away. I'll even pick up your Red Sox season ticket fee each year. That way they are waiting for you all summer and fall," Royston said, affectionately. "I know how much the Red Sox mean to you. You've had family season tickets all those years."

"Thanks," said Jack. "You sure know how to entice a new hire."

"Get her to S.D., boy, as soon as you can. I'll fax you some basic paperwork to get you officially on board. You will need to sign a confidentiality agreement about the work we are doing. Is that OK?"

"Sure," replied Jack. "I'll be glad to fax the signature and paperwork back to you. I'll 'hard copy' it back to you by FedEx."

"Welcome aboard, son! I'm pleased to have you on the team," said Royston, enthusiastically.

"Me, too. Glad to be a part of the project and the team," Jack said with a slight hesitance. He was scared that he might have just jumped off a bridge—a bridge to a new career and lifestyle. The whole package was too good to be true.

"I will need to inform my current employer in Boston of my decision to leave. I would normally do that after the trip to S.D. with Fawn, but I now feel confident that she will find San Diego attractive and be happy there."

Royston gave him all the latitude he needed.

"Take your time, son. Make sure she's happy with the new plans. You both need to feel totally committed to the move."

"Thank you for the offer and for the confidence in me. I think this will be a great opportunity for both of us."

"I agree, son," replied Royston. "Let me know how the trip goes with Fawn. Look at some land and houses. Get familiar with the surroundings! After you sign, I'll get you the project details you wanted. Fair?"

"Yes. We will. Thank you again," Jack responded.

"You betcha' kid. Talk to you soon."

Royston hung up and sat back in his leather chair in his home office in Texas. Photos of ballplayers and sports memorabilia surrounded him. He sat in the silence of the room. There was no one there but himself and he knew his plans were all coming together. All of the interaction with the scientists, with Jack and the medical doctors were finally coming to fruition. All the effort to build the perfect team was now there.

There would be a meeting in a week or so in San Diego. This time it would be the entire team, and Jack Danton would be introduced to the group as project manager of Project Samuel.

Twenty-two

Within a few days, Jack notified his boss in Cambridge that he had been offered a position on the West Coast and that he was leaving the company. Jack's decision was a surprise, and a substantial loss to his boss and to the Massachusetts-based contract laboratory. The staff planned to give a party for him before he left. The upper brass would also attend and wish him well. He had contributed much to the company financially.

In the meantime, Jack took his remaining vacation time and headed to San Diego with Fawn. He would personally introduce her to what he knew of the geographical area. They traveled the coastal route in a convertible. He impressed her with a Corvette from the rental car company, knowing Royston had promised him one of his own.

"Honey, how will you live without your beloved Red Sox?" she asked with concern, during the ride. "You've got those season tickets and all."

"Don't know, hon. The Padres are here at Jack Murphy Stadium, or whatever they call it now—QualComm, 'schmol'com or some big corporate name. They've been World Series contenders, ya know. They have Tony Gwynn!" he exclaimed. "They say he's the next Ted Williams. He almost hit .400 last year. I could easily root for them."

"What about the cost of living? Homes look very expensive compared to back east," Fawn said with genuine concern.

"Can we do it? Can we afford the lifestyle of southern California?" she asked.

"Well, hon, this isn't Boston and it will cost a bit more, but Royston is takin' care of us financially. The salary is awesome and the potential stock and bonuses should make it OK. Very OK."

Fawn was quiet as she enjoyed the scenery of the ride. He took her past the Gliderport in La Jolla, then up through Del Mar. The next day they would go south to Chula Vista and then north to Scripps Ranch. Poway was attractive to Fawn but too far inland and too far from where Jack needed to be for work. *Something in La Jolla or Del Mar would be best,* she thought. This would give Jack close access to the scientists involved in the project.

Fawn commented to Jack on how different the terrain appeared in southern California. In late summer the green hills of spring turn to brown. They often result in brushfires, which become serious threats to homes throughout California. Inland, the arid desert becomes readily apparent. Cacti bloom in spring but soon the area becomes even drier and more barren. This landscape seemed so different for Fawn who was used to a lot of green pines and the four seasons of New England. *If this is what Jack wants,* Fawn thought, *I'll go along with it.* She would follow him anywhere to make him happy.

Jack kept reminding her of how lucrative the job would be and how they would benefit from the successful research program that MacDonald had in mind. Fawn and Jack were not aware of the overall objective of the research, but both knew that many prominent scientists would be involved in the program. They were taking a chance and they both knew it.

Fawn commented on the MacDonald connection, and how she was uneasy about the speed at which everything had developed for the Danton family. She trusted Royston, but she still had some reservations about his impulsiveness and his impatience. She knew that the new job that he offered to Jack might not last forever and that the door was open for Jack to change his mind and return to the East Coast if he was unhappy. They would not have to sell their house back East; MacDonald offered to carry the mortgage on it. He didn't want Jack to have any burdens that might affect his dedication and efforts toward the new job at hand. *Therefore, "transplantation shock" to the West Coast must be minimized,* Royston thought.

133

Jack and Fawn would return home to Boston. There was nothing negative about San Diego in Fawn's eyes and they would return again after Jack's farewell party. The next trip to San Diego would probably be around the time of their wedding anniversary. That date was fast approaching. During both trips, Fawn met with the best Realtor in the area to look at homes in the San Diego area. They would eventually settle in Del Mar, not on the water, but close enough to see the blue Pacific.

"Hon, we'll find you a job in no time," he told her. "There are plenty of jobs in the area according to a headhunter that I have spoken with. I will get them to help you find something similar to what you had back in Cambridge."

"That's OK, honey," she replied. "Let's get you settled. Then I can start looking. I'd like to know the S.D. area much better so I don't have to deal with traffic and long commutes."

She began to realize that the move could be beneficial. Torrey Pines State Park was just south of Del Mar and easily accessible. Jack would no longer travel all that much on business. His focus was on the San Diego area except for an occasional meeting with Royston MacDonald in Texas. Jack would recruit most members of the final research team from the local area. He would add staff to the group that MacDonald had already started.

Jack would open an office for his project management in an executive tower on La Jolla Village Drive. It was next to the Hyatt Hotel and just off Interstate 5. It was easy access to both Torrey Pines Road, Del Mar and downtown San Diego. He would be able to be home in fifteen minutes, if needed.

Fawn would eventually develop friendships with their new neighbors. Many of them were the wives of doctors and lawyers who practiced locally and all were well-to-do. They would eventually get memberships at a health club and a golf course in the vicinity of their future home. The Dantons' lifestyle would change. Things would be more relaxed and, as Jack became happier, their relationship would become even closer. She was falling in love with him all over again. It showed at night when they went to bed. Four out of seven nights a week they made love.

Their future vacations would be to Mexico and Hawaii since their beloved Bermuda was too far away. If they wanted a winter vacation, Lake Tahoe, Colorado and Utah were a short plane ride away. They would have it all.

Twenty-three

Tom and Vicky Palmer were ecstatic that they might become parents in the near future. The doctors at the Fertility Clinic saw no anatomical reason why Vicky could not carry a baby to term. If needed, she would be given supplemental steroid hormone treatment to maintain pregnancy and insure a full-term baby or babies. She realized that her problem was physiological and endocrine in origin. The doctors had aided her in the ovulatory process by giving her multiple injections in order to produce ripe follicles with eggs.

Once the ovaries had been artificially stimulated to produce ova, the doctors would retrieve the eggs under light anesthesia. The procedure involved a surgical approach through the wall of the vagina. The series of injections often produced five to six ova per ovary. They would then add Tom's sperm directly to a laboratory petri dish containing some of the eggs. Tom was embarrassed since it would require masturbation to obtain the semen for the fertilization process.

"Oh, hon," Vicky told him, "don't look so pained by the procedure. Maybe they'll let me help." Tom did not respond and found little humor in his wife's comment. *That kind of stuff is private,* he thought. He didn't want some doctor tellin' him to go in the men's room and jerk off. He had asked the doctor if they could have sex and collect the semen in a condom. *Why not that?* he wondered. The doctor had advised them that that was not feasible since the latex of the condom was detrimental to the viability of the sperm. He would be provided a sterile cup for collecting the semen. The doctor also told

136

him that the process was confidential. He would have all the privacy that he needed. Even with the doctor's assurance, the whole thing was embarrassing for him.

Vicky was amused by his embarrassment. "You'll be OK, hon. I know you can do it, when the time comes," she snickered behind cupped hands over her mouth.

Dr. Bradshaw, the fertility expert at the clinic, and the medical staff would coordinate the Palmers' attempt at fertility enhancement. Vicky Palmer underwent all appropriate injections with the hormones necessary for production of the ova. In a matter of days, she entered the clinic at 8:00 A.M. on a Saturday and underwent extensive blood work and a procedure to visualize the ovaries for follicular development. It was clear that the procedure and injections had produced three mature follicles on the left ovary, and four mature follicles on the right, for a total of seven. Once they were retrieved by aspiration, they were placed in a sterile dish with a nutritive liquid culture medium to keep the eggs viable. Tom's sperm, which had been obtained earlier, would be added to the dish to fertilize the eggs. In a special incubator, the fertilized eggs would grow and divide until such time that they could be reintroduced into Vicky's uterus. That stage of development of the eggs would be about forty-eight to seventy-two hours after fertilization. The uterine lining would be in a hormonal state ready to accept the embryos.

Vicky could go home for the time being and return when the eggs would be reintroduced into her womb. It would be a far less invasive procedure than the retrieval. The doctors would place the eggs into the uterus, directly through the cervix by the vaginal approach.

Drs. Bradshaw and Sanchez were successful in retrieving the seven eggs and withheld three of them for storage in a frozen state. He felt that if the first blastocysts didn't implant in the uterus, they could repeat the procedure at a later date without Vicky having to go through the whole procedure again. The extra eggs, which were unfertilized, would remain cryogenically preserved under liquid nitrogen and would be stored in a special solution to maintain their viability.

Reintroducing four of the seven fertilized ova into Vicky would certainly be enough for a first attempt at pregnancy. She would have four children if they all implanted. Quadruplets would almost be manageable, compared to having septuplets. Actually, she and Tom had hoped for one or two anyway, and the odds were in their favor. Not all embryo transfers implant in the uterine wall. It might be that only one of the four would develop further.

After collecting the ova, Dr. Bradshaw left the hospital with a briefcase in one hand and a thermos bottle in the other. In the thermos were sterile vials of the extra, unfertilized eggs from Vicky. They were safely stored in special stainless steel cryogenic transfer containers. The vials would be placed in a special freezer in Dr. Bradshaw's laboratory where the eggs would be kept alive, but quiescent at minus 279 degrees Fahrenheit.

Days later, Vicky returned with Tom to the clinic for the reintroduction of the four fertilized eggs. All went well with the procedure and she remained in the hospital for a couple of days to encourage her to relax and have her remain quiet. The eggs were in the eight to sixteen cell blastocyst stage upon transfer. They had rapidly divided into a small cluster of little balls as expected. Each conceptus had developed in the incubator as planned. In an unstressed state, Vicky had the best chance of retaining the eggs; otherwise they might be expelled naturally from the uterus. She followed all the doctor's orders while in the clinic and went home in two days.

Tom and she smiled, but were teary-eyed as they left the clinic. They had their fingers crossed—at the thought of her becoming pregnant. The ultimate test would be a follow-up pregnancy test, which the doctors hoped would be positive. In a short time they would all know if the procedure had worked.

Twenty-four

Jack and Fawn had returned to Boston for his farewell party. Although Jack's boss in Cambridge was upset by his unexpected and rapid departure, he wished him luck in his new position.

"I know I can't keep you here, Jack," he said sadly at the farewell dinner, "but I must tell you that you have left us with a gaping hole in our marketing and sales effort. You made friends of your clients and they respected you. It's reassuring to know that you are not going to a competitor!"

"Not to worry!" Jack reassured him. "It's a totally different job and Fawn and I are really happy to have the opportunity to try the West Coast. Please visit us if you are in the area. I will miss all of you, and Boston. Thanks for the wonderful experience of working with you. You all were a critical part of the Cambridge team and our success."

Jack's boss in Cambridge knew that he couldn't match the salary and perks that MacDonald offered. He didn't know exactly what Jack's new job was, but he was aware of the salary that had made him leave Boston for California.

"Jack, in appreciation of your efforts and on behalf of this company, we want to give you something to hold you over on the West Coast . . . a little remembrance of Bean Town!"

Jack opened the gift-wrapped item, which was about fourteen by twenty inches. He surmised that it was something they had framed. *Perhaps,* he thought, *it's a picture of the Charles River and the Bos-*

ton skyline. He was totally surprised to see that it was something that he had always wanted.

"Thank you so much," he said sincerely. He didn't have to open it all the way to know that it was "The Boys of Boston"—a sports photo of Bobby Orr, Ted Williams and Larry Bird, taken when they had appeared together on local television. In the photo, they were holding their jerseys and smiling as they sat next to one another. All three autographs were clearly written with a blue Sharpie pen. It was a phenomenal piece of autographed memorabilia, surrounded by a cherry wood frame. It was authentic as evidenced by the NBA hologram logo at the bottom, right corner. The certificate of authenticity for the triple autographs came from the Ted Williams family in Hernando, Florida.

Jack was blown away by the generosity of his colleagues since he knew its value to be between $1,400 and $3,000, depending on the source. He looked forward to telling Royston MacDonald of his new acquisition.

There were other gifts and dinner at The Bostonian Hotel. Nothing else would match the photo of Boston's three greatest athletes in the sport of basketball, hockey and baseball.

Jack and Fawn would leave for San Diego in a day or so. He would miss his dedicated colleagues from Cambridge, but he also looked forward to starting his new responsibilities in San Diego. The prized autographed photograph would grace their family room above the California-style gas fireplace. It would be a wonderful reminder of their friends in Boston and the city and baseball team they had grown to love so much

⚾ ⚾ ⚾ ⚾

The return to San Diego by the Dantons coincided with their first wedding anniversary. As Royston had provided Jack with a few days off to settle in, the Dantons decided to use this time to celebrate their anniversary by finding a hotel on the cliffs overlooking the Pacific. Even though they had a new home, they wanted the sound of the ocean to be next to their bedroom. North of San Diego was a hotel not all that far from Carlsbad and the rooms directly overlooked the ocean below. Jack had stayed there once on a business trip. The coastal area was a nice place for them to be alone, and their renewed closeness had made them far more intimate than when they lived in Boston.

"Is this OK, honey?" she asked coyly and stepped out onto the veranda in the night air. She was wearing a peach camisole, which she had purchased at Nordstrom's at the Fashion Valley Mall, southeast of La Jolla. Below the camisole, a thong of matching color hugged the crevice between both cheeks of her buttocks. A triangular piece of fabric, smaller than a bikini, covered her front.

A candle on the patio table illuminated her figure with dancing flashing lights of yellow that came and went with the wind. Jack responded with a smile, "Where did you ever get that lovely teddy, miss? That is unbelievable, my love. Come over here!" he ordered her with tender passion.

She responded by handing him a glass of wine, then sat beside him on the chaise lounge. A cinder-block wall about five feet tall separated them from the adjoining neighbor's room at the hotel. No one appeared to be home next door.

"You like peach, don't you sweetheart?" she asked with a southern drawl just for fun.

"I should say I do, darlin'," he said. "You look spectacular in the night, my love." He was obviously aroused and she teased him by rubbing against his groin in a gentle but deliberate manner. She sipped her wine while stimulating him.

Jack was still dressed in sweats and a Red Sox T-shirt. "You never cease to amaze me!" he sighed. "You are an incredible hardbody."

It was a perfect San Diego night. The stars were above them and the night air clear as a bell. A partial moon was visible and shown above their bodies. There were no extraneous lights to dim the vibrant sky of stars. Soft music emerged from the bedroom by the veranda. The radio was set on an FM station and was playing new-age instrumentals by which one might go to sleep. The water and waves below varied in cadence that ranged from gentle to moderate. The wind rustled though the surrounding bushes and ground cover. A sound similar to tree frogs could be heard as background music above the softly playing radio.

Jack lay back in the lounge chair and pulled her close to him in a gentle but firm manner. She smiled ever so slightly as she leaned her chest into his face. Two pointed imprints in the peach-colored fabric arose from behind her camisole. Her nipples were erect and excited.

This was thelerethism at its finest, Jack thought. It was as if she was cold, but there was no evening chill. The after-shave from Jack's chest and neck was testimony to the shower he had taken twenty minutes earlier. She was excited by the clean scent of his skin and well-defined muscles in his arms and chest. He had no underwear on underneath his sweats and had left them off on purpose, well in advance.

"Oh you bad boy," she said with raised eyebrows as she reached inside his soft cotton apparel. "You have no skivvies on, boy! You naughty little boy," she whispered in his ear.

"Straddle me, sweetheart, please. I love you so much," he said in the heat of passion. He was breathing deeply and moaning in response to her lust for his body.

She obliged him, still clothed and teasing him as she lifted one leg over his body to sit directly on top of him. He lifted the camisole enough to reveal her erect nipples and gently kissed them as if he was a slowly moving windshield wiper—back and forth—back and forth. His tongue gently circled the areola of each breast and with a gentle sucking motion he totally aroused her. Her head fell back and her eyes closed as she gyrated above his pelvis, still wearing the thong and now moist from the erotic harmony of motion.

"You never cease to amaze me, Jack boy. I have never known this feeling before you," she praised him.

"You bring out the best in me, honey. I'm glad you enjoy me as much as I enjoy you. Just look at you! You glow in the night. Your face is flushed in the candlelight."

"I know," she replied in the heat of the moment, I need you inside me right now!" she said with clenched teeth and lips. She sucked in her own breath as if to hold it, in ecstasy. At that very moment she reached down with one hand and pulled her thong to the side and with her other hand she gently placed him inside her and lowered herself on him in a slow and methodical fashion. She was in no hurry to have him totally inside of her. The thong, once released, snapped against him in a pleasurable way. It would rest against him and her together. They would deal with the chaffing of their inner thighs later. The pain of irritated skin would not be felt in the height of the excitement. Pleasure superseded the pain and she gently bit his lower lip with each vertical motion of her pelvis.

"Hon, you get so wet so fast . . . you always get so wet," he whispered to her. She began to sweat ever so slightly and her skin glistened from the intense moment of passion. A fragrance of sex was aromatic, and mixed with his cologne and her perfume.

"Look what you do to me, Jack . . . you haven't been this large since we first dated. Must be the California air."

"Don't say another word, hon," he said with a higher voice. "I'm about to come." She sped up the motion in short and rapid strokes as they both came at the same time. Sweat poured off of her and he was completely soaked by hers as well as his own perspiration. His forehead was wet and sweat ran down his temples. He had ejaculated but was still erect for the moment. He couldn't believe that he was still hard.

Fawn took advantage of the moment and had multiple orgasms that would register on the Richter scale. "Yes!" she screamed . . . Jesus! . . . Yes! Yes! Yes!" she continued. Jack couldn't believe what she had accomplished and went silent. She eventually fell exhausted to his chest and whispered, "Happy anniversary, sweetheart."

He responded by kissing her forehead and telling her what a wonderful, sensual woman she was. She smiled and blew air across his face to cool him. She blew air back and forth with pursed lips and continued up and down his forehead and cheeks. He closed his eyes and enjoyed the human fan. He was still sweating from the elevation of body heat. His sweatpants were about his knees and for the first time he felt the abrasion from the thong that had rubbed against his inner thigh.

"Yipes!" he commented. "That sure smarts now."

"Me, too," she said, as she experienced her own chafed skin as well. "I've got some medicated powder in the bathroom. That should help," she volunteered.

Just then the light over the door of the adjoining veranda came on. It haloed the night sky. Fawn jumped off Jack and tiptoed into the bedroom adjacent to the veranda. She had nothing to cover herself with.

She lay on the cool white sheets of the bed as Jack scurried inside behind her. He crouched as best he could. They laughed at almost being caught outside by the hotel neighbor.

For the next couple of nights they would try and match the first night's accomplishments. Although they came close to repeating the moment, they could never reach that level of excitement of night one. The wine, the moment, the sky, the veranda and the camisole did it. Each morning, they were greeted by a wake up call of sea lions on the rocks below. The chatter of the males sounded like foghorns in the morning. It was the season for them as well and the bulls were looking for the sea cows of their harem. The Dantons would sleep late on the last day of their escape and then head down to the Gliderport in La Jolla to watch the hang gliders and paragliders catch the thermals off of the cliffs above Black's Beach.

⊘⊘⊘⊘

The short time that Fawn and Jack would have to celebrate their anniversary did not keep them out of reach of Royston. He would touch base with Jack by calling his new cell phone. It was important that Jack know of an impending meeting at the Hotel Del. There would be a discussion of the time lines and milestones needed to keep Project Samuel rolling forward. Jack would have to present the scheduling of the R&D efforts as well as the clinical parameters and protocol for the surrogate pregnancy. Additionally, Jack was responsible for recruiting the best technical staff he could find at biotech companies in the general San Diego area. The new hires jumped at the opportunity to make incredible salaries that exceeded that of the general technician benefits at their existing employers in the area. With the high cost of living in southern California, most of the trained technicians needed the extra income to survive.

Jack also recruited higher-level scientific staff, at the Ph.D. level, to assist Blackburn and Bradshaw in their research endeavors. He knew who was compatible with whom, and who was well trained in cellular and reproductive biology. On their mini-getaway, Jack had managed to balance Royston's needs with his quest to enjoy his anniversary with Fawn. They were still basically newlyweds in their own eyes and the recent move to San Diego made them feel that way again.

〇 〇 〇 〇

On the last day of their anniversary celebration, Jack and Fawn arrived at the large parking lot at the Torrey Pines Gliderport. The sport flying area had been in service for decades and featured soaring, hang gliding, paragliding and radio-controlled model gliders over the years. In recent years, there was an enormous interest by the locals in the sport of paragliding. Outside of the restricted takeoff and landing zone, Jack and Fawn sat at a picnic table and watched instructors and fliers converse near a small snack bar.

The Dantons noticed a young man preparing his comma-shaped paraglider for takeoff. Fawn was less interested than Jack and figured that the people were nuts to jump off a 300-foot-high cliff with only a thin piece of nylon above them. Jack, on the other hand, had parachuted out of a single-engine airplane once before and had loved to ski jump competitively during his youth. He had cocaptained the high school ski team, so height and vertigo were not issues for him, but he was older now and not eager to try paragliding, especially in front of his wife.

He couldn't resist chatting with the locals, however, to learn more about the special canopies and harnesses of the paragliding fanatics.

Meanwhile, Fawn picked up her copy of *Maggie May's Diary*, a steamy romance novel by New England author Tom Coughlin, that she had started reading on the cross-country plane trip. Maggie May's exploits reminded Fawn of home in New England and areas of coastal Maine where she had often visited. Fawn was glad for the chance to get back into the book, even though the settings and town names made her miss her family back East even more. In time she would revisit Boston, while Jack worked in San Diego.

She put her book back in her handbag when Jack returned from visiting with the locals. "Will you look at those crazies?" she said with concern. "Do they really jump off that high cliff to float into oblivion? They must have a *death wish!*"

"It does seem like a fragile piece of cloth over their heads," Jack agreed.

As an instructor nearby briefed a student on gliding, another young man put out his cigarette and donned a helmet. He had a parachute strapped on his back and an elaborate paraglider harness about him. With two raised arms he commanded the nylon canopy to rise into the wind off the ocean. He then turned and walked to the end of the cliff above Black's Beach. Almost at the edge, the canopy elevated and lifted him up in a vertical thermal. He sat back as if he were in a swing and turned the two-tone blue, winged device northward, sailing along the cliff's edge, rising and descending at will. Jack was amazed. He was not familiar with paragliders—only parasails and parachutes.

Jack asked Fawn if she wanted anything from the snack bar. He was thirsty and dehydrated from days of "anniversary" sex. She replied, "No thanks, hon."

He ordered a coffee and muffin for himself and returned to the picnic table. The paraglider had reversed his flight path and headed south along the cliff line. He blew a "ridge whistle" in his mouth, a signal to those on the ground that he was about to land nearby. He gently touched down on the grass and the canopy slowly deflated, falling to the ground about him.

The black man behind the counter reminded Jack that he had forgotten his change and added with a Jamaican accent, "Hey, mon, are you flyin' today, mon?"

"Nah . . . I'm watchin' today . . . just watchin'," replied Jack with a smile.

From behind, Fawn said, "The only flyin' he's doin,' is flyin' with me—and that's at night. It's our anniversary and I don't want to be a widow!" The man from the Islands laughed as he admired her, then said to Jack, "You be doin' some gooood flyin' on yo own, mon! She's a gooood-loookin' woman!"

A Bob Marley CD played in the background and music emanated from behind the snack bar. Two more paragliders launched and passed each other at different elevations over the ocean and beach below. One canopy was white and the other one yellow.

South of the gliderport and about 100 yards away was a walkway to the edge of the cliffs. Protective fencing cautioned pedestrians to stay clear of the edge. Jack and Fawn observed the beach-goers and surfers below. Fawn wanted to go down to the beach but it was unclear as to how one got there. *It certainly isn't accessible from where we're standing,* Fawn thought. *It is shear down a couple of hundred feet or more.*

Jack noticed a couple on the beach and suddenly realized that they were two men embracing, Black's Beach is a nude beach and "the boys" were naked. To their right were some topless women as well. It was quite a unique mix of sun worshipers for Fawn and Jack to absorb.

"Holy shit, Fawn. Will you look at that!" Jack remarked with surprise. "Those guys are a couple." By now, the men were on a blanket rolling around like two dogs. Jack found the sight unappealing. Furthermore, the girls were kissing and fondling one another.

Fawn responded with jest, "Jack boy. Think we better go now. This isn't the beach I had in mind, after all."

As they walked back toward the snack bar area, one of the instructors, who had noticed that Jack seemed interested in paragliding, asked him if he wanted to learn to fly. He suggested that they could do it in tandem—with the instructor and client flying together under the same nylon chute.

"Thank you, but no thanks. I've got no balls for this. I once jumped out of a Cessna 172 but that's about it. We had more fabric back then and many more shroud lines. I was also a lot younger."

The instructor replied confidently, "This is just as safe—perhaps safer. We have more control with these gliders. The margin of safety is better today than it ever was."

Jack laughed, "Doesn't look safe to me, or to my wife of one year. We want kids someday and you have to be alive for that to happen."

"I've got kids!" the instructor said. "Hell, I take them up there with me!"

"If it's so safe, why do the fliers wear reserve chutes behind their back?" Jack asked sarcastically.

"Backup chutes, man! Just a precaution!" was the reply. "You just saw that guy do it and land safely. You sure you don't want to learn?"

"Not today, thanks. Perhaps another time," Jack said patronizingly.

"Yeah, perhaps another time," Fawn piped up. "Perhaps, 2046, honey!"

"The name is Wayne. What's yours?" asked the instructor.

"Jack. Jack Danton. Pleasure to meet you," responded Jack in kind.

"Well, Jack. Let me know when you are ready. We'll be here for you!"

"Thanks for your card, Wayne, I'll keep you in mind."

The serenity of the paragliders quietly soaring above and the background Bob Marley island music was shattered by the sound of a cell phone ringing at the next table. *There is no escape from the obnoxious little devices,* Jack thought. A group of visitors from a foreign country babbled on the phone, while they watched the paragliders.

Fawn and Jack left in disgust. The noisy telephone conversation by the spectators ruined their mood. The Dantons would drive north along the coast and find a beach to walk for a while.

Twenty-five

Soon after his anniversary celebration, Jack was well immersed in his work. Jack and Drs. Dwayne Blackburn and Robert Johnson agreed to meet at the Forensic Toxicology Laboratory in downtown San Diego. The purpose of the meeting was to discuss Royston MacDonald's Project Samuel. MacDonald had insisted that the scientists collaborate as soon as possible on the research project. Royston had asked Jack to join them because he had no real knowledge of DNA analysis.

"Well, where do we begin, Dwayne?" asked Jack.

"Can I see the hair samples?" Johnson asked Dwayne.

"Sure, Bob," Blackburn replied. "Here they are. Now, don't drop them. MacDonald will kill us!"

"Hell, they almost look like the same hair . . . just different years written on the vials," Johnson added.

"Yeah, they are supposed to be from the same person—supposedly from the renowned Boston Red Sox icon, Ted Williams," commented Blackburn. Jack concurred.

"This is incredible!" Johnson said. "You mean this Rizzo guy collected hundreds of these samples over the years?"

Jack nodded in agreement, "He cut the hair of Red Sox players, managers, celebrities and politicians for more than forty years."

"Jesus! Who else did he collect hair clippings from?" Johnson asked, in amazement.

"Don't know, but Royston hinted that JFK and other Kennedys stopped by Rizzo's shop as well."

"You mean *the* JFK and RFK brothers?" Johnson asked.

"Suppose so! Roy never told me or Jack about the entire list of initials that he had acquired. Each vial apparently had the initials and the supposed year of collection. JFK could have been there in the early 1960s, or even earlier in the late '50s, when he was a congressman," Blackburn added.

"Holy shit!" Johnson exclaimed, "Wouldn't that be somethin' if he had JFK's hair clippings!"

"Yeah, Bob, but that would freak me out," said Dwayne Blackburn. "I attended Kennedy's funeral in 1963." Danton was impressed. He had been a mere baby at the time.

Dwayne paused, then continued, "I was there when the caisson and casket went by on the bridge to Arlington National Cemetery. I was also there in front of the Capitol building when John-John saluted his father's coffin. I can still feel the chill of hearing the caisson wheels bounce over the cobblestones during the funeral dirge."

Dwayne was lost in thought. He then continued as his mind returned to the present. "A bunch of us fraternity guys drove down from college in New York—on Long island. We just wanted to be there. It created an everlasting memory. Having a sample of JFK's hair would be eerie. After all, he was one of four presidents who have been assassinated." Dwayne's mind seemed to wander off again as he stared at the large clock on the wall of Johnson's laboratory.

"Yeah, I guess that would be strange," Johnson added.

Returning to the task at hand, Johnson fumbled with the two vials that Dwayne Blackburn had given to him to look at. He held them up to the light.

"So . . . Bob," Dwayne asked, "what is the procedure for comparing the two vials? Do you need all the hair for the analyses?"

"Nah," he replied. "Just a little will do. But we need to run multiple samples on each vial for validation. We want to be sure that both hair collections came from the same person. I'm concerned about the source of the clippings."

"Why?" asked Blackburn.

"Why? Because, they may be contaminated by other hair. We don't know if Rizzo swept the floor to collect them or took the hair cuttings from a clean apron or drape that was wrapped about a client during a haircut. You know, when they cut your hair, they put a drape or apron around you, so the hair doesn't go down your shirt collar. A sample from that garment would be relatively clean—as compared to one from the floor. If they were from the floor, there could be hair from other people in the vial. Understand?"

"Sure," Dwayne replied, "don't want someone other than Ted in those vials!"

Johnson continued, "If the samples are off the drape, as I suspect, they could be pure DNA from Ted Williams. Off the floor, they could be ten different people! But look!" As Johnson held them up to the light, he said, "They look pretty much the same—hair color matches—so that's a good start."

Blackburn conceded that he hadn't thought of contamination in the vials. "Hopefully this dude, Rizzo, gave us clean samples."

Johnson reassured him that the samples looked similar in texture as well. They would soon know the answer since the DNA profiling would show inconsistencies if different hair samples from two or more origins coexisted in the vials in question.

"What's step one, doctor?" Blackburn asked with interest, "I've extracted DNA but have never analyzed it for sequencing. Our lab doesn't have your analytical hardware."

"Well, I won't try to get too deep for you—it might bore you—all that science," Johnson responded jokingly, knowing that Blackburn also had studied this field.

"I can handle it!" Blackburn retorted, with a smile.

"OK," Johnson said. "Over ninety-nine percent of DNA is the same in all people. It's the other percentage that makes us different as individuals. It's much easier to analyze samples that are tissue or blood—hair is tougher to evaluate. As you know, DNA from live tissue fragments 'extracts' more easily. That's usually what we get in the lab." Shaking the vials gently he added, "Hair is mostly dead cells and very dry. In this case, the stuff has been dead for years! It was dehydrated before it was collected in the Rizzo barbershop. As I said before, we need to break open the epithelial cells in the hair. Fortunately, there are some hair follicles in there as well. Look. See the end of some hairs. That little piece at the end is like a root. Having those cells from the follicle will help. Hair is modified skin. For example, the horn of a rhino is really compacted hair that is derived from its skin. Each hair cell that you see in the vials has a nucleus, which we need to extract, but it is dehydrated. Follow?"

"Yes," replied Jack, "So, we need to reconstitute it to a hydrated state? Put the water back in it."

"Correct!" said Johnson. "Normal tissue or blood is ready for extraction, but hair must go through several steps to retrieve the DNA in the nuclei of the cells." Blackburn was in agreement.

Johnson continued as Jack got a basic tutorial in hair cell physiology.

"First, we need to break up the epithelial cells and the membrane that surrounds each cell. We homogenize the hairs for a period of time in buffer. The buffer solution will do the trick. After that, we need to centrifuge the homogenate that we created in the buffer. It's like homogenized milk, in a way; everything is in suspension. It stays there until we spin it down at high RPMs in a centrifuge and a pellet forms at the bottom of the tube. The clear liquid stays above the pellet. Follow?"

"See," Blackburn added, "we decant off the supernatant liquid, and the pellet should remain behind."

"Right!" said Johnson. "The nucleus of each hair or follicle cell will layer together in what we call a 'Ficoli gradient.' The genetic material from each hair cell will rehydrate and pack together when centrifuged at high speed . . . follow?"

Jack was fixated by the procedure and lecture. "Sure," he said, "so . . . among the gammish at the bottom of the tube is a pure layer of nucleic DNA from Ted?"

"Right! If all goes well we'll have the DNA to analyze. It will be waitin' for us at the bottom of that little centrifuge tube," Johnson said with confidence as Blackburn nodded in agreement.

"What then?" Jack asked.

"After we decant off the supernatant top liquid, the DNA pellet at the bottom is removed and saved. We can then play with it!" Johnson added.

"Play with it? What do you mean?" asked Jack.

"Well, this is where we have some options. . . . We can analyze it by PCR analysis which will give us the sequence of DNA for ol' Teddy Ballgame. We'll know exactly what he is made of . . . *genetically*, of course."

"Really?" Jack asked. "You can get all of that information out of that hair sample?"

"Oh, yeah . . . it's got it all. Royston wants us to prepare some samples for microinjection, as well. He wants some extracts of the DNA to go to Dwayne's lab at Torreyana College. Dwayne and Bradshaw will get to play with the stuff in some mouse eggs, I guess," Johnson said.

"So . . . Project Samuel is a cloned mouse, ya think?" Jack asked.

"Don't know yet—doubt it actually—think Roy is planning something bigger. The mouse is probably for practice. Don't really know," added Johnson. "Royston just wants us to send the samples to Bradshaw's animal lab."

"That would be odd," remarked Jack, "Ted's DNA in a mouse!"

They all laughed.

"Ya know, Dwayne, Royston has some strange ideas, sometimes," Johnson said coyly. "I'm just doin' what he requested," he added while rolling his eyes.

"OK, so when do we start the analysis?" Jack asked. "Today? Tomorrow?"

"Tomorrow," was the response. "We'll start tomorrow. That is of course if the "druggies" downtown don't get too rowdy and kill someone tonight. If they start shootin' one another, I'll be busy with autopsies and such. Precedence. Ya know?"

"I understand the priorities. We'll call you in the morning to see how we are doin'," responded Blackburn. "Why don't you lock up the sample vials here for the night. Store them in your file cabinet. Would that be OK?" Blackburn asked.

"Sure . . . put them right here. They'll be safe here 'til mornin'. I'm the only one with the key."

"A-OK. I'm outta here. I'll call you in the mornin'. OK?" Blackburn asked. "You coming, Jack?"

"Oh, Jack, here's a recent article for you to bone up on. It's a publication from last year on DNA extraction. It gets into a little more detail," added Johnson.

"Thanks, Bob, I'll read it tonight. See ya later."

"Bye, for now, gentlemen," responded Johnson.

Dwayne Blackburn and Jack proceeded to leave the forensic lab, and each headed north on Route 5. Dwayne still had a lawn to mow and flowers to plant. The remainder of his Saturday would involve playing with the kids, as well. He needed to accomplish a lot before Sunday morning. If Johnson had a slow night in the pathology lab, he thought, then the two of them would be involved in "extracting Ted" early the next day. Jack headed home to see Fawn. Weekend chores awaited him as well.

Johnson would end up staying at the lab for a while that Saturday. There was laboratory prep work to do for the anticipated Sunday morning extraction and analysis of the Ted Williams's hair samples. He wanted everything ready to go, if they were to begin the DNA extraction the next day. He had family and chores at home as well, but E. Royston MacDonald had suggested some urgency with the project at hand. Johnson also anticipated that MacDonald would be calling to see how the Saturday meeting went with Blackburn and Danton. Once updated, MacDonald would then contact Jonathan Bradshaw at the fertility clinic, to advise him of the status of the mouse experiments. That way, another meeting between Blackburn and Bradshaw could be scheduled separately and without Johnson. Once Johnson confirmed the DNA structure from the two vials, Blackburn and Bradshaw could practice the nuclear cellular injection technique into the ova of mice. After they established a level of comfort with the technique, MacDonald would reconvene the group and present to them Phase II of Project Samuel.

An hour after Blackburn and Danton had left the Forensic Toxicology Laboratory, Johnson began preparing the next morning's glassware in the DNA biochemistry lab. The phone rang on the laboratory wall. As expected, it was Royston. Johnson would spend the next twenty-seven minutes briefing him on the meeting that he just had with Blackburn and Jack. Johnson, sounding reassuring, commented,

"Mr. MacDonald, we will begin the extraction tomorrow . . . Sunday. Yes, I'm sure . . . I will keep you abreast. Yes, Roy!"

Johnson was shaking after the call. Much of the telephone conversation was Johnson *listening* to MacDonald. He knew that this was top priority for the Texan. MacDonald had also indicated that a new shipment of mice had arrived for quarantine at Torreyana College and that the practice microinjection studies needed Johnson's DNA analysis data confirmed before they could proceed further with the preclinical animal experiment. Although Johnson was wary of the time frame in which MacDonald wanted to do the study, he assured Royston that he would begin his own tasks early the next day. He confirmed that Jack and Dwayne wanted to return on Sunday.

MacDonald had emphasized to Johnson that a lot was at stake on this research program and time was of paramount importance. The DNA extraction procedure would need to be validated on Sunday. For the first time ever, Johnson felt the "heat" from his financial benefactor. He had never personally experienced that before, but he knew from conversations with colleagues, that when MacDonald said, "jump!" . . . people *jumped!* Their asses and jobs depended on it.

What is Royston's complete agenda? Johnson wondered. For the first time ever, Johnson tossed around the word "ethics" in his mind.

The curiosity of the overall scope of Royston MacDonald's focus would surely weigh heavily on him for the next couple of days.

Twenty-six

Jack, at MacDonald's suggestion, called a meeting of the senior scientists who had been working on Project Samuel. They normally met monthly at the Hotel Del Coronado, but this meeting was to put to rest the rumor that they were in competition with other international labs with similar goals. The philosophical discussion was to review what was known in the research area of cloning, and to bring everyone within the group up to date on the status of the technology involved in Project Samuel. They also planned to review the milestones set for the program and to discuss potential glitches in meeting the target dates that MacDonald, Jack and the fertility staff had set.

The first part of the meeting was devoted to a discussion of the state of the art of cloning, in general. All scientists were responsible for keeping up with the published literature in journals and for reviewing critical data that might suggest detrimental effects of the known procedures to date. No one wanted to produce monstrous effects during the development of the first cloned human fetus, or the development of its major organs during the first trimester.

The round-table discussion began with individuals relaying pertinent information to the rest of the group. They discussed ethical or regulatory issues garnered from the TV news, newspapers, and scientific journals, or from direct telephone discussions or conferences with fellow scientists at other institutions.

Dr. Jonathan Bradshaw, the British reproductive biologist from the local Torito Bay Fertility Clinic and Torreyana College, was quick to comment on an article from a Los Angeles newspaper, which focused on stem cell research. It was becoming a focus and fashionable medical topic during a U.S. presidential campaign year. Stem cell research and cloning were closely linked.

"Gentlemen," Bradshaw began, "I saw an article that suggested that the National Institutes of Health (NIH) in Washington is now condoning the use of public funds to sponsor research on the extra embryos that infertile couples do not need. Once the donor is pregnant, there is little need for the additional embryos frozen in reserve. Often they are discarded and many NIH scientists feel that there is the need for stem cell research that may eventually benefit mankind. Even Christopher Reeves, the actor, supports this since nerve cells for transplant could evolve from that exploration."

He continued by stating the official positions of many members of Congress who objected to the basic research.

"Obtaining stem cells from these embryos is at the heart of the debate. We all know that major organs are created from the basic stem cell. Replacement organs for human use might be created for curing disease-states like diabetes, cirrhosis, or spinal injuries that paralyze. So the question is, what to do with the extra eggs from the fertility treatment . . . the ones that they freeze after they have been fertilized by the father's sperm? NIH wants to utilize the embryos and Congress want to dispose of them. It is unethical they say, to use an embryo in a frozen state of suspended development."

The group was focused on ethics and felt that *science* prevailed since the embryos would be thrown out or wasted anyway. That discussion would generate interest in other dilemmas of the day.

Another scientist had photocopied a recent newspaper article on cloning. It was more relevant to their task at hand. When it was discussed at length, many members of the team became nervous that other labs were also on a mission to clone a human. The most apprehensive of the group was Royston MacDonald who thought he was ages ahead of any other research groups. He was ahead, but only in the United States. He wanted to be first to succeed with cloning a person, and wanted the Nobel prize, as well. Royston felt compelled to expound upon the thought.

"You know colleagues, and for those who might not be familiar with the difficulty in cloning a human, it is not an easy task. Sure rodents have been cloned and farm animals, too. 'Dolly' the sheep was the end product of a long series of failed studies back in 1997. It was *that* major achievement that fostered the idea that man might be next in line." The scientists that sat around the conference table were enthralled with his knowledge. They did not know that Jack Danton provided Royston with review articles and that he synopsized the newspaper articles as well. Royston MacDonald was totally in tune with all ethical issues and medical breakthroughs of the day. It was part of Jack's job to keep Royston informed.

Royston continued, "No one knows of our plan for Project Samuel. No one knows the preliminary success rate we have had with lab techniques in rodents. Most people have felt that man could not be cloned in our lifetime. I hope that you will prove them wrong. There are people in other countries that have actually signed up to be cloned, or to have their relatives cloned. They know it will cost millions to have it done. There are people who have lost children at a young age by disease or by accident. These people want their child back. We know that scientists in the U.K., Canada and Italy are trying to clone a human. They are actively pursuing this."

Everyone was amazed by Royston MacDonald's passion and conviction. They were psyched by his drive and charisma. He unified the team and reinforced the quest to achieve this miraculous goal. With that, Jack stood up and added some other thoughts. "I have read recently that there are religious zealots that actually believe that *we*, yes, *we*—you and me—are clones from extraterrestrial beings!" The idea caused chuckles in the room. Dr. Bradshaw added to that, "Yes, they are known as the Raelian Movement and are headed by a man named Rael." Meeting attendees were shocked by that revelation.

Another scientist interjected, "I have read that most of our contemporaries think that the *maturity* of the science of cloning is less than five years away, especially for the human, yet we seem to be ahead of them. Because of what we know in rodents, sheep and cattle, we should be able to achieve this goal well before the predicted five years." He exuded confidence in the group. "Since the human is another mammal, we will probably succeed well before their projected target date."

Bradshaw became more serious. "We cannot count our chickens yet," he added. "We are on a good track with this, but it is not an easy task. We do not know if a healthy fetus can evolve from an altered egg. There are indicators in the lower species that some animals age prematurely, especially the sheep. There are some animals that have developed enlarged organs from the procedures. You have mostly heard of the successes to date. We don't know what transpired in the earlier failures."

Jack Danton interjected, "In a way, we are rushing to make history. We are rushing here because some countries are banning the procedures we are going to be doing. Right now, the U.S. and Japan are considering prohibiting the research. Guidelines are being discussed. Britain, Israel and Germany have already passed laws that affect human cloning. Basic research is about all that may be allowed in Britain; however, they show signs of being more liberal in the future."

Bradshaw added, "Even the people in Scotland that created Dolly the sheep, started with about 300 sheep eggs and succeeded in only getting about thirty embryos to form and implant in a total of thirteen sheep. The success rate of embryonic development, once in the uterus, went from 10 percent to 1 percent over time. The success rate is not high."

"What of the nonhuman primate? What has been achieved in the monkey, the baboon or the ape?" someone asked.

Bradshaw cited the fact that a research group at the Oregon Primate Center had already attempted monkey cloning. "The embryos died a few days after transplant. That is not a good sign, since we are primates, as well. If it doesn't work well in the monkey, it may be a sign that it won't work in us . . . the *human species*. In Oregon, they were able to successfully clone jellyfish DNA into monkeys. The resultant baby monkey glows green in the dark like a jellyfish in the ocean." That enlightenment brought levity to the crowd.

Jack piped up again. "If it takes hundreds of DNA-injected eggs to achieve one successful pregnancy in sheep, and numerous surrogate ewes to carry one clone, there may be serious odds against us that a human-cloned embryo will take hold in a surrogate mother. It might take years, and hundreds of DNA-modified eggs in many women to succeed with Project Samuel."

By now Royston himself was getting depressed and nervous with the conversation and the direction of the analyses. He felt that morale would be impaired in the whole group by the current discussion.

"Gentlemen, we are on the forefront of science. Our labs are different than those elsewhere. We have the finest scientists, the finest facilities and the best preclinical and clinical operations. We purposely hired all of you in order to succeed with this program. I don't think we need the data from monkeys to succeed at our project. Monkeys differ from humans and there are many species of monkeys. Each primate species differs reproductively, and their behavior and physiology differ as well. Monkeys have a high rate of spontaneous abortion; something we scientists can't easily control. Some perfectly good monkeys just naturally lose their babies early on. There is a high attrition rate; perhaps 30 percent chance of them not going to term with their young. Maybe this affected the current monkey data! Man is different," he insisted.

The attendees agreed that the monkey might not be a good indicator of how a woman would respond to carrying a surrogate human clone. They listened intently as Royston MacDonald loosened his collar and became more casual and comfortable. He focused on them, and gestured with his hands and arms to make his point.

"I have confidence in all of you and your approach to this novel science to date. Jack Danton has helped pull together a great team; all of you here! We have studied the literature, refined the technical procedures a thousand times, talked directly to the most noted colleagues in a multitude of scientific fields, and now it is time to fish or cut bait! Creating organs from stem cells for potential transplant is one thing. Creating a whole new body with all organs intact, is another! Cloning a human will be the next major accomplishment in medicine and in all mankind! It will precede a cure for cancer, heart disease, Alzheimer's and AIDS! It will happen because those other diseases are far too complicated and have parameters that constantly change.

Cures vary with each type of cancer or with the virus that might mutate daily."

He continued, "A pregnancy is far simpler to achieve. The uterus doesn't give a damn whose egg is inside it! The brain doesn't know either," Royston said, red-faced and shaking with enthusiasm.

"You have been brought together to advance the science of human reproduction and birth; to go beyond the natural occurrences that we take for granted, i.e., simple conception, pregnancy and the birth of a new individual. We have every chance of succeeding on this program . . . and we will!"

Royston sat down, flushed and winded. Bradshaw quickly stood up. "We can't do any better than we have done folks," he said. "We know the science as well as anyone out there and our approach is plausible and unprecedented. If we succeed from the lab to the clinic and generate a new being, there will not be one country, one continent, one official, one person of the human race, or one lowly tabloid reporter or national news commentator that will not know who we are . . . forever! Project Samuel will hopefully succeed the first time, but if it doesn't, we will continue our quest until it does!"

With that, everyone was enthused and started to clap. They decided to break for coffee and pastries, and some took a walk into the patio and garden area of the Hotel Del. They all needed fresh air.

Later that night they agreed that they needed to achieve their goals before the U.S. government banned the research altogether. The sense of urgency was there to succeed the first time. They had come far in achieving a *team* approach, the validated science at the laboratory level, and now were ready to apply their experience and knowledge to the "clinical" situation.

Royston retired to his room. There was no way he would allow the Italians, the Canadians or anyone else beat *his* team to the Nobel prize and the re-creation of one of the finest baseball players to ever play the game.

161

Twenty-seven

Teresa Cordero had become comfortable with Royston MacDonald and Dr. Sanchez and after being accepted into the surrogate program, she was treated as royalty.

A tentative date was projected for the placement of a surrogate embryo in her uterus, although the actual procedure in the lab had not yet begun. Under the guise that she would be carrying an infertile couple's child, Teresa anxiously awaited the laborious clinical tests needed for the future intrauterine instillation of the developing embryo. Dr. Bradshaw of the fertility clinic, in collaboration with the other scientists, had retrieved an "extra" Vicky Palmer egg from the freezer in the reproductive physiology laboratory. The Palmers had no knowledge of this devious act. It would undergo the microinjection of the isolated DNA extracted from the hair in a vial labeled T. W.; a sample of which E. Royston MacDonald had acquired from the Rizzo collection. The DNA had been isolated by Dr. Johnson in the forensic lab downtown and transferred to the lab at the fertility clinic in La Jolla. The two "T. W." vials from different years matched in DNA sequencing. The dates were years that Ted Williams played for the Red Sox. It was naturally assumed that they contained his hair clippings and follicle cells in both vials, although there was no definitive proof of that supposition. Even if it was not Ted's sample, the DNA was from the same person. Since Joe Rizzo had told MacDonald that he used to cut Ted Williams's hair, the cloning team felt that it could be none other than Ted's hair in those vials.

With Ted Williams in his eighties and living in Florida, the only proof that the DNA from the vials was his from forty years ago would be to compare the results to a current sample of DNA. MacDonald knew that it was out of the question. He had no way to do that. The plan was secretive and unknown to the outside world, including Ted's family. They could easily research his blood type but that would not help in comparing his DNA of today with that of the vials in question.

What amazed the team was that they had actually managed to extract DNA from the hair. It was questionable in the beginning that the procedure would work. DNA from nonliving tissue is often fractionated and inappropriate for cloning studies. They attempted the DNA isolation and extraction anyway. The presence of hair follicles in the sample increased their odds of success.

Laboratory scientists in the preclinical animal lab had practiced placing other DNA extracts, obtained and isolated from a technician's blood sample, directly into rodent eggs. They were confident that they could also perform the procedure in a *human* ovum, since most mammalian eggs were of similar size and structure, whether mouse or elephant.

Royston had not told all of the team members that the egg was from Vicky Palmer's ovaries. The Palmers would eventually be blessed with twins generated from their own fertility procedure, and it was the number of children that they had hoped for. They naturally assumed that all extra eggs from her ovaries had been destroyed since they were unfertilized and there were no further plans by the Palmers to increase the size of their family.

$$\oslash \oslash \oslash \oslash$$

"Dr. Sanchez, will I know the actual family that I am carrying the child for?" asked Teresa.

"No. I'm afraid that is confidential, Teresa," he said. "The parents would like to remain anonymous for the child's sake." He felt ashamed that he was lying to her.

"That is sad, doctor. But I would imagine that they probably think that I would want to keep it. This perhaps makes it easier for all concerned," she surmised. Tears formed in her eyes.

"I'm sorry, Teresa. That is the way they wish to have it. We must honor their confidentiality. That is why we have strict rules and procedures. Some of those papers you had to sign."

Sanchez was remorseful over her duress. He knew that he was not being forthright with her, but he could never divulge the source of the egg as Vicky Palmer's.

"Teresa, has your menstrual cycle been normal this month? I'm referring to the number of days," asked Dr. Sanchez.

"Yes, doctor," was the reply. "Nothing has changed."

"That is excellent, Teresa. Everything then, is proceeding well, and on target."

They would continue to monitor her cycle for another month, so that they were sure of the optimal time to introduce the egg into her uterus.

The embryo containing the extracted DNA from the T. W. vial would be transferred into Teresa's uterus three days after she had ovulated. At least that was the clinical plan. With her normal menstrual cycle of twenty-eight days, the date of her own ovulation would be anticipated to be around day thirteen or fourteen. Since she often felt mittelschmerz, ovulation would be fairly easy to predict. Three to four days after that would be the time that her natural ovum would reach her uterus. Since she was not having sex, there was no chance that her own ovum would be fertilized or implant in the uterine wall. The uterus at day three after ovulation would be receptive to the DNA-altered egg. That would be about day seventeen of her cycle. By then, the uterine lining would be engorged with a blood supply to support the placental development and a fetus. Her natural hormone, progesterone would have made the womb receptive to any developing embryo, including the one that the doctors planned to instill into her uterine cavity. The uterus was not fussy about whose egg it was, as long as it was of human origin.

The scientists involved were ready for the challenge. If successful implantation of the modified egg occurred and an embryo grew inside of her, they stood the chance of global praise for the accomplishment, or ridicule for playing God. Their success meant the Nobel prize for medicine, they thought. That was always E. Royston

MacDonald's dream. He had the money to buy success, both in laboratory equipment and scientific salaries. It was a small investment in biotechnology for him since he was filthy rich from his Texas oil business. In his own devious mind, he was also now well on his way to buying, indirectly, a Nobel prize.

⊘ ⊘ ⊘ ⊘

In complete secrecy, the MacDonald team proceeded with the DNA modification of Vicky Palmer's ovum once it had been removed from its frozen state. The cryogenic medium that kept the egg viable was both nutritive and protective against freezing. Without that protection, it would self-destruct after thawing, splitting open and releasing its own nucleus into the solution in which it was maintained.

"Close the door and lock it, please," MacDonald said to the last scientist who entered the lab. Through glass windows, the group of scientists watched the trained technician work in a specialty hepa-filtered laboratory hood and incubator. It was merely a sophisticated box with a vertical sliding front glass door and specialized gloves that maintained sterility inside the chamber. Filtered, purified air entered the chamber and the atmosphere was 100 percent free of solvents or other toxins and microbes.

"He's got the micro pipette ready for the replacement of the DNA," Royston said with exuberance. "Will you look at that? You can actually see the egg in the petri dish on the TV monitor above. Look up everyone."

No one spoke. Only MacDonald would comment. A special binocular dissecting microscope of the highest magnification was used to visualize Vicky Palmer's donor ovum in the dish. Once focused, the stereo-camera attached to the microscope projected a perfectly normal egg on the TV screen. A highly calibrated device guided the micropipette containing the DNA in solution toward the egg. It lay suspended in the nutritive medium that surrounded it. The dish was maintained at human body temperature, which is about 37 degrees Celsius. While a second glass pipette with suction gently held the egg in place, the fine-tipped DNA micropipette punctured the side of the egg with a pin prick. The technician, who had months of practice injecting mouse and rat eggs, expertly controlled the operation. This was a critical phase since he had never before attempted to remove existing DNA and then reinject new DNA into a human ovum. It seemed all the same to him because it looked like any other mammalian egg. Once the egg's outer lining (zona pellucida) was penetrated, the technician guided the probe into the center of the single cell. Vicky Palmer's own DNA was removed and subsequently the new T. W. DNA was deposited into the nucleus. Careful withdrawal of the micropipette was critical since the natural capillary action of the glass tube could remove some of the material that needed to be left behind.

"Damn!" said Royston with glee. "He did it! He actually did it!" Everyone remained silent until the technician turned and gave a thumbs up. He was hidden behind a sterile outfit of clothing and face shield. The still camera attached to the stereomicroscope captured the moment. A video camera recorded all of the transfer procedure for posterity. If the ovum survived the mechanical trauma and began to divide into multiple cells, the cameras would record that as well.

They viewed the modified egg for a moment and then the petri dish was placed back in the incubator to encourage the cellular division of the newly genetically altered egg. The entire procedure was quick and mimicked a single sperm fertilizing the ovum. Sperm normally cause a similar cellular reaction in natural fertilization. The puncture seals itself and a reaction takes place in the zona to prevent other sperm from penetrating the outer shell of the ovum. In that manner, only one sperm fertilizes an egg in natural mating. In a similar fashion, the micropipette and an electrical pulse mimicked the same reaction without the aid of a sperm.

Once the petri dish was returned to the incubator, the door was closed and a red indicator light lit up to maintain the temperature of the internal chamber. A separate ON/OFF indicator light showed that the unit was functional. The red thermostat light remained illuminated when it was heating. It went off when the preset temperature was maintained inside the incubator.

MacDonald began to jump around like a child and hugged the technician who emerged from the sterile laboratory. "You did it, kid. You made history today!"

The young technician beamed with pride. "Thank you, Mr. MacDonald. It was very much like the other eggs we've done before—you know—the mouse ova. I've done about one thousand transfer injections of mouse ova in anticipation of this day."

The scientists congratulated each other and accolades were passed around for a wonderfully coordinated team. Jack Danton stood in the corner of the room in awe of the whole event. He knew he was responsible for a portion of the project management that resulted in this phase being successfully accomplished.

Royston congratulated him on his contributions to the day's success. "Jack, it's all about to happen. We are one step closer to fame."

He looked back at the monitor and yelled, "Replay the bastard! Let's see the video again!"

With the click of a remote, a VHS video of the entire procedure was repeated. It was clear that no DNA nuclear material leaked after the egg was punctured. *It's artificial fertilization at its best!* Royston thought. Blackburn, Bradshaw and Johnson, the DNA expert, were elated. Other technicians approached MacDonald in unison and asked if T. W. stood for something. What was the source of the DNA that they had instilled in that egg?

Royston was silent and stared straight ahead. He looked at Jack Danton and smiled. He then looked at the other scientists and said quietly, while gesturing with open hands. "Gentlemen, there is reason to believe that we have created the first cloned human. That human is a 'noted' individual."

They looked at Royston with wonderment.

"Noted? *Who* is 'noted'?" they asked.

"Gentlemen, we have reason to believe that we have just re-conceived Theodore Samuel Williams, the noted Red Sox Baseball player from Boston."

There were gasps among the crowd of technicians and junior scientists.

"Seriously, sir? . . . *the* Ted Williams?"

"Yes, gentlemen. *The* Ted Williams. *The* Teddy Ballgame. *The* Splendid Splinter!"

"Sir?" asked the technician, who injected the egg.

"Yes, son?"

"But Ted is not dead, sir. He is alive in Florida. He is still alive! What if he finds out? Are you telling me, I just created Ted's clone?"

"That is true, gentlemen. He is not aware of this feat today. He will probably never know of this feat. If we are successful with the pregnancy, there will be a genetic copy of Ted growing up in San Diego, just like the original Ted Williams did. If the Nobel Committee in Stockholm recognizes us for this accomplishment, they won't even know the individual's identity for years. We will not and cannot tell them. In time, they will know."

The room was silent since some of the team members were not aware of the DNA's origin. Most people thought it was Royston's DNA with other initials on the vial of hair designed to mislead them. Royston took command. "Gentlemen. You are not to say a word to anyone. Wives, friends, colleagues are off limits concerning this accomplishment today. Report back here tomorrow. That's twenty-four hours from now. If the egg has cleaved and divided into two cells, we will have been successful. If not, we have lost our first attempt to clone a human."

"All we can do is hope that it works," added Blackburn.

MacDonald was given a copy of the videotape by a technician. He could watch it in his room at the hotel, as much as he wanted.

MacDonald had hired a security guard from a local "rent a cop" company in San Diego. The guard and a scientist would be at the lab twenty-four hours a day. The scientific staff took turns accompanying the guard. The guard was located outside the door to the lab and the scientist remained inside the lab for the most part. The guard was not aware of what he was protecting. He didn't know that it was a cloning laboratory and that it was off limits. He just figured it was a biohazard area and he was to stay out.

The guard began his watch shortly after the team left the laboratory. "What's in there?" he asked a scientist. "You got animals and stuff in there?"

The scientist just smiled and told him that there were microorganisms and viruses in there. That would keep the guard's curiosity at bay.

"You don't want to be in there!" the scientist told him. "It's OK for me to be in there, because I've got a protective jumpsuit and a shower in there," he added.

"OK, man. I'll stay clear of there. I don't want no germs and stuff," replied the guard with eyes wide open. "Is that some sort of 'speriment goin' on in there?"

"Sort of," the scientist replied. "We have some stuff growin' in the incubator and need to make sure it's OK twenty-four hours a day."

The guard sat down in a chair next to the door to the lab and began to read *People* magazine. He would be content to just sit there and look at the celebrity pictures. The patch embroidered on the arm of his uniform read ACME SECURITY—SINCE 1970. Below that, were words that read: YOUR PARTNER IN CRIME PREVENTION.

The guard had no idea that he was protecting potential Nobel prize material in the laboratory. He had one responsibility and that was to keep everyone out except the designated scientific staff with proper identification. The members of the team were the only ones approved to enter; even *they* had a rigid schedule to cover the lab around the clock. If there were any problems, MacDonald was to be contacted directly by the guard or the scientist on duty.

$$\oslash \oslash \oslash \oslash$$

MacDonald had taken the rest of the staff out for a celebratory dinner at the restaurant in the U.S. Grant Hotel at Broadway and Sixth Avenue in downtown San Diego. MacDonald would cover the tab for the evening. Alcohol was served in moderation given the task at hand for the next few days. Everyone would need to be alert especially if there was a problem at the lab. Until the embryo was instilled into the surrogate mother, everyone was to be available and retain functional mental faculties. Excessive drinking was prohibited.

"Here's to the team!" MacDonald said as he toasted the group at the celebratory dinner table. One glass of champagne would not affect the members.

"You folks did what was needed today and that was just the beginning. As you know, tomorrow will be a critical step, which will determine if the project is going forward."

"Congratulations to you, Roy," added Sanchez. "You have made this a reality! Without your foresight and the project management of Jack Danton, this would not have been possible."

"Here, here, I second that," came a voice from the other end of the dinner table. They all clapped for one another. There would be shrimp and filets and Pacific lobster tails for everyone. Dessert would be a selection of bananas Foster or baked Alaska.

MacDonald had direct telephone access to Teresa Cordero and he excused himself from the dessert selection during dinner. He contacted her and told her that she would be hearing from the Torito Bay clinical team as early as the next day. There was a good possibility that she would be receiving the surrogate embryo within seventy-two hours. The *in vitro* fertilization procedure was in progress and she would be needed on the seventeen day of her cycle.

"Wonderful, Mr. MacDonald," she said with glee. "I am ready when you are."

"Thank you," he replied. "I will be in touch as well—right after Dr. Sanchez updates you. Good night, Teresa. Sleep well."

Royston returned to the table and pulled Sanchez aside for a confidential discussion. MacDonald basically reiterated the importance of the impending embryo transfer. He asked him to call Teresa and to make sure everything was all right. Sanchez did better than that. He left the U.S. Grant Hotel and headed directly over to see her.

⊘ ⊘ ⊘ ⊘

On the East Coast, the Rizzo family in Boston attended Catholic mass in memory of their father, Joe Rizzo Sr. It was the one-year anniversary of his death. The priest at the church highlighted his notoriety in a fitting tribute. The eldest son read an eulogy that he had written.

Joe Rizzo Sr.'s former barbershop was converted to a delicatessen, which served pizza and Italian hoagies, or submarine sandwiches. There was no indication there that a barbershop ever existed. The candy-striped barber pole was auctioned at a local consignment shop. Eventually, Royston would acquire it for his collection in Texas.

After the anniversary mass, the family visited Joe's grave and left flowers from the family garden and photos at the marble stone. They would go to Sunday brunch in the Italian North End of Boston. They would feast at La Familia Santini Ristorante on Hanover Street. Pasta fagoli, calamari, tutte mare and cannolis were served family style. Mrs. Santini, a friend of the Rizzo family, would personally serve them.

The first anniversary of Joe Rizzo's passing, ironically correlated close to the potential date for the embryo transfer to Teresa Cordero. That, of course, would only occur if the ongoing incubation procedure was successful.

MacDonald had sent the Rizzo family a warm, religious card and large basket of fruit. He would not forget the Joseph Rizzo anniversary date. He was familiar with Italian customs and feasts and anniversary masses.

Twenty-eight

The scientific team and fertility specialists were at the laboratory the next day when the technician placed the petri dish with the DNA–injected ovum under the binocular stereomicroscope. The room was silent. It had been only twenty-four hours since the egg was placed in the incubator. If successful, it would be divided into two cells of equal size within the spherical zona of the egg. In a short time it would then multiply to four cells, then eight and sixteen, and so on.

The microscope light that illuminated the culture dish from beneath the microscope stage, cast a vertical beam of light through the dish and into the lens and oculars. As the laboratory technician adjusted the focus, an enlarged image appeared until it was that of a two-celled circle of human protoplasm in its earliest stages.

The room erupted in joy as the cleaved ovum came into view on the monitor and was photographed and videotaped for the first time.

"Yes!" screamed Royston. "I can't believe my eyes!"

The DNA micro-insertion process had resulted in a two-celled human creation, at least in a laboratory dish. Voices rang out with excitement and everyone present and witnessing the event had to comment on their spectacular achievement. *Life had been created by mankind . . . a human life in its earliest stages.* It would need to attach to the uterine wall of Teresa Cordero in order to evolve beyond the cellular stage in the dish. In two more days, the morula would become a blastocyst, or ball of multiple cells; a stage that normally embeds itself in the endometrium of a woman's uterus.

"We did it!" screamed MacDonald. "We actually did it!"

As he jumped up and down like a child, the floor shook from the enormous weight of his body. The egg in the dish was jostled from the excitement and commotion in the room.

"Calm, everyone! Calm! Please!" barked MacDonald. "Everyone adjourn but the technician, please."

The technician would rapidly return the cloned embryo and culture dish to the incubator. Proper temperature was needed at all times for the embryo to grow. Vicky Palmer's ovum had just become the carrier of a completely new individual; unrelated to her but complete in all DNA sequencing for another human being. It was not just a human clone, but a probable and potential DNA copy of Ted Williams. Basically, it was an artificially created *twin* of the now elderly man; a twin created more than eighty years into his own life. It was being performed without his knowledge.

Drs. Sanchez, Blackburn and Bradshaw had tears of joy from the preliminary results of the incubation. Sanchez, who was deeply religious, reflected on what he had always believed to be God's creation. He justified the excitement and the ethics of the moment by saying to himself that it was still God's act . . . another of God's miracles or a helpful mystery of God's actions.

"Wait," said MacDonald as the room became silent. "We have not achieved our goal as yet. In two days we hope to be able to place a multicelled embryo into a young surrogate woman. *That* will be the day to celebrate."

"Yes," said Jack with confidence, "but today is equally as awesome. Just look at what has been done here. We have the proof. We have the photos and video of our accomplishment."

Sanchez spoke up in a philosophical manner. "This, my colleagues is a photo of something that Ted's *own mother* never saw when she became pregnant with him. She only saw the end result of procreation, or felt him kick inside of her. We are now observing firsthand what the mother of an actual baby never gets to see. Mrs. Williams, rest her soul, has never seen what we have just observed. A small part of her and her husband is in that laboratory dish. It's their genetics that created Ted, and his clone."

Blackburn brought things back to reality. "Listen up, please! We must not be overconfident. This is only the first step in the Project Samuel creation."

"Yes," added Royston. "He is right. We still have a long way to go. We will check this at twelve-hour intervals from now on. You are all requested to be back here for each twenty-four-hour period, if you so desire. I don't want everyone here for each twelve-hour viewing. That would be too disruptive."

Jack Danton sat quietly and in awe of the moment. *I am here by simple fate,* he thought. He was there because E. Royston MacDonald liked him and had faith in him to be part of the team. If, in the end they were successful in creating an actual fetus that was a "live" birth, Jack Danton would be as famous as everyone else in the room.

A beaming Royston asked, "Jack, my boy! What do you think?"

"This is earth-shattering. You have pulled it all together. You have Ted Williams literally 'in the oven' over there," replied Jack.

"Actually, son, you folks did it all. I merely had the interest and the finances to play with the concept of creation. That may offend some people in the end. However, once science created the cloned mouse, cow, sheep and goat, the scientific minds of our day set the precedent for today's achievement. We merely took their technology and moved it forward to *man.*"

"Right, sir, you have gone beyond the animal and barnyard. This will be the accomplishment of the century—perhaps of the millennium!" said Jack with excitement. He shook Roy's hand.

No one on the team would sleep that night. They had to go home to their families and still say nothing. That would be the hardest thing to do. How could one not brag about what they observed today?

If the success continued in the forthcoming days and months, there would surely be ridicule from some scientists, the Vatican and the pope. It would also be of concern to the president of the United States, the right-wing Christian element of the southern United States, and other noted scientists who wondered if there were hair clippings hanging around from Hitler, Charles Manson, Ted Bundy—other psychiatric anomalies of the world. On the other hand, open-minded individuals would see value in the new technology at hand. After all,

174

people who had lost their children from disease, accidents, viruses, HIV, or terrorism and war, might be able to recreate their child from strands of hair that they saved from their first haircut. They may have had their blood or a tissue sample stored somewhere as well. The DNA from those samples could be introduced into other surrogate women and carried to term.

Royston's quest was less grandiose. He merely wanted the notoriety of the accomplishment to go on his gravestone and he wanted to be in history books like the J. Paul Gettys and Rockefellers of the world. He wanted the Nobel prize for medicine or physiology especially in the Nobel centennial year. It would be a follow-on to Watson and Crick and their British colleagues that figured that DNA was real, solved its structure and proposed the model of the double helix. The double helix contained the coded genetic entity of a person or animal.

"Here's to Watson and Crick!" someone shouted. "They started this whole thing and they are still with us today."

"We owe that British team a thank you!" another technician yelled above the others.

No one knew that MacDonald had met James Watson once when Watson had presented a talk at a conference. If the surrogate pregnancy was successful, MacDonald wondered what Watson's response would be to the feat. For now, it didn't matter. MacDonald was not at a stage to tell anyone of their preliminary results.

Twenty-nine

Jack Danton spent time researching the prerequisites for being considered for a Nobel prize. He was interested in the selection process but had no clear idea as to how it all came about. Royston MacDonald had made things sound easy, just like cloning. The process to Nobel notoriety, however was complicated and had rules and statutes specific for Nobel consideration. If they were anticipating fame, they needed to know the details. Jack took it upon himself to research the process thoroughly. Some evenings, he would spend hours on the Internet researching general information on Alfred Nobel and the Nobel Foundation. Once he was competent with the information, he would convene a meeting of the research team and present a synopsis lecture on what he had learned.

Searching the Internet, Jack was able to find an official Web site for the Nobel Foundation. It contained the history and specifics of the nomination process and the various award categories. Jack took copious notes on the detailed process after he printed the material from the site.

Alfred Nobel, a noted chemist, died December 10, 1896. Based on the desires in his final will and testament, a foundation was established in June of the year 1900. The foundation was charged with the task of honoring Nobel's last request. At first considered controversial, the foundation finally became a noted accolade in memory of the man. The handwritten "Testament of Nobel" included sections that Jack practically memorized. It fascinated him like poetry.

Testament of Nobel

*The whole of my remaining realizable estate shall be dealt
with in the following way. The capital, invested in safe secu-
rities by my executors, shall be annually distributed in the
form of prizes, to those who, during the preceding year, shall
have conferred the greatest benefit to mankind. . . .*

"The 'said testament' was to be divided into five equal parts,"
Nobel had clearly stated. Annual awards covered the fields of physics, chemistry, physiology or medicine, literature and peace (the fraternity of nations). The field of economics would be added to the list
of categories in 1968, after which the Nobel committee decided to
never add another category.

The Nobel awards each year involved the countries of Norway
and Sweden, depending on the category. The physiology and medicine award was under the jurisdiction of a three to five person committee at the Karolinska Institute in Stockholm, Sweden. A Nobel
Assembly of the Institute decided the annual award of prizes for physiology or medicine for works during the preceding year.

Jack was fascinated by the procedures and the fact that time was
also a factor. After all, it was not as if someone could accomplish
something of value to mankind, and then receive the award the next
week!

Royston's quest to become a Nobel laureate would most probably be considered and recognized the subsequent year. Cloning the
first human would certainly be considered relevant should the documentation be supportive and scientific credibility established. The
process required that a "written work" of the accomplishment be a
prerequisite for Nobel consideration.

Jack read through the statutes carefully. The Royston MacDonald
team of scientists would exceed the number of people that could receive the Nobel award. Each award category was limited to three per-
sons or fewer. Royston would certainly be considered one of them.
The other team members, if they won, would be selected at a later
time. The principal scientists, such as Drs. Bradshaw, Blackburn,
Johnson, and Sanchez, could all qualify as contributing scientists to-

ward the overall success of Project Samuel. Jack Danton knew that he was not a candidate, but he was still a critical member on the overall team.

All Nobel prize awards undergo "expert scrutiny" and must be of "outstanding importance." Jack had noted that some previous Nobel laureates for medicine covered the related research areas of genetics and embryonic development. *Cloning was certainly a combination of both sciences—increasing their chances,* he thought.

With major breakthroughs occurring in the research areas of HIV, AIDS and central nervous system (CNS) diseases in the centennial year, there would certainly be many nominees for the Nobel prize for medicine or physiology. Potential vaccines were moving forward in AIDS research and the abolition of plaque on the nerves of the brain was a major accomplishment for Alzheimer's research. *Would those people win?* Jack wondered. *Who would nominate the Project Samuel team if it was successful? Would a prominent scientist in the field endorse the controversial project: the cloning of a human?* After some thought, Jack concluded that famous scientists in DNA research would probably line up to "endorse" anyone who might accomplish this incredible biological feat.

If Fawn were nearby, Jack had to go off-line. He did not want her to be privy to the secret research program that MacDonald had in progress. She wondered why he was on the Internet so often, and so late at night.

The deadline for nomination of the Nobel prize was February 1 of each year. Jack calculated the approximate date that Teresa Cordero would deliver. The timing would be close. If she was late in delivering, they might miss the deadline. A written account of the accomplishment would need to be detailed on paper for the review committee in Stockholm, as well. Royston had assured Jack, that if they were successful in their clinical phase with Teresa, they would meet their deadline. A cesarean delivery could be performed if her due date was near the deadline. Jack felt uneasy about that ethic, since there would be no justifiable medical need for that kind of surgery. It would be performed to satisfy E. Royston MacDonald's quest for fame and the Nobel prize. That part of Royston's ambitious nature did not set well with Jack Danton. He just hoped that a natural delivery of the baby would prevent the need for unnecessary, elective surgery.

Jack was responsible for coordinating all research data and paperwork relevant to meeting the requirements for submissions to the Nobel committee in medicine. That way, if they were successful with Teresa's pregnancy and near the February deadline, they would have minimal paperwork left to complete. Typing in the baby's name and the specific statistics of the baby's birth would be all that was needed. Jack had compiled all the data on the DNA extraction and the micro-injection of the egg. The clinical intrauterine procedure and the actual pregnancy, would follow. The combination of the biochemistry, the preclinical animal studies and clinical study data (Teresa's pregnancy) would always be up to date as the information was generated. The document merely awaited data from the eventual pregnancy. Royston had insisted that the project information be digitally camera-ready for worldwide distribution over the Internet, at a moment's notice.

The actual date of the Nobel prize awards was always December 10th—the anniversary date of Alfred Nobel's death. It is a date referred to by the Nobel committee members as the "Festival Date of the Foundation."

Jack was surprised at the value of the Nobel awards. The cash prize was generally about one million dollars per award, divided and shared by one to three people. There was also the famous gold medallion, complete with Nobel's facial profile embossed upon it. A formal diploma accompanied the historic accolade. The medal was considered the most noteworthy award. Kings and heads of state often bestowed it on the annual recipients. This year, Swedish King Carl XVI Gustaf, would present the awards.

The Nobel prize was first awarded in 1901, therefore the year 2001 was considered the 100th Anniversary for the dissemination of Nobel awards. Royston MacDonald desired to be one of the 100th Anniversary Nobel winners.

Jack envisioned himself and the others attending a reception in the Nordic Museum on December 9th, the Prize Award Ceremony in the Stockholm Concert Hall or the Globe Arena. A glorious "Nobel Banquet" was known to follow the ceremony in the Hall of Mirrors, in the Grand Hotel in Stockholm, or in the Golden or Blue Hall of the Stockholm City Hall. Jack and Fawn had never been to Sweden and he pictured her in formal attire, and he in his tuxedo and tails. He daydreamed about the grandeur of them winning the prize. *Feasting in the Grand Halls with 1,200 celebratory guests and prior Nobel laureates would be a highlight in his life,* he thought. It saddened him not to be able to share his daydreams with Fawn.

"Are you coming to bed, honey?" Fawn asked one evening. "You've been on that damn computer all night. What about me? Press my buttons instead of the keyboard, Jack boy!" she teased.

Jack was startled by her presence in the den and quickly clicked off the Nobel Web site. (He had already made a "bookmark" of the site so he could easily return to it later.) Jack heeded the request by Fawn but could not get out of his mind the possibility of being part of the most famous medical team in the world.

Jack retired to the bedroom. His mind was still on the Web site for the Nobel Foundation. Fawn had caught him at an intense moment in his research endeavors. He faked his way through the sex act, and then felt guilty afterward. He was becoming possessed by the Project Samuel quest of Royston MacDonald, and Fawn was noticing the difference in his attentiveness. She thought that he needed to start paying more attention to her or their relationship would deteriorate. She still wanted a family and she wanted to be sure that his physical desire for her was still there, as well. If it wasn't, she would begin to question their future together.

Thirty

Teresa Cordero had moved from her North Park residence that MacDonald had set up for her to the inn at Torrey Pines in La Jolla. She would now spend the next two days near the clinic where she would potentially receive the developing embryo. That is, if it continued to divide and multiply as planned. The Torrey Pines Inn was close to the clinic facility and she could be there at a moment's notice. The doctors needed that flexibility in order to maximize the proper timing of the embryo transfer. She checked into her room at the inn with enough clothes for two or three days. It was necessary for her to be at the clinic because had she remained in North Park, she might be caught in traffic at the optimum hour of egg transfer. All her meals were on site and she could relax in a room with a view of the public golf course. Just outside her room was the ninth hole of one of the two golf courses. She could read and walk about the grounds as long as she carried a cell phone and pager.

Royston continued to stay nearby at the Hotel del Coronado. He preferred that over the condo in La Jolla. Jack Danton was at home and would take Fawn to dinner at Jake's on the beaches of Del Mar. He was accessible by phone as well. Fawn knew that the team was busy with a project that had Jack on call for the next few days.

He and Fawn were finally able to have a decent conversation over dinner.

"Hon, do you think I might be able to go to Boston for a quick visit?" she asked. "My parents are having a gathering of older Italian cronies there and I should attend. I know you are busy, but would you mind if I went back East for three or four days. I could also make sure our other house is still standing."

"Sure, hon. That would be fine and probably a nice break for you. I'm sorry I can't go with you. They have me on call."

"I know, sweetheart. You've been kind of busy and preoccupied with your work," she responded, looking a bit dejected.

Jack felt bad. He took her hand over the dinner table and said with love, "You know, this project is so consuming that I've neglected the best thing in my life . . . my wife."

"That's OK. I understand. You are there for me all the time," she said. "Royston needs you now. I can wait. Well—maybe we could have dessert at home tonight," she offered with a smile. The candlelight on the table reflected off the perfect bone structure of her face. Her eyes were bright from the flickering flame.

"You read my mind, Fawn, dear," he said with raised eyebrows. "I think I'll have the dessert with the most whipped cream. Maybe *splurge* on all those calories," he chuckled.

"Jack boy. You amaze me. Let's get out of here. I'll need to run into Ralph's Grocery on the way home to get your topping of pleasure," she said with a soft voice. He laughed and felt himself get an instant rush. His libido became intensified at this point. He had visions of the movie *9½ Weeks*—a sexual fantasy with food.

The valet brought their car around front and Jack and Fawn headed for a local grocery store. He could hardly wait to get home. Perhaps they'd "christen" the new love seat in the family room.

After "dessert," Jack would check the Internet, where he could arrange for Fawn's round-trip flight to Boston on-line.

Fawn departed the next evening from Lindbergh Field. She would not know anything about the impending critical time period for the cloned embryo transfer. Jack was still not allowed to share specifics of the project. Jack dropped her off at the USAirways terminal for a red-eye flight to Boston. The night flight east would maximize her time in Boston. She could sleep on the plane and a family member from the Italian North End would pick her up at Logan International Airport early the next morning. She would check on the house that she and Jack owned and spend time with old friends and relatives. She would also visit her old health club and work out. She already missed the green foliage of the East Coast.

After Jack had dropped her off at San Diego Airport, he used his cell phone to call Wayne, the Gliderport instructor. Jack thought they could meet up at Croce's in the Gas Lamp District of San Diego. With Fawn away, Jack could learn more about paragliding. Perhaps Wayne was available to hang out for an hour or two. Wayne was glad to oblige and was pleased that Jack had called him.

"Hey, nice to see you again, Jack," Wayne said, as he arrived at the bar. "Pleasure's all mine," replied Jack. "Thought you could tell me more about the paragliding/parasailing thing," Jack added. "My wife is off to Boston for a couple of days and maybe I'll get brave while she's away."

"Gees, Jack, you don't want to do that without her knowledge!" Wayne said sincerely. "That wouldn't be fair and I couldn't do that to her," he continued. "You should wait till she returns, don't you think?"

"Yeah," said Jack, feeling guilty. "I guess you're right."

They spent a half hour talking about the sport and what famous celebrities the instructor had taught to fly off the cliffs near Torrey Pines. Eventually the conversation turned to baseball. Jack's T-shirt read PETE ROSE—HIT KING and it sparked the conversation. Adjacent to the two men at the bar was a man from Cincinnati, Ohio. When he noted the Pete Rose shirt he interjected with pride, "One of the greatest players ever!" He had on a Red's baseball cap and was probably old enough to have seen Pete play and manage.

"Yeah, you're right. His records will never be broken!" Jack yelled back over the noise of the jazz band in the corner of the bar.

"Too bad about the hall—ya know, the hall of fame. Poor Pete may never make it into the hall. The bastards still accuse him of bettin' on the team. Don't think he did."

Wayne added his two cents. "Did you read the commentary by Jon Saraceno in *USA Today*? Damn! He went right for Pete's throat in that article. Saraceno must have been a major leaguer, right?"

All three men laughed and ripped the sportswriter Saraceno to shreds. Jack loved to talk about Pete Rose. He knew him personally and found him to be honest and forthright. That didn't matter to some people. He was a marked man by the former commissioner of baseball, Bart Giamatti. It carried over in the later years to Bud Selig, the reigning commissioner.

"4256!" the man from Cincinnati said confidently. "Who the hell will get that many hits? Griffey? McGwire? Sosa? None of them will come close. Hell, they won't play long enough to match Pete's record. They'll take the money and run before they'd play as long as he did!"

Jack and Wayne agreed with the stranger. Jack had studied and practically memorized all of Rose's records and knew that he deserved to be in the hall at Cooperstown. Jack had once hired Rose to do an autograph session for a company function. It was a phenomenal afternoon and night with the "Hit King." Rose admitted that he gambled, but said convincingly that it was never on baseball. He cited the fact that he had bet on "Monday Night Football," just like everyone else. Jack believed him and often maintained contact with Rose's agent.

Jack Danton's home was filled with Pete Rose memorabilia including baseball cards, plaques, photos, bats and trinkets such as the famed Pete Rose candy bar. Jack had Rose autograph everything he owned related to the man's career. *If he was such a bad guy, why the hell did they name a highway to the ballpark after him—Pete Rose Way,"* Jack wondered.

Jack and Wayne listened to the man from Cincinnati talk of the days of the Big Red Machine. It was a famed team of 1975 with Griffey Sr., Concepcion, Bench, Rose, Morgan, Perez and others who played for the glory of the game. It didn't matter that Jack was a Red Sox fan and Ted Williams was his hero. He appreciated talking about the boys of summer anytime.

"You know how Rose got dubbed 'Charlie Hustle'?" asked the man.

"No! How?" replied Jack. Jack knew, but didn't want to hurt the man's feelings.

"Well, I'll tell ya. Rose got walked and still *ran* to first base! He *ran*! It was Mantle and Whitey Ford that found that amusing and dubbed him Charlie Hustle. Rose hustled! Ain't nobody today that hustles like Pete did! Nobody!" The man who had been drinking for a while, almost fell off his stool as he gestured dramatically with his hands. Jack and Wayne caught him before he fell and straightened him back up on the seat.

"We need another Rose in the game," the man mumbled. "These assholes today . . . all they want is money and glory. They don't give a shit about the game. They're makin' twelve million a year and sit it out when they have a friggin' hangnail!"

"You're right," Jack agreed. "We need another Rose in the game. Maybe someday there'll be another Pete Rose."

"There is his son, Pete Jr., but he's got a little ways to go!" The man from Cincinnati added. "Petie Jr. is still in the farm league. Dammit! We need to *clone* Pete Sr.!"

With that, Jack became alert and refocused on the day. The word "clone" brought him back to reality for the moment. He needed to get home since they would be checking the embryo in a few hours and he was on call, as well.

Jack wondered if Royston MacDonald had acquired a Pete Rose hair sample, from the Rizzo acquisition. *If so, did he have plans for cloning an All American baseball team?* he wondered. Before they left the bar, Jack and the man from Cincinnati exchanged business cards. In a week or so, he would mail him a Pete Rose autographed 1980 World Series baseball. Jack had a couple of extras from the autograph signing and was pleased to send it to a dedicated Rose fan. The man would surely be surprised by his generosity. Jack would include a note with the baseball. It would say: "To a 'real' Pete Rose fan—nice to meet you in S.D.! Regards, Jack Danton."

Thirty-one

The successful attempt to microinject the T. W. DNA into the donor egg precipitated a chain of events, which would have Teresa Cordero arrive at the clinic seventy-two hours after the DNA procedure in the lab. Each day the egg continued to divide as anticipated. They were at the sixty-hour stage and the embryo was now a small cluster of cells rapidly dividing and not easily counted. It was dividing into a new individual in the petri dish. After the team had confirmed that the new life *in vitro* was on schedule, they left the lab. The guard remained with a technician for the night. For two hours they did nothing but play cards. The responsibility for keeping an eye on the incubator was a simple task for the next twelve hours.

In the early evening, the phone rang for Royston MacDonald. It was his dedicated cell phone for emergencies. He was in his room at the Hotel Del. That number was a special number and had never rung before throughout the project.

"Yes!" Royston answered in anticipation of a problem.

"Sir? This is guard Thompson at the lab. There's been a problem down here!"

"What?" shouted Royston. "What is the problem? Is it serious?" He was shaking from the call.

"The power, sir, went out in the lab. The lab with the incubator and your virus."

Guard Thompson did not know of the surrogate embryo and he had been told that it was a microorganism or virus in the incubator.

That way he would not question the research that was actually going on in the lab. He would be too scared of the supposed virus.

"Damn! Who's there? Get the scientist on the phone!" Royston ordered the guard.

"I'll get the technician, sir. Hey, mister!" the guard yelled, "He wants to talk to *you*. Now!"

"Where is the tech?" screamed Royston. Other hotel guests could now hear his booming voice on the next level down in the hotel.

After the technician answered, Royston peppered him with questions.

The technician responded apprehensively, "Sir, we had a brownout and the emergency auxiliary power came on. The incubator was only off for microseconds. The small backup generator that handles the lab kicked on, as expected."

"Are you sure it was our lab that was affected?" yelled Royston, whose whole project was in jeopardy. "Is it still running? Is the generator still running?" he repeated loudly. "Speak up, son! How's the incubator? Is the light on, dammit?"

"Sir, the generator is on and functional. I'm looking right at it. It's running OK. . . . Hang on. . . . Sir, the main power is back on! The central power is back. We are fine, sir."

"Good, son, I'll be right down in a few minutes. I'll come over. Call maintenance and have them there when I get there. Get them at home if you have to! I want to talk to them."

The technician would call the emergency number for the maintenance staff as soon as he hung up with MacDonald. The telephone numbers were posted on the door to the lab. An electrician and a facilities manager would come to the laboratory as soon as possible. They had heard about MacDonald, and his critical project.

"In the meantime, boy, find out what the fuck happened to the power. I'll be there in no time. Call me back while I'm on the way— that is, if you hear about the loss of power!"

"Yes, sir, I will find out what happened," the technician replied, flustered. A deck of cards was strewn on the floor from the excitement of the blackout. The guard scrambled to gather them and hide them before Royston would arrive.

MacDonald hung up and paged Max, the limo driver. In two minutes Max would be waiting and have the car door open outside the front portico of the Hotel Del.

The technician was shaking and checked the incubator every thirty seconds. Nothing seemed altered by the brownout and no power surge occurred on the restart of the power from the main line. Sometimes a fuse might blow during the restart. That would shut down the incubator, and lab in general, and potentially affect the status of the developing embryo's temperature control. Temperature inside the incubator was critical or the dividing egg was subject to detrimental hot and cold temperature changes. A few minutes without proper temperature maintenance could affect the embryo and ruin Project Samuel.

The technician called MacDonald's cell phone number less than three minutes after the crisis. He caught him, still in the car and crossing the Coronado Bay Bridge to San Diego. He would update him on the problem at the lab and cited that the brownout was the result of an increased usage of electricity in the area. Air conditioners and other appliances in the vicinity were in use due to the high heat and humidity of that particular day and evening. Their usage stressed the system. The electrician would explain the details to Royston when he arrived. The electrician could also suggest additional ways to protect the power to the lab.

When Royston entered the lab, he was breathing heavily due to his enormous size and the fact that he had run from the limo to the facility. He would check everything himself and at the electrician's suggestion, call a local generator company that provided supplemental emergency service to hospitals and critical medical research institutions.

Within an hour, the company had arrived and had run massive power cables to the building power station and transformers. A micro switch would respond if the power went down and the massive 25,000 KW diesel-powered generator would kick on, if needed. The generator sat on a flatbed truck outside the building. MacDonald paid for the unit as well as for a maintenance man to be there from the generator company, for the next forty-eight hours. The hired hand would not leave the flatbed's side. MacDonald had everything covered and paid the generator company a premium price for this emergency service. After the forty-eight hours, they could leave. If all went well, the embryo would be inside Teresa Cordero's womb in two days and the emergency generator would no longer be needed.

"Now we're set," Royston said smiling to everyone involved. "I'll be at the Hotel Del Coronado. Keep me posted. You've got the number! Call me if any little thing goes wrong—and I mean *any* little thing!"

Max took Royston MacDonald back to the hotel. It would be a terrible night for sleeping. They all had experienced much anxiety from the adverse experience at the lab.

Everything appeared to be back on track, and there were only a couple of days left before the embryo transfer would be attempted. While in the car, MacDonald called Jack Danton. He briefed him on the electrical problem and told him to keep in touch with the lab. He wanted Jack to oversee any other issues that might arise.

Jack assured him that everything would be under control. Project Samuel was not to go down over an electrical circuit failure.

Thirty-two

Dr. Sanchez visited Teresa the evening before the actual instillation of the embryo into her uterus. She arrived at the clinic in advance and would stay there until the procedure was completed. If the cleaved egg was ready at seventy-two hours after DNA injection, her menstrual cycle would be in perfect synchrony with the stage of embryo development. The uterine endometrial lining would be most appropriate and receptive for embryo transfer.

"Teresa, how are you doing?" Sanchez asked.

"Fine, thank you, doctor," she replied. She was sitting on the edge of the hospital bed dressed in a johnny.

"Teresa, I want to tell you that you are an integral part of this wonderful event. You will carry a child through nine months and birth, if all goes as planned. Right now, it all looks promising for the embryo transfer to occur tomorrow. Fertilization was successful and the embryo is at the right stage. We'll know more in the morning."

"I am happy to help someone have a child," she added with a beautiful smile. "Especially a couple that is childless and not capable of conceiving a baby."

Sanchez smiled and then told her that he would next see her in the morning. He wished her a pleasant evening's rest.

"Thank you for stopping by, Dr. Sanchez," she added. "Everyone has been so nice to me."

"Well," he said, "You are a special woman and everyone likes you a lot. You are the perfect patient for this surrogate pregnancy."

"I feel special, doctor," said Teresa, blushing.

"Teresa, I will examine you in the morning. We will draw some blood and perform some routine tests. If all is well, you will receive the donor egg in the early afternoon. It will be a painless procedure and actually very quick."

Teresa replied, "Doctor, I am a bit nervous. Do you know if these procedures ever have complications?"

"No," he replied in a reassuring way. "Normally, this is like having a vaginal exam . . . like a Pap smear. It is almost as simple. If there is pain, it will be during the placement of the egg in the uterus. The cervix of the uterus has no pain nerves but sometimes the uterine muscle is stretched slightly to enter the womb. That would be the only pain. You may feel some discomfort during the procedure and we can give you pain medication if you need it. We prefer not to if at all possible, but we would if you requested some."

She felt better knowing it was like the Pap smear procedure. She had one performed every year or two, in the past. The biggest fear to her was the cold speculum that they used to access the cervix. When Dr. Sanchez promised that his speculum would be pre-warmed, she laughed.

"Good night, Teresa. Have a nice, restful sleep. Should you need anything, please feel free to ask an assistant or nurse for their help. They are here to assist you."

"Good night, doctor, and thank you," she replied warmly.

"Bye for now," he replied. His footsteps clicked against the tile floor as he left, stopping first at the nurses station to advise them of his departure, as well as his anticipated arrival time in the morning.

Teresa turned on her side in bed and stared at the wall and window. She was still nervous and that made her tired. She cast her eyes at the TV screen above the end of her bed. A typical American family situation comedy was on TV and she knew that the family portrayed in it was not like her *own* family in Mexico. Life was much harder for them in Mexico and there was little laughter in her native town. It was hard to laugh when you were struggling for food or competing with seagulls at the dump for something to eat. Her brothers had to find food there when she was young.

Still bothered by all the written information she was given in advance of the procedure, she studied the instructions once more and looked hard at the diagrams and graphics. The surrogate patient manual was very helpful and thorough. She was close to dozing off when a nurse came in to check on her and to say good night.

"Good night to you," she replied.

"Everything will be fine ma'am," the nurse added. "We do these procedures all the time. It's a piece of cake. You'll be home shortly after the procedure."

The nurse left the room, leaving the door slightly ajar. A small beam of light radiated through the opened portion and streamed across the bed.

Teresa pressed the remote for the TV to shut it off. The room became darker as the TV flashed a kind of good night. No sound, no visual distractions and no visitors made for a very comfortable environment. Staring at the ceiling, she pulled the top sheet up to her neck with both hands and feeling secure, soon fell sound asleep.

Royston MacDonald called the nurse's station shortly thereafter. He wanted to know about the patient, Ms. Cordero.

"She is asleep, sir. She dozed off a couple of minutes ago."

"Thank you. Let me know if anything changes from the planned agenda," Royston said. "I'll be there in the morning with Dr. Sanchez."

"We will see you in the morning, Mr. MacDonald," she replied.

Royston sat in his hotel room and thought of the next day's agenda. He could not wait for the latest results of the developing embryo, or the procedure the next day. He would go to the lab during the night, and have the technician on duty show him the cleaved egg. It would be at the blastocyst stage and ready for transplant. He would not tell anyone he did this and reminded the guard and scientist on duty to keep his visit a secret.

Royston just could not let go of any aspect of Project Samuel. His heart, blood and soul were in the project. Everything depended on the next day. *Everything.*

Thirty-three

Fawn called Jack in San Diego. She already missed him, although she was happy to spend a little time back east. She was able to network her old friends and still check on the second Danton home, north of Boston.

"Miss you, hon," she said genuinely. "I didn't think I would feel so lonely in such a short period of time."

"That's nice of you to say that, babe. I miss you, too," he replied. "Are you having a good time?"

"Yes," she answered. "How's the project going? I mean—how's work? Is the project going well—the one that you were worried about?"

"Yes. It is fine and we are very busy. The procedure is scheduled for tomorrow and everyone is pretty nervous tonight. The whole program is critical to Royston. He is betting on this new procedure that we can't yet talk to anyone about. It's proprietary."

"Really? What procedure?" she asked with interest. "Royston knows science?" she joked.

"No, not a lot of science. Not enough to hurt him! But the finest cell biologists and reproductive physiologists in the community surround him. I helped him pull the team together."

"Well, whatever you folks are doing, I hope that it works out! I'm proud of you anyway, sweetheart."

"Thanks, hon, I love you, too. I'll get back to you tomorrow. OK?"

Jack and Fawn hung up and he sat there thinking for awhile. His job with Royston and their potential fame all depended on tomorrow's embryo transfer to Teresa's womb. He opened a beer from the refrigerator and turned on CNN's "Headline News." He would watch it for hours. He found the women at the CNN anchor desk attractive. They were competent professionals and he admired that. They dressed well and presented the subject matter without bias. After a while he lay down in his bed missing his wife. He dozed off for the evening and kept his cell phone and pager next to his bed. If Royston needed him, he would be ready. Tomorrow would arrive in a few short hours.

Due to the difference in time zones, Fawn was three hours ahead of him. She was in need of sleep but she sat up in bed thinking about things in general. She would head back to San Diego in a day or so. Her airline ticket was flexible and she missed Jack terribly. Before she had gone east for the short visit, they reminisced about the fun they have together. They also entertained the thought of starting a family. Awake, she thought of how much Jack's connections in his day-to-day job and travels brought to their relationship. She admired his celebrity connections at work and during his free time.

Jack and Fawn had been enjoying the San Diego scene, especially at night. They were both avid folk music aficionados. Jack, who dabbled in acoustic guitar, was friendly with The Kingston Trio. She reminisced about a concert that they had attended in the summer.

"Hon," he had told her back then, "the Trio's coming to town. They'll be at Humphrey's by the Bay on Shelter Island."

"Really? That's great! Will we be able to see them?" she asked enthusiastically.

"Let me call George Grove, hon. Perhaps he can arrange for some good seats!"

George was the banjo player and a guitarist in the group. Jack had known him for a number of years and they often got together in Boston when the trio was in town. Jack and Fawn would do dinner with him at Union Oyster House near City Hall Plaza. George was impressed that the restaurant was the oldest, continuously operating restaurant in the country. In addition to enjoying the great seafood, they often sat in a special dining booth on the second level. It was the booth that President John F. Kennedy requested when he was in town. Inspiring conversation seemed to come out of that particular booth.

The straight-backed seats resembled benches or an antiquated class-room desk.

Jack and George Grove stayed in touch by e-mail and often hooked up whenever their travel plans were similar. Jack had even played with them on stage in Anaheim, California. It was an impromptu performance and luckily Jack was familiar with the tune, the words and the chords. It was about a guy named "Charlie" riding on the MTA—a true Boston protest song from decades earlier.

Humphrey's by the Bay was a great venue near Shelter Island Marina. The limited seating of the outdoor concert area allowed for an intimate performance by any act. Acoustic groups shined at that venue. Interaction with the audience was facilitated by its smallness.

George Grove was not an original member of the group but replaced in kind a founding member of the group. That member was Dave Guard who later in life died of lymphoma. A number of musicians replaced Guard over the years, and George was the most musically talented of them all. A superb voice and gift for stringed instruments made George the man to harmonize with Bob Shane and Nick Reynolds. A thoughtful person and avid songwriter himself, George Grove treated The Trio's fans with the utmost respect. If he could get you seats up front, he was happy to oblige.

Jack had called George in Nevada, Fawn remembered, almost asleep.

"George, how goes it? This is J. D. in San Diego."

"Hey, Jackson, what's up?" replied Grove.

"See you're comin' to S.D. and hope to get to see you. Me and the little bride of a year!"

"Neat!" replied George. "Need tickets for Humphrey's? Passes, too?"

"Yah, you folks already sold out the venue. Can you help?" asked Jack with concern.

"I'll check with the boys, see what's available, and get back to ya. I'll e-mail you if there is a problem. Otherwise, just meet up with us in the late afternoon. Sound check is at 5:00 P.M. Gotta run man! Plane to catch—off to D.C."

"Thanks, George, you're a good guy! See ya soon."

195

"Bye for now. Love to Fawn—my second favorite woman!" replied George Grove in haste.

Fawn was flattered by George's affectionate comments. She remembered that Jack had met the trio back in the 1970s when they passed through Vail, Colorado, for a couple of days. It was the Kingston Trio that had inspired Jack to take up a musical instrument. Jack grew fond of the five-string banjo and later, the guitar. Jack thought that the trio had never been properly recognized for their contributions to the music industry. They had been awarded only two Grammies, and that was in the 1950s. *They really deserved a Lifetime Achievement Award by the NARAS music industry,* Jack thought. They toured for over forty plus years and drew excellent crowds. Their performances were humorous and entertaining. Fawn always liked Bob Shane's jokes between songs; the timing and delivery of his material was perfect.

Fawn fought to stay awake as she lay there missing her husband and the great times they had together.

She and Jack had discussed another topic before she had left to go east for a few days—starting their family. She was becoming fond of San Diego and getting to know the town quite well. She knew that Jack's job was awesome and that he was doing well with Royston MacDonald, and Royston's pet research program.

The evening with the Kingston Trio was like icing on the cake for both of them, she remembered. *What could be better than their current life,* she reminisced, half asleep. The beaches, the restaurants, their West Coast home, and hanging out with famous people, were becoming a common occurrence for both of them.

She recalled the ride home after the concert. "Jack boy, I'm really lovin' San Diego. How about you, hon?"

"This is heaven sweetheart—you, me, the job—the whole scene," he replied as he drove up the interstate.

"Ya know, I've been thinkin'. With all the good things happening in our lives, maybe we should think about doin' the 'kid thing'," he whispered to her as she sat quietly in the passenger seat.

"Really, hon? You serious? Are you ready for children?" she looked at him with amazement. She was stunned by his comment, but also pleasantly surprised by his sincerity.

"Think so, babe. Think it's time to start tryin'," he teased her back. *Tryin', meant a lot of practice to get things right,* he thought to himself.

"What's your take on that?" he asked gently.

"Well, sweetheart, there is the biological time clock thing to consider. Maybe we should decide on a family before we are old and cranky!" she joked back.

"We don't want to be raisin' them when we are old. They are a lot of work and quite an investment. It takes about 100K to raise them ya know," she added.

"Them?" he asked. "You talkin' multiples?" raising his eyebrows in the dim light from the dashboard of the car.

"Yes," she replied. "I can see us with two. Raisin' a single one is painful for the child. Two would give them interaction at a young age. That's important, the experts say. What do *you* think?"

Jack indicated that two would be reasonable, but wondered how they would get free to do the things they used to do in Boston, and now in San Diego. *There was no way they would be free of the enormous responsibilities in raising one or two for that matter,* he pondered.

"Maybe the team you work with could guarantee a boy and a girl," Fawn continued. "That would be perfect for me!"

"That's not really what the team does, hon. They are experimenting with fertility enhancement in infertile couples, not offering children of a particular sex. They think cloning is the future."

"Cloning? You mean humans, or animals—cows and stuff?" she asked.

Jack was reluctant to get into it since MacDonald had sworn him to secrecy.

"Cows, pigs, cattle in general," he told her. "The human cloning will eventually happen, but no one has been successful at that as yet."

"Maybe they will clone you, my dear," she joked, "so I can have a younger, exact copy, 'boy toy' of you when you are old and impotent."

"Jack laughed, "Now, that's a great idea. I can watch you 'do me,' or a *clone* of me, from a wheelchair, I suppose. You, my dear, are a sick woman. Personally, why don't we start tonight with the baby thing."

"Are you sure it's not the wine talking, Jack dear?" she asked.

"No, hon, it's not the wine. I want to create a miniature you—a little girl, just like my lovely wife."

"That is so sweet," she said, leaning on his shoulder.

"But I don't want to be cloned!" she added, "I don't want any one of your friends playin' with my DNA!"

"I'm the only one who will play with your DNA," he jested. "Just little ol' me! There's only one of you, Fawn, and that's the way I want it."

Jack and Fawn felt very close that evening. They had decided to start a family and she was in love with the idea. They turned into the driveway and barely made it into the house with their clothes on. They would "practice" for two hours.

The daydream over, Fawn lay in her bed in Boston remembering the conversation they had after the Kingston Trio concert and the trip home. She would be heading back to San Diego in a day or so. The timing would be right for her menstrual cycle. She wanted to be near her husband to be able to love him and have a chance to get pregnant. She had been off the pill for a month and her normal cycle had returned. There was a good chance that she might get pregnant that following month.

The few days she had in Boston were enough and she wished to return to San Diego. Her husband missed her just as much.

Fawn finally fell asleep, dreaming of Jack.

Thirty-four

Dr. Sanchez visited Teresa early the next morning. He spent time with her, describing the schedule for the day.

Teresa Cordero was moved to the fertility clinic surgical suite in the late morning. The transfer of the DNA-impregnated ovum was performed on schedule, exactly seventy-two hours after the egg had been modified. She would feel nothing during the procedure. The clinic staff was confident that the embryo that was transferred would be retained. There was no indication that the transfer fluid leaked out the cervix of the uterus. The free-floating embryo would eventually adhere to the endometrium of the uterine wall. Teresa remained in her hospital room and rested for two additional days.

Royston was not in the surgery room when the procedure took place. He remained nervously close by in the conference room and awaited the fertility doctor's input.

Dr. Sanchez entered the conference room and brought MacDonald up to date. "All is well, sir," he said with a smile. "She's back in her room and there was never any doubt that the transfer went as well as we had planned."

"Good!" responded Royston almost ragged from anticipation. His armpits and white dress shirt were soaked from perspiration. "Did you check the pipette? Did you check to see that the egg was transferred?" he asked anxiously.

"Yes, sir, there was nothing residual in the transfer tube. The embryo and transfer medium went straight into the uterus. Microscopic

evaluation confirmed that there was nothing remaining in the pipette—
nothing, sir."

"Good," said Royston as he sat back down from pacing the room.
"When will we know? When will she be pregnant? When do you
confirm the pregnancy?"

"Sir, we will know in due time. It takes a little while. The egg
needs to implant. Once the embryo implants, hormones will be produced that end up in the blood and urine. We can detect them early
but it takes a couple of weeks or a month to be sure."

"Can the test be wrong? Can she show a false positive?" Royston
asked. He had read much on the commercial pregnancy tests of the
day. The hospital would use the most sensitive tests known.

"Not often, sir. It is rare to have a false positive test," replied
Sanchez. "But it can happen. Let's see what transpires. All looks promising to date. She was at a perfect point in her cycle to receive the
embryo. She has a better than 80 percent chance that it will take."

"Eighty percent?" replied Royston. "I need 100 percent, doctor.
One hundred percent!"

"I know, sir. We are all rooting for 100 percent, as well," replied
the doctor nervously.

"You've done well, Sanchez. You've done well. Sorry, I'm just a
bit antsy."

"We've all done well, sir. All we can do is watch and wait," replied Sanchez with confidence.

Royston stopped in to see Teresa before he left the clinic. He
talked to her in private with her door closed.

He then left and returned to the Hotel Del. He would have a cocktail and get some rest. There was nothing to do but wait and each day
would be the most painful time of his life. He would receive updates
continuously from the clinic personnel. He would also make sure that
Jack Danton was his ambassador and on full alert. He needed to have
Jack update him on all aspects of Project Samuel. They would meet
every day until the pregnancy test results were known.

When Fawn arrived back in San Diego, she discovered that Jack
was too busy to spend much time with her during the next two weeks.
Royston was most demanding at this time of the project and Jack was

on call perpetually. Fawn spent much of her time reading at the beach or shopping for the house. She was content to add furnishings to the spare room. It was an office and library now, but could eventually become a family room. Everything she envisioned for them as a couple was now focused on their commitment to become parents. Jack was happy that she was preoccupied with furnishing and decorating their home. He had such heavy and demanding responsibilities at this time, that he needed a wife that understood his mood swings as she did. She also understood Royston's demands on Jack's time. MacDonald was paying the tab for their incredible lifestyle and Jack was compensated well for his dedication. If Project Samuel succeeded, there would be major bonuses for key personnel to appease the frustrating moments of separation from family during the program. In the end, with success, everyone would be not only rich, but would also become famous.

Thirty-five

The implantation of the embryo coincided with the midpoint of Teresa's menstrual cycle. She would normally expect her period some fourteen or fifteen days later. That would be day twenty-eight, if she were not pregnant. Teresa was in touch with Dr. Sanchez every day and sometimes twice a day. No physical problems were noted throughout the time she awaited the pregnancy test confirming that the embryo had implanted in the womb. There was always the concern with only one egg transplanted, that the pregnancy might not take hold. Normally, in surrogate women, multiple embryos are transferred to ensure that at least one is successful. These doctors were not about to try more than one egg in Teresa. Nothing in the scientific literature was known of what might happen with a cloned human egg transfer. Would it behave normally? It was also not their desire to have multiple Ted Williamses developing inside Teresa Cordero.

Before her next expected menstrual flow, the clinic would draw blood and collect urine samples from Teresa. If there were a hint of human chorionic gonadotrophin (HCG) in either sample, they could detect it immediately. All pregnancy tests were now sensitive for minute quantities (twenty-five international units) of HCG. The other steroid hormones of pregnancy could also be monitored. In two or three weeks, the lack of a menstrual period would suggest pregnancy and that the transfer procedure had been successful.

⚾ ⚾ ⚾ ⚾

The phone rang in Royston's room at the Hotel del Coronado. He had booked the hotel for the month, just to be around during the critical clinical phase of the project. There was no need to be in Texas at this time; the oil business basically ran itself. Two weeks had passed since the embryo transfer.

"Hello," he answered, with anxiety.

"Royston!" said Sanchez with exuberance, and with Bradshaw by his side, *"You're a dad! You're a dad,* sort of. Teresa's implant took! She's pregnant!"

"What?" screamed MacDonald. "Are you for real? This is no joke or prank, right?"

"No joke, Roy!" added Sanchez. "The test lit up positive. There is no doubt. We ran it twice. She's poppin' HCG at record levels!" Dr. Bradshaw could be heard in the background whooping it up.

"We did it! We did it!" E. Royston MacDonald shouted.

Royston finally came to his senses. He was pacing with the phone to his ear. He was dazed. The embryo had successfully implanted and Teresa Cordero was pregnant. *No other woman had ever been pregnant with a cloned human embryo.* The scientific team knew of none in any literature that they had reviewed. Even in Europe, there was only speculation of a potential human pregnancy by cloning.

"Oh . . . my . . . God!" MacDonald said slowly and deliberately. There was genuine amazement and excitement at both ends of the line.

"Convene the group at the Del immediately," he barked. "Have Danton call everyone and meet me here in an hour . . . or earlier!" he ordered. "Have everyone paged! Does Teresa know yet? Have you told her?" asked Royston more calmly.

"No, Roy, you didn't want us to tell her right away. Remember?" asked Sanchez.

"Right . . . right. Sorry, I forgot. You can tell her after we hang up, then come to the Del right after, please," Royston said courteously.

He sat back in his easy chair in the Hotel Del suite and cried tears of joy. *It really did happen,* he thought. *It wasn't a dream after all.* He was numb at the idea that another milestone had been reached. The first milestone was the egg that cleaved after the DNA injection; the second was the successful embryo transfer, and the third milestone was the implantation of the embryo in the uterus. Now there was the confirmation of pregnancy.

Other milestones were still needed, i.e., maintaining a pregnancy and delivering a healthy child. Even with that formidable task ahead, Royston was beside himself. *How will I be able to wait nine months for this child?* he thought. *Could he do it? Will she go nine full months or eight or seven? Will the child be normal? Will it survive?*

His mind was spinning. He was talking to himself. Then the ultimate question crossed his mind in fright! *Would the child who was to be born, be Ted Williams? Look like Ted? Play ball like Ted?*

Royston dug out a book on Ted Williams and stared at Ted's baby picture. "This is what the child will look like," he mumbled. He could not take his eyes off the picture—a six-month-old Ted Williams.

Royston would shower and shave and dress to the nines. He was ready to celebrate the event with his colleagues. They would be arriving one by one in an hour.

MacDonald would meet with Jack Danton and Dr. Sanchez in advance of the others.

He called the Hotel Del caterer and events coordinator and asked that he meet him in his suite immediately. Royston told him to set up the Wellington Room and have Dom Perignon, caviar, lobster tails, shrimp, raw oysters of seven varieties and assorted top-shelf liquors, plus hot and cold buffet items. The event coordinator ran from the room and coordinated the event in less than an hour. House chefs were put into high gear to meet Royston MacDonald's demands. The caterers would charge Royston double the normal cost for his extravagant impromptu reception. He did not care. An hour later, all would be set up, tables draped and food presented among arrangements of bird of paradise flowers. Thirteen thousand dollars later, Royston was ready for his noted colleagues and guests. The Project Samuel team was there, but absent Teresa Cordero.

⚾ ⚾ ⚾ ⚾

She sat quietly in her room at the Torrey Pines Inn. With Dr. Sanchez about to arrive, she waited patiently for some news of the pregnancy.

Good or bad, she wanted to know. Sanchez had called in advance to say he was coming over. She did not know the reason, but the timing would indicate that perhaps a lab test was complete and he had some results for her. She was nervous.

Dr. Sanchez arrived at the door of room 31 and was smiling. He handed Teresa a folic acid tablet and said, "Eat this!"

He then hugged her and told her the good news, the exceptional news. She was so excited she had to sit down. Her heart was racing and she patted her stomach gently. "That is a pill you now need to take daily, so don't forget it. Here is the rest of the bottle," he said with a smile. "It is for a healthy baby, Teresa. Congratulations! You are about to become a surrogate mother."

Teresa had been taking multiple vitamins with folic acid prior to Sanchez giving her the bottle. She was aware that she would eventually need that special vitamin supplement.

Dr. Sanchez did not stay long at the inn and told her that he and Royston would be in touch. He had another meeting to go to and he congratulated her on her pregnancy. He did not tell her he was meeting with MacDonald at the Del, for a celebration.

"I want you to rest a while, please," he said before leaving. "This has been exciting for you, Teresa. It is exciting for all of us. Every surrogate pregnancy is a celebration," he added.

"But this one, is a special one. You are special, the baby is special and the whole fertility team is special! I must go but again, congratulations!"

"Thank you, doctor. You are wonderful, too, and I am very happy that a child is inside of me. Thank you."

Sanchez departed the inn parking lot and drove from Torrey Pines Boulevard to Genesee Avenue. Once on Interstate 5, he proceeded south. He was fifteen minutes from the Hotel del Coronado, and in a matter of minutes the champagne would be flowing at Royston MacDonald's impromptu function.

Thirty-six

Teresa experienced little morning sickness in the first three months of her pregnancy. She progressed as well as any normal woman carrying a child at that stage. Between her third and fourth month, she began to show a bit. There was a subtle increase in her waistline and small bulge by her navel. By the fourth month, the pregnancy would be readily apparent. Everyone on the project team was happy to know that she was doing well. The press and the general public still had no idea that there was a woman in San Diego carrying the first cloned human being. Even Teresa didn't know and Royston wished to keep it that way.

Teresa spent those early months in her home in North Park, a few miles from downtown San Diego. Royston MacDonald, as promised, covered all expenses of the house. The 3000 block of Utah Street was a typical neighborhood and it was only a couple of blocks from Ted Williams's boyhood home at 4121 Utah. Teresa often walked around the neighborhood and ventured downtown to shop. The coffee shop and local Salvation Army store on University Avenue were nearby. She liked visiting with clerks and people she met on the street. The Salvation Army store was more entertainment than anything. She would peruse the counters of gadgets, trinkets and glassware. She often saw baby clothes there and would check out an OshKosh piece or two. She knew she shouldn't buy for the baby, but the urge was there. Adult clothing racks had little to offer the pregnant woman, even though she occasionally found a cute maternity garment there.

Teresa followed the clinic's regime for nutrition and exercise. She was in good shape during both the first and second trimesters. The clinic's personnel reminded her often to take her prenatal vitamins and folic acid, especially during the early months. At home, she would often talk to neighbors, or simply watch TV. Sitting on the living room couch, she would sing to the baby in Spanish and English. "I will sing to you, young one," she would say. Then she would hum a tune or lullaby. The baby was calm during those times, as if it was hearing its surrogate mother's voice from the inside. Teresa often did cross-stitch. She hoped to have them framed for the baby's room.

"Now, sweet child, you are a gift from God. I will take care of you for a while. I am your mama for now. You will know your real mother later and she will love you even more than me. I will be your temporary mother, and you will be fine. You will be fine." The moments of communicating with the baby made Teresa feel good as well. She was becoming the natural mother in a way. The more she interacted with the fetus, the more she felt as if it was her own child. It calmed her to talk to him. She was beginning to feel little tingles during those months as well. There were subtle movements in her abdomen. At that point, the baby became surprisingly real to her.

As a young woman she had attended church with her parents when she was growing up in Puerto Nuevo, south of Tijuana. Therefore, on Sundays she attended the Catholic church near her new home. It was there that she met Wanda.

Wanda had a ten-year-old son, Randy. She became attentive to her new neighbor and concerned for the baby. When she visited Teresa, she often brought her fruit and a magazine or books. Randy enjoyed sports and played second base in Little League at Ted Williams field. Teresa and Wanda would root for him at the games, and Teresa began to understand the game of baseball more thoroughly.

"Your baby will play here someday as well," said Wanda with an encouraging smile. "All the kids in the neighborhood play here, in time. It is the thing to do here when a child is eight to twelve years old, Teresa. Every child wishes to be discovered here as the next Ted Williams!"

Teresa looked puzzled. "Ted?"

Wanda realized that she might not know of Williams.

"Who is Ted Williams?" Teresa asked.

"Ted Williams was a famous Red Sox baseball player in Boston, but he grew up here in San Diego. He was and still is very famous, Teresa. He used to live near us on Utah Street. All the local kids think that they will play professional baseball someday. That is their hope, their dream. They know Mr. Williams lived here as a boy, and they hope a baseball scout will discover them as well. Everyone must have a dream."

"I know little about baseball, Wanda. Tell me more about Ted Williams. My brothers played ball in a sand lot in Puerto Nuevo, but the girls were not allowed to be with them. We played dolls elsewhere."

"This park was named after Ted Williams, and years ago he stopped by to visit his old neighborhood and to say hello. Ted Williams was the most famous person to come from North Park. I have many books about him. I will let you borrow them. Better than that, I will get you copies."

During breaks in the game, Wanda continued to enlighten Teresa about Ted's life. Her pride in Williams was almost overbearing. Teresa was interested, but did not care to know everything about the famous ballplayer. Wanda would always add a bit to the story of Ted, especially in the weeks that followed.

"Teresa, you will find that many neighbors know of this man. He is elderly now and retired to Florida to fish. He has been ill as well. They say he had a stroke. If you read and learn about him, you can talk to most of your neighbors and meet new friends. Maybe you will find a man or husband, if you can talk about baseball," Wanda said laughing and rolling her eyes. Teresa was cordial but wasn't really interested in finding a man, especially while pregnant with someone else's child. She cared little about baseball because she was unsure of the sex of the child. *What if it was a girl?* she wondered. *Do girls play baseball, too?*

Ted's parents moved into their home in 1920 when Ted was five years old. Except for the later renovations, which he paid for as a major league ballplayer, the house remained similar to how it looked in 1920. Teresa, Wanda and the neighbors still lived very much like Ted's family did years ago.

One big difference between now and then was that May Williams, Ted's mother, was involved in The Salvation Army. She was always in downtown San Diego or Tijuana as a missionary. She got home late and Ted was often waiting in the dark, with his brother Danny, to get into the house. He would still be swinging a baseball bat at that late hour.

Wanda asked Teresa, "When is your birthday, dear?"

"It is actually next week," she responded. "Why do you ask?"

"I think I would like to bake you a cake. You have no one here to celebrate your birthday with. Would that be OK?" asked Wanda.

"Sure, that is very nice of you, Wanda. You are always very kind to me and I never seem to be able to repay you," responded Teresa, feeling a little guilty.

"There is no need to repay me for anything. I like you and our friendship. You are a kind neighbor too. You bought Randy a new baseball to practice with. That was kind!"

Wanda would host a small birthday party for Teresa. A couple of neighbors would attend as well. They too, seemed to focus on Ted Williams at the party. In the end, two of the gifts were books on Williams, his life and times. In time, Teresa would find the noted ballplayer's life interesting. More intriguing to her though, was that she would find his mother's life of interest as well.

⚾ ⚾ ⚾ ⚾

A day after the birthday party, Wanda received a telephone call. The caller ID said: "Coronado CA."

"Wanda," the voice said, "how are you?"

"Fine, sir, I am fine, and you?" she replied.

"Fine," he responded. "Did you give Teresa the book—the one I sent you about Ted Williams?" he asked.

"Yes, I did," she replied. "We gave it to her for her birthday yesterday. She seemed interested and is reading it now, I think."

"Good!" said the voice on the phone. "Encourage her to read it, please."

"Yes, sir!" Wanda added, "and thank you for the check. It was a nice surprise and very helpful this month. I've never been paid for being a 'good neighbor' before."

"Enjoy it," said the voice on the phone. "You are a good neighbor, Wanda. Be nice to her and you and Randy will be rewarded. By the way, how's his batting average lately?"

Wanda was pleased that the man asked.

"He's at .285 and doing very well. He hit two homers the other day. He really appreciated the book that you sent him. You know— the one that Ted wrote called *The Science of Hitting*. He practically read the whole thing at one sitting, and he learned a lot from it!" she boasted. "He'll be at .300 soon!"

"It is a great book. All Little Leaguers should read it, Wanda. They would learn that one must swing slightly up, not level. Ted knew that! You can't hit it 'out' swingin' level!"

"It must have worked, since he got those two homers," she laughed.

"Wanda, I've got to run now. Thank you. I'll call you again next week. My best wishes to Randy. Please send him my congratulations on the two homers."

Wanda returned to her laundry chores and did a load of clothes for her son. He had another baseball game that evening and his uniform needed pressing.

⚾ ⚾ ⚾ ⚾

Teresa, in her spare time, became engrossed in one of the two books about Ted Williams. The book *Hitter* by Ed Linn was very intriguing. A second book called *Ted Williams—A Portrait in Words and Pictures* by Johnson and Stout, would be the next book she would read. Wanda continued to encourage Teresa to read about Ted. Teresa was still more interested in the life of Ted's mother, and her unusual career, than in baseball. The woman was fascinating in that she was listed as a housewife on Ted's birth certificate, but she was really a career woman in the Salvation Army. Teresa read all she could about May Williams and felt a kindred spirit to her, knowing how other mothers lived in that neighborhood.

Ted Williams's mother, the former May Venzer, was of Mexican-American and French-American descent. Teresa was amazed that Ted was one-quarter Mexican and she found joy in telling Wanda about that fact. Sam, Ted's father, was of Welsh and English descent.

May was known as "Salvation May" or the "Angel of Tijuana." As an active lieutenant in the Salvation Army, she was often found wearing a bonnet and carrying a tambourine as she collected money for "the cause." She worked far from North Park and her children raised themselves, or close neighbors influenced their lives. May lost her commission with "The Army" when she married Sam Williams. Sam was not in the Salvation Army fold and was a photographer who often took passport photographs for sailors, Teresa had learned.

When Ted was five, his family moved into the home on Utah Street in North Park. A wealthy benefactor bought the house for them, one biography had noted. Teresa thought that odd and coincidental that Royston MacDonald was covering her expenses and house costs in a similar fashion. She never told Wanda that, but sensed that she already knew that the home was *gratis* for Teresa. Wanda knew that Teresa did not work while she was pregnant. Wanda never brought any of that up for discussion.

May and Sam Williams never reimbursed the benefactor for their home, because May Williams gave all her money to the Salvation Army. Sam's business was not very lucrative so he was of little help financially. Teresa sensed that Ted's family was poor and that the boys, Ted and his brother, Danny, basically raised themselves. One brother would succeed in life, and the other would end up in jail. Danny was apparent trouble, according to historians. It was clear from the Williams's biographies, that May and Sam were distant and their marriage would not last. May would eventually raise the children alone and Sam moved to San Francisco when they were divorced.

Many times, friends teased Ted about his mother's activities in the "The Army." He would hide behind the drum that she played in the Salvation Army band. She would hand out the army's publications and collect money in her tambourine. She ministered to the underprivileged, the drunks and the whores downtown. Her religious influence on Ted, as a boy, would take its toll and he would eventually rebel when he was older. Teresa found this parallel of interest. She was religious while young and hoped any child she had would seek religion as well, when he or she was older. Ted replaced religion and the influence of the Salvation Army, with baseball. That became his life. Soon he became a star baseball player, even as a teen.

Teresa read that his mother finally bought him a glove. He would attend Garfield Grammar School and Horace Mann Junior High. He would then enter Hoover High where Mr. Caldwell, a coach there, nurtured the boy's interested in baseball. Teresa began to understand the influence of the local schools and local people on the life of Ted Williams. She went to the library and read voraciously about him and his mother. Even in his junior and senior years in high school, she read that Ted's batting average was .583 and .406, respectively. Teresa was no expert, but understood that those were extraordinarily high batting averages. Wanda had influenced her well.

Ted's mother had named him Teddy Samuel Williams. The "Teddy" came from Teddy Roosevelt. Ted's father claimed to have served in Roosevelt's Rough Riders regiment. Ted's middle name was for May's brother, Samuel, who died on the last day of WWI. Ted's father's name was Sam as well. Ted's birth date was listed as October 30, 1918 in one document and August 20th in another. It was listed as August 30th on yet another. Later in life, Ted would change his name from Teddy to Theodore, and establish August 30, 1918, as his date of birth. He changed it because October 30th interfered with baseball season, one book had noted. Teresa found the whole scenario weird. Her baby was due late in the year as well. It could possibly coincide with a Williams birth date. Teresa wrote the coincidences down. The similarities in her life and May's were uncanny.

Teresa was amazed that May Williams was honored as San Diego's Woman of the Year and that she was known by virtually everyone in San Diego, including residents in North Park. Ted's father had gone to the Bay area, so May attempted to raise the kids alone. Teresa, without a husband, was not unlike May Williams, she often thought. The neighborhood men became Ted Williams's surrogate fathers— especially one who lived behind their home on Utah. *How will my surrogate baby grow up?* she wondered.

She would also learn that Ted's mother died in 1961, one year after his professional playing career ended. That was reassuring to Teresa—that he had his mother in his life for a long time.

Teresa put the biography down and cried. For the first time, she realized that she was basically carrying a child alone, and at a very young age. She cried all night and slept poorly. She would never tell Wanda that the book that she gave her for her birthday, made her sad. Teresa saw so many parallels between herself and Ted's mother and their respective homes, that she became possessed by the resemblance of the lives. She knew that she would never be part of the Salvation Army. There was no way that any future child of hers would be abandoned on a daily basis, especially during his or her young life. Love, attention and nurturing would always be there for any children that she might bear, and raise, in the future.

Thirty-seven

E. Royston MacDonald and the physicians at the fertility clinic had led Teresa Cordero to believe that she was carrying the child of an infertile couple. Well into the second trimester, she felt comfortable with her home and its free amenities. By the seventh month of her pregnancy, she felt a part of the neighborhood and had developed a number of close friends in the area. She would go to the new cinema, visit nearby convenience stores, and browse in the local gift shops for fun. University Avenue was a short walk away and offered her opportunities and a convenience store for needed household staples. If she wanted to go to the Fashion Mall near QualComm baseball stadium, Royston provided a limo for her. A simple phone call brought her access to other parts of the city. North Park was nice but didn't cover all her shopping needs.

Royston MacDonald occasionally visited her.

"I feel a part of the neighborhood," she had told him. "This is my home now and I am comfortable here in a nice part of San Diego. I have made many friends. I am the only person of Mexican descent here on Utah Street, but I feel like everyone cares about me. They often ask me how I am feeling and how the baby is."

"That's wonderful, Teresa. You look great and appear very healthy. I'm glad that you are happy here as well," commented Royston. "You seem nice and relaxed and that is important."

"There is no stress in this quiet neighborhood," Teresa responded with a smile.

Since the successful implantation, Royston had spent half his time in San Diego, and half in Texas. He often stopped by to check on Teresa. He made a point to call in advance and ask if that was OK. She assumed that the real parents wanted to know how things were going. There were, however, no real "future parents."

"Does anyone bother to ask of your husband, Teresa? Do they pester you with questions or cause you to be upset. If so, please let me know," inquired Royston.

"I feel fine. The doctors at the clinic are pleased with my progress. Their concern is, as if it were my natural child. Everyone comments on how well I have gone through the early and mid-months of this pregnancy. They say I look beautiful and am a natural mother."

"You do look beautiful, Teresa. You are radiant with beauty. It is called 'bloom.' Your color is magnificent and you carry the child well," Royston added.

Royston who was standing, walked back from the kitchen area of Teresa's house. His finely polished shoes clicked on the tile floor of the passageway to the living room. Teresa sat on the couch and awaited his return. He gave her a small glass of water and sat nearby her.

"Thank you," she said with a smile. "I was a bit thirsty. How did you know?"

"Ah," he said quietly, "you must maintain hydration. You always need water otherwise you can have contractions prematurely. I thought you might like a drink," he said thoughtfully.

"I do get tired," she volunteered softly. "It is not always easy carrying this extra weight around. I have back pain and have to go to the bathroom more often. Maybe the water is not such a good idea," she laughed. He laughed with her, then he got a bit more serious.

"Teresa, there is something that I must tell you. It is about the natural parents of Samuel. I mean the baby."

"Samuel? It's a boy?" she asked with surprise.

"Yes . . . ah . . . we think it is. The team of clinicians has been calling him Samuel or Sammy for short," Royston responded while caught off guard.

This was Teresa's first knowledge that the sex of the child had been determined. She wondered why the name.

215

Royston quickly moved to the subject at hand. "Ah, you asked if the parents ever ask about the child, or your pregnancy. Yes, they *did*, and often," he said using the past tense.

"Did? Do they not ask anymore," she asked with furrowed brow.

"Teresa, we have recently been informed that the natural parents of the child that you carry inside you, were . . . ah . . . in a terrible accident—a car accident," he said slowly.

"What? The parents are hurt, or *worse?*" she raised her voice a bit and with concern.

"Teresa, we do not know a lot of details but there was an accident on the Interstate, north of San Diego."

She stood and stared at the wall. She was distraught and placed her hands on her forehead, almost covering her eyes.

"Are they OK? Are they in the hospital?" she asked as her hands lowered and clasped her belly. Without intention, she appeared to be comforting the child within. She wasn't aware of her own actions. A sharp pain ran across her abdomen and deep inside her stomach.

"Teresa. Please sit down," he said as he moved next to her on the couch.

"Teresa. I'm afraid that the husband was killed in the accident. A mini sand storm from the side of the road swirled over the road like a tornado and many drivers were blinded. A half-mile north and south of the windstorm it was clear. They went off the road and the car flipped. It came to rest near a gully—a drainage gully."

"Oh, my God," she gasped. "What of the mother? What . . . ?"

Royston's body shook from his fabrication of the story, but he composed himself. He saw that she was withdrawn and truly sad. He did not want her to go into labor right in front of him. He thought for a second and then responded quickly to her question about the mother.

"Teresa, the mother is in a coma at UCLA Medical Center in L.A. She was airlifted there and is in good hands. She is on life-support but her condition is guarded or grave. There were massive head injuries and she lost much blood at the scene of the accident. By the time they got to her and used the jaws of life to get her out, she was in a coma," Royston added. He began to feel sick from the story he had concocted. He could not tell her any other way. It was in his master plan.

"A decision will be made next week whether or not to remove the respirator from the mother. She has no brain function, but her heart is beating. She is essentially brain-dead, to her physicians. She would never have a quality of life that is normal. Sadly, there is no way that she would be able to raise a child if she survived."

"Oh my God! This is so sad. I feel sick," she said, beginning to weep and covering her face.

Royston touched her arm and then held her close. She believed his sincerity, or what she perceived to be his sincerity. She had never known him not to be honest with her.

She looked up with dark brown eyes that were now bright red from crying.

"What does this mean for me—for the baby?" she asked with head bowed. "What will happen to my baby? Oh, my poor little one." She grimaced from a contraction deep in her abdomen.

Jesus, he thought. *What will happen? Will she lose this child right here?* he thought anxiously. He stood up and paged Dr. Sanchez, and had him come to North Park immediately. Sanchez had just finished an exam of a patient and headed to North Park by cab. Along the way, he called Royston's cell phone. In the physician's bag were sedatives, a uterine relaxant and other analgesic medications, if needed. He was disturbed at what Royston had told him. If the conversation released adrenaline, the woman could go into contractions. That would be premature at this stage and might result in fetal distress. In either case, the baby could be in jeopardy from the mother's anxiety.

"Driver, please go faster!" he demanded of the cabbie. "This is an emergency!" Sanchez was nervous. The driver did as he was told and came close to getting into a crash himself.

Royston was able to calm her down. "Teresa. There is nothing to worry about. I know that you are sad for the parents, but we still have this blessed child to be concerned about. Please relax for the moment. I have called Dr. Sanchez. He will come here to check you over. I know you are distressed and I am sorry that what I said saddened you.

"Teresa, there will not be need to terminate the pregnancy. There will be no late-term abortion. You will receive the remaining $2,500 dollars, the second installment, that we promised you—no matter what happens."

Her heart was pounding from the verbal trauma of Royston's shocking information and the baby moved abruptly from the internal physiological changes that occurred with Teresa's stress. *Teresa is certainly frightened now,* he thought. He was genuinely concerned. She was breathing deeply and unconsciously stretching her body out to alleviate the cramps.

"That doesn't matter . . . the money . . . it no longer matters. What happens to the little boy inside me? Their baby? The one you always affectionately call Samuel."

"Teresa, there are options here regarding the child," said Royston with more fabrication. "The child could be placed for adoption, for one thing," he baited her.

"Oh no, sir. He is like my child to me. I could not allow the little one to go to a foster home or be adopted by strangers."

"But, Teresa," he added, "he is not your child. You are the carrier of someone else's baby, right?"

"Yes," she replied, "but I love this little one as if it were mine. Can I not keep the child and raise it, on behalf of the original parents?" she asked with desperate eyes.

"Yes, that may be possible, I suppose. It would seem that you are a good mother. You have carried this baby for some seven months now and it seems like it was almost your child genetically," he said, watching her response. He had achieved his goal of enticing her to keep the baby, and perhaps raise it in North Park.

"Would you want to raise the child alone, Teresa?" he asked. "You have no husband or father figure to help. Wouldn't that be tough on you and the baby?"

"I have raised my brothers and sisters, almost on my own. I know what children need. More than anything they need *love* and *encouragement.* I am capable of providing *that.*"

"I know you have done your family well," he replied.

"I can go back to work and get day care for Samuel. I also have neighbors who would help. You said it would be nice for him to grow up in North Park. I love North Park as well."

Royston kept the conversation going. She seemed relaxed now and the baby was quiet inside her. She was focused on the baby's future, not the apparent loss of his "real parents."

"Are you sure, Teresa? Why not think about it? You are young and the child will need a father, a male role model. You know, someone to play sports and trucks with the boy," he suggested.

Royston had created the scenario that he wanted. He desired for her to keep the baby, and raise him in North Park—the same North Park and same neighborhood in which Ted Williams grew up. Royston was the only one to know the total Project Samuel mission. This conversation was planned well in advance.

Teresa became silent. She now reflected on the near total loss of the child's supposed parents. She was exhausted. It was all so overwhelming to her. Royston saw her pensiveness and decided to add one more thing. "Teresa, there is one more option."

"Sir, what's that?" she asked quietly.

"I think under the circumstances that rather than have you work, I would offer to pay your expenses to raise the child. Basically, I would pay you to be his mother. He would be your son, in essence, and you would not have any bills," he added.

"Mr. Mac Donald, that is very generous of you. Why would you do that?"

"Teresa, this child means the world to you and to me. I feel like I am the father of this child. It is a miracle in the making. I want only the best for him and you," he said with a reassuring voice. "Why not sleep on it and let me know. This is a major decision for you in life. Having a child while in your twenties is a lot of work. I want you to be sure that you can do this," he added with theatrics. He was the consummate actor at this time. *There is no way,* he thought, *that she will not accept his offer.*

"Teresa. You're young and the child may tie you down. Remember, raising Samuel will be a full-time job. There's little time off and massive responsibilities at your young age. Can you do it?"

"I am strong and mature. My parents had little time for me and my brothers and sisters. We are all stronger today, because of their neglect."

"You will want to see America and not be tied down by a child," he stated. "People at your age travel."

"Mr. MacDonald," exclaimed Teresa, "I am happy as I am now. When he gets older we can travel—together—and see America."

With that, she placed her hand on her belly and patted it. She looked down with a subtle smile and said in Spanish, "It's OK, Samuel. You will be loved. I will love you, as your mother would have. God bless your mother and father."

Royston was not sure what she said in total, but knew it was designed to be of reassurance to the baby. She did not share what she had said with Royston, but told him it was a little prayer for the baby.

At that moment, Dr. Sanchez arrived and was winded from rushing from the taxi into the North Park home.

"Mr. MacDonald," he exclaimed. "I came as fast as I could. Teresa, are you OK? How are you feeling?"

"I am better, doctor. I feel OK now. He is quiet and I can rest now," she answered.

Dr. Sanchez gave her a physical exam. All parameters seemed normal for her and the baby's heart rate. He advised her to take a pill to calm the uterus. That way she could rest more easily that night. The pill was the newest version of a Ritodrine-like drug, a uterine muscle relaxant. She would not experience any contractions while the drug circulated within the body.

"I need to lie down now, please," she requested. Royston and Dr. Sanchez saw no reason to stay any longer. Teresa needed sleep and so did the baby. They would call her in the morning and Sanchez assured her that he would be on call if she needed him. Royston hugged her and patted her abdomen. Everything was back on track. His size dominated her petite little body, even while pregnant. Both he and Dr. Sanchez went out the front door and walked down the three steps to the sidewalk.

One block over, MacDonald heard kids playing ball in the park dedicated to Ted Williams. He decided to see whom the diehard kids were, to be playing in such reduced-light conditions. Royston and Sanchez looked up at the sign on the chain-link fence that listed the accolades to Ted Samuel Williams, otherwise known as Ted, The Kid,

The Splendid Splinter and Teddy Ballgame in Boston. Royston called Max the limo driver on his cell phone. He would be there in a matter of minutes to pick up MacDonald and Dr. Sanchez.

MacDonald and Sanchez sat in the bleachers for a few minutes until the limo arrived. Royston smiled to himself regarding the conversation with Teresa Cordero. He almost felt bad about the fabricated story of an accident on the Interstate, near L.A. *She is such a sweet girl and will make a great mother,* he thought. Since she had no idea she was carrying Vicky Palmer's host egg or that the embryo had been genetically altered, his guilt was overshadowed by the possibility of winning the Nobel prize for medicine. In time, Teresa would be as famous as the research team for creating the *first* cloned human— one that was a notable person and star athlete as well.

As the limo arrived, Royston chatted briefly with one young player. He and Sanchez then entered the long dark sedan. The children watched as both men entered the limo and it slowly drove away.

"Who was that?" one boy said to another.

"I don't know," replied the boy. "Someone with lots of money. And he was *huge!*"

"How do you know he has money?"

"You saw the car didn't you? Rich people have those cars, you idiot. And besides, he gave me a $20 bill as he left."

"What? He gave you money. You took it? From a stranger?" the boy asked.

"All he said was: 'Here son, treat your friends to some ice cream. You kids play ball well,' and then he left with the other man." The boy held up a crisp $20 bill for all to see. They decided to go to the corner store and get the ice cream. They left the field not knowing who E. Royston MacDonald was, or why he was there watching them play baseball. Someday, when they were eight years older, they would know who he was.

Thirty-eight

In the last two months of her pregnancy, Teresa had not only agreed to MacDonald's proposal that she raise the child, but she was temporarily moved back to the inn at Torrey Pines in La Jolla. With a month and a half to go, she would be closer to the clinic if something went wrong or if she required medical attention. She occasionally had Braxton-Hicks contractions and, although this was not an issue, the doctors felt that they could monitor her better if she was close to their facility.

Teresa sat quietly in her room at the inn. Her room was at ground level and overlooked the famed Torrey Pines Municipal Golf Course. The patio off the entrance to the room was framed by two hedges and had a lounge chair and two molded white plastic chairs on the cement stoop. Her view out the doorway was that of the eighteenth hole on the south course. The steps and patio were covered in green Astroturf and the room was comfortable, but a bit antiquated and small.

Torrey Pines was an old resort and famous for many championship tournaments. It was the only public course that qualified for a national PGA tournament. The best of the best played there, especially for the Buick Invitational. Even Tiger Woods played there. Teresa could wander the periphery of the grounds, the sidewalks and frequent the restaurant and rustic lobby of the inn, styled after a Vermont cabin. She spent most days relaxing, talking to close friend from North Park on the phone and watching the local duffers careen their golf balls off the side of the inn when they sliced the ball. She had cable TV and a constant breeze from the Pacific bathing her room. The sun set outside her doorway.

One particular morning, the rising sun to the east cast its early shadow on her patio. Some of the staggered-start golfers would play the eighteenth first, in order to allow everyone to finish in a reasonable time. To get to the tee, they had to use the cart path or sidewalk in front of her room. She was pleasant and greeted them each morning. "June gloom" or marine air, migrated easterly off the ocean and a light fog blanketed the course at 6:00 A.M. The golfers would start playing anyway.

When alone, she would bet with herself whether the foursomes would hit the green on their second shot. There was one water hazard that posed a real threat for each approach shot. One member of this particular morning's foursome had hit the green three feet from the pin. She was amazed that it practically looked like a "TV shot." He almost holed the nine iron approach.

Teresa stared at the people playing the affluent game and wondered how her earlier life had been so poor, in money and in quality of life. Her parents ran a small restaurant in Puerto Nuevo, sixty miles south of Tijuana. They served American tourists Pacific lobster and Superior Mexican beer—all for eight dollars. She was happy that the reward for carrying the surrogate child was so high. To her, five thousand dollars was a lot of money. She had plenty of free time to ponder how she would use the money for herself or her family.

Day in and day out, for the remainder of the pregnancy, Teresa would remain in her Torrey Pines room. She was pampered and monitored by the clinic staff once or twice a week. Her blood pressure and temperature was taken often and occasionally they would check her blood chemistries for deviations from the norm. She took her prenatal vitamins from day one. Folic acid was supplemented in the early months as well, to insure the proper development of the baby's nervous system. This was critical in the formative and early stages of pregnancy. The blood pressure (BP) recordings were most critical in the last couple of months of gestation. Some pregnant women note a rise in blood pressure toward the end of the third trimester. Preeclampsia and potential eclampsia (toxemia), a known rise in BP, often necessitates the need to perform a cesarean section on the mother. The baby would need to be removed surgically to reduce the mother's blood pressure. To date there had been no rise in it.

A couple of weeks passed and Teresa was now quite bored with the inn and golf course surroundings. It was no longer novel and she yearned for something else to do. She was depressed from being alone and cooped up in her room most of the day. Her only friend, Emilio Juan Rosero, was the dishwasher from the inn—a thirty-year-old man of Mexican descent. He would stop by to see her after his shift was done and they would chat. She was comfortable with Emilio because he spoke Spanish.

∅∅∅∅

E. Royston MacDonald called the Torito Bay Clinic each day to see how Project Samuel was progressing. Dr. Sanchez would brief him on Teresa's medical charts. It was just a matter of time before the baby would arrive.

"Doctor, what is her status today. Is she doing well?" Royston would ask. He was becoming a pest.

"Do you think she will go to term?" he would ask. Royston wanted the child *out* so that the world would know of his accomplishment. Ultrasound had confirmed that it was a boy and that all was normal. He knew that after seven months, there was little to worry about. If the baby were to be delivered early, he could have an excellent chance at survival. Modern neonatal care pediatrics had pretty much perfected any problems with immature lungs during premature births. There were ways to treat the condition and therapeutically mature the lungs with steroids, if needed. Obviously, the longer she carried the child, the stronger he would be at birth.

"Roy," Sanchez replied to MacDonald, "Teresa is progressing well. There is no reason to believe that she will not go to term with the baby. She has had a *classic* textbook pregnancy to date."

"I know," replied Royston. "I am eager to see this miracle child."

"We have her most recent ultrasound. You will be happy to know that the baby still has all digits that you saw in the first scan. His estimated weight is appropriate for the eighth month of pregnancy."

"That is awesome doctor—you damn well need ten fingers and ten toes to be a ballplayer," barked MacDonald.

"Yes, I guess so," responded Sanchez. He felt like he had patronized MacDonald and now the Texan was slightly irritated with him.

"Doctor. I have to go. I have a meeting with Danton and some of the other scientists. Keep me posted, doctor!" instructed MacDonald.

"Yes, I will." Royston's abrupt departure worried Sanchez.

⊘ ⊘ ⊘ ⊘

Emilio stopped by Teresa's room to say hello after his shift was over. He thought the world of her and knew she was bored with the room, and with the pregnancy. She was now getting more uncomfortable with the extra weight. The baby would sometimes position himself on a nerve. It was suggested by the medical staff, that it was probably the broad ligament that supports the uterus that the baby had decided to park himself on. She had discussed the occasional discomfort with Dr. Sanchez and there was little they could do to relieve the pressure.

Teresa was sitting in the chair when he entered her room. Uncomfortable, she moved from side to side and even tried to shift the baby by pushing her abdomen with her hands. Samuel was determined to remain comfortable on Teresa's nerves. "Is the baby boxing with you again, Teresa?" asked Emilio with concern.

"Yes, he doesn't want to move off that spot and it sometimes hurts. I'll be OK," she said with assurance. She shifted her position one more time and the baby kicked. She laughed at his rejection of her rearrangement. "There!" she said with a smile, "I think it is better now. He's comfortable—and now, I'm comfortable."

Emilio smiled gently. He could see that her smile was special. She was a beautiful woman when she was not in pain from the uncomfortable position of the baby.

"Here!" he said as he passed her a large paper bag. "This is from my garden—my trees," he said with a smile.

"Thank you, Emilio. How did you know I like this fruit? You amaze me with your kindness and thoughtfulness."

He responded, "It was nothing—some oranges, grapefruit and avocados. There are plenty more for me at home."

"Really?" she added. "It looks like you picked the whole tree for me," she laughed out loud. "I hope there are some left for *you!*"

Teresa was impressed with his kindness and stepped into the kitchen to get a knife to slice a grapefruit and orange. The oranges were blood red inside and the grapefruit was pink and sweet. She was in heaven.

Emilio always reminded her to take her vitamins. It was as if he was the father of the baby. He rented a room north of the city in Poway. It was a ride from La Jolla, but it did not bother him very much. Teresa wanted to see where he lived. He claimed that there were dozens of fruit trees there; an old established orchard. She thought that he might take her there after the baby was born. They had coffee and pastries on the patio and chatted about their homeland. It turned out that Emilio knew of her parents' restaurant in Puerto Nuevo. He had once run a cleaning service near there and used to clean the old mission across from the restaurant. Oddly enough, it was the same mission where Teresa was baptized.

Each day, Emilio and Teresa's friendship deepened. He brought her gifts practically each day he worked. She looked forward to his visits and conversations since they had much in common and enjoyed each other's company.

Emilio was not surprised when Teresa shared her story with him. He did not criticize her for carrying another person's child, especially for money. He was more sympathetic to the fact that the parents were killed in the crash. She mentioned that the mother was finally allowed to expire when the respirator was turned off.

Emilio did not question Teresa's motives or ethics in the surrogate matter. He knew well that her family in Mexico was struggling to put food on their table. Teresa was kind of a martyr to him. He actually commended her for taking on the added responsibility of the new child that was near term.

"You are a brave woman," he said to her thoughtfully. "You have friends that will certainly help you when the time comes. I will be happy to help you, too."

"Emilio, you are a fine person for thinking of me so much. You always bring me nice things. It means so much to me."

"Teresa, it is easy for me to help. I would only go home to nothing but myself. *You*, Teresa, give me something to look forward to."

She smiled gently at him and realized that he was an honest and generous person. He left shortly thereafter but promised to stop by again in a day or so. It was dusk and the golfers were done. Teresa sat in the cool evening air and watched the sun going down in the west. She could hear laughter from the lounge on the golf course. The golfers were drinking beer and telling stories again. The stories were of their wonderful golf shots from the day. It happened every night about that time. It would continue until 11:00 P.M. or midnight.

The following morning, at 9:30, Teresa ventured to the pool on the grounds of the inn and rested on a wooden lounge chair. There was no one else there that early in cool morning air. The pool attendant had just cleaned the filter and vacuumed the pool bottom. He soon departed the area. With the clink of the gate lock, he was on to other chores.

Teresa stared at the blue lane lines at the bottom of the pool. The surrounding trees and palms reflected in the shimmering water. It was mesmerizing.

I feel terrible, she thought. *The baby is quiet this morning.* Normally, the baby was active at this hour. The longer she stared at the lane lines, the more ill she felt. She began to sweat, but it wasn't from the heat of the day. She felt a wave of nausea and came very close to vomiting. She looked up and straight ahead to ward off the nausea. Staring at the pool bottom gave her vertigo.

Teresa headed back to her room and quickly called the clinic. The phone number was direct to Dr. Sanchez's office.

"Hello," she said, "I am Teresa Cordero. I need to speak to Dr. Sanchez, please."

"I'm sorry, Ms. Cordero, the doctor is in surgery. Can I have someone else help you?"

"Is there a doctor on call? I need to ask him some questions, please."

"Certainly. Can you hold," was the attendant's response. "Dr. Bohta, Dr. Sanchez's partner is on call ma'am." Moments seemed like minutes to Teresa.

"Hello, this is Dr. Bohta. May I help you, Teresa?"

"Doctor, the baby has not moved much this morning and I feel ill. I almost threw up a few minutes ago and I am concerned." Teresa spoke with anxiety, "I don't know if something is wrong, or if it's just nerves."

"We are sending a car to pick you up. We will be there shortly. I will come myself. Please lie down until we get there. Please drink a glass of water and wait for us."

Bohta let Dr. Sanchez know of the phone call and Sanchez was nearly finished with surgery. He asked someone else to close the incision and he would be there to assist Teresa if she needed any emergency medical treatment.

Dr. Bohta was quick to get to Torrey Pines. He and a clinic security guard used the fertility clinic car that resembled a police car. They would make rapid time in the emergency-looking vehicle.

Bohta was familiar with her charts and her records. MacDonald insisted that all staff be aware of Teresa Cordero and this particular pregnancy. Once he arrived, he felt that she should come into the clinic for a more thorough exam. Her heart rate and blood pressure was a bit high and she had a headache. They would analyze her urine for albumin; a potential observation in toxemia of pregnancy, or preeclampsia. There was slight edema in her lower extremities. Bohta knew the clinical signs and quickly had the security guard rush them back to The Clinic at Torito Bay. Dr. Bradshaw of the reproductive group would be brought in as well. The symptoms were clear.

Was she rejecting the fetus, or was this a transient, abnormal incident? he wondered.

Sanchez and Bradshaw greeted her at the clinic and went behind closed doors in examining room number 1. They questioned her about her morning; what she had eaten and what she had to drink. They also asked her about any unusual activity or exercise. The baby showed no signs of fetal distress as yet and his movements were normal.

"I see nothing wrong at the moment, Teresa. The baby's vitals are OK. Are you feeling better?" she was asked.

"Yes, Dr. Sanchez, the nausea has gone away and the headache is less intense," she replied, reassuringly.

"That is good, my dear—that is good to hear." Sanchez whispered to her, "I think you'll be OK. That was a scare. Sometimes Teresa, the mother is poisoned by the child. It is foreign protein to the mother. If this happens late in pregnancy, it sometimes means that the baby must be removed by cesarean section to get the mother's elevated blood pressure down."

"Doctor, you are scaring me." She cried out, "The baby is not ready yet. He still has a month to go!"

"Teresa," he reassured her, "if we needed to deliver the baby, it would be OK. Young Samuel is eight months and healthy. This would not be a problem. If necessary, we have pediatric specialists and incubators to help him. Samuel is fine. His heart rate is fine, and your blood pressure is back to normal. Sometimes these things happen."

Teresa was silent. She was tired from all the commotion and the conversation. Little did she know that Royston was contacted and was well aware of the situation. He would await Sanchez's call back. The impromptu surgical team and surgical suite was no longer on call. Sanchez had ordered it staffed, and at the ready, if needed. Code Blue, an internal, staff emergency team, was no longer needed.

Emilio had stopped by Teresa's room, only to find that Teresa was nowhere to be found. He was gravely concerned and checked her room each hour. She did not return that evening.

Where could she be? he wondered. It was not like her to just disappear. He could not sleep that night. He would go to work early the next day and check out her room again.

Teresa, at Dr. Sanchez's recommendation, spent the night at the clinic. The urinalysis came back negative for albumin. She was not preeclamptic, otherwise she would have experienced serious seizures and there would be a profound effect on her and the baby.

Teresa returned to Torrey Pines the next day, and was ordered to have strict bed rest. She was to remain quiet for a couple of days. She had no desire to go anywhere anyway. She avoided the pool area and kept her shades drawn on the windows. The drapes by the door were closed to block her view of the golf course. She began thinking about the events that had led up to her episode of nausea—her banned involvement with a man.

As usual, Emilio had stopped by to see her the day before. Neither one had realized that they were slowly falling in love. It was natural. He was so attentive and she was lonely.

"Emilio?" she said quietly.

"Yes, Teresa?" he responded in kind.

"Do you have a friend? I mean—a girlfriend?" she asked, cautiously and without seeming to pry.

"No, not now. I once had one, but she married my friend. I was very, very sad then," he replied almost in tears.

"Where is she now? With him in Mexico? In the U.S.?" she asked, with real concern.

"No . . . she is no longer. . . . I mean she died . . . a while ago . . . in a car accident. Her husband is now alone, too. He lives in Mexico. He was drunk and they went down a ravine. He killed her, by drinking too much."

He looked out the patio doorway, and away from Teresa. There were tears in his eyes. The sniffles gave it away, and she hugged him as best she could.

"Emilio, I am so sorry. I didn't mean to pry. You must have loved her a lot," Teresa said sadly.

"I did Teresa, I did! She is in heaven now. . . . Away from him. . . . God took her home," he said, emotionally, then walking to the bathroom for a tissue.

"Emilio, could you ever fall in love again?" she asked him anxiously.

"I already have, Teresa. More love than I thought I could have."

"Oh," she said, sadly, "with whom?"

Emilio noted her bowed head and said, "Teresa, I'm in love with you. I have fallen in love with you," he repeated.

"Oh Emilio, you are so caring. You have looked after me for two months now. It is sad because I am with child—someone else's child," as she walked away and stood with her back to him.

"That is OK, Teresa. I love you anyway. You are a nice person to carry this child, especially for someone else," he spoke reassuringly.

"I wish I had a loving husband to help me raise this little boy. He will need a father in time," she cried.

Emilio sat silently. He was in love with the beautiful young Mexican woman right in front of him; a woman who was pregnant and unwed. He walked over to her and hugged her. She leaned her head into his shoulder and held him close. The baby separated them but they were still able to embrace.

Emilio's shift at the kitchen was over for the day. He would visit with her that evening. He had nowhere to go and didn't want to leave her, even for a minute. At one point during his visit, she had the incredible desire to make love to him. She needed to feel like a woman. She had no one in her life and Emilio was special. She had heard that pregnant women enjoy sex even more. She knew her desire was real that evening and she passionately kissed him. He responded in kind. She was embarrassed to undress in front of him. She knew her belly was large at this point but it did not matter.

Emilio was slow and gentle with her. He did not want to harm the baby. Intercourse in the later months could induce labor. Her most comfortable position was on all fours, or on her side, with him behind her. He satisfied her needs.

"Oh my God, Emilio, you feel wonderful. I had forgotten how it felt," she cried out. She covered her mouth with her hand as she experienced orgasm. He followed in short time. She then lay back on the bed with him beside her. She was exhausted but so pleased by him. Her face was red from delight and he was sweating. She kissed him gently and thanked him. She knew he was equally satisfied.

Under the most unusual circumstances, they had found one another, and they were now both in love. Had she not stayed at Torrey Pines, she probably would not have met him.

As she lay there on her back, the baby was quiet and sedated. It did not move. It seemed natural that the baby was quiescent. The baby had just taken a "Disney-like ride" in the dark; sort of a Space Mountain experience. Both Emilio and Teresa laughed at the fact that the baby was quiet.

"He's moving again," she said quietly, "Can you see him kick?" she asked with a smile.

"Yes, he's a boy all right—a real soccer player with that kick. I have always wanted a child, Teresa, a little boy."

"You will have your little boy, Emilio. You will have one. God will bless you with a boy," she assured him.

Emilio went home to Poway that evening.

Once Emilio had found out that she had gone to the hospital, he was concerned that *he* had caused the medical problem by the pool—the nausea and the headache that she had experienced. Teresa avoided mentioning to the doctors that she had sex the night before. That was forbidden in the surrogate mother's contract. Anything that might initiate a premature delivery of the baby would be taboo. Fortunately, the problem she experienced was unrelated to the sex act. The doctors were unsure of the reason for her preeclampsic-like syndrome but they would keep an eye on her in the next couple of weeks. Their diagnosis was temporary dehydration.

The doctors assured Royston MacDonald that Teresa was OK. Sanchez would check on her the following day.

MacDonald had retired for the evening after hearing of her episode. He was restless, but deep in sleep. He tossed and turned, and snored loudly from his enormous size—especially when he slept on his back.

Thirty-nine

With a final push and grimace, the newborn emerged into the new world with a hearty wail. The cord had wrapped around his neck, but he was not in jeopardy.

"Is he OK, doctor?" Teresa cried out. The baby was only partially out and could not be easily seen from her position on her back. Sterile disposable drapes surrounded her groin and under her buttocks. The expression on the doctor's face could not be seen from behind the surgical mask. The cord was cut rapidly and the baby whisked away to the anteroom. Nursing assistants left her side and headed for the room adjacent to the delivery table. The surgical lights blinded Teresa. Her main view was the ceiling, however, with the wailing she knew that the baby was delivered.

She felt almost alone there. No one seemed to be with her, at least within her view.

"What?" she screamed. "What is wrong? What is wrong with the baby?" she said in a panic. "Where is my baby?" she cried out. Teresa was delirious from the people scurrying about her. A nurse returned to her side.

"Wait a moment, dear. The doctor will be right back," a nurse assured her. The nurse grasped Teresa's hand tightly. "He'll be right here, dear. Just wait." The nurse's surgical mask of blue was now loosely around her neck. She smiled at Teresa and held her hand tightly. The lights in the ceiling now shown down on her pelvic area. The placenta still needed to be delivered.

"Is he OK? Is the baby OK? Where is the doctor? Dr. Sanchez! Where are you?" she screamed.

"Relax. Please, Teresa. The doctor is nearby. We have things under control," the nurse said, trying to console her.

Just then the doctor reemerged from the anteroom and informed Teresa that there was a problem with the baby. He was perturbed.

"What problem?" she asked with tears flowing. "Is the baby dead? Did the baby die? Tell me!" she demanded with eyes wide open.

"Shut up!" the doctor said forcefully. "The baby is not dead! The baby is missing some limbs. This sometimes happens," he said to her sternly. "Do you take drugs? Did you take drugs at any time? Ones that were not prescribed?" He demanded an answer.

"No, doctor. Honestly, I have done nothing wrong! I tell you. I did nothing wrong! Oh, my baby!"

"The baby's arms are missing, Teresa. We have seen this with some mothers that were exposed to certain drugs. It is similar to the effects of a drug known as Thalidomide," he added with a stern look.

"I have taken nothing doctor—only the prenatal vitamins that you told me to take," Teresa cried out, as the placenta was delivered.

"The ultrasound showed it was OK. Why are there no arms?" she screamed. "Oh, my poor little boy . . . no arms!"

"Damn it Teresa! You fucked up. You screwed the baby up!" Sanchez screamed at her. "You have ruined my fame, the Nobel prize. You bitch!"

At that very moment, Royston sat up abruptly! He was sweating profusely and his heart was racing. He was shaking from fear, and gasping for breath. He startled himself with the *dream* that he had just experienced. *A baby with no arms!* he thought. *His baseball player, Samuel—with no arms!*

He sat on the edge of the bed. His hands rested on each side and supported his huge frame. He was in his T-shirt and underwear. His head hung low in the dark. The clock on the night table flashed to a new setting. It was a red digital glow of 4:03 A.M.

"Shit," he said. "I can't believe I dreamt that," he mumbled to himself. "For Christ's sake!" he continued, "what a horrible fucking dream."

He was nauseated from the nightmare and headed for the bathroom. He did not throw up, but he was sick from the scenario that his subconscious brain had fabricated. *It was a dream from hell,* he thought. *A baby—with no arms? His DNA Nobel prize, award-winning, Ted baby!* The nightmare was so real that Royston was in a stupor. He could picture the child with no arms. *Sure, there were ballplayers with disabilities,* he thought. *Pete Gray and Jim Abbott had similar problems and were successful. But not Ted Williams!*

"Ted needed both arms to bat, dammit!" he murmured. *This is Ted Williams number two in Teresa's belly, not any third-rate ballplayer!*

The earlier emergency medical problems with Teresa had probably precipitated the nightmare for Royston. He was stressed-out by the fact that she had the problem by the pool and had to be checked out at the clinic.

He leaned back against the pillow and thought for a moment. *What if there is a problem when she delivers in a month?*

If so, it would affect cloning research for years. It would make him the laughing stock in the business. There would be no Nobel prize, no notoriety, no fame. He dabbed his face with tissues from the nightstand. The sweat had poured out of him, from the nightmare. He was disgusted with the sweat ball on the end of his nose. The sheets were soaked from perspiration and he could no longer lie back down.

Royston rationalized that everything was OK. There was no need to call Sanchez to see if there was an issue. Besides, Sanchez would think he had lost his mind. MacDonald would only share his dream with Jack Danton the next day. He could be trusted not to tell anyone, and Royston needed to tell *somebody.* No longer able to sleep, he poured himself a drink from the mini-bar in his room. He would have two at 4:30 in the morning. He thought of reading a book to take his mind off the nightmare. The book would *not* be the current Stephen King novel that he had started reading. He grabbed a magazine instead, which contained an excerpt of a book on Joe DiMaggio's career.

Teresa Cordero lay in her bed in her room at Torrey Pines. It was 4:15 A.M. and she was comfortably asleep. The nightmare that Royston had experienced was not even close to the real life scenario at Torrey Pines. She and the baby were asleep.

The third trimester is the major growth phase for the baby and all twenty digits—two arms and two legs were doing what they were supposed to do. In the darkness of the amniotic fluid, Samuel was in the characteristic prenatal position with one thumb near his mouth. He only kicked once or twice, a feeling that would not wake his mother.

$$\oslash \oslash \oslash \oslash$$

Jack Danton reflected on the fact that there was a woman carrying the first cloned human. It was during a meditative moment that the accomplishment finally hit him. He had the science background. He was trained in physiology and understood the genetics of the situation and accomplishment to date. Ethically, he had some concern over the total implication of the research. *After all, it is one thing to clone a cow or sheep,* he thought, *but cloning a human who resides in Florida, seems like a final step in the evolution of man.* It was one thing to create replacement organs or parts that might be needed to cure disease or replace an organ that was damaged. It was another thing to actually create a total new being.

On one occasion when Royston MacDonald had gone back to Texas for a few days, Jack Danton met with Dr. Robert Johnson from the forensic lab. He rarely saw much of Johnson as part of the team, but Johnson had helped in the extraction of DNA from the hair samples. The ethical quandary that Jack questioned could be discussed with Johnson—in private. Jack could not discuss the project with Fawn. That was a Royston MacDonald mandate! But, he still needed someone to bounce his concerns off; someone from the research team. Jack would meet with Robert Johnson one evening.

"Bob," he said shyly, "what will be the implication of this, now that someone is pregnant with a human clone? Does that bother you?"

"No, not really," replied Johnson without reservation. "Why? Does it bother you that we were successful to date?"

"Don't know," replied Jack, "but it was on my mind. It's a massive step forward in science. I suppose that some people would take issue with what we are doing."

"Jack, you knew it would happen. With all the success in Massachusetts and in Scotland with farm animals, you just had to know that it would happen, in time."

"Yes, I figured all those steps would lead to something someday, but now *it has happened* and we are part of that success. It is scary to think that *man* has been created without help from above," Jack replied with a furrowed brow. "This isn't a farm animal. It is a human, and a *special* human, at that!"

"You're right, Jack boy. You're right! This is a powerful step forward. It is the equivalent of Neil Armstrong stepping onto the moon in July of 1969. It had to happen. If we didn't accomplish it, someone else would have. Ya know?"

Jack responded with, "I guess it was in the cards, so to speak."

"All in all, it was a miraculous accomplishment, Jack. The cards were dealt when they cloned the first mouse. It was just a matter of time. Once DNA was discovered, it became feasible."

"I guess you're right, Bob. It's just so incredible that a cell could be modified to do this."

Bob interjected, "It's not all that novel, you know!"

"What the hell do you mean, not that novel?"

Bob took a sip of his beer. "Really? Look at twinning. Look at identical twins! Cloning is natural in many ways. Identical twins have the same genetics. The same egg splits into two people who are exactly the same as each other. It is only the environment and how they are raised that makes them a bit different. People twin all the time and that my friend is a natural clone!"

"Guess you're right," replied Jack. "This clone, however, is a twin born eighty years later! That to me is different. If the original person had a disease or propensity for a disease, so will this child! Maybe that makes it unethical if we create a person and know roughly what he or she might die of later in life."

"Not really, Jack, the clone might be killed in a car crash rather than whatever the original might have had! Relax."

"OK, OK, Bob. But we do know that Ted Williams had a stroke or two. The new kid will have the same genetics and the potential for cardiovascular disease, right?"

"Maybe, Jack boy. Maybe you are right! We probably won't be around to hear about it."

They both laughed and ordered another beer and a burger at the café. They were sitting outside of the restaurant on Fifth Avenue in the Gas Lamp District. It was a Friday night and many people were milling along the street next to their table. Bob and Jack would catch some of the conversations of passersby and joke about them. The café was a great place for people-watching.

Occasionally a street person would stop by the café and beg for change. The waist-high fence did not stop the homeless from asking for handouts from restaurant patrons seated next to the sidewalk.

"Spare change, please?" the desperate man asked Jack. "Spare change?" he repeated with his hand across the fence and almost in Jack's face. Jack gave the guy a dollar. "Thank you," the man said as he shuffled off.

"Ya know, Jack, that dude makes 30K a year from saps like you," Bob Johnson said sternly.

"What do you mean 30K? The guy is desperate! Just look at his clothes," he said defensively.

Johnson fired back, "He does! He makes some serious money here. Tax free, my boy."

"You're kidding, right?" asked Jack.

"Nope. He makes quite a nice little bundle from this street alone. I've seen him before. I saw the same guy last week down near Dick's Last Resort, a few blocks south of here. He was in a wheelchair that night. The bastards switch off and a new guy sits and wheels along the sidewalk."

"You're kiddin'!" said Jack, shocked. "You mean they fake the disability thing and then walk away, all the richer?"

"Yep, you been had, dude! It was a kind thought, but save your change for the parking meter."

"That scumbag!" replied Jack. "How could he do that?"

"Easy. No one wants to work today. They want the buck the easiest way they can get it!" added Johnson.

"I want my friggin' dollar back!" Jack said feeling stupid.

"Too late, Jack! He's gone."

Jack was amazed by the fact that not all these people were destitute or deprived. He had always thought that the Boston homeless were for real. Now he questioned them and the San Diego homeless, as well.

Jack shifted the conversation back to the earlier discussion. "So Bob, you're an expert at this DNA stuff. Do you think the baby will come out normal? I mean, Teresa's in her eighth month and doing well it seems, but who really knows? I suppose some fetal anomalies could occur later on, right?" asked Jack.

"Don't foresee any problems, Jack—certainly not at this time. The ultrasound looks good. The kid looks fine. Hey, did you catch that? I called him *the kid!*"

"Yeah," laughed Jack. "Williams was known as 'The Kid.' That was cute, Bob."

"Hang on—look at that chick. Is she fine or what?" Bob commented about a passerby.

"Mighty fine!" replied Jack. "This town of San Diego is loaded with that stuff!"

They finished their beers and burgers and requested the tab for their meals. Jack covered the expense since it was basically a business discussion. He was pleased that Bob was willing to discuss his concerns over the ethics of Project Samuel.

"Hey, we better get goin'. It's gettin' late and I need to get home," said Bob. "Jack, do you feel better about this whole thing?"

"Guess so," replied Jack. "It's only a twin, right? But hell it's Ted Williams, for Christ's sake! Not just some ordinary Joe like you or me!"

"Yeah, that's true," said Bob. "It's not some regular guy. If this kid grows up to be Ted all over again, perhaps he'll beat Ted's records from the '40s and '50s. You know, Jack, Ted lost many years of ball playing during WWII and the Korean War."

As they walked down Fifth Avenue toward their cars, Bob added, "Had the man been able to play during those years, he may have easily established records more difficult to surpass than the ones he did set. As it was, he achieved a single season with a batting average of over .400. So far, no one has matched that record!"

"You're right. He might have hit more than 521 home runs, as well," Jack surmised. "No problem. Maybe Samuel will play for the Red Sox someday and beat his 'twin's' record!"

Bob laughed, "You've been drinking too much, Jack. Time to get home."

"Catch you later, Bob, and thanks again," Jack said as he unlocked his car with the remote security device. It made a *beep-beep* sound as he approached the door.

"Keep the faith, Jack," Bob added from the next parking space. "I'll be talkin' to ya."

"Have a nice trip home, Bob. Maybe we can do this again. It was fun to hang out with you," Jack replied. "I'll call you next week."

Both men headed home to their wives. Jack felt better. He no longer saw the project as a complex, ethical question. *After all,* he thought to himself, *it wasn't Charles Manson, Hitler or Bundy that they had cloned. It was Ted Williams, the most famous Red Sox player of all time. It was—The Kid.*

Forty

Teresa, at eight months pregnant, was patiently awaiting the arrival of the baby. She was increasingly uncomfortable and the fetus was becoming more active. She was sitting alone in her room at Torrey Pines Inn when the phone rang. A friend called her to say that a local newspaper in San Diego was touting the fact that a human cloning study was in progress in a fertility clinic in the area. The clinic was in La Jolla and her friend knew that Teresa was in a surrogate pregnancy program in a La Jolla clinic. The coincidence of the details was frightening to her friend. The article was preliminary, but hinted that the mad scientist doctors were possibly creating monster children. Rumors had surfaced to the local press.

Frightened by the call, Teresa decided to phone Dr. Sanchez immediately. *A cloned child? A local clinic in La Jolla? What was a cloned child?* she wondered as she dialed.

"This is Dr. Sanchez, Teresa. Is there something wrong?"

"No, doctor, nothing wrong with me, but, my friend called to tell me of a clinic in La Jolla creating monster children. She talked of them cloning a person. . . . What is cloning?"

Sanchez was taken back by the conversation and wanted more details of what her friend had said. He was shocked by her information, and could not understand how there had been a "leak."

"The newspaper talked of a clinic out this way. That they were experimenting with humans—human babies," she added cautiously. "Is that true, doctor? Do you know of anyone doing this?"

Sanchez was silent. He was caught totally off-guard. His mind raced as to how a leak would have gotten out. He was not prepared to tell her of Project Samuel. They had misled her all along regarding the origin of the egg and the ultimate goal of the surrogate pregnancy. He was now on the spot.

"Teresa, what are you talking about?" he hedged.

"Teresa, I need to go. I have been paged and need to respond," he lied, speaking softly. "I will get back to you, dear. I'll call you this afternoon."

Sanchez stared at the wall. Who would have discussed the project with the press? How would a reporter find anything out about the project? Everyone was sworn to secrecy concerning Project Samuel. It could not have been a senior member of the team, he felt.

Teresa called her friend back to ask which paper the story was in. After getting the name of the newspaper, she went to the lobby and asked for a copy. There were various papers on the coffee table. The *La Jolla Journal* had the article on page 1A:

LA JOLLA AREA CLINIC IMPLICATED IN HUMAN CLONING RESEARCH!

It went on to say that other local biotech companies were hiding research in cloning; the cloning of the first human. A reporter had received a call from an animal activist, and member of the APS (Animal Protection Society). The person had infiltrated the biotech company as an employee and had video of the animal research in mice. The reporter's calls to the clinic and to local hospitals for verification turned up nothing.

The article continued: "the pregnant woman is being secretly held in La Jolla. The woman harboring the first cloned human is suspected of being of Mexican descent."

The article went on to say that the successful pregnancy was generated from years of research on small rats and mice. The experiments were genetic alterations of animals, which offended APS members. The APS Web site became a billboard of the cloning issue. "Many animals have died in the attempt to create a human life," the article continued, quoting an APS member. The article emphasized that the clinic—The Torito Bay Fertility Clinic—would be the target of an APS protest.

Teresa sat in the chair in the lobby. The newspaper draped over her lap slid off because of her expanded stomach. A recently hired desk clerk picked it up for her and noticed that she was forlorn.

"Ma'am," he said, "are you OK?"

Teresa looked up, but said nothing. She was paralyzed by the words "Torito Bay" and the phrase "woman of Mexican descent." She aptly fit the description. The desk clerk became concerned and mentioned the woman's response to his staff.

◔ ◔ ◔ ◔

Dr. Sanchez paged the senior staff team, Royston and Jack Danton. The page was urgent. He paced in his office at the clinic. He needed to talk to Royston MacDonald immediately, and to Teresa as well. She would expect a call back and he knew she was under stress. Stress could affect her and the baby.

Royston called from The Del and Jack from a golf course. All agreed to meet immediately at the Torito Bay Clinic where there was a private conference room.

Royston was shocked and devastated by the leak, and its potential damage to the program. He had the concierge at The Del get him the newspaper in question. The bellman gave it to him as he left the hotel and entered the waiting limo. Inside the car, Royston was out of breath and experiencing chest pains, which he did not relate to the driver. Max could see that Royston was in distress over something.

"Fuckin' APS!" Max heard him murmur in the back. "Who is the cunning little bastard that got into Mesa Biotech and shot his or her mouth off?" he sputtered as he read. "Some damn college student at Torreyana?"

Royston cocked his head back in the rear seat and closed his eyes during the ride. He called no one and spoke to no one. Someone on his staff had squealed about *the project. Who wanted the world to know the secret of the first human clone?* His mind was spinning. *What if the rest of the press got the word? The TV stations? The research community?*

He would be dead meat, and so would his business, Mesa's and the clinic's. *What about his chance for the Nobel prize? Damn!* he thought. *There it all goes.* His head was pounding. His blood pressure was up so he took a Cardura to knock it down. He grabbed a glass of water from the decanter in the back of the limo and took a second tablet. Max remained silent. He had never seen Royston so angry and upset. Something awful must have happened, he surmised.

Royston guessed that it was not a senior scientist that had caused the problem—a technician perhaps, but not a senior scientist such as Blackburn, Bradshaw or Johnson. Technicians were known to be APS "plants" in research organizations. They were often hired under false pretenses, then brought in cameras, videos and audio recording devices to record procedural errors and potential mistreatment of the lab animals. Most films were doctored later to look worse than they actually were.

Was it a caretaker of the vivarium/animal facility, a cage washer, or a technician who knew of the DNA injection technique? wondered the stupefied Royston.

∅∅∅∅

Teresa Cordero returned to her room at Torrey Pines. The walk from the front lobby to the darkened and dreary hallways seemed to take forever. Part of the walk was outside of the buildings, but the fragrant flowers near the pool meant nothing to her today. She figured that the newspaper article was talking about her but she had no idea what it meant. *What was cloning, anyway?* she thought. *Was she carrying an altered monster child that she had been told was normal? If cloning was evil, what had she gotten herself into? Why had Sanchez not called her back?*

Teresa's friend had called her again after consulting her home medical encyclopedia. The definition of a clone frightened Teresa immensely. The description "of an individual derived from a single cell and identical to the parent" made her nauseated. She had no idea what that meant. She never took a biology class, nor knew the specifics of a cell. She immediately thought of an experimental monster inside of her.

Teresa's friend tried to calm her down, but Teresa was crying. Her abdomen became hard from her fright, and she was breathing heavily and more rapidly. Anxiety had set in because she had not heard back from Dr. Sanchez.

Five minutes later she began experiencing hard painful contractions. They occasionally went from high in her belly to low. She timed their frequency as she remembered reading about in her copy of the popular book *What to Expect When You Are Expecting.* They were not Braxton-Hicks contractions that sporadically appear during the latter stages of the third trimester. *These are real,* she thought. She decided to lie down, and would call her friend back if nothing changed.

Emilio was working in the inn's kitchen, and his shift would not end until early evening. Teresa rested and was still scared by the phone call from her friend and her eyes were red from crying. The contractions continued at ten minutes apart and increased in intensity. Thirty-five minutes later there was wetness between her legs. It was ever so slight and she thought she had urinated on herself. Shortly thereafter there was a gush of fluid. It was a bit cloudy and had smatterings of blood in it. She sat up staring at her thigh area and was shocked by the amount of fluid that had saturated the bed. *Her water had broken!* she thought. *This means labor!* She knew the scenario from the book about pregnancy. This meant she was delivering!

She called her friend back and Teresa was hysterical.

"Calm down, Teresa. . . . Please calm down. I will help you!" said the friend. "How far apart are the contractions?" she asked.

Teresa was in severe discomfort and was crying again. She did not know how dilated her cervix was, but it was enough to allow for the amniotic fluid to flow. The cervix was not "ripened" for delivery. Her friend told her that she would call her back immediately, and for her to stay calm.

Three minutes passed.

In the distance, Teresa could hear sirens and they were getting louder. Her friend had hung up on her to call 911 and had the good sense to mention Teresa's room number. Her friend had also alerted the hotel front desk of the problem, which resulted in two employees running down the darkened hallway to Teresa's room to assist her. A threesome of golfers on the ninth hole saw the commotion of hotel staff running into the patio area and one golfer, a physician, came over to assist. He calmed Teresa until the rescue squad arrived moments later.

The paramedics rushed their gurney in and out of the room. One was on the radio with a local emergency room and an IV was started in Teresa's left arm. If medications were needed in transit to the hospital, the IV route was the easiest way to administer them. Dextrose and water was dripping into her arm. She was somewhat dehydrated. At eight months pregnant, she could have the child without much concern the EMTs thought. A critical factor was whether the fetus was in distress from being thrust against a cervix that was not relaxed enough to facilitate delivery. Hard labor against a stiffened cervix was not desired during parturition. In critical cases, labor might need to be arrested by the administration of a uterine relaxant drug, or an emergency cesarean might be needed at the hospital.

The EMT noted that Teresa's blood pressure was elevated. Conversations between the ambulance crew and the local E.R. doctor surmised that she was possibly preeclamptic, in shock or in premature labor. Her blood pressure needed to be lowered immediately. The rescue vehicle was a minute from the hospital and her condition and vital signs seemed to be more stable.

Emilio had heard the sirens from the restaurant area, and noticed flashing lights out the side of the kitchen window of the inn. He knew that the emergency personnel rushing to that hotel were heading toward the area of Teresa's room. Sensing that she might be in trouble, Emilio took off his dishwasher's apron and threw it in the washtub where he was scrubbing pots and pans. He slipped on the greasy floor as he ran out a screen door. He hit the pebbled area outside the door and one knee slid on the grass. He was out of shape and panting as he saw the gurney being placed in the back of the ambulance, about fifty yards away. Teresa saw him from afar and gestured slowly with her left arm. The attendant asked her to keep the arm still. The IV was in that arm. The door to the emergency vehicle was closed quickly and the ambulance headed for the exit onto Torrey Pines Boulevard.

Emilio stood in silence as the flashing red and white strobe lights of the ambulance became smaller in the distance. He knew she was in trouble but did not know why. In all the confusion, he prayed for her.

After a few moments, Emilio went to her patio and room. The door was still open and the curtains in the doorway were moving gently in the breeze. Inside the room were a hotel attendant and a front desk clerk. They were changing the bed linens and Emilio could see moisture on the white bed sheets.

"Is she OK—the woman who was here? Is she OK?" he asked, sadly.

"We think so, Emilio. She apparently went into labor a little while ago. They think she is ready to have the baby," one woman responded.

"Baby? She can't have it now . . . too early!" he blurted out in a panic.

"Do you know her, Emilio? How do you know that it is too early— too early for the baby?"

Emilio stammered at the question. "I don't know . . . I mean I saw her once. She told me she . . . she . . . was not due till next month," he said, trying to sound calm.

"Oh?" asked the desk clerk, who looked at the maid on duty and shrugged his shoulders. They finished the cleanup and secured the door.

A minute after the hotel staff left Teresa's room, the cell phone that Royston had given Teresa, rang on the night table.

"I can't reach her," Dr. Sanchez said to MacDonald. "There isn't any answer there," he said in dismay.

"Dammit! Try the front desk!" screamed Royston. "She has to be there!"

The phone rang at the inn lobby. "Torrey Pines Inn, please hold!" was the response.

"No! I can't hold. Connect me to the Cordero room! This is an emergency!"

The attendant was shocked by the caller's demands.

"This is Dr. Sanchez, Teresa Cordero's obstetrician! Please connect me immediately! Do *not* . . . put me on hold!"

"Doctor, I'm sorry, Ms. Cordero is not there. I can't connect you, sir. You may leave a voice-mail in her room if you wish."

"Where is she? I don't want voice-mail. I want her!" he shouted into the mouthpiece.

"Doctor, she was taken by ambulance to the local hospital. She was in apparent labor, we believe," the clerk said with apprehension.

"Labor? Hospital? What hospital?" demanded Sanchez. "This is *my* patient! Where the hell have they taken her? *I am* her doctor! Who took her, and where?"

"I don't know, sir," the clerk said shaking. "It was a 911 call and an ambulance came. I guess the local La Jolla hospital is where they might go. No one has told us, doctor."

The man at the front desk was battered by more questions and was frustrated by Sanchez's intrusion with the operation of the lobby. People near the desk sensed that he was on the phone with a lunatic customer or a "house complaint."

"I'm sorry, doctor. I can't help you. People are lined up here and I need to attend to . . ."

The doctor had hung up in frustration.

"Where is she?" Royston asked. "Did they say? Which hospital is she in?"

"Don't know—they don't know! I'll find out," Sanchez said.

Royston grabbed the phone from Sanchez's hand. He was pissed that they had not learned anything yet.

"Uh, 911? . . . hello. This is E. Royston MacDonald. I have a question. No . . . this is not an emergency," he said calmly. "I have a friend that was just taken to the hospital from Torrey Pines Inn. Might you know where the ambulance went—which hospital?"

The voice at the other end quickly responded and caught him off guard. "Are you a relative, sir?"

"No! I'm not a relative, dammit! A close friend!" he said by mistake. *He should have said yes to being a relative,* he later thought.

Sensing Royston's frustration, Sanchez tapped Roy's shoulder for the phone.

"I'm Dr. Sanchez from Torito Bay Fertility Clinic. The woman is my patient! Please tell me where she is!"

"Yes, Dr. Sanchez, I know your name. I didn't know you were there. How can I help?"

"Ma'am, thanks. Do you know which hospital received Teresa Cordero?" he asked speaking with a professional tone.

"Doctor, I believe they thought that La Jolla General was closest, and that she was in labor. Do you need me to assist you in anything, doctor?"

"No thank you. If someone should call, I'm on my way to La Jolla General."

"Yes, sir, I copy! Good luck with your patient."

Sanchez hardly heard the last words of the woman's voice on the phone and he and Royston raced to the limo. Royston told Max to hurry. "Head for La Jolla General, Max. Please hurry!"

Max peeled out of the parking area at Torito Bay Clinic and raced toward La Jolla General located in the center of town.

Teresa Cordero screamed in the back of the ambulance. One contraction was severe and her back arched to relieve the tension on her stomach. She requested a painkiller and the emergency medical technician radioed the doctor in the awaiting E.R.

"Doctor, she is requesting some pain relief; the contractions are severe."

The response from the E.R. doctor was to administer a few milligrams of a limited infusion of an analgesic, and a uterine relaxant. It would be added to the dextrose/water IV drip in her arm. They confirmed that the BP was still high and her pulse was racing. An obstetrician on staff at the hospital was paged for the E.R. When the ambulance arrived, there was an emergency response team already in place.

La Jolla General Hospital was also a trauma center, and had immediate access to various types of physicians and specialists. The surgery unit was always prepared for emergencies and a skeleton surgical staff at the ready.

"Where does your husband work, ma'am?" asked an EMT in a soft voice. "We need to let him know where you are."

"I have no husband," she grimaced.

"A relative nearby, perhaps?" he asked.

"No. My immediate family is in Mexico. I only have friends nearby. One of them called you, I believe."

The EMT rechecked her BP and pulse.

"Is the pain going away?" he asked as he adjusted the rate of flow of the IV into her arm.

"Yes," she nodded.

"I am a surrogate mother for an infertile couple," she stuttered. She became very tired from the ride and all the commotion.

"Surrogate?" he responded in amazement. In all his years on the Rescue Squad, he had never run into this scenario of a surrogate pregnancy.

"Wow! You're carrying someone else's child. That is so nice of you to help them," he replied, assuring her that everything would be OK.

"Yes. It is nice." She faded again and almost passed out.

"Please rest, ma'am. We'll be there shortly. One more turn ahead," he said reassuringly.

"Teresa," she said back to him. "I am Teresa."

"OK, Teresa. Hang in there. We are almost there. I can see the hospital from here," he said to her with a smile. She felt secure in his care.

"Emilio? Emilio?" she whimpered quietly. "Please call Emilio. Someone call him," as her voice faded off slowly.

"Emilio?" the EMT recited back. "Teresa. Who is Emilio? Where is he?"

She was now almost asleep and the EMT leaned over to hear her whisper, "The inn, the Torrey Pines Inn. Emilio—kitchen help."

The EMT made a quick note of the information that she had given him. The ambulance was now at the E.R. entrance and backing into position. The door was open and numerous members of the critical care staff were gowned and waiting. Teresa was rushed into the E.R.

Once freed of his responsibilities, the EMT grabbed a cup of coffee from the nurses' station. He called information and then punched in the number for the inn on a pay phone. He would follow through with Teresa Cordero's request. It was the least he could do.

Emilio would be summoned to the front desk of the inn, to respond to an emergency telephone call.

$$\oslash \oslash \oslash \oslash$$

An emergency room doctor ordered the staff to draw 10 cc of Teresa's blood.

"Type and cross-match—*stat!* Get a second IV going—stat!" he commanded the E.R. nurses. Teresa was now under strong observation lights. Stirrups were positioned at the end of the exam table, and her legs were elevated. The obstetrician gently examined her vaginally for cervical dilation. The cervical opening was still small and some uterine contractions were apparent.

The results of the blood work showed she was type A+ with no Rh factor incompatibility. Slight fetal distress was apparent on the fetal monitor. With essentially a nondilated cervix, and occasional contractions, the obstetrician ordered the surgical suite ready and a consultant pediatric pulmonologist brought in. The E.R. physician surmised that if a cesarean section was needed, the baby might have underdeveloped lungs requiring assistance. He did not know her due date; however, he knew that immature fetal lungs often lacked the phospholipids (L/S ratio) necessary for proper lung inflation and normal breathing of a newborn. He would take the precaution of bringing in a pediatric expert.

An ultrasound evaluation showed the baby was inverted, so that it was breech. There was no way that the baby would be delivered naturally in that position—certainly not if it was stressed. The baby's position was causing part of her pain. The head needed to be down and locked in the lower part of the cervix. That would induce natural dilation of the cervical opening. Without the baby locked into position, the cervix would not relax sufficiently to the ten or twelve centimeters needed to deliver Samuel by the vaginal route.

Royston MacDonald and Dr. Sanchez arrived a few minutes after Teresa had undergone the rapid evaluation in the emergency room. Sanchez burst in demanding to see his patient. He was quickly informed that she was upstairs and not in the E.R. The doctor on duty said that a decision had been made by an obstetrician and the chief of staff to perform a cesarean section. Sanchez was flabbergasted. He had been given no prior medical information and had assumed wrongly that Teresa was having some contractions that might dissipate with time.

"You can't do that! She is my patient. I demand to see the doctor in charge and to see my patient, Teresa Cordero!" he shouted unprofessionally. Royston was just as upset and the doctors questioned MacDonald's presence there at all.

"Doctor! Who is this gentleman? I need to speak to you in private. A consult. The other man will need to wait in the lobby." Royston objected loudly to being banished to the lobby of commoners awaiting other patients and refused to leave. A security guard sensed à problem between the men and came over to the attending E.R. physician.

"Doctor, is there a problem here?"

"No, thank you. I have it under control."

The security guard was reluctant to leave the doctor with the two men, but stepped back to observe the situation from a short distance.

At Sanchez's request, the physician finally allowed MacDonald to be included in the briefing on Teresa.

All three men stepped into an annex room, off the E.R. suite.

The doctor was quick to point out that Teresa had come there in dire straights. He updated Sanchez on her blood pressure, contractions and the fetal distress of the baby as assessed by the trauma team.

"Teresa will need emergency surgery to remove the baby by cesarean, doctor. She and the baby's life are threatened as we speak. She is almost eclamptic and a seizure could occur at any time. As attending physician when she came in, I had the finest specialists here ten minutes ago. There is no doubt that she and the baby are stressed. A delivery of the child is taking place right now in the obstetrical surgery unit."

Sanchez and MacDonald were stunned by the apparent crisis at hand. It was not just premature contractions, but a critical situation for both mother and son. It was at that point that Royston asked Sanchez to update the doctor on the surrogate pregnancy.

"Doctor," said Sanchez. "This is no regular pregnancy. It is critical that this child be saved from distress. It is a surrogate pregnancy for another couple. Teresa Cordero is merely the *carrier* of the child."

"Only the *carrier?* Is *that* what you call her? A *carrier?* A woman in her eighth month—whose life is in peril, as we speak!"

Sanchez apologized for his seeming cold and callous description of the mother.

"Doctor, I am sorry. We are all excited by this situation. I was merely letting you know that this is a *prized child* from the Torito Bay Fertility Clinic Program. It is imperative that we see this child born and check the mother," Sanchez said.

The doctor stared both of them down and said with venomous eyes, "All children here are 'prized' as you say, and so, doctor, is the *MOTHER!* I will tell you that in the case of a duel for life at this hospital, the mother's life has priority—a sad rule necessitated by hospital regulations and the internal ethics committee."

Sanchez was upset and said, "Doctor, that child must live, mother or not. She is not even the real genetic mother!"

The E.R. doctor grabbed Sanchez's arm firmly and told him to leave immediately. The guard took notice.

"Guard!" he said firmly through the door left ajar, "Escort these gentlemen out—right now! This doctor is not licensed to practice here, and I don't want him near this hospital or the patient who arrived a few minutes ago!"

"Yes, sir. Gentlemen? You will have to leave right now! Follow me."

Sanchez shoved the guard away and screamed at the E.R. doctor. "Who is the medical director here? Who's in charge? I demand to know! You are holding my patient against her, and my will, and I want to talk to the top man here! I demand it!"

Royston was irritated by everyone's behavior, including Dr. Sanchez, and asked diplomatically if the hospital director could meet with him. He volunteered to wait in the lobby with Sanchez for permission from the hospital director or chief of staff of obstetrics.

The E.R. doctor reminded the two men that he alone was *in charge* of *that* aspect of the facility—the E.R. and all its ramifications. He advised them that they could seek the advice of the director, but they were not to be found anywhere near the delivery room or surgical area.

He then excused himself and headed for surgery. His footsteps echoed on the tile flooring as he abruptly pushed open two swinging doors that lead to the hallway and elevator. The guard led the two men to a courtesy house phone that would get them the operator, and the hospital director. He remained by their sides while they made the call.

$$\oslash \oslash \oslash \oslash$$

Teresa Cordero mumbled under the effects of a presurgical sedative that was now in her cardiovascular system. She was relaxed and barely awake. The pain was less severe and the uterus quiescent for the moment. The uterine relaxant was doing its job and the baby was no longer being driven violently against the stiffened cervix.

A doctor stood beside her gurney in the hallway on the second floor. He awaited permission to enter the surgical suite.

A nurse quickly appeared and said, "Doctor, we are now ready."

"Thank you," he said. "We have no time to waste. Help us here, gentlemen."

Two assistants that were gowned-up in greens, had emerged from the scrub room and wheeled the gurney into the awaiting suite. Gigantic surgical lights were located in the ceiling and shown down on the pregnant woman, and the stainless steel surgical table. Surgeons and surgical nurse assistants surrounded her.

Dr. Bower was the chief obstetrical surgeon, and had been an obstetrician for thirty years. His distinguished-looking white sideburns could be seen behind the green sterile mask. He wore glasses and appeared to be pleasant to Teresa. He had been called in as part of the trauma team.

"Teresa, I'm Dr. Bower. We are going to take good care of you and your baby," he said.

"You have a pretty name," he added trying to relax her even more. He leaned forward and spoke softly, "The reason why you are here in surgery is that your blood pressure is still a concern to us and the baby is showing signs of fetal distress—it needs to come out now. Unfortunately, dear, you are in no position to deliver the baby naturally. Your cervix is not dilated enough for the head and shoulders to pass. The baby is breech as well—rear first. If you did not have the elevated blood pressure we would have tried some drugs to help relax the cervix, but it is too late for that and we will need to do a cesarean section."

She sensed Dr. Bower's fatherly concern for herself and the baby. She guessed that he was probably a grandfather himself.

"Doctor Bower, I am aware of a cesarean. Please don't scar me for life," she said, thinking of her own self-image for a change.

The doctor reassured her that the "bikini cut" he would perform would be low and transverse, as to cross her stomach very low and below the hairline.

"You will still wear bikinis, dear. Not to worry," he joked with her. "No one will see or know you had the procedure," he said reassuringly.

"Teresa," the doctor said, awaiting the anesthesiologist to finish his rapid setup. "Did something happen today that may have caused this emergency?"

"Yes," she replied, "I am scared of the *monster* inside of me!"

"What monster, Teresa? There is no monster inside of you. I saw the ultrasound myself. You have a very normal baby girl in there."

"A baby girl? What?" she said, with eyes wide open and in a panic. It was as if the surgical premedication had worn off.

A nurse overheard the conversation and quickly reminded the doctor that the ultrasound showed *an appendage* in the genital area, and that the baby was definitely a *boy*!

"I mean a boy, Teresa. We've been in a rush and I haven't spent much time reviewing all the tests. The earlier delivery today was a girl. Isn't that correct, nurse?" the doctor said quickly.

Teresa continued to be fixated with the monster idea. "Doctor, this baby may be a monster, the newspaper said so. They said it was a monster, a clone."

Looking at the attending nurse to his right, Dr. Bower was confused. *Clone? Monster? Newspaper? What the hell was this young woman talking about? Did this premedication have a side effect of hallucinations?* he wondered.

Because of the speed at which the baby needed to be removed from her abdomen, the anesthetist would use inhalation anesthesia instead of an epidural injection in her spine. The general anesthesia would be quicker to initiate and Teresa would reach the "surgical plane" of unconsciousness necessary to open the abdomen and uterine wall in a rapid manner. The baby would be removed before any significant concentration of anesthesia could cross the placenta. An epidural injection, on the other hand, might cause the mother to experience some respiratory difficulties if the anesthetic migrated vertically within the spinal fluid. The speed of surgery was now of utmost importance.

Dr. Sanchez and MacDonald paced back and forth in the reception area. The hospital director was still not available. He would finally show up but it would be too late for Sanchez to reach Teresa before surgery commenced two floors above them.

Forty-one

At 7:01 P.M., baby Samuel, the first cloned human, was delivered by cesarean section by Dr. Bower and without the presence of Dr. Sanchez and E. Royston MacDonald. The twenty-two inch, eight-pound four-ounce boy was taken into an examining room to the right of the surgical suite. Dr. Bower had no idea of the ramifications this delivery would have on his obstetrical career. His personal life would also change forever.

Teresa was still anesthetized and would not see the actual birth of Samuel, but the child was totally normal, complete with ten fingers and ten toes. He screamed like any other child and wiggled in the mixture of blood and uterine fluids that emerged when the womb was surgically opened.

Teresa Cordero would remain in surgery to undergo closure of the incisions in the uterus and the abdomen. The process would take another twenty minutes. As promised by Dr. Bower, the abdominal scar would be low and hidden from view.

Teresa's blood pressure returned to normal values shortly after the surgery, but she would be in the recovery room for a couple of hours. She would not be alert enough to see the baby right away.

In the reception and lobby area of the hospital, an Hispanic man arrived through the front entrance. It was some distance from the E.R. or the surgical suite upstairs. He sat there for a few minutes until he got up the courage to see the receptionist. He was afraid to ask for the patient, Teresa Cordero—a new patient in the maternity ward. Emilio

Rosero thought that he recognized the two men near the telephones. He had seen their faces before, but waited for them to move on before approaching the reception desk. He thought it odd that a security guard was standing near them. Emilio read a Latino magazine in the waiting area, and hid his face behind its cover.

Forty-two

The Project Samuel team, the Torito Bay Clinic, the directors of La Jolla General and the San Diego community in general were fast becoming aware of the attention that had been directed to their region of the United States. News and supposition about a cloning project was now spreading across the country. Implications of human cloning research were now widespread. The Associated Press newswire added to the confusion by releasing excerpts of the potential ethical issues, if cloning existed. It was timely for the AP since Britain had just OK'd the use of human cloning "in basic research situations only." Creation of an individual, full-term baby was not approved in the United Kingdom. Even with Samuel in his crib, no one in the news was aware that he actually had been born. Jack Danton would eventually enter Samuel's birth data into the Nobel supportive documents for the annual prize nomination.

The press releases written by the local animal-activists in California had caused the board of directors of the various facilities involved in the controversy to meet separately and then together to handle the newly generated commotion. It involved La Jolla General, the Torito Bay Fertility Clinic and Mesa Biotech. A potential nightmare for Royston's team was being spawned by the news media.

More information from the animal activists was circulating on an Internet site. It claimed that a famous sports figure, supposedly in baseball, was being cloned in a Mexican woman. This piqued the interest of the entire sports world as it spread from sports magazines to celebrity magazines. It was the buzz on network sports TV shows on cable TV. *Who was cloned and where?* The press wondered, *Was it Ruth, Gehrig or someone else?*

Seemingly unaware of the full impact of the news releases, Royston MacDonald and Dr. Sanchez celebrated quietly, after they had been advised by the staff of Samuel's birth. But they had not seen the child yet. They knew that no matter what, a live birth of Samuel meant fame and eventual wealth for them.

Teresa Cordero was still in the recovery room when she awoke. A nurse brought the baby to her. It would be the first opportunity for Teresa to see the baby that she had carried. Dr. Bower would be seeking answers to the news reports that implicated both La Jolla General and now his patient in the historic event.

Dr. Bower had restricted all visitors and photographs of the baby until the controversy was resolved. Only hospital staff were permitted in the room.

"Dr. Bower. Thank you for my beautiful child, Samuel. He looks so normal; as normal as a child can be," she commented with a smile, as he slept in her arms. "He is not a monster, right, doctor? They said he would be a monster. My son is healthy now and I am so happy!" she added with elation.

"Monster, Teresa? You have no monster!" the doctor replied, admiring the child's handsome face.

"Teresa," he said, "You and the baby are doing well, but you know that in surrogate pregnancies, you cannot keep the child that you bore. You really weren't supposed to see him, either. By contract, the child goes to the rightful parents," he added sadly.

Teresa was quick to acknowledge that she knew that; however, she needed to tell Dr. Bower of the car accident. She told him that the biological parents were recently killed in a car crash. Dr. Bower did not remember such a crash and looked confused. *He certainly would have been aware of such a tragedy had there been one in the general San Diego area,* he thought.

"Dr. Bower? Does my doctor, Dr. Sanchez, know of the baby being born and delivered by cesarean?" she asked. "Does he know of Samuel? He is my doctor at the fertility clinic."

"Yes, Teresa. Actually, they are here and wish to see you. Dr. Sanchez and another gentleman have been waiting for news of the birth for quite some time. They were very anxious and caused some commotion downstairs. I had to restrict your visitors due to the fact that you required emergency surgery, and isolated recovery," he informed her.

"Was the other man, Mr. MacDonald?" she asked politely.

"Yes, Teresa, I believe his name is—*a Mr. MacDonald*. What is his relationship to you? A relative? He is not a doctor, but he seems somewhat knowledgeable in medicine," he commented sarcastically.

"He is a wealthy man from Texas. He hired me for the surrogate mother program at Torito Bay. So he has interest in baby Samuel."

"Why do you call the baby 'Samuel'?" he asked. "Is that a family name?"

"No, Dr. Bower, that is the name the clinic people affectionately gave him, while he was in my belly. They thought it was cute, I suppose. I do, too. I will keep his name Samuel. It sounds like a classy, famous name. Don't you think?" she asked Bower.

"Yes, Teresa, it is a classy name!" he replied, while smiling at the child.

"Teresa, do Dr. Sanchez and Mr. MacDonald work together, in some fashion?"

"Yes, Royston MacDonald is involved in research. He is on the board of the fertility clinic and has much money. He is a wealthy oilman, they say."

Just then, the baby made a soft sound and appeared to be slowly waking up. He stretched and yawned and then went back to sleep, tightly cuddled in his mother's arms. She looked at him for the moment and kissed his forehead. She loved this child so much. *It is a miracle*, she thought.

"Teresa?" Dr. Bower continued. "You talked of cloning and monsters when you arrived here. Do you think you were delirious from some of the drugs? What do you remember from yesterday and last night?"

"Doctor, there was an article in the newspaper that caused my friend to call me yesterday. She said the description sounded like me.

It concerned a cloned baby and a surrogate mother. The description in the paper was. . . . It was—*me!* Is my baby a clone, doctor? Does it look like a clone to you?" she asked him in rapid-fire questioning. "What is a clone, doctor? A monster? It all scared me."

Dr. Bower looked puzzled by her comments. It wasn't the medication that she was given, after all. She was genuinely scared of something. *What is the fertility clinic up to?* he wondered. *Did she actually have a cloned baby? Why were Sanchez and MacDonald so interested in this baby?* Bower was mystified by the whole conversation with her.

"Did your contractions start prematurely after you heard of the newspaper article? Is that what happened?" he asked her, with piqued interest.

"Yes," she replied quickly. "They happened right afterward! I became scared by my friend's phone call."

Dr. Bower was now deep in thought. An assistant came into Teresa's room and told him in confidence, that news organizations and protestors had been gathering outside the hospital holding signs during the last few hours. Local police had been called to keep them at bay. Remote TV crews from local broadcast stations were appearing outside the hospital facility, as well.

Bower began to piece the story together. He was trying to evaluate what Teresa had told him, with the fact that Sanchez and his friend were cohorts at the fertility clinic. The news article and the fact that protestors and the media surrounded his hospital was making his supposition a reality. Bower needed answers *quickly*—to mollify the press. *Only two other people have the answers,* he thought.

Bower concluded that Torito Bay had a cloning project in progress, and that he just might have delivered by cesarean, the world's *first cloned human.* He pretended to examine the child, touching every digit and his face. The child was perfect—all postpartum tests were normal for pulmonary, renal and liver function. The Apgar score was high. He could not take his eyes off this *unique creation.*

"Is everything OK, doctor? Is Samuel OK?" she asked in fright. "You are spending a lot of time examining him. Are you sure he is OK?"

"Teresa, this is a beautiful, healthy child. A perfect boy," he replied reassuringly.

"Doctor, was there anyone else who came by to see me?"

"Yes, they tell me that a gentleman of Mexican descent has been downstairs all night. He slept on the couch in the lobby. He asked for you. . . . Did you expect a relative?"

"It is probably Emilio, a friend. I had asked that someone call him when we got to the hospital. The ambulance attendant might have called him. If it is Emilio, may I see him? Is he still here? It would be nice to see him."

Bower replied with a smile. "I will have someone check downstairs. If he is still there, I will have him sent up—though I wish him to wear a mask and to gown up. He will need to scrub his hands as well. The baby is fragile and he should not get too close. Please do not let him handle the baby just yet. Germs can transfer easily and we want Samuel healthy," Bower said, suspecting that he was protecting a unique baby. *He was.*

Five minutes went by and Emilio entered shyly, his eyes shifting back and forth around the room. His hat was held tightly in his hand. He briefly hugged Teresa and congratulated her on the birth of the baby.

"Are you OK? Is the baby OK?" he asked with concern.

"Check over there, Emilio. I am fine. Do not get too close, but you may look. I just put him down in the bassinet. Isn't he beautiful?" she asked him.

"He is beautiful, Teresa, just like his new mother. He is so perfect, in every way. Look at those long fingers. He will play piano, I'll bet. Children with long fingers, Teresa, become piano players—famous surgeons or ball players. Yes!" he said with conviction. "He looks like a ball player!"

"Say 'hi' to Samuel, Emilio," she said. "Samuel, say 'hello' to Emilio."

With that, Emilio looked down at the sleeping child and made the sign of the cross as if he were in church. The baby was wrapped snugly in a blue blanket and wore a small, blue, knitted cap on his head. The blanket made him feel like he was still within his mother's womb and the hat kept his temperature stable. Babies can lose body heat through their heads.

"Teresa, I am glad you are OK. I was scared when the ambulance came. God bless *you* and the child." Emilio kissed the crucifix about his neck chain and went over to her. "Bless this child," he kept saying. He was as excited as a real father. It was as if Samuel was *his* baby.

Emilio did not stay long and thanked the doctor for allowing him to visit. He saw little of the protesters' signs on the way out to the parking lot in the back of the hospital.

When Teresa saw the baby begin to stir, she decided she would nurse him because the situation was so special. A nurse brought Samuel to her to hold, and moved the bassinet closer to her bedside. *Had I given birth to this the child for his natural parents,* she thought, *I would not have had the chance to see him, or have had the chance to hold and nurse him.* She was engorged with breast milk and colostrum and knew he was ready for nourishment. She relished the fact that he was actually attached to her, and a hungry young man, at that. She fell asleep while nursing, but her grip was sufficient to hold him close. No one would remove this baby from his new mother. The bond was natural.

Dr. Bower returned later to say that Sanchez and MacDonald were still there and wished to say hello. Teresa had no knowledge of what a miserable night they had experienced, trying to get approval to see her and the baby. Dr. Sanchez's comments to the attending E.R. physician's face the previous night were not found acceptable. Sanchez had basically told him that "if it had come down to saving the mother or baby, that the baby had priority." That incensed the E.R. doctor and resulted in the hospital director and chief of staff delaying approval of their visit even longer. Besides, Dr. Sanchez was not cleared to practice in La Jolla Hospital. His practice was solely at Torito Bay Fertility Clinic.

Dr. Sanchez was the first to enter the room where Teresa was awake and recuperating. The baby was nearby in the bassinet. Sanchez looked at Teresa warmly and congratulated her, but his mind and eyes were on the bassinet. She, in turn, was fearful that they might take the baby. Sanchez could see a life form in the plastic isolation tub beside her bed. He smiled as Royston entered just behind him. MacDonald was all smiles, as well. They were masked and gowned as Emilio had been , but the smile lines seemed to exceed the protective mask over their faces. They said little but stared at the creation in the blue blanket, seemingly dumbfounded.

"Samuel," they each said from a distance. "Welcome, Samuel!"

They each hugged Teresa and congratulated her for what she had accomplished. She was less willing to hug them back. She was irritated that Sanchez had not returned her phone call until she had a crisis and emergency surgery. He was apologetic about that and kept telling her that he was sorry. *He does not seem all that genuine,* she thought. Both men remained focused on the crib and the newborn.

The mood soon shifted to a very analytical Teresa Cordero. At that moment, Dr. Bower returned to the room.

"I have a question for you both," she said firmly to Sanchez and MacDonald.

"Yes, Teresa?" said Sanchez with interest. "Is it about the pregnancy, or the baby's health? Are you in pain from the surgery?"

"No, Dr. Sanchez! *That* is not the question!" she emphasized loudly, with conviction.

"What is the name of the child's parents? You know—the ones that died in the car crash. What is their *name*? I can't seem to recall," she said emotionally.

By now she had tears in her eyes. "What is their *name?*" she reiterated with clenched teeth.

Both MacDonald and Sanchez stepped back and looked at each other in confusion. They knew that she was irate.

Teresa screamed at them, "Roy? What was their *name?* Do *you* know?"

At that point the baby stirred from the elevated voice, and Dr. Bower spoke up. "The parents of the surrogate baby? Can you recall their names? I think she wants to know who they were—the ones who died in the crash."

"Ah—not at the moment," said Sanchez, hesitating. "Ah—Their last name escapes me. We do so many surrogate pregnancies that. . . ."

Ah . . . I confuse the parents' names, but not the children," he laughed nervously. No one else laughed.

Bower was shocked at the men's response.

"You mean to tell me that the parents of this child were killed within the last month and you can't remember their names? I, for one, don't recall hearing of this tragic accident. Nor has my staff. They did not come to this hospital or any hospitals near San Diego. We checked with our colleagues in the general area."

Bower was on a roll. He fired questions at both of them as if he were at the O. J. Simpson trial, then voiced a casual statement to set them up: "There are no parents for this child, are there, gentlemen? There never were any parents of this child, were there? There was no automobile accident was there? No one died, did they? Did they? Answer this woman!" he demanded.

The two men flushed with embarrassment and were speechless.

Teresa looked at them sternly and sat up as best she could. It was obvious that she had pain in the abdomen from the sutures. It caused her to grimace. The Tylenol was wearing off.

"*You bastards!*" she shouted, with daggered eyes. "You lied to me! I thought you liked me, and then . . . you . . . you . . . bastards lied to me. What have I created here? Where are the parents of this child? Who's egg was it? Who's sperm was it? This child! Who are his natural parents? I demand to know!" She was adamant about getting the answers.

The baby awoke from the commotion and began to whimper.

"Teresa, Dr. Bower, please listen. We will explain everything. We can explain . . . "

Bower cut him off. "Can you explain the *newspapers*—the *protestors* outside this hospital at this very moment—or the fact that no accident occurred?"

MacDonald had had enough berating and ventured to comment.

"Hold it! Just hold it a darn minute! Let me comment! This can be explained and yes, there is some *joy* to this moment. This child next to you, Teresa, is 'the most famous child' in the world. *His birth* is only surpassed by the birth of the Christ child! You have every right to lambaste us with questions, to insult us with accusations, to scream obscenities if you wish." He took a deep breath. "You and the baby are famous today. You became *famous* nine months ago and you are even *more famous* today, than back then.

"And you, Dr. Bower—you and your staff, and this institution, are famous as well! All of you and this wonderful child by your side, have made history. It is a first-ever event! A first-ever event! No one in the world has ever achieved what you see in front of you! Ever!"

Bower and Teresa listened intently. There would be a two-hour briefing of the entire matter. In the end, tempers would settle down, everyone basked in the glory of the incredible event that had transpired before them, twelve hours earlier.

Dr. Bower, by shear fate and necessity, and Teresa Cordero had become unwilling accomplices to the birth of the *first cloned human being* in the world.

At Dr. Bower's request, the mother and child would be moved to the North Park home at one the next morning. Both were fit to leave and a registered pediatric nurse would be available to assist Teresa and the child for a while. Accommodations were made for the nurse to stay with the neighbor, Wanda, nearby.

The hospital had all they could do to deal with the protesters and news organizations. With Teresa and the baby out of the hospital and secretly living in North Park, the heat of controversy might temporarily be taken off the various institutions in the La Jolla area.

In this way, the hospital could honestly say that there was no mother or cloned baby at its hospital.

☕ ☕ ☕ ☕

Fawn paged Jack and was glad when she got his return call. She was a bit stressed over the news on TV when she saw that Mesa Biotech, Torito Bay Fertility Clinic and La Jolla General were featured. Fawn was aware that Jack was preoccupied by the controversy at hand. He was the only person in the research team that had media training to deal with the press.

Talking to members of the news media required evasive action on certain questions that might pry into the confidentiality between research organizations and clients.

Fawn was somewhat miffed with not knowing what his job really entailed. It was OK to be secretive on certain things with work, but this recent issue was something that almost seemed unethical. She was concerned that her husband's new job had a life of its own and that he might be in serious trouble. Animal rights activists and self-designated ethics groups were congregating in La Jolla and his name would be bantered around the world in time. She did not want their personal life infringed upon, and this occurrence stimulated massive attention to the Danton name.

Jack had just returned from an intense news conference. The local media wanted to know everything about cloning, a potential surrogate mother and La Jolla General Hospital, in general. Jack had stalled everyone and had met with Royston and Sanchez to plan the next strategy.

"Honey?" she said with concern. "What the hell is going on at La Jolla General? The local news has been covering protestors there and at Torito Bay Fertility Clinic. Does this have to do with Royston and you?"

Jack hesitated with the question. His head was spinning from the barrage of questions that he had experienced earlier.

"Honey, can this wait? I can't talk for long, but this mess here *does involve us.* I just can't get into specifics."

"Specifics?" she raised her voice. "Why can't you tell me? I see these protestors as endangering your life! What the hell is up?" She had one hand on the hip of her jeans and the other rose with defiance into the air. The phone was locked between her head and shoulder, and she was searching for some paper and a pen.

"Honey," he continued, "this is not the time to get into it, but yes, there has been a fertility program here that involved one particular individual and cloning. I am sworn to secrecy, by Royston. No one knows anything outside of the research team," he continued in a calm voice.

"Well! If no one knows what the hell is going on, then who is the stoolie, animal rights person that they just interviewed on TV? Who the hell is *that* person and who the hell is this *Mexican chick* that's carrying some baseball hero's clone?" she exclaimed. "There is some animal rights chick—who must have been on Royston's secret team—that should not have been. She was tellin' all the press about mice and rats and babies and a surrogate pregnancy. The Mexican woman is supposedly carrying a human clone of a famous ballplayer for Christ's sake. Come home and watch the news and tell me the truth about what's going on!" she continued to rage.

"Dammit Jack! I'm your wife of one year and you can't tell me what the hell you've been doin' with these scientific oddballs. Can't you trust your wife? If not, then who the hell can you trust?" she continued.

Jack had never heard Fawn so angry. His head pounded from her furious interrogation.

"I'm sorry. I will update you when I get home. I'm sorry. We were told by MacDonald that no one—absolutely no one—was to be told of the project: Project Samuel," he said. He knew Fawn was hurt by the fact that there was something *this* important to the world in general, and he could not elaborate further on it.

"Honey," she said, depressed, "how could you keep this from me. Who was I going to tell? I'm your damn wife and honesty is everything. We swore and vowed honesty," she said with dejection. "You gave up a good job for this nonsense? This exposure?" she cried out.

"Fawn, dear. Listen! I will tell you all about it tonight. This is bigger than life itself. Trust me! This is bigger than anything in life as you know it. Please let me explain. There was a cloning, and yes it was someone famous. The press has no idea about what happened or who was cloned. The baby was born today, a month premature, and yes it was at La Jolla General. You are the first to know—it is Ted Williams who was cloned! The new baby is a genetic copy of Ted. Project Samuel was named after Ted."

"Ted? What the hell does *Samuel* have to do with Ted?" she said, with her mouth open in amazement.

"Ted's middle name was Samuel. He was named after his uncle, and also his father. Both were named Samuel. Even Ted doesn't know about this baby, honey. History was made today! The first human clone was born—and it was another Ted! It's a genetic copy of him."

"What? Ted doesn't know? He didn't approve of this, did he? What did you do—collect his sperm while he slept?" she asked sarcastically. "Jack, what you did was deceitful and fraudulent. They will nail you guys! It is unethical to use someone's DNA, especially when they are still alive. Dammit! Jack, Ted Williams is still alive! You took me to Fenway! We saw him. Remember?"

"Honey, the DNA came from the Rizzo collection. It came from the hair clippings that old man Rizzo kept of ballplayers whose hair he cut. The damn hair was decades old and still had Ted's genetic code locked in it."

Jack became antsy. "Honey, this is Nobel prize material. No one has done this before! Ted will be flattered that he was first. He calls himself 'the greatest hitter that ever lived,' and he was. He has vanity," Jack added in justification.

"Jack! If you think he will be flattered, then call him! Call him after we hang up and tell him—he's been cloned! It's the only ethical thing to do! And the Nobel prize? Who are you guys kidding? They'll get you guys for theft of DNA, for deceit, for lying and for non-sanctioned science! You won't get the medal or the money—just ridicule!"

"I really must go, hon! Royston is paging me. I really must find out what he wants." Jack hung up abruptly. Fawn was depressed. She could no longer watch TV and surmised that this was just the beginning of a lifelong nightmare. It would go on for years.

She decided to go down near the ocean and have a cocktail at a local club that she and Jack frequented for dinner. She might not even have alcohol. She just needed to sit and think about the conversation. She parked her car and walked into the bar of a restaurant on the beach. The bartender sensed that she wanted solitude. She ordered a wine after all. One cocktail would not hurt, she felt.

Fawn was in the bar no more than two minutes when a handsome V-chested man approached her and offered to buy her a drink. The bartender sensed that it was a bad time for him to be talking to her, but his warning went unheeded. The stud noted the ring on her finger, but she was alone and he took a chance on meeting a beautiful and sexy woman. She turned heads often and she was a downright "piece of ass" to him.

"May I sit here and buy you a cocktail? Barkeep! Put her wine on my tab, please." There was no response from Fawn.

"Do you come here often? I've never seen you before," he tried again.

Fawn looked at him with lustful eyes and raised the glass of wine to her lips. She backed it off her lower lip. She licked her lips and moved her tongue over the rim of the glass slowly from left to right and then back to the left. The man, in heat, almost wet his pants from the fantasy inspired by her the tongue on the rim of the wine glass.

Fawn slowly lowered the glass and smiled. She took the glass of merlot and dripped some on his bar tab.

"Here, its on your tab now, asshole!"

She then dumped the beet-red liquid remnants on his crotch and yelled, "Fuck off, hard on! I can't do you! Why, you've got your 'period' today, Mr. Studly!"

Fawn picked up her purse, slid some money toward the bartender, and walked out. She never looked back but there was a smile on her face, wider than a highway. The embarrassed man headed in horror for the men's room. He looked as if he had been "Bobbitized."

He looked at the bartender and was in shock. The bartender shook his head at the stud and laughed. "Tampons are in the machine in the ladies room, fella. You just messed with a committed woman. Her name is Fawn and she's pretty well committed to her husband, Jack!"

The other patrons just roared at the brazen stud. Fawn was long gone and actually felt much better now. The audacity of the fool to try and make her, when all she wanted was some quiet time to review Jack's conversation from the earlier phone call.

Twenty minutes later the stud exited the men's room. He spent that time washing his pants and drying them under the blower for drying hands. It would be weeks before the bartender would see him again.

On the drive back home, she traveled the coast highway and took some curvy roads for fun. She was keyed up—first, by Jack's call, and then by the asshole at the bar.

Along the way she thought of the surrogate mother. Jack had mentioned that none of the doctors at La Jolla General knew who was cloned. He did not know that both Teresa and Dr. Bower had been briefed. As she drove she felt sorry for the Mexican woman. She knew the name of Teresa and hoped to meet her someday. Jack had mentioned on the phone that Teresa did not know about the project, all through the pregnancy. She sensed that Teresa would need a real friend soon. *Maybe she could be that trusting friend,* she thought.

Fawn wondered if Teresa would sue the clinic and the participants. After all, she was thrust into a charade for monetary gain, and lied to for more than nine months. She was a guinea pig for an unapproved procedure—one that was discouraged in science around the world. *God,* she thought, *is supposed to create life! Teresa was reduced to an oven for experimental purposes—all for the sake of money.* Fawn drove unusually fast until she saw a cop parked by the side of the road. He noticed her speed but chose not to pursue her. She slowed down and decided to go home. All she needed to know now was what was next on life's new agenda from hell.

Jack had left a message for Fawn after his call with Royston. He wondered where she was and why she didn't answer. The message said, "Honey, Teresa will be heading home to North Park after midnight tonight. They will send her home in a doctor's personal car. Somebody's SUV with blacked out windows—so no one will notice. After we get her settled, I will be home. We think that we may be able to escape the press and settle her into the house before people find out who she is or who the baby is."

Fawn mumbled to herself after listening to the message. "Foolish husband! Every Tom, Dick and Harry will find out in time. The press will scour the land to find out where this woman went. Animal activists, the news and North Park locals will sense what has happened. Once they realize that it was Ted Williams who was cloned, they will know where to look. North Park was his boyhood home—you foolish man!" she said, pacing and talking to herself.

"This will ruin us, Jack," she practiced saying to Jack when he got home.

Jack was no slouch. He knew he was in trouble with Fawn. She was obviously hurt and pissed off by the secrecy of the whole cloning issue. He had always been open with her. *Now she might not trust me anymore,* he thought. That was an awful feeling, especially when they had recently decided to have children.

The timing of the whole episode was poor. Fawn had tested her urine with a home pregnancy kit, and was, in fact, with child. She was excited, but would not tell him until the current critical situation was over. It would spoil the joy of sharing it with him—that *they, too,* were going to be parents.

Forty-three

In Boston, one of Joe Rizzo's children, Joe Jr., called the Texas home of E. Royston MacDonald. He had his number from the time that Rizzo's will went to probate. Joe Jr. assumed that Royston might be there in seclusion. Most of the Rizzo children had read Royston MacDonald's name in the newspaper. It was associated with the potential cloning of a child in California. They knew all too well that Royston was involved in biotechnology, but they didn't know he was messing with a controversial research area.

Joe Jr. needed to talk to Royston immediately. The article had indicated in the newspaper that the DNA source was from a hair sample of a famous person. Joe Jr. knew damn well that Royston had acquired all the hair samples from his father's barbershop when he bought the collection of memorabilia.

Joe Jr. tried to reach Royston many times on his private line. There was no answer in Texas. Joe Jr. and his family would keep trying. Eventually, they knew they would talk to Royston. At least, they hoped so.

Forty-four

Jack Danton finally got home from North Park. Fawn was asleep, but she awoke when he kissed her forehead.

"I'm back, honey," he said quietly.

"Glad that you are home," she replied in a somewhat drowsy state. She had just fallen asleep. She was more relaxed now and sat up against the pillow. He was sitting on the side of the bed, kicking off his shoes.

Fawn wanted to share the news about her pregnancy and didn't care about the events of the day.

"Jack, dear. I thought that you should know that my period was late this month. I think you did the job! You are going to be a dad! I think the thong-on-the-patio trick did it!"

"What?" he replied with a proud smile. "Are you pregnant?"

He hugged her tightly. "Are you sure? That is such great news. When did you find out?" he asked.

"I did the home pregnancy kit yesterday, and in no time flat, the blue line appeared. I tried it again and the same results happened. Looks like the *rabbit died*, hon!"

"Rabbit died?" he asked.

"Just an expression from the old days, honey," she replied with humor. "Are you excited?"

"Yes," he replied. "I'm ecstatic! I was hoping we would have a family. I love you so much, Fawn." He kissed her again and nuzzled up to her belly. "Hi there, baby!" he said with a smile. "Boy or girl? Care to guess?" he asked.

"Won't know that for some time, hon," she said with a gleam in her eye. "Week twenty is when we can determine the sex, for sure. Right? Could be a boy. That's *my* guess."

He replied, "Yeah. Week twenty! We should know for sure. A boy? That sure would run in the family, so that's as good a guess as a girl," he laughed. "It will be one or the other."

"Well, Jack. Your pregnant wife of a day or so was 'hit on' to-day—by a stud muffin at the beach bar."

He looked confused. "What are you talkin' about? Stud muffin? Beach bar? You're not supposed to drink with a baby inside of you!"

"Well, after our phone conversation, I went to Jake's to unwind. I needed a break and a cocktail to relax. I never did drink the wine! I wasn't there two minutes when some Mr. Studly sauntered over and wanted to be my best friend for the afternoon and evening."

She relayed the entire scenario to him and they roared at the out-come. "You should have seen this guy's face when the wine hit his crotch!" she laughed. "He was mortified that I bagged him so bad."

Jack responded in support of her accolade, "I'm proud of you, hon! Great job fending off those perverts who hit on pregnant women! You must have had pregnancy rage hormones already!"

"No, honey. It wasn't hormones already. It was the fact that I love you so much and this jerk had the audacity to hit on someone who just wanted her space. Guys just think that if you're sitting there alone, that you're there to get laid! I wasn't. I just wanted a simple glass of red wine. He thought that he could just come over and bother me. Why do men do that?"

Jack reminded her of how they met. "Fawn? If you recall, I did the same thing! You were so beautiful and everyone loves your look. Him hittin' on you doesn't surprise me at all."

"I wasn't wearing a ring then, Jack. Today I had my wedding ring on, so what was his interpretation of that?"

"Guess he just wanted to *poke you,* baby! Some guys are pigs!" he responded.

"Better come to bed now," she encouraged him. "It's been a long day for both of us. Let's get some rest. You'll surely be dealin' with the press tomorrow and you will need some sleep."

There was a pause, and then she piped up, "Jack, do you have any ideas for a name for a boy, or a girl?"

"A name for the baby? Already? Ah, maybe," he replied.

"Is it your mom's or your dad's name?" she asked.

"No, hon, let's find some new names. Perhaps one that is unique to Boston. A Bostonian name!" he suggested.

"Why Bostonian?" she asked with puzzlement.

"Well, hon, I think I'd like to go back there. I've had enough of sunny San Diego. We now have a nice nest egg from this job with Royston. The bonuses were massive on Project Samuel. It's time to take some time off, perhaps."

"Really? Back home? I was hoping we could go back some day."

"I want our child to be raised in the East. I like the four seasons and the greenery. It gets pretty dry out here and brown," he said.

Fawn was shocked by the revelation and asked Jack, "Are you quitting the Royston gig? Aren't you happy being a part of history?" she asked.

"No, I may not have to quit him. We talked recently and he hinted that he might get hooked up with a Cambridge biotechnology company that likes his research support. They figure that he may be a future Nobel laureate! I don't need to work for a while and we could head back and see what's new and different. Take our time, check things out and then settle in for good."

"Really? You mean after all of this controversy, he is going to continue with programs such as Project Samuel?" she asked with surprise.

"I think he just might. He's astute enough to know that California and San Diego will vote this kind of research right out of here. Even if it will benefit those parents that have lost children and want to have the same child back. They will ban it! California is first in the nation to ban anything. They just label it *Proposition 2½, 65* or whatever, and send it to the voters. The next thing you know, it's an environmental concern or bad for dust mites! They'll protect anything in this state. They're all friggin' Republican conservatives!"

"What about Texas?" she asked. "If he has all that land down there, why would he not move his operation there?"

"He might," Jack said raising his eyebrows. It could be Boston or Texas. Hell, he could build his own biotech company down there and call it "Surrogate, Inc." The damn state of Texas is so big, it would take years for them to find him!"

Fawn was tired now. Her anger had dissipated with the conversation of the baby. They were up later than expected. "Hop in bed, hon. It will be morning soon," she said lovingly. "Boston, eh?" she reiterated. "How about Chelsea if it's a girl, or Quincy if it's a boy?"

Jack turned and hugged her. He jokingly responded with, "How about Roxy for Roxbury, or Matt for Mattapan!"

She laughed.

"Go to sleep, mama and baby!" he whispered.

He lay back on his pillow but his brain would not rest. He knew that Royston was headed to Boston or Texas on the red-eye that evening. *What is he up to?* Jack wondered. *Why did Royston not get concerned that he desired to return to the Boston area?* Jack just *knew,* that Boston was the next biotech hub, not Texas.

Jack eventually fell asleep lying against Fawn's back. One of her legs was locked over his.

∅ ∅ ∅ ∅

The next morning Fawn asked Jack if she could meet Teresa. She explained that she thought that Teresa could probably use a friend. Jack called the new mother and arranged for Fawn to visit her in North Park. Teresa welcomed the opportunity to meet Jack's wife. Even though Jack was part of the team that had lied to her, she was never upset with him. It was Royston and Sanchez with whom she was disappointed. Teresa was anxious to show off Samuel. Fawn, in turn, could tell Teresa that she, too, was now with child.

Teresa would be flattered that she was the first outsider to know. They would become good friends from that day forward. Fawn and Jack would eventually be Samuel's godparents.

Forty-five

MacDonald had disappeared the night that Teresa returned to North Park from La Jolla General. He did not respond to pages by any of his colleagues. He had secretly taken an overnight flight to Boston. Jack Danton was the only one who knew that he had left San Diego. Jack would meet with the Project Samuel team members to organize the Nobel prize committee papers for nomination of the prize for medicine. An anonymous sponsor from the United Kingdom would submit the final paperwork to the evaluation committee.

Royston had purchased all of the first class seats on the evening jet so that he had that section to himself. He wanted no one around him. He asked the flight attendant to please keep people from using the forward cabin bathroom. No one from the economy section would pass the curtain. Neither the flight attendants, nor the pilots knew who he was. They assumed he was a wealthy eccentric.

E. Royston MacDonald's plane landed in the predawn darkness at Logan International Airport at 7:30. The air was cool and brisk. There was hardly anyone on the flight from San Diego, and he was casually dressed. His clothes were wrinkled from the long flight and he looked very tired. He had not slept well, even though he had the first class cabin to himself.

He left the plane and walked up the jet way with only a carry-on piece of luggage. It would only be a one-night stay at best.

In a month or two, Royston and some colleagues would hear of the Nobel prize awards selection and he was confident that his achievement would at least be recognized and nominated. *He had worked hard at accomplishing the greatest biological quest of modern day science,* he thought. He smiled at passengers in the gate area thinking all the time that they did not know who he was. He knew that they would in time. He would be very famous in a month. His ego could be no larger.

Royston said nothing during his journey through Terminal C. He quickly descended the stairs to a waiting stretch limo that Max had arranged for him back in San Diego. Max's friend, a black gentleman named Cliff, waited for Royston to appear. Cliff held a sign that read MR. SAMUEL. The limo lights along the side of the car were reminiscent of the old coaches of yesteryear. Their dim glow reflected off the side of the shiny, highly polished, black Cadillac sedan. Inside the car was a tray of coffee, pastries and juice for Royston.

"Good morning, sir," said the driver. "Have a pleasant flight?"

"Yes. Thank you," he said, shaking Cliff's hand. "Max tells me, *you're the man,* in Boston! That you will take care of me, Cliff."

"Max is a good guy, sir, and yes, I'm at your service. Max did not know where you wanted to go, sir," he said opening the door.

Once inside, Royston thanked him for the breakfast setup. *It is nice of Cliff to do that,* he thought. Since it was 5:00 A.M. by Royston's watch, but 8:00 A.M. in Boston, he was appreciative of the coffee and breakfast array.

"Where to, sir?" was the question from the front seat.

"Brookline, Cliff. Take me to Brookline, out Route 9."

"Don't mean to bother you, sir, but to any particular place?"

"Yes, Cliff. Please head out toward Fenway Park, and we can get on Route 9 west from there. Take me to Sacred Heart Cemetery. It's out there somewhere west of town."

Royston had no idea where the cemetery was, and had never been there before. He had called ahead and had spoken with a caretaker who gave him some general information about its location, and a particular gravesite.

The traffic was not too bad that morning and the sun was brightening the sky over the harbor in Boston. The thirty-five-minute ride gave Royston time for reflection. He had Cliff pass by Fenway ballpark and then stop in the general area of Joe Rizzo's former barber-shop. Royston emerged from the car and stayed long enough to peer into the windows of the shop. The sign above said RIZZO'S PIZZA AND SUBS—BEST PIZZA NORTH OF THE BRONX. There was a neon sign above the Coca-Cola-sponsored Rizzo's Pizza sign, but no real indication that a barbershop had ever been located there.

Royston looked up and could see the spot where the candy-striped barber pole once hung. He always wanted it for his memorabilia collection in Texas, and that is where it ended up. It needed to be in his Texas collection of Joe Rizzo artifacts. The red and white stripes on the pole were faded but still there. Royston had wired it in his display so that the candy stripes would illuminate and rotate. On the Rizzo shop outside wall was the old electrical wire, which had been severed. The employee of the neon sign company had probably cut that when the new pizza sign was installed. The wire hung and waved slightly in the morning breeze.

Royston saw that the shop was closed at that hour, and opened at 11:00 A.M. He surmised that the Rizzo family boys, in keeping with the tradition of the old man, ran the new sub shop. Above the deli, where Joe Rizzo Sr. once lived, was a sign in the window that read, APT FOR RENT. Royston was pleased that the kids had at least kept the building, and were running a business there. *If that is true, it's a nice continuum of tradition,* he thought.

Looking to the right of the deli counter, where people ordered pizza, Royston noticed three photographs on the wall. One was of Joe Sr. with Ted Williams and autographed by Ted. The other two photos were of Mo Vaughn and Jose Canseco, both ex-players for the Red Sox. *Perhaps they bought subs or pizza there?* he thought. He hoped that they had.

Royston laughed at the Mo Vaughn photo since old man Rizzo would have never cut *his* hair. "Mo shaved his head for Christ's sake!" he mumbled.

Cliff overheard Royston laughing in the cool morning air.

"Sir, everything OK out there?"

"Yes," was his reply from the shop doorway. "Everything is just fine," Royston smiled. He chuckled to himself and wrote an unsigned note on a piece of paper and slipped it under the door. The note said, "You need Nomar Garciaparra's autograph on your wall! Now *that's* one that will be worth something in a few years!"

Royston returned to the limo, and went silent for the duration of the ride to the cemetery. He loved the photo of old man Rizzo and Ted Williams and would love to own it, but he knew that it belonged in the sub and pizza shop, forever. He surmised that the next time he would pass through Boston, the collection on the wall would be greater than what he saw today. *After all,* he thought, *it's in the Rizzo family's genes to collect these wonderful pieces of autographed history.*

The entrance at the Sacred Heart Cemetery came up abruptly, a few miles outside of town. They were now in Brookline, Massachusetts, the town where JFK grew up. Royston walked up the cobblestone driveway and had Cliff wait back by the entrance of the cemetery. Royston could read the stones, since the sun was bright over Boston. No one was around except a lone caretaker who came in early to open the gate at Royston's request. He gave the man a $100 bill for his troubles and the man directed Royston straight ahead to cemetery section 13.

Four rows in was a simple gravestone with a cross and name embossed on the granite vertical marker. On one side of the stone it read RIZZO, and on the other side were the names of Joe Sr. and his wife, Rose. Their respective dates of birth and dates of death were listed below each name. As is an Italian custom, a small glass-encased picture of the two of them on their wedding day adorned the grave. The glass holder was glued to the stone.

"Rest in peace, Joe and Rose," he whispered to himself. "I think I'll be headin' for Stockholm soon because of you, Joe. I owe it all to you, my friend," he whispered at the cold stone marker. "I owe it all to you and your collection of memorabilia. Thank you."

Royston became very reflective and philosophical. It was as if there was no other quest for him now, in his life. He had done what he had needed to do. He thought for a moment and murmured, "I'm also here, Joe, to tell you that you will live again. Joe, *you* are next for the project. Guess what, Joe? You will see Ted play again; right here on earth! I owe it to you. I have *your* hair sample, as you requested. It is stored under lock and key. The funeral home director obtained it during your wake. I have done what you had asked, Joe. We actually extracted your DNA last week."

He continued to talk to the stone. "Joe, Ted was born again this week. I came here to tell you of the incredible feat. His new name is Samuel, and he will be your contemporary when you appear again. I imagine that you will be physically born again, in ten or twelve months, if all goes well. The woman who will be your surrogate mother lives in Boston, not Calabria. But that is OK, Joe. That will be OK. You will grow up in Boston, like you did before.

For now, Joseph Rizzo Sr. Rest in peace. Rest in peace."

Forty-six

Emilio was with Teresa immediately after she and the baby returned to North Park. He missed her greatly while he worked at the inn and visited her when he could. Their love grew deeper and he finally stayed in North Park more than he was in his apartment in Poway. He was helpful with the baby, and was able to help her escape the house if the papparazzi or press decided to seek her out.

"Emilio?" she said one night. "I've grown close to you. Do you think we'll be together someday? Perhaps when Samuel is grown?"

"Yes, Teresa. I wish to be with you, and with him, even now!"

"Really?"

"Yes," he said again. "I love you and him. He will need a father. Can I be his father? Can I be your husband?" he said shyly, almost fearing her response.

"Are you proposing to me, Emilio? Are you asking me to marry you?" she asked.

"I do want to marry you someday. I want to be with you and Samuel, day in and day out."

"Why, Emilio? You have freedom now. You would not have that with me and the baby."

He was sincere and pious with her. It was like a religious experience between them. He looked at her and said simply, "Teresa, he is a part of you, and I wish to be a part of you."

"You are a wonderful man, Emilio. I think that you should move here to North Park and live here," she suggested.

"What about the doctors and Mr. MacDonald? Would they approve of that?" he asked.

"Emilio, they have nothing to say about that! They lied to me and I was going to get a lawyer to sue them for fraud and deception. Dr. Bower wanted me to do that as well. I dropped that idea after they agreed to let me keep Samuel, and to leave me alone. Royston MacDonald has had his glory. There is one more thing that he needs. It is the Nobel prize! Let him have the Nobel prize and all its money! That's all he ever wanted anyway. The paperwork on the baby says that Samuel is all mine. They can not take him away."

"Really," he smiled back. He held her close. "You mean they will leave us alone?" he asked. "Will MacDonald or Sanchez or any of them see Samuel?"

"I agreed, Emilio, to allow them to see Samuel from time to time. It is at my convenience and Samuel's. It is only fair that they see him. They created this bundle of joy," she added. "Besides, Royston has agreed to pay all Samuel's expenses—the expenses to raise him. He is covering this home as well, but the house will be in my name. I do not have to go back to work."

"Wow, that is very nice for you and the baby."

"Yes, Emilio, and you can be part of that, as well. There will be a trust fund for the baby. He will have all his schooling and college expenses paid for later on. I plan to send him to local schools just as Ted Williams attended. He will have to know his heritage, and his heritage is here, in North Park. I will raise him here."

Emilio was amazed at how strong this woman had become. She knew that she wanted to right the wrong that had been done to her. He was ecstatic that they might be together after all. She was just as thrilled that he wanted her in his life.

Emilio expressed his desire to still work and contribute his fair share where he could help out. *He would find work in North Park*, he thought. That money would probably be sent to Teresa's family in Mexico. She had already sent them the final $2,500 from Royston.

Emilio would save some money and buy Teresa and the baby a piano. He thought that Samuel's hands were perfect for becoming a pianist. Teresa kissed him and thanked him for the kind thought.

She thought, *a concert pianist? Maybe?* After all, no one would force Samuel to be a baseball player. But, if he leaned that way, he would be encouraged to play piano and ball, as well.

Forty-seven

The whole world quickly caught wind of the cloning controversy in the United States. The research community was abuzz with the rumor that there was a human clone in California. The researchers in the United Kingdom were especially surprised, but pleased that their technology may have been used in human cloning for the very first time. They surmised that the U.S. team had garnered the technical expertise and advantage from the international symposium where the British team had presented data at the Washington and Bethesda conference, the previous year. The Brits had felt they had perfected certain microinjection procedures that would make it easier for scientists to alter the human egg. Electrical simulation was a critical phase. The problem for them was that one year earlier, British law prevented them from applying the technique to a human egg. It was deemed unethical and the government was quick to discourage anyone in universities from attempting the creation of human life in a petri dish or test tube.

They were right. It was the proceedings in Bethesda, Maryland, that aided the Project Samuel team in achieving its success.

Now that it had been achieved, the researchers in the United Kingdom were anxious to nominate the U.S. team for the Nobel prize in medicine. The U.K. scientists certainly had the credentials to nominate, but needed the printed documentation for submission. Ultimately, when the birth was confirmed, Jack Danton would provide them with the manuscript that he had put together from the very beginning of the project. It would be considered an official publication preprint that would eventually appear in the biology journals, *Nature* or *Science*. Since there was nothing to hide now, Royston and Jack approved of their colleagues in the United Kingdom submitting the formal nomination. The Nobel committee would then need to determine if there would be one or more recipients in the U.S. team, if they in fact actually won the centennial award.

❄ ❄ ❄ ❄

While Teresa was pregnant, Emilio spent hours talking to her about her pregnancy, and later her ordeal with the premature delivery. He often made notes from their get-togethers at the inn at Torrey Pines. He did not know the details of the science of obstetrics, but focused rather on her mood and emotions during their discussions. His diary became a story in and of itself, from her pregnancy to her emergency ambulance ride and the eventual cesarean section.

Emilio had never shared his notes of her with anyone. He felt that, when Teresa finally delivered, he would give her a "written gift" of what she went through and experienced. It might provide her with solace and even humor, at a later date. He left nothing out, including the evening that they made love. It was noted in his diary as "the day that they fell in love."

Teresa surmised that Emilio was preparing something for her as a present. From time to time, he had asked more personal questions than she wanted to hear, or answer.

Emilio was keen enough to realize that the MacDonald research team was being considered for the Nobel prize. He did not object to doctors and scientists getting this grand award for what they had accomplished. He knew that they were smart and gifted to have created life in the face of God. He also knew, in his own mind, that they were *mere instruments* in the creative process. For him, it was *God* who made them successful. He was a devout Catholic and truly believed that God gave the team a hand in their success.

In his spare time Emilio would visit the local library in North Park where he befriended a library assistant who helped him learn more about the Nobel prize.

She helped him with the English words, when he had difficulty. She often searched the Internet for him, since he knew very little of computers, or the Web.

In December, Emilio mailed a package to the Nobel Foundation in Stockholm, Sweden. That package contained a handwritten letter and a diary.

A month would go by without a response from the Karolinska Institute.

The various Nobel committees in Sweden and Norway met to decide the winners of the Nobel prizes in all categories. There were seven submissions of noteworthiness in the category of physiology or medicine. The committee in Sweden had the responsibility of selecting the winner of that particular category. It took them weeks to review the information in each submission. The nomination of Royston MacDonald and his colleagues was most impressive and thorough, thanks to Jack Danton and the U.K. sponsors. Everyone nominated in each of the six categories desired to be the centennial winner.

The submissions for physiology or medicine included researchers from Kenya who worked on an AIDS vaccine; biologists from the U.K. who had solved cell-to-cell communication pathways; NIH/US researchers who had isolated the debilitating plaques in the nerves of Alzheimer's patients; and other noted discoveries in breast cancer, cardiovascular disease and medical device technology. Also in the piles of documentation and submissions was a small package from North Park in San Diego, California.

🥖🥖🥖🥖

E. Royston MacDonald was in Texas when the call came in from Sweden. It was the official call, and he and two members of the Project Samuel research team were awarded the Nobel prize for medicine.

"Congratulations, Mr. MacDonald," said the Swedish gentleman.

"Thank you, sir," was Royston's reply. He was speechless. He had wondered what he would say or do if he had won. He could say nothing at all, except, "Thank you!"

Royston was shocked, stunned, proud, and humbled all at once. He had achieved his quest. He was informed that he would be hearing

289

from other officials about the awards, the formal proceedings and the banquet. The caller also reminded him that a formal presentation and lecture would be requested shortly after the awards. He could present his talk at any point over a six-month period. Generally, they preferred the presentation be earlier than later for continuity. That was protocol.

"Mr. MacDonald, the awards committee also selected two of your colleagues for their contributions to the overall accomplishment. They are Drs. Blackburn and Bradshaw. We will call them separately. Many people contributed to your successful program, but the Nobel committee can only acknowledge a maximum of three people.

Congratulations again, sir! You are free to contact the press at your leisure. We will notify the worldwide press as well."

Royston sat back after the call and cried. He was alone in his library at the mansion. His household help would be the first to know. There was excitement everywhere in the mansion. He needed to compose himself before he contacted the others.

He thought of the whole scenario from start to finish. It really had happened. All the flak about ethics and restrictions on human cell research fell by the wayside. He basked in the glory of the moment. He realized in his own mind long ago that he had contributed to the field of physiology and medicine. *All the people who questioned his motives were idiots!* he thought. The only selfish part of the whole plan was the utilization of Ted Williams's DNA in the study. He could have used his own, or JFK's or anyone's, to try to achieve the goal, the birth of a human from an altered egg. There were hundreds of samples in the Rizzo collection. He could have tapped any one of them including Babe Ruth. He chose Ted Williams for fun. He was his favorite ballplayer hence Ted was his first choice.

Once he calmed down, Royston called Jack Danton. "Jack, my boy, we did it! We won the prize!"

"Holy shit!" was the response at the other end. "Congrats, Roy! When did you get the call? Tell me! When did it happen? What did they say?"

"Just now, son. I just hung up with the gentleman from Sweden! We damn well did it, son! Thank you for your help, Jack boy!"

Jack responded like a school kid, "Who can we tell? Can I tell Fawn?"

"Son, you are free to tell anyone and everyone. It's official! Tell any damn person that will listen. Bradshaw and Blackburn are co-recipients. Swedes are calling them now. I'm about to get drunk, son—right here in my own Texas villa! We're goin' to Sweden, son! All of us! We're goin' to Sweden!"

Jack congratulated him again and said, "Roy, go for it. Have the time of your life! We'll see you soon and thanks for the great news!"

Jack was beside himself. He didn't know what to do next. He needed to call everyone he could think of. He was Royston's media man and he wanted the team to know before the press got wind of it. In the next hour, he would cover everyone that mattered on Project Samuel.

Fawn was first to hear the news from Jack. Royston would call Teresa. He did not want her to find out from anyone else.

Forty-eight

December tenth, the day selected as the day to disseminate the awards each year, was fast approaching. The Nobel Foundation's Festival Day was like a holiday. In both Sweden and Norway, the committees had decided and notified all winners. The press had already published the names of the distinguished recipients well in advance of the gala event.

A woman from England would be awarded the Nobel prize for literature. The first of the million dollars was hers, alone. Two men shared the glory for chemistry. They were from two different institutions. One was from the former East Berlin, and the second from the western side of the former wall. The Berlin Wall had long been gone, but the two countries' separate research programs were not previously known to each other. They both had isolated the structure of, and had synthesized a newly discovered central nervous system neurotransmitter. The Nobel prize in economics went to a woman from the United States. She had created a computer model that predicted the financial decline of the eastern block countries in advance of their financial demise. The model would be used to identify other countries in financial trouble. The Nobel prize for physics was indirectly related to medicine. The study of calcium depletion and its effects on the mechanics of bone could have easily been considered for the Nobel prize for medicine, as well. The mathematical analysis of structural defects and resultant bone breaks in osteoporosis qualified a male and female researcher for the Nobel prize in physics.

The peace prize (or fraternity of nations) was simultaneously being awarded in Oslo, Norway. It was no surprise that the secretary general of the United Nations was awarded his medal in Norway. His quest to solidify Northern and Southern Ireland as well as his efforts to neutralize the Middle East conflict was acknowledged as an insurmountable task at times. He worked tirelessly to accomplish forward progress in both geographic areas.

The most impressive, but controversial accomplishment was about to be awarded. It was one of the most dramatic moments in the entire history of the Nobel prize.

E. Royston MacDonald, Drs. Blackburn and Bradshaw stepped in unison onto the stage at the concert hall to have their medals bestowed upon them in recognition of the 2001 Nobel prize in medicine. All members of the Project Samuel team were in the audience. The three men were greeted with cheers and a standing ovation that lasted for minutes. Each man would receive one-third of a million dollars. They were cited as having accomplished the most significant task of modern biology—*the creation of man by cloning*. The value in the achievement was seen as the utilization of various individual biological sciences (DNA extraction/sequencing, embryonic development and obstetrics) in combination, to achieve the creation of a new human. Successful delivery of a human baby that had been cloned was, in and of itself, worthy of the prize.

The three gentlemen left the stage to the applause of the entire gathering. Controversy could wait. The U.S. team of researchers had now broken a biological barrier, once thought impossible and unethical to cross.

Man had been cloned!

Just as guests began to exit the hall to commence the banquet at city hall, the chairperson of the Karolinska Committee quickly halted the mass exodus. There was confusion amongst the entire congregation in the hall since all the awards for the year had been presented.

"Ladies and gentlemen," the chairperson said loudly, "we, the governing body of the Nobel Foundation and Award Committee of the Karolinska Institute, have one more prize," he said. The crowd was stupefied and grew quiet. The prizes had all been presented in accordance with the current Nobel statutes. *What category had they added?* There was a hush throughout the hallowed hall.

"Ladies and gentlemen. In recognition of an incredible accomplishment in physiology, we deem it necessary in the 100th anniversary year of the Nobel Foundation to award a separate physiology prize in addition to the prize for medicine." MacDonald, Blackburn and Bradshaw looked at each other in total confusion. The yearly award was either in medicine or physiology, and not both categories in the same year.

"Fellow distinguished researchers—the Nobel committee awards the Nobel prize for physiology to a person who has contributed the most to the betterment of mankind, by creating the *most well-known baby* in the history of mankind. The Nobel prize goes to Ms. Teresa Cordero-Rosero for her role in the development and birth of baby Samuel, the first cloned human. Please welcome Teresa, Samuel, and Teresa's devoted new husband, Emilio."

The Nobel committee had recognized Emilio's sponsorship and documentation of the event, after all.

The Stockholm Concert Hall erupted in massive applause and to a standing ovation for more than twenty minutes. The baby cried from the noise and Teresa wept on stage. She was handed a check for one million dollars. The medal was placed about her neck, and the king of Sweden gave a smaller commemorative one to Samuel. They each received a Nobel certificate, as well.

The only person present who was not surprised by the announcement in the entire arena was Fawn Danton, standing by her husband and near term herself. She blushed with pride for her friend, Teresa, and for baby Samuel. Beside them, stood a smiling Dr. Bower from La Jolla General in California.

Jack leaned over to Fawn and said, "Hon, I'll bet you knew of this surprise award, didn't you?" She smiled back at him and whispered in his ear as they stood there applauding, "Jack, I guess we're even now. Next time, you'll trust *me* with your own little secrets, hon!"

Emilio watched proudly as his new wife and baby were recognized and complimented by the international gathering of world guests, dignitaries, and former and current Nobel laureates. A celebratory banquet followed for 1,500 people in the Golden Hall of the Stockholm City Hall. Samuel's crib was strategically placed next to his mother's seat at the end of the head table. He would not know of his own fame or for that matter, his mother's fame, until he grew older. He, after all, was a normal baby, and slept through the entire banquet.

Epilogue

Eight years later, E. Royston Macdonald and his San Diego driver, Max, parked his limo on a side street to the left of "Ted Williams Field" in the North Park section of San Diego. There, Royston got out and walked the short distance to the chain-link fence that surrounded the Little League ballpark that was set between homes. It was a stone's throw from Utah Street. He peered inconspicuously through the fence's web of metal that rattled and rang out every time someone touched it, or a baseball recoiled off the backstop.

Ten to fifteen kids of varying sizes and ages were playing late in the afternoon, on a perfect day in San Diego. Royston stared at one particular player who was about eight years old. He appeared young in facial features, but tall for his age. *He is lanky,* Royston thought. The boy fidgeted a lot while in the outfield and sometimes sat down. Appearing bored with his teammates, he would yank pieces of sod from the ground. The kid was always anxious to bat and appeared impatient with the other kids.

When called by his friends to take batting practice, he ran in from the outfield with excitement, almost skipping and hopping in anticipation of his time at bat. He had energy, a drive and desire to get in front of home plate. He swung the bat wildly in the batters' box, in anticipation of being the next to hit.

At the plate, the young man who fellow players called "Kid" was the most popular player there. He towered over the others. His swing of the bat was a fluid motion that left every knowledgeable baseball fanatic or observer in the bleachers talking about the boy from North Park, with the Ted Williams swing. The young boy seemed to prefer hitting left-handed, but sometimes switch-hit from the right side. Unlike most children taught "level-swinging" lessons from Little League coaches of the past, this boy swung upward with precise timing.

It was as if he sees the stitches on the ball approaching him, Royston thought. He swung the bat hard, like no other kid on the field. The bat ended up behind his back after each follow-through—hit or miss.

Max stepped up to Royston and stood beside him at the fence. He looked at Royston with a tear in his eye.

"Sir? Ya done good! . . . He's your boy, ya know," Max said confidently and firmly.

Royston had no response other than a subtle smile as Max turned and walked back to the limo. Royston never took his eye off the boy and stared straight ahead, capturing each moment.

Royston walked slowly over to the bleachers and sat for a while. He remained there alone, and purposely sat on a dried-out slab of wood—on the highest seat in the stands. Every time the kid swung from the left side, the ball sailed out to right field, or over the fence. He seemed to miss very few pitches that were over the plate. It was as if he had established a "hit zone" that he favored over the rubber pentagon-shaped mat. Otherwise, he would wait for the next good pitch.

Royston stayed for about twenty-five minutes and for the most part, went unnoticed in the bleachers.

But, at one point, the kid at the plate noticed the large man in the stands. The kid smiled at him after Royston gave him the thumbs up following a "blast" over the right field fence. The kid was proud of himself. *He has confidence and determination!* Royston thought.

Royston took some snapshots of the boys through the fence, before leaving the ball park. On the way past one youngster, he gave the boy a $20 bill and said, "Here son, treat your friends to some ice cream." The kid was ecstatic at receiving the money. As Royston headed for the limo, he told the same kid to put some extra "jimmies" on "Sammy's" ice cream cone. The boy ran over to the tallest player and said, "Hey, Samuel, that man just bought us some ice cream! Come on everybody, let's go to the corner store!" They all cheered wildly.

Samuel watched as the limo departed on the other side of the field. It drove off slowly, with the large man snapping pictures out the rear side window. It then turned toward Utah Street.

"I've seen that man before," Samuel said, smiling. "He usually wears a big ten-gallon hat and watches us play. I wonder if he's a 'scout' or somethin'? I sure hope so."

"Perhaps!" said a friend. "He sure is rich!"

"I know that man!" Samuel said, "I just know that I know that man," he said smiling and laughing, as they ran to the convenience store.

On the way out of the neighborhood, Royston's limo passed by the 3000 block of Utah Street. It went slowly past Samuel's home. In the front window, Royston could see what appeared to be a glass candelabra on a piano top, and Teresa was hanging some baseball uniforms on the clothesline in the backyard. They appeared to be small baseball uniforms with the number 9 on the back. She had a playpen in the yard next to her as she hung clothes. Royston smiled. He knew that she and Emilio now had another child, one of their own. She had kept her promise of staying home to raise her children. She did not go back to work. Unlike Ted's mother, Teresa was there for Samuel when the school day was over, and when dinner was ready.

Max took Royston to Lindbergh Field in San Diego. Royston's plane left for Texas promptly at 7:00 P.M. He would have the photos from that day in North Park developed when he got back home to Texas.

Postscript

I wish to acknowledge separately

Mrs. May Venzer Williams,
(d. 1961)

mother of

Theodore Samuel Williams, a Boston Red Sox icon.

Mrs. Williams was a revered Salvation Army lieutenant in San
Diego and the mother of two sons, Teddy and Danny.
"Salvation May" Williams (the Angel of Tijuana) was often ostra-
cized for her religious beliefs, daily commitments to the "Army"
and the public's misperception of her lack of motherhood
responsibilities.

Rest assured May Williams, that you *were* a *good mother* and there
will only be *one, Theodore "Samuel" Williams,*
the greatest hitter who ever lived.

About the Author

J. P. Polidoro, Ph.D., is a vice president of business development for a company in the biopharmaceutical industry. He has been in the medical related field for thirty-five years. A reproductive biologist by training, Polidoro was awarded his master's and doctoral degrees from the Department of Veterinary and Animal Sciences, University of Massachusetts at Amherst, Massachusetts. He earned a bachelor's degree in biology from C. W. Post College in Long Island, New York.

Polidoro is also a noted songwriter, guitarist and performer, known in the world of folk music as the "The Good Dr. Jack." He has produced six albums of his own material to date. He also collects sports memorabilia and autographs.

Polidoro lives in Laconia, New Hampshire, with his wife, Brenda. He has five children.

Project Samuel is Polidoro's second novel. His first, *Rapid Descent: Disaster in Boston Harbor*, a thriller mystery about a doomed commuter flight from Logan Airport to New Hampshire, was published in 2000.